Are you in the mood for giveaways, discount books, excerpts, and more? Sign up for Scarlett's newsletter here.

www.scarlettscottauthor.com/contact

Nobody's Duke

League of Dukes Book 1

By
Scarlett Scott

Nobody's Duke

League of Dukes Book One

Published by Happily Ever After Books, LLC
Print Edition
Edited by Grace Bradley
Cover Design by Wicked Smart Designs

For more information, contact author Scarlett Scott.
www.scarslettscottauthor.com

A widow with secrets

When the dangerous men who killed her husband in a political assassination threaten Ara, Duchess of Burghly, the Crown assigns her a bodyguard. But the man charged with protecting her is no stranger.

He's Clayton Ludlow, the bastard son of a duke and the first man she ever loved. Eight years after he took her innocence and ruthlessly abandoned her, he's back in her drawing room and her life.

This time, she's older, wiser, and stronger. She will resist him at any cost and make him pay for the past.

A man with a broken heart

She's the only woman Clay ever loved and the one he hates above all others. When Ara brutally betrayed and deceived him, leaving him with a scarred face and a bitter heart, he devoted himself to earning his reputation as one of the Crown's most feared agents.

He wants nothing more than to finish his assignment so that he can remove all traces of her from his life forever. But walking away from her for good won't be as easy as he thinks.

As secrets are revealed and danger threatens Ara, Clay discovers that the truth is far more complicated than deceit. Once she's back in his arms where she belongs, he'll wage the biggest fight of all to keep her there.

Dedication

Readers, this one is once again for *you*.

This said, … he wished to have me in his sight
Once, as a friend: this fixed a day in spring
To come and touch my hand … a simple thing,
Yet I wept for it!

Elizabeth Barrett Browning, **Sonnets from the Portuguese, 28**

Chapter One

London, 1882

TO SOCIETY, SHE was the Duchess of Burghly. To her husband, murdered by a Fenian's blade, she had been Araminta, formal and proper and beloved by him in his way. She had loved him equally in her way. Sweet Freddie, with the heart of an angel and the desire to change a world that would never understand or accept him.

She was all too familiar with the way the world treated hopeful, unsullied hearts.

"Ara."

She had been hopeful and unsullied once.

When she had known the man standing before her in the drawing room of Burghly House. When she had loved him. When she had been…

"Ara."

There it was again, spoken with such dark vehemence that it almost vibrated in the air, sending unwanted tendrils of heat licking through her even after all the years that had passed. That name, that bitter reminder of who she had been, spoken in the voice that had once sent a thrill straight to her heart…it was her undoing.

Ara had not realized she had clambered to her feet until her body swayed like a tree caught in an aggressive wind. Faintness overcame her. Her vision darkened. The palms clenching her silken skirts were damp, hands trembling.

He was taller than she remembered. Broader and stronger. He had always been a mountain of a man, but he had grown into his bones and skin, and the result took her breath despite her fierce need to remain as unaffected by him as possible. His eyes, cold and flat, burned into her. His jaw was rigid, his expression blank. A vicious-looking scar cut down his cheek.

She wondered for a moment how he could have received such a mark.

And then she reminded herself that she did not care. That he had ceased to be someone she worried after some eight years ago, on the day she had waited for him with nothing more than a valise and her foolish heart. He had never come.

The agony of that day returned to her a hundredfold as she stood in the gilt splendor of her drawing room, stabbing at her with the precision of a blade. Hours had passed, day bleeding into evening, and she had waited and waited. The only carriage to arrive had been her father's, and it had taken her, broken and dejected, back to the place from which she had fled.

"Your Grace, are you well?"

The voice of the Duke of Carlisle, edged with concern, pierced her consciousness, reminding her she had an audience, lest she allow her dignity to so diminish that she allowed *him* to see the visceral effect he had upon her.

She swallowed, tamped down the bile threatening to curdle her throat, and turned her attention to Carlisle. "I am as well as can be expected, given the events of the last three months, Duke. I thank you for your concern."

He inclined his head. "I am deeply sorry for the loss of your husband, madam. He was a bright star in the Liberal party."

"Yes," she agreed, a tremor in her voice that she could not

suppress. Speaking of Freddie inevitably festered a resurgence of horror and sadness. He had been a good man, an estimable husband to her and father to Edward, and he had not deserved to die choking on his own blood in a Dublin park. "He was."

Carlisle's lips compressed into a pained frown. "I cannot begin to fathom your grief, and I apologize for our unwanted presence here today. If there were any way to keep you free of this burden, I wholeheartedly would."

"The grief is immense," she whispered, all she could manage past the knot in her throat.

How she hated that it wasn't just her sorrow for Freddie that paralyzed her now and stole her voice. She felt *his* stare upon her like a brand. He had not moved. Had not spoken another word save her name, and yet he seemed to have stolen all the air from the room.

"As I was saying prior to Mr. Ludlow's arrival," Carlisle continued with a formal tone, "it is with great regret that I find myself tasked with informing you that there has been a threat made against you by the same faction of Fenians that murdered your husband. To that end, the Home Office has assigned an agent to ensure your protection."

Carlisle's words sank into her mind as though spoken from a great distance.

...a threat made against you...

...same Fenians that murdered...

...an agent to ensure your protection.

Her breathing was shallow. Her fingers fisted in her skirts with so much force that her knuckles ached. Still, the weight of *his* burning gaze upon her would not lift. Her entire body felt achy and hot and itchy and chaotic all at once.

"Would you care to elaborate on the nature of the threat?" She kept her eyes carefully trained upon the Duke of Carlisle, but it was impossible to keep *him* from her peripheral vision.

He filled the chamber as much with his presence as with his massive size.

The Duke of Carlisle, despite his reputation as a depraved reprobate, was the unexpected liaison between herself and the department of the government responsible for informing her about Freddie's murder and the investigation into finding his assassins. Their previous meetings had been equally stilted, revolving around his sympathy for her loss and any new information regarding the Fenians who had plotted Freddie's death.

In the murky days following her husband's murder, she and Edward had been removed from Dublin with an armed escort, but she had imagined that they had left all danger behind them in Ireland.

"Assassination, Your Grace." Carlisle's tone was quiet but deadly serious.

Those three words, so succinct and cold, struck her heart.

Edward could not lose both his parents in the span of three months. Her heart squeezed at the thought of her son alone in the world. Her beautiful, kindhearted boy. She would do anything to protect him.

Her mouth went dry. "I see." She paused, attempted to collect herself, an odd mixture of discomfit at *his* continued presence and fear swirling through her. "My son, Your Grace? Has he been included in the threats as well, or do they only pertain to myself?"

"Your son was not referenced in the threats, Your Grace," Carlisle said.

"*You have a son*?"

She flinched, the angry lash of *his* voice striking her. Still, she would not look at *him*. "I do not understand the reason for your…associate's presence, Your Grace. Indeed, I would far prefer to conduct this dialogue with you in private, as befitting the sensitive nature of the circumstances."

Ara refused to say *his* name. Refused to even think it. Would not speak aloud the true nature of what and who he was. A bastard. The half brother of the Duke of Carlisle. The man she had lost her heart and her innocence to. Her son's father.

No. Freddie had been Edward's father, the only one he had ever known. And it must—*would*—remain that way until she went to her grave.

The Duke of Carlisle appeared unperturbed by her uncharacteristic outburst. "Pray forgive me again, Duchess, but Mr. Ludlow's presence here today is necessary as he is the agent who has been assigned to your protection."

"No!" The word left her in a cry, torn from her, vehement.

But what surprised her the most was that it was echoed by another voice, dark and deep and haunting in its velvety timbre.

His.

Her gaze flitted back to him, and the stark rage she read reflected in the depths of his brown eyes shook her. Beneath the surface, he was seething.

"I will not guard her under any circumstances, Leo. Find someone else," he sneered. "Anyone else."

And then he turned on his heel and stalked from her drawing room, slamming the door at his back.

CLAY'S FEET COULD not carry him far enough or fast enough away. *Damn it all to hell.* Damn Leo to hell. But most of all, damn *her*. Time and distance were not panaceas, but they had been his sole comfort, and now even that would be stolen from him if he allowed it.

He could not allow that. She had broken him once. Never again.

The urge to strike something or someone—to smite and thrash with a violent savagery borne of all the fury flashing inside him—had never been stronger. Eight years and she had not changed. If anything, she had grown more ethereal. She had always been lovely, with her pale skin and coppery curls, the blue-violet eyes framed by long, dark lashes that stared at a man as if they could see into the dark pit of his soul.

Ara, his Ara.

No. Not my Ara.

Not any longer.

Nothing had made that clearer than the day she had confessed to her father that the Duke of Carlisle's bastard son had taken her innocence. He could feel the blade of the knife slashing his cheek as if it were yesterday. Could still smell the fetid breath of the man who had marked him for life. His scar ached and burned, a permanent, visceral reminder of why he could not even breathe the same air as the woman he had just turned his back upon.

"Clay."

The commanding sound of his half brother's voice halted him, but his cessation of movement was an act of duty and nothing less. If he had his way, he would be halfway across London by now, putting as much distance as possible between himself and the woman he had once loved.

Fists clenched, he spun around. As tall and dark as Clay though not as broad, Leo had nabbed the fortune of being born on the right side of the blanket, which upon their sire's death several years prior had made him the rightful duke. Though he was three months Clay's junior, he was also his superior in the clandestine ranks that had been created by the

Home Office known simply as the Special League.

Those twin facts would always rankle.

He waited for Leo to approach him, trying to temper his rage.

"Where the hell do you think you are going?" Leo demanded without preamble, irritation twisting his countenance and rendering it even grimmer than it ordinarily was.

Calm yourself, Clay. She can likely hear everything from where she waits in her gilded little drawing room. Do not give her the pleasure of knowing how much the sight of her affects you after all these years. You can never again allow her to see your weakness.

"I respectfully request to be assigned elsewhere," he clipped.

Leo did not miss a beat. "No."

He resisted the urge to roar or slam his fist into his brother's face. "Allow me to rephrase. I am not requesting. I am demanding."

Leo flashed him a small, severe smile. "Once again, no."

"I cannot guard her." The low confession was torn from him.

He did not want to admit it. Not aloud and especially not to his brother, who traded in the weaknesses of others. Blood they may share, but Leo did not yield for anyone. He had inherited his mother's icy temperament and sternness, where Clay had his own mother's soft, giving heart.

Or at least he had, once.

"You can and you must," Leo insisted. "You are aware of what happened to the duchess's husband."

The Duke of Burghly, the Chief Secretary for Ireland, had been stabbed to death in a Dublin park in the midst of a spring afternoon, along with his undersecretary. They had been beset by men wielding surgical knives, all the better to inflict deathblows. Whilst the men responsible for the outrage had escaped, evidence pointed in one direction only: the Fenians.

"Of course I am bloody well aware, Leo," he said, fists and jaw still equally clenched. "But that has no bearing upon my presence here in her home. I cannot—will not remain here. The League is rife with other agents. Choose another one."

"No one else is you, Clay. You can and will accept this post and guard her, because you must." Leo paused, lowering his voice. "I know the two of you share a past, but I had not realized you still have feelings for her."

"I don't," he denied with force. Too much force.

He had feelings for her, in truth. Loathing. Anger. Rage. Betrayal. Those were the sorts of emotions she had left behind along with the scar. And just like the mark upon his flesh, they would disfigure him for his lifetime.

"Then there is no reason why you cannot accept the position." Leo's tone smacked of finality.

Yes, damn it. There was *every* reason.

"I cannot be in proximity to her, Leo." There, he admitted it. Just seeing her had shaken him. If he had known she had become the Duchess of Burghly, he never would have even deigned to come to Burghly House at all. She was like a broken rib, hurting him with each breath, a danger to his lungs. "You deliberately misled me in bringing me here."

"I did not mislead you," his brother argued, keeping his voice quiet so it would not carry back to the drawing room. "I acted in the best interest of the Home Office, the Special League, and the duchess. You must consider the matter rationally, Clay, and not with your heart."

"I am being as bloody rational as I can be when it pertains to that woman," he growled. "My heart has naught to do with it, of that I can assure you. My patience, however, my anger, my sanity…those things cannot withstand being in her presence for longer than I have already endured."

Leo remained unmoved. "We cannot afford to allow the Fenians to claim another victim. The assassination of a duchess here on English soil, coupled with the bombings we have endured and foiled, would spark fear and pandemonium."

An assassination.

Ara's assassination.

Her *murder.*

The sobering thoughts chased the heat of his rage, replacing it with a numbing chill. As much as he loathed not just the sight of her but everything she had done to him—her betrayal and her willingness to toss him away like an outmoded gown—the notion of her meeting her end in the same gory fashion as the duke made bile churn in his gut. The threats made against her were not just real; they were possible. The Fenians wanted Irish home rule, and they were not above terrorizing, bombing, and killing anyone they imagined stood in the way of their cause in an effort to gain it.

An ingenious part of their evil strategy was to bring war to England without ever sending an army. Small groups of plotters had already invaded towns and ports. A bomb last year in Salford had killed a young boy when it exploded. Other bombs had exploded in Liverpool, and various plots had been uncovered and stopped throughout London.

Now they had begun a different prong of attack, targeting government officials like the Duke of Burghly. And like his widowed duchess. Ara was being threatened by the most ruthless, fearless, and dangerous sort of men: those who perceived they had nothing left to lose.

But even so, she was not his responsibility. She had ceased being his *anything* the day she had chosen to destroy him. He would not save her. The burden was too great for him to bear.

He shook his head. "I am sorry, Leo, but any other League member is as suited as I am for the role, if not more so. I cannot pretend I would be able to maintain indifference and guard her as will be necessary. Forcing me to do this is both unwise and dangerous to the lady, who is deserving of the basic right of safety, no better or worse than any other person."

"No one is as suited as you, Clay." His brother's dark gaze was unrelenting. "You have thwarted dozens of assassination attempts. Your work protecting the Duchess of Leeds was commendable, and you had no problems settling yourself into a more domestic setting than you have been previously accustomed."

The Duchess of Leeds had been the victim of a murderous plot, and he had served her well. In so doing, she had become his friend. She possessed the heart of an angel, with a willingness to take in all the stray beasts of London, but she had been different. She had not been Ara.

He had never loved her.

And it did not matter how much time had passed. He had not forgotten a moment of the time he had spent with Ara. Kissing her, holding her, the wildness of her burnished curls tangling around them. The soft giggles he could coax from her lips with his wandering mouth and hands.

He shook himself free of the memories, cloying like ivy, threatening to choke and overrun him. "My history with her renders it an impossibility. What of Strathmore? He would be an excellent man for the job."

"He is otherwise occupied," Leo said curtly. "I grow weary of your objections, brother, as they are all immaterial at worst and flimsy at best. You are the man I have chosen, the man the Home Office has chosen, to protect her."

"I don't give a damn," he thundered as the last, fine filament of his control broke. "I will not do it."

"Sodding hell, Clay." His brother fixed a dispassionate frown upon him. "I did not wish to do this, but you have left me without a choice. If you do not take on this task, you will be suspended from service. The Home Office requires you to perform this duty, and they will not accept anyone else. Do you not think I already tried to substitute another, knowing of your past?"

His heart thrummed faster, his chest rising and falling, each breath harsher than the next. He had never supposed Leo would attempt to protect him in such a fashion. Though they had come of age side by side, Leo possessed not a modicum of maudlin sentiment, or so Clay had always supposed.

"Suspended from service," he bit out, as though the words tasted bitter and ugly in his mouth. For they did. His work in the Special League was what had given him purpose these last eight years. Because of her, it was all he had. And now because of her, he also stood to lose it.

How bloody fitting.

"I am sorry, brother." Leo's somber tone said more than his apology could convey.

He swallowed the bile that had begun in his stomach and worked its way into his throat. "I do not have a choice, do I?"

Leo's lips compressed. "I am afraid not."

He spun away, stalking down the hall, intent upon inflicting damage upon the first inanimate object he spied. With his fists. But there was nothing in sight that he could punch, aside from damask-covered walls and tables rife with bric-a-brac. Pictures of her. Pictures of her husband. Of the two of them with a small lad.

He could not face them, so he turned back to the fate awaiting him. His life had never been his to rule. Why should this assignment be any different? He would do what he must. Because there was no other option.

"Very well. I shall do it." He gave a terse nod, feeling a heavy weight descend upon his chest as he acquiesced. It held the finality of a death sentence, and he had never felt more like a man being informed of his impending swing upon the gallows.

"Good man." Leo strode to him and clapped him on the shoulder. "I know what this is costing you, Clay, and do not think that I don't appreciate it. I will continue to assert pressure for you regarding the creation of a peerage."

Following his previous assignment, there had been rumbles that he may be rewarded for his service to the Crown with a title. Clay knew better than to hope for such an eventuality.

"Do you think I give a damn about gaining a title?" he asked dismissively, his lip curling. "I never have, and I never will."

But that was a lie, and he knew it. For if he had possessed a title, he would still have Ara. He never would have lost her.

"Even so," Leo said, "you deserve recompense for your service. There is no man better."

"I am doing this because I must and for no other reason," he persisted. "But I do not like it, Leo. And neither will I forget it."

His half brother gave him an odd little smile then. "Let it be just one more to add to the vast catalog of black marks upon my soul."

Clay could only hope it would not also be a black mark upon his.

Chapter Two

Eight years earlier

WHOEVER HE WAS, he had been the most beautiful young man she had ever seen. But she supposed she would never get to know his name.

Ara had been watching him for three days in secret. On this, the fourth day, she lingered hours past the appointed time, and still he did not come.

The first day had been purely unintentional. She had been engaging in the impulses her father so reviled by wandering as far away from Kingswood Hall as she could possibly find herself. She had ridden a feisty mare to the edge of Papa's sprawling country seat, all the way to the woodland that had always held her fancy, and had tethered her mount to a tree so she could wander about in unabashed joy at her freedom.

Papa was not at home and would be gone for the next fortnight at least. Mama was prone to the megrims. Her brother Cecil had gone abroad. Her sister Rosamunde was happily being the Countess of Somerset, off with her husband or one of her paramours.

Which left Ara in possession of a great deal of free time and an unprecedented lack of chaperoning. Perhaps it was because she had already had two seasons, and at one-and-twenty, she was expected to make a match soon with the Marquess of Dorset. Whatever the reason, she would not complain.

For Ara did not like the Marquess of Dorset. And she did not like Papa's disapproving frowns and insistence she marry the odious man. Dorset was ten years her senior, and he had an irritating way of talking above everything she said, as though he could not even hear a word she spoke.

But she did like the mystery gentleman in the woods with his strapping form, his dark hair, and his broad face, an arresting complexity of strong angles and chiseled perfection. She had been seated on the forest floor, her back against a large old tree trunk, reading a book, when the snapping of branches and rustling of leaves had alerted her to a presence.

From the moment he had first appeared, jogging and stripped down to nothing more than a shirt and plain dark trousers, performing all manner of athletic feats she supposed served to enhance the lovely strength of his body, he had robbed her of breath. She had looked upon him, and something in her belly had tightened. Her mouth had gone dry. A tingling sensation had blossomed in a forbidden place. She had wanted to know him.

But to her shame, she had simply watched him in silence, drinking in his body's fluid motions without alerting him to her presence. She had stayed silent and still as moss until he had gone, jogging away as if he had never been at all.

The second day, she made excuses to Mama and returned in the hopes she would see him again, though she told herself she simply wished to go for a ride and take the country air once more. She had been about to leave in disappointment when he had appeared, bounding into the forest with his vitality and his magnetism and his formidable size. He was so very enormous, the sort of man who would dwarf her. As she watched him, she had wondered what it would be like to be held in such large, long arms. To be cradled against that broad chest. To be touched by a man who was strong enough to do anything he wished.

Dorset was not strong or vital. He possessed a paunch that spoke of his fondness for spirits and a thinning pate. Occasionally, spittle collected in the corners of his lips as he spoke, and she found it revolting.

For three days, she watched the unknown young man perform his athletic coups in silence from her hiding place, dreaming of emerging and speaking to him. Of introducing herself, though she had not possessed an inkling of what she would have said.

And finally, on the fourth day, when she had summoned up her courage enough to storm forth from the shadows of the forest, he did not materialize. She had appeared at the same place where her father's lands bordered with the Duke of Carlisle's, at the same time, and had waited for what seemed like an eternity. Still, he had not come.

Ara sighed. Perhaps it was time to return home.

A stick snapped behind her, and she scrambled to her feet, spinning about.

There he was.

This close, she could see him even better. Could appreciate the slash of his nose, the fullness of his lips, the regal ridges of his cheekbones, the wideness of his jaw. There was a wildness about him, a ruggedness, and a draw that made her long to be closer. To be so close she could touch him, could trace the breadth of his shoulders, the column of his neck. His hair was black as ink and so long it nearly brushed his shoulders, falling in luxurious waves. His eyes were dark, focused on her now with an intensity that stole her breath all over again.

"How many days have you been watching me?" he asked.

She felt a fiery rush of shameful heat coloring her cheeks.

Dear heavens. How could he have known? He had never once even glanced in her direction, and she had been so careful—so very, very, careful—not to move or rustle or make even the slightest sound that would alert him to her presence.

She summoned all the frost she had in her being, which was a feeble fraction in the face of his great, pulsing fire. He was like the sun blotting out everything else in the sky. "I beg your pardon?"

He stepped closer, and she could smell him. Man and sweat and leather and musk. Nothing had ever smelled better. She wanted to press her nose against the Adam's apple of his throat, inhale the essence of him directly so she could recall it wherever and whenever she wished.

A smile flirted with the corners of his lips. "You heard me correctly. How many days have you been watching me? Three by my count, though I daresay it could have been more. I tend to get lost in my own thoughts."

He had thoughts? How odd, for he owned all of hers at the moment. She could not think of anything but him. Something deep inside her, some unknown and primitive part of her, said this was the man for her. That he was hers and she would be his.

With great effort, she shook free from his spell, chastising herself. *Oh, do cease being a ninny, Araminta! Little wonder everyone is always thinking you so silly. You cannot fancy yourself in love with a man you do not know.*

But it was not that she thought herself in love with him, not precisely. Rather it was that she felt, in that moment, with just the two of them, she could love him. One day. That this queer, indefinable rightness she felt in her bones meant something. All foolish, all so naïve. Little wonder her father ever despaired of her making a match when she could not help but to spin tales about a man she did not know while the suitors who vied for her hand were always uninteresting and unwanted.

Swiftly, she recalled he had spoken to her. That he was awaiting her response.

He knew how many days she had watched him. Knew she had watched him all along, and yet he had never shown even a hint of awareness of her. How humiliating to have been caught ogling a stranger in such fashion. If Papa ever learned of her disgrace, he would never forgive her.

"I have not been watching you," she lied, tipping up her chin in defiance and daring him to gainsay her.

His smile deepened to a grin, and her heart thudded so loudly she swore he must have heard it. "You *have* been watching me, and we both know it. You may as well dispense with your prevarication, for it is futile."

She rather supposed it was.

Feeling out of her depths, she huffed out a small breath, staring at him, wishing she could read his eyes and know his thoughts. "What have you been doing?"

He raised a brow. "Truth at last? I have been training."

"Training," she repeated, frowning as she tried to comprehend precisely what that meant.

"Also, I have been giving you something worth watching." He had the audacity to wink then, the knave.

Her heart sighed.

He was beautiful.

And he was hers.

She decided there, in the shade of the trees, that whoever this man was, she was going to marry him.

Chapter Three

HE WAS HERE.

Sharing the same roof.

Inhabiting the same space.

Ara stared blankly out the window of her drawing room. Outside, London bustled about its day. The sun attempted to pierce the fog. Carriages rumbled, taking the fashionable to and from their homes on St. James's Square. How mundane, all the world continuing, breath by breath, minute by minute, hour by hour, day by day.

But there was an interloper in her home. An unwanted presence. The last man she had ever wanted to see again.

He had not returned to the chamber yesterday following his cold retreat. The Duke of Carlisle had entered alone, informing her Mr. Ludlow would be settling into guest apartments forthwith, and that for the foreseeable future, he would be charged with acting as her attendant. A handful of other sentries would be added as guards as well, but all would answer to Mr. Ludlow.

"You are to trust him in all matters," Carlisle had said solemnly. "He is here for your protection."

Trust him in all matters. That was the trouble. She could not trust the man. Not ever again, though she had been foolish enough to do so once. All she had managed to gain was a broken heart and her beautiful son.

A choked sob escaped her lips even now, one day removed from the awful conversation. When he had stormed away, a great, soothing relief had blanketed her in the calming air of his absence. She had been convinced he would not remain, and she would be free of him.

But then the Duke of Carlisle had dashed her hopes and set her on edge. She had requested, as politely as she had been able to manage, a different guard. Anyone else would have sufficed.

"Mr. Ludlow is the only man I would entrust with your protection, Your Grace," he had told her. "The Home Office has issued its decree, and until the conspirators responsible for the duke's death are jailed, I am afraid you will have to accustom yourself to this temporary way of life."

How was she to accustom herself to *his* presence in her own home, the one place of refuge she had remaining to her? The last place she felt safe? The knowledge he was here vibrated the very air, as though he were a ghost haunting her rather than a flesh-and-blood man. She had lain awake well into the night, thinking of him, four doors down the hall eight years after the first time she had seen him in the forest.

She should have run that day rather than lingering to watch. If she had only known, she would have fled. She never would have returned. Ara pressed her heated forehead to the cool pane of glass. Perhaps she was growing ill. Her lungs felt tight in her chest and she was so very warm all over.

"Your Grace?"

There was the voice, dark and delicious as chocolate. And like chocolate, she wanted more. She wanted to taste it on her tongue. *No, no, no.* Gads, where had that errant thought emerged from? She tamped it down, down, down. Buried it good and deep inside herself where it belonged. Pressing a hand over hear frantic heart as if to absorb the beats, she spun to face the source.

He had entered her drawing room without her hearing, and now he stood within arm's reach, those dark eyes burning into hers. He seemed somehow taller today than he had yesterday, his frame wide and formidable and barely civilized, contained in a dark coat, silver waistcoat, black trousers, and a simple neck cloth.

"I beg your pardon for the intrusion," he said into the charged silence. "I knocked several times and you did not answer."

He had knocked? She hadn't heard, so lost had she been in the turmoil of her thoughts. But she did not wish for him to know that. To sense her inner weakness toward him. To know that just the sight of him made an old and pathetic part of her long to throw herself into his arms.

His arms had once felt like home.

She tipped up her chin. "I answered you. Perhaps you did not hear."

He stared at her, saying nothing, his fathomless gaze scouring her as if he could mark her with it or swallow her whole. "I heard nothing, madam," he said at last. "You need to sharpen your senses."

How dare he take her to task? His curt words stung.

"My senses are already sharp enough." They were horribly aware of *him. My God.* She could even smell him, and his scent was familiar and yet new. Musk and leather and potently masculine. A shameful surge of warmth pooled in her core.

For some reason, she recalled what he had once done to her there with his mouth. With his tongue. Her cheeks heated but she maintained his gaze with the greatest effort. What in heaven's name was wrong with her? She was feverish. Yes, she must be coming down with something dreadful. Surely that was the answer, the only reason she felt flushed and odd. Her perplexing state had nothing to do with *him*.

How was she to endure his presence at Burghly House when she could not even bear to think his name?

"Madam, your senses can never be sharp enough when there are seasoned killers determined to hunt you down and murder you." His tone, like his statement, was savage. Grim.

She flinched. "I do not understand what my..." she trailed off, unable to say the word *murder* aloud, for it made Freddie's awful, violent end too real. It made the danger facing her more genuine. It made her chest go tighter still. She cleared her throat and began anew. "I do not understand what my death would accomplish. Freddie's position made him vulnerable, but I have no role in the governing of Ireland, nor have I ever spoken publicly on the matter. What could they possibly want with his widow?"

"You do not wish to know what they could want with you." He came nearer to her, crowding her with his scent and his body and the memories he provoked, memories that lingered like stars in the morning sky as the sun rose. Dazzling glimpses into what had once been. "For now, all you need trouble yourself with is the indisputable fact there is an enemy who wishes you ill. I understand that you are accustomed to silk and tea and drawing rooms, but the men who murdered your husband do not give a damn about your insipid world. They detonate bombs that kill children. They carve innocent men to death in the middle of a park. They do not care about anything more than their desire to gain Irish independence by any means necessary. They will spill your blood and laugh upon your grave if it gives them what they want."

As the vicious volley of his diatribe lashed her, he continued forward until there was no distance at all. He moved with the grace of a predator. Like a lion.

She stepped back. Once. Twice. Her skirts met the wall.

Her head found the cool, slick hardness of the window. She swallowed. Her hands fisted in her skirts, shaking. If he was trying to intimidate her, he was succeeding. If he was attempting to frighten her, his mission was accomplished. But that did not mean she would allow him to see her vulnerability even for a moment.

She pinned him with a glare. "Come no farther, sir. You have already encroached upon me, and I do not care to be crowded by servants."

There. She had done it. Used her knowledge to cut back at him. Dredged up the past to wield against him.

His nostrils flared. "Understand this, Duchess. I am not your servant."

She took pains to keep her expression one of icy condescension. "Nor are you my equal. I did not give you leave to speak to me as though we are acquaintances, for we are not."

We were, once, whispered her foolish heart. *More than acquaintances. So much more.*

"I will speak to you as the situation merits," he said, his voice as cold and dead as the winter ground. "If I am to conduct my duty here, I will need your cooperation. In case you have not realized this, the danger to you is very real, else the Home Office would not have placed six men here alongside me."

Of course it was. Thinking again of the faceless, nameless men who had slaughtered Freddie made a sea of sickness churn inside her. It chased away the heat and left her impossibly chilled. She shivered, rubbing her arms.

He noticed. "If you are cold, Your Grace, I will see that a fire is built for you."

It was early spring, a time of damp, cool mornings. A time when the hope of renaissance remained elusive. Burghly House had been built in the beginning half of the eighteenth century, and its cavernous chambers never seemed to warm. For some reason, it had not ever felt like home to her. Even less so now that Freddie was not there to fill it with his infectious laugh and indomitable sense of humor.

He had been such an optimist.

Always believed the best of everyone around him.

Look at where his optimism had landed him.

"I want you to build it," she said.

The moment the demand left her lips, she wished she could recall it. Indeed, she did not know why she had uttered it aloud. One moment, she had been swept away in memories of her dead husband, and the next she had been speaking. She did not even want *his* continued presence in this chamber. Why, then, would she require him to linger?

Because you can, came the knowing voice inside her once more. *Because you are relishing the power you have over him, to make this big man feel small.*

He stiffened. "I beg your pardon, madam?"

Here was her chance to rescind the order. To dismiss him and send him away from her. But somehow, she could not.

"The fire. I wish for you to build it for me." The cold of the outdoors leached into the glass pane. She felt it through her hair. It was calming and comforting. It made her bold. "If you are to remain here at Burghly House, you may as well make yourself useful."

She waited, hoping for his mask to crack. For his lip to curl. For him to rage against her, tell her to go to the devil, for him to leave the drawing room and this time never come back. Instead, he stared at her.

He stared and stared, raking his dark gaze over her face, lingering at her throat. The silence swelled, growing heavy. His eyes dipped lower, lingering on her breasts as if it were a caress. She felt it, felt the heat of his perusal, her breasts tingling and her nipples tightening into stiff buds behind the protective cover of her corset.

And then his gaze fixated upon something, darkening. His jaw tightened. She knew what had caught his attention without looking down. It was her mourning brooch, gold and carved jet with glass trapping the lock of Freddie's hair.

His eyes flicked back to hers, his countenance as impassive as if it had been hewn from rock. "Ring for a servant to build the fire, *Your Grace*."

He spoke her title as if it were an epithet. As if it tasted tart upon his tongue. He was a duke's bastard, but she had become a duchess. He may have rejected her all those years ago, leaving her behind as if she had meant nothing to him, but she had achieved the status he would never have.

The realization gave her no joy. All she knew was the same acrimony he emitted.

Abruptly, he gave her his back and quit the chamber. The door closed softly behind him. Not a slam, but worse in its deadly calm.

Perhaps she had chased him away after all.

She turned back to the window, looking upon the busyness of the street below, and tried to ignore the pang the notion of his departure left in her heart. He had not even been here for one day, and he had already torn the fragile peace she had erected in the wake of Freddie's death asunder.

Ara shivered again, but it wasn't from the undeniable chill in the air. And no fire in a grate could quell it.

SHE WAS BENEATH Clay's skin. In his blood. Like a contagion. She had been another man's wife. The reminder had been a harsh but necessary rebuke. She carried a lock of her husband's hair, pinned with pride to the mourning weeds she wore in his honor.

He had never been her husband. He had been her lover. Her secret. Ultimately, her shame. The man she had rejected. The man she had marked forever.

Clay stalked down the main hall of Burghly House. It was not the finest home he had ever been inside, and nor was he unaccustomed to opulence and wealth. He had lived in a home that was larger, grander, and more ostentatious than this one. But that had been a lifetime ago, when he had believed he would ever have a hope of being perceived as something more than his father's bastard son.

The son to be pitied.

The son to be reviled.

The one who would never be good enough. Who would never quite be able to rise above the ignominy of his birth. To the polite world, it did not matter that Leo's mother's marriage with their father had been loveless and arranged or that Clay's mother had been their father's true love. Love was not good enough when it came to the quality, and it was a lesson Clay had learned as a lad but one that nevertheless ached like an old wound—like his bloody scar—even after all these years.

But Ara's scorn burned hotter than all the fires of condemnation combined.

He wanted to hate her, but her tremor had reminded him that she was only human, all too fallible. What he actually hated was the cold that touched her. The fear that infected her. Despite her icy hauteur, he had seen the terror in her eyes.

He wanted her to be warm.

Even though he should not. Even though he had told himself, as his gaze caught on the lock of her dead husband's hair she displayed above her heart—the heart that should have been his, damn it—that he would not do as she bid, he knew he could not leave her to the chill.

He located a footman dressed in the distinctive Burghly livery of scarlet coat and black trousers and stopped the young man. "You will build a fire in the drawing room. Her Grace is chilled."

The fellow bowed. "Yes, my lord."

"Mr. Ludlow," he corrected, for he knew his place here. He was not, and nor would he ever be a lord. He was a commoner. A baseborn bastard. He was the brawn, the fighter, and the killer. He was not what Ara had chosen. He was not a duke. He was the darkness. The reflection of what a duke could never be.

He was nobody's duke.

"Of course, sir," the footman said, his Adam's apple bobbing nervously in his throat.

"Why do you tarry, lad?" he barked. "Attend your duties at once."

"Yes, Mr. Ludlow." The footman bowed again and fairly fled in the direction of the drawing room.

It occurred to him that he had yet to interrogate the staff. He needed to make certain none of them would pose a danger to Ara. If the Fenians had managed to either plant themselves amongst the ranks of the Burghly House domestics or sway a domestic already in her employ in some fashion, it could prove ruinous. This house was to be their stronghold.

She had to be safe here.

He had to keep her safe here.

He followed the lad, doing what he had sworn he would not. She bid the footman enter at his knock, and Clay stepped back over the threshold. Back into her realm. She stood at the window once more, her back a stiff, elegant line, her wasp waist more pronounced by the sweeping train pooling in a fall of silk and ribbon around her. Glittering jet ornamentation called attention to the graceful column of her throat, the carefully wrought upsweep of her copper curls.

Why did he recall how soft those curls had been when they had fallen to her waist, when they had brushed over his bare chest? He did not want to remember. He wished to hell with everything in him he could forget. That he could remove the memories of the stolen moments they had shared a lifetime ago, but they were as intrinsic to him as his organs, and they would not part from him.

"You are here to build a fire, I presume," she said coolly, without bothering to turn to face the person who had entered.

By God, had she not listened to a word of the stern warnings he had just issued? There were murderers who wanted to slaughter her just as they had the duke, and she did not even look to see who had intruded upon her solitude.

"Yes," he bit out grimly, a heated surge of anger rising in him at her lack of regard for her own safety. Was she daft, foolish, or merely defying him out of spite?

His voice pried her from her vigil. Her eyes were wide when they collided with his, her expression startled until she quickly replaced all emotion with her customary hauteur. Who was this stranger she had become? Every inch of her was a duchess.

Her face remained the same, but beyond that he could not recognize even a hint of the Ara he had known. Of course, that Ara had proved a lie.

"Why have you returned, Mr. Ludlow?" she demanded in a frigid tone.

His gaze flicked to the servant, who had the beginnings of a fire kindling in the grate, before returning to her. "It is my duty to remain near to your side, madam."

Something flashed in those violet-blue orbs, but just as quickly, it was gone. "No, Mr. Ludlow, it is not."

He would not argue with her before the domestic. He did not want the staff to become aware of the enmity between them, for it would undermine his authority in the household, and the last thing he needed was to perpetuate any vulnerability. "I am afraid the matter is not open for discussion."

She paled. "How do you dare, sir?"

He said nothing, maintaining his silence.

The longer the quiet between them stretched, punctuated by the scraping and toiling of the footman stoking the fire, the more pinched her lips became. At last, a roaring, snapping fire filled the fireplace, sending a burst of warmth into the chamber. The servant bowed and excused himself.

They were alone. Again.

With nothing to stop him from giving in to his instincts to take her in his arms.

Nothing except his sanity, that was.

The door had scarcely clicked closed behind the footman when she unleashed her ire upon him. "If you returned thinking to offer me further remonstration, you may go, Mr. Ludlow. I neither require nor want to hear your warnings concerning the ruffians who plot against me."

"Ruffians." The bitter bark of his laughter was torn from him. "The men who want you dead are barbaric murderers, Your Grace. The sooner you acquaint yourself with your new reality, the better each day shall go for you."

"I am already more than acquainted," she snapped. "Do not think to condescend to me or I shall contact someone at the Home Office myself and have you removed from this post for insubordination."

"How amusing, Your Grace." The smile he gave her was equally dark and mirthless. "Do you not think that I have already attempted to have myself removed from this most unwanted post? Did you not imagine I would have done everything in my power to avoid being tasked with the protection of the woman I loathe?"

She froze at his queries, going paler still at the last. Was it his fanciful imagination, or did he see hurt in her expression for a fleeting moment? And if so, why? She had to know he would hate the sight of her after what she had done. After not only her betrayal but also his scarring. To this day, he did not know whether or not the knife to his face had been her idea or her darling papa's, but if he ever needed a reminder of why she could not be trusted, he only had to look upon his reflection.

Did she view the evidence of her treachery with shame, he wondered, or with pride? His scar burned and throbbed on his cheek. For a moment, he could feel the blade again, slicing through his flesh, leaving behind the permanent mark of his stupidity. An *aide-mémoire* he could have done without.

"If you do not wish to be here, then why do you remain, Mr. Ludlow?" Her question cut through the grim silence that had descended.

"Duty," he answered swiftly. "Unlike most, when I make a vow, I honor it."

Damn it. He had not meant to speak with such candor. Had not meant to even hint at their shared past. Their shared sins.

She inhaled as if he had struck her. "Forgive me, Mr. Ludlow, but I seem to recall a vow you did not honor. I will ask you again. Why do you remain here if you do not want either this task or my loathsome presence? Why are you here now, within this chamber, with me?"

How dare she suggest he had not honored his every vow? He had made many vows to her, and he had remained true to them all with the exception of one. *I vow to you I will always love you, Ara. You will have my heart forever and the century next.*

But of course he had stopped loving her. He had needed to after what she had done to him. To them. He could still recall each word of the letter she had written as if it had been branded into his skin.

He ground his jaw. "Do not presume to speak to me of such matters, madam, when the evidence of your duplicity is plain for all to see."

"How dare you?" She moved at last, stalking forward, her skirts swishing, fire in her cheeks.

He knew what she intended before she had even reached him. He caught her wrist easily, deflecting the blow she would have delivered. How small she was, how fine-boned beneath his grip. His hands swallowed her. If he exerted enough pressure, he could crush her as if she were as delicate as a baby bird.

He could not hurt her. Would never hurt her.

"It would not go well for you, Your Grace, were you to strike me," he warned.

"I want you gone!"

Her anguished cry echoed in the room, the first real display of emotion she had shown since he had first laid eyes upon her yesterday. Did she hate him that much? Or, like him, did she hate the weakness that lingered?

Unlike time and the two of them, her scent had not changed: vibrant summer blossoms of a rose merged with a hint of orange. It hit him then, along with a wall of memories. Dancing in the forest, her eyes laughing up at him, stealing his first kiss from her soft, supple lips. Riding with her beneath a black velvet sky studded with glittering stars.

How brilliant the future had seemed then. How rife with possibility.

No longer.

Here he stood looking down upon the ghost of the girl he had loved, a vast, gaping chasm of emptiness threatening to consume him. He released her wrist. Took a step back from her because it was necessary. He feared he could not control himself where she was concerned here in this moment, with the tension and the pain of the past vibrating around them.

"Do not dare to attempt to strike me again, madam," he seethed. "And do not keep your back to the door. From this moment forward, you will trust no one. Assume everyone wishes you ill, myself included. Though it grieves me to say it, if you wish to survive until the bastards behind your husband's death are caught and clapped into gaol, you need me here. The Home Office has decreed it, and it is my duty to remain. That is why I am here. The very instant the danger has passed you, I will be gone from your life forever, and that is one vow I can promise you I will uphold above all others."

He did not wait for her to speak, for he could not bear to hear another word. With a curt, mocking bow, he took his leave of her for the second time. He could only hope the Fenians who had murdered Burghly would be caught.

Soon.

Chapter Four

Eight years earlier

HIS NAME WAS Clayton.

Ara had tried it out on her tongue in the privacy of her chamber. She had written it on her sketchbook in charcoal. She had penned it into the margins of her journal as if it were the lyrics to a favorite hymn. Over and over again, small and neat, large and dramatic, sometimes with a flourish, sometimes accompanied by a heart. What silly doodles. What foolishness.

She was old enough, wise enough, to know her heart could not possibly love him already after having met with him in secret each day for the last fortnight. And yet, she could not stifle the emotion bubbling up inside her, like a kettle filled to the brim upon a hot stove.

She was boiling. Threatening to overflow. He was all she could think about. His name, his face, his hands. They were so large, the fingers so long and thick and handsome. Could fingers be handsome? Yes, she decided, they could. For if anyone had a question regarding such a notion, they had only to look upon Clayton's hands.

They were lovely and gentle, sculpted perfection. Capable of anything really, but most of all tenderness. Though he had not touched her with them, she had lain awake at night in the loneliness of her chamber and imagined those strong, masculine hands upon her. Lifting her nightdress. Skimming over her ankles and calves. Caressing her in the place only she had dared trespass upon, though she knew how wicked it was.

But if it was wicked, why did it feel so lovely and pure and good? This was ever a conundrum in Ara's mind, one she had put to her mother. Mama had blanched and urged her to never again speak of such a despicable thing.

And so, Ara had learned her lesson. She would never again ask her mother about such matters. Instead, she would enjoy *despicable things* without worrying about the rightness or wrongness of them. For indeed, no gentleman had ever made her feel so many *despicable things* as Clayton.

She felt them now as she allowed her mind to wander to him while she awaited his presence in their appointed meeting place. He was so strong. His lips were beautiful, as was his smile. What would they feel like against hers? Would he dare to kiss her? Would she dare to let him if he did? He had been a perfect gentleman upon each of their clandestine meetings. Nothing he had said or done had suggested his heart beat for her in the same fashion hers did for him.

But she liked to believe they had an unspoken bond. An understanding.

From the moment he had come upon her in the forest that day, they had spoken to each other with a candor and an ease she had never known. She was one-and-twenty years of age. She had taken her curtsy at court, had experienced her comeout. She had been courted by suitors who inspired not even a flutter in her belly or a pounding in her heart. Nothing and no one compared to Clayton.

Or, as she had begun to think of him recently when she was mooning over him in the privacy of her chamber each night, *Clay*. Yes, that was the perfect name for him. Far more suiting than the rigid and overbearing Clayton.

She tried her new sobriquet for him in the welcoming shade of the forest. "Clay." A dreamy sigh escaped her as she waited, hoping he would return as he had promised he would.

It had been fourteen days since he had discovered her watching him in the forest. Fourteen days since they had spoken for the first time. Fourteen days since everything had changed.

"Lady Araminta."

With a squeal of surprise, she spun about to find him, her beautiful man. She had not heard him approach, but she had learned in the short time they had known each other Clay was adept at being stealthy. If he wished to be heard, he would be. If he chose to remain elusive, no one would have an inkling he had approached.

Heat rushed to her cheeks as she realized he must have seen her pacing about, sighing his name to herself as if she were a young girl who had just seen her first gentleman.

"Call me Ara if you please," she corrected him, furrowing her brow. "It suits me ever so much better. If only I could convince my family of the same. They seem to enjoy making light of my irritation."

Oh, Lord. She was rambling again. Saying too much, allowing her inner nervousness to surpass her poise and grace. He came nearer to her, handsome in a way that was almost reminiscent of nature itself. He was rugged and beautiful, raw and angular, a force.

"Ara." He smiled then, striding forward. His teeth were even and neat.

She wanted to kiss him. Or for him to kiss her. Anything, any action on either of their parts that resulted in their mouths fusing would be lovely. It would be enough to change her world forever, she was sure of it.

And, she hoped, to change his as well.

They were meant to be together, the two of them. She knew this with the kind of certainty that told her the sun would rise each day. She felt it deep in her heart, in her bones. In her soul.

"I do like the way you say my name," she whispered, watching with wide eyes as he stopped only when his boots brushed her skirts.

She wanted more.

"I like the way you say mine." He touched her chin then. Just a small, brief caress.

And she melted. "Clay. Won't you kiss me?"

He shook his head, his dark regard growing intent. "I would not presume to take such a liberty, nor am I fit to do so. You deserve far better than a lowly man such as me. You deserve everything, in fact. All the stars and the moon, the sun, every flower, every diamond, each ruby. Were it in my power, I would give you all those things."

The ferocity in his tone struck her heart. "I do not want those things, Clay. All I want is you."

And your heart. Please, please, say it can be mine.

He exhaled, the sound harsh. "You do not even know me, my lady."

But of course, she knew him. They had shared a great deal about each other these last two weeks. He liked to read poetry best. He was a talented rider. Hunting had never appealed to him. His favorite color was copper, like her hair. He did not enjoy sweets, though he could not resist fruit, especially pineapples. He had one brother.

"I know you," she argued, daring to reach up and cup his whisker-roughened cheek. "Moreover, it would not be taking a liberty if I give my approval."

He shook his head, shrugging away from her touch and putting some space between them. "What you ask is impossible. I am not who you think me."

She frowned, following him, confounded by his sudden withdrawal. "You are Lord Clayton, the Duke of Carlisle's son. I have already told you I do not give a fig about the feud between our fathers. Their old enmity belongs to them and not us. We cannot allow it to ruin our friendship."

Or—she dared hope—their courtship.

Clay's father the duke owned the lands bordering her father's estate, but for reasons her father refused to divulge, the two men detested each other. The quarrel was the reason for the reticence she sensed in Clay from time to time, she was sure.

"I am not Lord Clayton," he bit out grimly, plucking the hat from atop his head and flinging it to the forest floor.

A trickle of unease licked down her spine. It occurred to her for the first time that perhaps he had lied about his identity. Mayhap he was a groomsman or a steward for the Duke of Carlisle. She would not have known the difference, having never been introduced to any of the duke's household. He could have led her along quite easily. And she had lapped up every word he spoke like an eager little kitten. Because she had lost her heart to him somewhere along the last fortnight of furtive meetings.

Her every day revolved around when she could sneak away and what subterfuge she might employ so she could see him once again. She passed the hours from their goodbye to the moment she saw him again filled with desperate longing.

She touched his coat sleeve, needing to feel his reassuring strength and warmth. "Have you deceived me, then?"

If he had, she did not care. It did not matter to her who he was. She would forgive him. She would find a way to be with him. For now that she had known him, she could not fathom her life without him in it. They were like two halves coming together to form the perfect whole.

He stiffened but did not move away from her this time. His countenance was hard and harsh, so different from the young gentleman she had come to know. "I am Clayton Ludlow."

She blinked, her brow furrowing. "I am afraid I do not understand, Clay. That is precisely how you introduced yourself on the first day we met."

"I am a bastard," he bit out, the words emerging like a feral roar, torn from him, it seemed. "Specifically, I am the duke's bastard. Not a lord. Not *Lord Clayton*. I will never be a lord. Nor will I ever be truly welcomed in drawing rooms or ballrooms. There will not come a day when those who see me do not look upon me with scorn, knowing I am the product of sin."

His revelation took her breath. But not because of who or what he was. Rather, because of the resigned manner in which he disparaged himself. It was as if he believed he was a monster to be shunned. That he was unfit, lesser than because his father had not married his mother. He could not help the circumstances of his birth. Tears welled in her eyes, unshed. For him. For the burden he had borne his whole life, the burden he would always carry.

"Clay, it does not signify," she began, but he cut her off.

"Yes, it bloody well does," he hissed, raking those long, beautiful fingers through his rich, dark hair until it stood on end. "I was wrong. So damned wrong to allow this to carry on for as long as I did. I should not even have besmirched your reputation by speaking with you. I do not know what I could have been thinking. You must not—*we cannot*—associate with each other any longer. I am so sorry, Ara, but this has to be goodbye. It must be goodbye for us."

"No." She launched herself at him then, without a second

thought. Without a moment of hesitation. Straight into his chest she went, her arms looping around his lean waist and holding tight. She breathed in his delicious scent. His heart thrummed.

"Ara, release me," he growled, tugging at her arms in an attempt to dislodge her.

"No," she repeated into his coat, turning her face until her ear rested above that reassuring thump. She locked her arms tighter. "Never."

He caught her elbows and pulled. "This is not proper, and if the earl were to discover I have been meeting with you in secret, he would have my hide and you would be ruined. We need to forget we ever met. I am not for you, and you are far too good for the likes of me."

"You cannot say that," she cried with feeling, still holding on to him with all her might. "I will never, ever forget you. I do not care if you are not Lord Clay. I have never wished to be a lady anyway. All I want is to be happy."

Mama was a countess, and she was not happy. Rosamunde had become a countess as well, and each time Ara saw her, the grooves of sadness alongside her eyes had grown deeper. Titles and wealth and comfort did not make a contented heart.

His hands slid from her elbows to her upper arms, gripping, but not with enough pressure to hurt her. Rather, it felt as if he was not sure if he wanted to set her away from him or bring her closer still. "It is easy for you to say so, when you have been treated with respect all your life. You are your father's rightful daughter. You are a lady. No one will ever look upon you with disgust, as if you are a shameful secret that should have been locked away."

He was right. She had never experienced what he must have endured, and she could not fathom the pain he must know, being treated as if he were less worthy than anyone else by mere virtue of his birth.

"You make me happy," she whispered, stroking him tentatively at first. Just a swipe of her right palm over the indent of his lower back. Then higher, up the rigid curve of his spine where corded muscles flexed beneath her touch. And then her other hand could not resist moving as well, following the same path, not halting until she reached his powerful shoulders.

So much strength contained in one man.

His arms and his large, lean frame dwarfed her. But she had never felt more safe or alive.

"I cannot make you happy." His voice rumbled against her ear, mingling with the steady, reassuring throbs of his heartbeat. "I cannot bring anyone happiness. I am a curse."

But his hands too had shifted, one cupping her shoulder, the other curling about her nape. He did not wear gloves, and his bare skin upon hers sent a shiver of something wonderfully sinful tremoring all the way to her toes and then back up her body once more, settling between her thighs.

The *despicable thing* had returned.

"You're wrong," she told him, daring to tilt her head back and look up at him. "You bring me happiness, Clay."

Their gazes clashed, his dark and angry and fraught with a host of emotions she could not begin to read. He was so handsome, so beloved, and she ached just looking upon him.

He caught his full lower lip in his teeth, worrying it, and how she longed to kiss him there. To set her lips upon the flesh he tortured. To soothe it. To take away his every pain.

Clay let out a low groan. "Do not look at me in such a fashion, I beg of you, my lady."

"In what fashion?" she asked innocently, allowing her gaze to stray once more—quite intentionally—to his mouth, for it had seemed to provoke him.

His tongue replaced his teeth, flicking over his lip. He blew out a gusty sigh. His fingers had begun to slide upward, settling in her carefully pinned coiffure. "You are an innocent, damn it, and you have not the slightest inkling of how I could destroy you. I am not someone you should know, Lady Ara."

But he could never destroy her. She did not believe it possible. And neither could she resist him. He was Clayton Ludlow, and he was temptation, and she knew without a doubt he was the only man she would ever love. The realization settled in her heart, and she welcomed it.

"I do not care if you are a lord," she told him, her voice firm, nary a trace of doubt shadowing her words. "I do not care about anything other than that you are Clay, *my* Clay. Seeing you fills me with warmth. Thinking of you makes me smile. I spend all the time I am not in your presence wishing myself back in it until I am here again, with you."

"Damn it, Ara, do not do this." His chocolate eyes begged. "I am trying to be a gentleman, to send you away from me with your innocence and your reputation intact. I cannot be the man for you."

She did not want her innocence.

Did not want for him to be a gentleman.

Nor did she care for her reputation.

Nothing and no one mattered but the man in her arms, the man who was looking down upon her as if she were the most perfect and revered thing he had ever seen.

Her life had been lonely and empty before him, her future prospects an abysmal marriage like her parents shared—a match made in reason and not in love, doomed to make both parties miserable. She did not want to spend the rest of her life hiding in her chamber, feigning megrims because she could not bear to face what she had become. Now she had found something different. Something right. And she was not going to allow it to slip through her fingers.

She hooked her arms around his neck, rocked onto her toes, and fitted her lips to his. With a low sound of need his mouth took hers, claiming and hungry and seeking. Shocking. Unlike any other forbidden peck she had ever received from a previous suitor.

His tongue swept past her lips, delving into her mouth. Decadent and absolutely delicious. It made *the despicable thing* quiver and burn inside her.

But just as quickly as he had branded her with his kiss, he dragged his lips from hers and set her away from him. A vicious curse rent the air. He stared down at her, his chest heaving, his eyes darker than obsidian.

"I am no good for you, Lady Araminta," he said finally. "Do not come looking for me tomorrow, as I will not return. It is for the best. For your own good."

And then he spun and stalked away into the forest, disappearing as if he had never been there at all. She stared, unseeing, holding two fingers to her lips.

Chapter Five

"MAMA!"

Ara bent, arms open, as her beloved son hurtled toward her. His long arms wrapped around her, and he nestled his face into the smooth silk of her mourning bodice. She caught him, burying her face in his head of dark, unruly curls and inhaling. He was growing taller every day, and soon she would no longer need to bend at the waist to embrace him at all.

If he took after his father, in no time, he would surpass her in height. Already, she saw the signs. His arms and legs were lanky and awkward. Even his neck seemed too long for his body, as if preparing for the frame he would one day grow into. Nothing about him resembled her at all, except for his eyes. He would become a strapping young gentleman, towering over her.

How odd to think that the babe she had carried in her womb and held lovingly in her arms would one day become a man. Would he resemble Clay even more as he aged? The thought pained her, but she could not help but to wonder.

Regardless, it would little matter, for Clayton Ludlow would be long gone from both their lives at that point. He would never be the wiser.

Why did the notion cause a pang in her breast? An ache that would not dissipate? She did not wish to think about it.

Did not wish to feel. Instead, she turned all her emotions toward the thin body in her arms.

"Edward, my love." She hugged him tightly, grateful he was not yet of an age where he did not wish to hug his mother. He was still innocent and young enough to think she could do no wrong and the world was a fair, safe, and lovely place.

Ah, innocence.

"Mama, you are squeezing me far too tightly," he complained.

Perhaps there went her supposition he still felt she could do no wrong. Just as well, for she most assuredly could do wrong. And she had. But she had spent the last eight years doing her best to ensure none of those wrongs would come home to roost.

She released her son, smiling down at him as a surge of maternal protectiveness rose within her. Nothing could have prepared her for the love in her heart the moment she had first gazed down upon her babe in swaddling. His face had been red and wrinkled, his hair a dark tuft that had reminded her painfully of Clay, but her heart had sung. Being a mother gave her, all at once, both the greatest joys and the greatest frustrations she had ever known.

She could not resist ruffling his dark locks affectionately. "And how is my favorite gentleman today?"

"Growing weary of his studies," he grumbled. "I wish to go outside. It feels as if we have been trapped inside these walls forever."

Essentially, they had. Their time of mourning had stretched, each day slowly less bleak than the last. And then, just when their lives had at last begun to settle back into a semblance of normalcy, the Home Office had sent its emissaries and its dire warnings of threats against her life.

Resentment surged inside her, clawing up her throat until she longed to scream. How dare those villains murder Freddie? How dare they take a young boy's father from him? As if their crimes were not heinous enough, they then sought to take his mother as well. The injustice of it all made her want to lash out. To smash something.

But she was not a violent person.

She was a mother, and she had to be strong and calm now for her son.

She had not yet told him about the danger facing her, and she was not sure she would. Each time the words rose on her tongue, she swallowed them down with the bile, unable to shatter his fragile world once more.

"The weather outside is unseasonably chilly," she told him lightly, "and the fog is particularly atrocious. I should say it is not a day for the out-of-doors."

Edward frowned, his expression looking so much like Clay's stern visage that it took her breath. "It is almost always foggy, Mama. I do not care. I want to stretch my legs."

"You are stretching them now, my darling boy." She tried to keep the worry from her voice, but she feared it bled through. Her concerns were twofold now: the Fenian threat and Clayton Ludlow both. She had not realized, until Clay's abrupt return to her life, just how uncanny the resemblance was between true father and son.

He had not met Edward yet, and now she was more certain than ever that she must keep that introduction from occurring. If he suspected the truth, she did not know what she would do. She could only hope her marriage to Freddie would vanquish any suspicion from his mind. But one had only to look at Edward and Clay to see they shared the same blood.

"I want to run, Mama," he said. "I want to run in the

gardens."

Yet another trait he and Clay shared: a love of physical motion. Before Freddie's death, she had smilingly sent Edward outside whenever his boisterous nature required freedom and movement. But things were different now. There could be hidden dangers lurking for him outside. Anything could happen, and she would not risk her son. He was all she had.

"You are the duke now," she told him quietly, and though it was true she ought to encourage him to begin accustoming himself to his future duties, she hated the lie. "You must remember your position."

"Papa is the duke, not me." Edward's lip trembled. "I miss him."

Tears welled in her eyes, and she gathered her son against her once more, embracing him every bit as tightly as before in spite of his earlier protest. "I miss him as well, my darling. But we must be brave together. Papa would want us to be brave. And he would be so very proud of how strong you have been. You will make an honorable and good Duke of Burghly. This I know with all my heart."

Freddie had been their pillar. He had always been ready with a smile or a quip. His wit and his heart were unparalleled, and he had been so very generous with both. There had never been a doubt in her mind that he loved Edward as if he were his own son. When he had offered her his unconventional proposal, he had made it clear to her he would accept her babe—male or female—as his own. And he had. He had more than lived up to every promise he had made on that day.

Until his death. Even in death, he had made certain she and Edward would be protected.

"Do you think I can be as fine a man as he was?" Edward asked solemnly.

The anguish on his small countenance made her crumble

inside, but she refused to allow it to show. Instead, she smiled and cupped his face. "I know you can be, for you already are."

"Thank you, Mama," Edward whispered. "I hope you are right. Papa always said you know better than anyone else, and I must trust you in all matters."

Dear Freddie. Of course he would have said so. In truth, she did not know better, and she had committed more sins in her lifetime than she could count. She was not a good person. She was no one for her son to pattern himself after.

Something twisted painfully inside her chest then. A river of guilt deluged her, rushing over the grief. Edward had lost the only father he had ever known, but his flesh-and-blood father was somewhere beneath the same roof. She had deceived her son for seven years, and for a mad moment she wished she could unburden herself to him now. To reveal to him his father was Clayton Ludlow.

But she could never, ever do something so foolish.

If Clay discovered Edward was his son, she had no way of knowing how he would react. Already, he was icy and aloof. He spoke to her as if being in her presence was abhorrent. If he found out she had kept his son from him for all these years...

Then again, perhaps he would not care. After all, he had left her without a word. Abandoning her to face her father and her shame alone. Leaving her with no choice but to accept the proposal of any man who offered. Ara had done the only thing she could. That she and Freddie had found each other at all was a miracle, and she would forever be grateful to him for being the best man she had ever known.

A truer and finer gentleman than he had never lived.

Blinking back tears, she released Edward with great reluctance. "There now, you have turned me into a watering pot."

"Papa was always smiling," her son observed with a gravity that belied his age. "He would want us to smile too, Mama. He always hated when you cried."

Yes, he had. Much to her shame, there had been days when—despite the fulfillment of being Edward's mother and despite the comfortable companionship she'd shared with Freddie—she had been miserable. Days when the past and what might have been had returned to swallow her whole. Freddie had always managed to chase her doldrums in one fashion or another. Sometimes, with chocolate. Others with bawdy jokes.

She smiled sadly to think back on those innocent days. Her old self would not have been able to fathom what lay ahead. Indeed, she could scarcely wrap her mind around it.

"You make me smile now," she told her son. "I love you so very much, my darling boy."

"I love you too, Mama," he said, looking down at his shoes, shuffling them as if embarrassed.

Who was this young man he was turning into before her eyes? Was it Freddie's death that had manifested it, or was it merely a part of growing into a young man? She could not say, but either way, her heart hurt.

"We will go on an excursion soon," she told him suddenly, wanting to chase the sadness from his eyes. "Anywhere you like, I shall take you. Think on it, and then we will go."

He beamed. "Thank you, Mama."

She fixed him with a stern look. "Now off with you, my love. You must return to your studies. I shall see you in a few hours, and I expect a report on everything you have learned."

Looking lighter, his shoulders not stooping quite so low with the weight he carried in the wake of Freddie's death, he bowed. Then he was gone, leaving her alone in her sitting room with only her guilt and her sadness to keep her company.

DAMN IT ALL to hell.

His bloody cat was missing. Clay had searched his apartments, sinking to his knees on the plush woolen carpet to peer beneath the bed, looking atop furniture, beneath chairs. Anywhere he could conceive of the feline hiding, he had examined. After half an hour of thorough searching, he had reached the conclusion that someone—likely a Burghly House chambermaid or other such domestic—had inadvertently allowed Sherman to escape.

The little fellow had a fondness for freedom, and Clay could not fault him for it. Lord knew he longed for the same, and more than ever now he was forced to do his duty in such proximity to the woman who had betrayed him. But since he had been keeping Sherman's presence to himself, locating the feline could prove all the more difficult.

Today marked his third at Burghly House.

He grimaced, making one last, cursory search of his chamber before he ventured onward in his quest. Three days of being within the same walls as Ara. Two nights of sleeping a scant few chambers away.

For the differences between them and the ugliness of their past, she might as well have been in another country rather than just at the opposite end of the hall. She was as far removed from him as she had ever been. At least on this second go around, he had the benefit of knowing precisely where he stood with her.

She had no longer wanted him when she finally realized it would mean giving up her title and her riches. She had seemed so innocent and good when he had first met her in the forest joining their fathers' lands, and he had been a fool to believe in her protestations that his bastardry did not matter to her.

Like any man hungering for more than he had been apportioned, she had been a siren's song for him. The beautiful earl's daughter with violet-blue eyes and fiery hair, with the sweet kisses and beseeching gazes and the promises he never should have believed.

Hell yes, he had believed every one of them. But the blade of a knife had dispelled his disillusions just as swiftly. For when she had truly understood that doors would close to her, that she would not be treated to the manner of respect she was accustomed, that she would not possess the prestige and wealth she desired, she had betrayed him.

Your blood for the blood you spilled, the man who had sliced open his face had said coolly. *The earl considers the debt paid now. You will never speak to Lady Araminta or look upon her again.*

On that day, he had made a firm promise to himself he would never again be weak. On that day, he had begun fashioning himself into the hardened man he had ultimately become.

How ironic, then, that the warrior he now was—the trained assassin, the man who could wield a blade or pistol or the strength of his hands with lethal results—was now searching for one errant feline.

"Sherman," he called one last time for good measure, lest he linger in the chamber all day, trapped in the muck of his past.

The cat did not materialize, not so much as the hint of a meow or a swish of a tail. Clay exited his chamber and stalked down the hall, knowing from past experience the first place he ought to look was outside. The furry devil adored fresh air, and he considered an opened door his own personal invitation.

Sighing, Clay made his way to the first floor of the stately house. He had enjoyed a productive start to his stay here. He had added six additional guards after an inspection of the periphery of the home. He had interviewed servants. Most importantly, he had kept his distance from the duchess.

He had not seen her since their clash in the drawing room the day before. Since then, he had taken each of his meals in his chamber, for he did not wish to break bread with her. The ears and eyes he had on the streets of London had reported to him that for the moment, all appeared quiet on the Fenian front. Authorities were doing their damnedest to run those responsible for Burghly's death to ground—as well they should—so that was likely the reason for the silence.

He could only hope after the passing of a fortnight without incident, he would be permitted to leave this unwanted post far behind him. If there was no hint of further acts of vengeance upon the duchess, and if the Fenians retreated to lick their wounds, and if the most alarming thing to have occurred thus far during his stay here was the disappearance of his bloody cat, he could not imagine any means by which Leo or the Home Office would compel him to stay.

The longer he remained here, the more dangerous it was to his sanity. To his restraint. To his ability to keep from either kissing or throttling the Duchess of Burghly. *Damn it*, he hated thinking of her as her title, for it seemed so far removed from the girl with the bewitching smiles and the tender kisses. The girl who had defied her father to sneak away and meet him…

But then, that girl had been a fantasy.

And the fantasy had become the duchess.

And he remained the duke's bastard.

Hopeless, all around.

He made his way to the door that led to the gardens and exited, expecting he would find the cat somewhere within the neatly kept labyrinth of shrubbery. It did not take him long to hear a familiar meow, but he was not quite prepared for the discovery he made when he rounded a well-manicured hedge.

There, on a stone bench, sat a young, dark-haired boy, holding the missing cat in his lap. Long-limbed and thin-framed, he was a collection of awkward angles that rather put him in mind of himself at a younger age. It had not been until he'd gained his twentieth year that he had finally begun to grow into his own massive frame, and even then, it had taken more years for him to build his muscles and strength.

Clay stopped. He recognized the boy from the pictures he had seen on his first day at Burghly House. The same pictures he was forced to walk past each day, only now he had become more adept at ignoring them.

It was the lad.

Her lad.

The sight of him was akin to a blade sinking into Clay's gut. Ara had a son. Of course she did. She had also had a husband. Another life that spanned far more years than the stolen weeks they had once shared. His rational mind knew these undeniable truths. But the sight of him, in vivid color before Clay, holding his bloody cat, took that knowledge and made it real. So real it burned in his gut and the backs of his eyes.

The boy looked up at him, his expression wary. "Who are you, sir?"

Canny of the little fellow not to trust anyone. Clay supposed that was the way of things now the lad's father had been murdered. He approached the bench, flashing what he hoped was a reassuring smile. He had no inkling of what to say to children. Possessing a scarred visage and a massive form did not precisely endear him to them.

He bowed. "I am Mr. Ludlow. Perhaps a more apt question would be who are you, and why have you stolen my feline?"

The boy's eyes went wide, and here at last was the resemblance to Ara in the blue-violet gaze. "I am the Duke of Burghly, and I do not thieve cats, sir. I found him wandering in the halls, and as we were both lonely and in need of sunshine, we decided to tour the garden."

How strange to think Ara's son—this pale, sad-looking youth—was a duke. Clay bent and gave Sherman a head scratch. The cat rose on his hind legs with a sound of approval that was half purr, half meow. "Did you have a dialogue with him, Your Grace?"

The lad blinked, his brows snapping together. "Of course not, sir. He is a cat and cannot speak."

He scratched his chin, feigning perplexity. "How very odd, then, that you would know he was lonely and in need of sunshine."

"I surmised," the lad said, looking proud of himself.

"Ah, clever fellow, Your Grace," he said. "For a moment there, I was convinced you were capable of speaking cat."

The lad laughed, giving Sherman a long stroke over his back. The traitorous cat showed no inclination to leave his new friend's lap. "You are making a sally, Mr. Ludlow."

"Yes," he admitted, realizing he was actually enjoying this odd little exchange. The boy's dark hair caught his attention once more. For some reason, he had imagined the lad's hair would be copper like his mother's. "Does anyone know you are here in the gardens on your own?"

"Are you one of the men who has come to protect us from the bad men who murdered Papa?" the lad asked instead of answering his query. "I overheard the servants talking."

The question took him by surprise. "Yes," he answered simply. "I am. And this furred menace is my most trusted partner. He was a gift to me from a friend with a talent for rescuing stray animals. His name is Sherman."

The lad nodded. "Sherman. I do think the name suits him, though I had him in mind as Mr. Patches. He is a most agreeable feline, sir."

"Most discerning of you, Your Grace," he intoned seriously, "for his full Christian name is Mr. Sherman Patches."

Ara's son smiled at him again, this time revealing a missing front tooth. "You are strange, Mr. Ludlow, but I think I like you. I know I like Mr. Sherman Patches. Only do not tell Mama you have him here. I asked her for a puppy a few days ago, and she told me animals do not belong inside the home."

"Is that so?" He patted Sherman on the head once more, recalling the household schedule. The boy was to be ensconced with his governess in the schoolroom at this time, which strongly suggested the governess was not performing her duties. "Then he will have to be our secret, Your Grace. Now unless I am mistaken, you ought to be at your studies. Is that not right?"

The lad looked sheepish. "Yes, but Miss Argent sometimes snoozes into our Latin books, and then I come out here to the garden. You won't tell Mama, will you?"

Clay had two men stationed on the perimeter of this side of Burghly House, but he did not like the thought of the lad wandering about unchaperoned. What the devil was his governess doing falling asleep in the midst of his studies, anyway?

"From now on when you wish to venture into the garden, find me and I shall accompany you," he offered.

"The bad men will not come to our gardens, will they, Mr. Ludlow?" the lad asked, his face ashen.

The boy's question brought a lump to his throat. He did not want to like this boy, who was half Ara and half another man, and yet he did. No young child should have to fear for his safety in his own home.

He met the boy's gaze, so like his mother's. "Not while I am here, Your Grace. Now come. We must return Sherman to my apartments before he is spotted by your mama, and we must also return you to your studies."

"Very well, Mr. Ludlow. I suppose I have been outside taking the air long enough."

Clay scooped his cat into his arms.

Devil take it, what was that infernal warmth blossoming in his chest?

This will not do. It will not do at all.

Chapter Six

Eight years earlier

THERE SHE STOOD, illuminated in the beam of light filtering through the tree boughs overhead so her hair glowed with fire. Her hat dangled from her fingers, suspended by trailing satin ribbons, and she wore no gloves. Her riding habit was vibrant blue. She looked like a goddess fashioned of ice and fire.

Clay knew damn well he never should have returned for her. He should have left her here, knowing inevitably there would come a day when she no longer waited for him and she would move on with her life. She would find a gentleman who was worthy of her, one who was suitable for her to wed. Some earl or duke. Perhaps the heir apparent. A man who could give her jewels and silk gowns. Who could escort her to the most fashionable balls and soirees.

But he was selfish. He wanted her more than he wanted to take his next breath. And so, he had come back to their meeting place deep in the forest connecting her father's estate to his, hoping she would be there at the appointed time, as always. He could not halt his forward motion now. He was like a cannonball shot from a gun, speeding his way to her, hell-bent upon destruction.

Her destruction. His.

He was not the man for her. But his heart was stubborn,

and it damn well refused to listen to his head. Here he was, hers for the taking even though he knew it was wrong.

"Clay," she murmured when she saw him, opening her arms and running to meet him.

He caught her against him, burying his face in her sweetly fragrant locks as she pressed hers to his neck. Nothing smelled as lovely as Ara, warm and soft and sun-kissed, rose blossoms, woman, everything forbidden. Everything he had ever wanted and never dared to dream could be his. It had only been one day since she had kissed him, and it had felt as if a lifetime had passed.

How could he ever bear to let her go when it seemed as if she was the other half of him?

Something hard and small distracted him then, a sharp corner cutting into his thigh. *What the devil?* It seemed to be coming from her dress.

"What are you hiding in your skirts, Ara?" he could not resist asking.

"Oh!" Flushing and sending him a coy smile as she stepped back from his embrace, she reached into a hidden pocket in her gown and extracted a small, red leather volume. "This is for you, Clay."

Warmth suffused him as he accepted the book. No lady of his acquaintance had ever given him a gift before. He looked down at the volume in his hands. "Poems."

"These are not just any poems." Her smile widened to reveal a slight dimple in her left cheek. "This book is from my favorite collection. There are two volumes. Now you will have the first volume, and I shall have the second. Two pieces that go together."

His heart thumped as he opened the cover and read the inscription she had left for him. *To Clay from Your Ara. When you are ready for Volume II, you know where to find it.*

Something trickled through him. His gut clenched. He looked up to find her watching him intently, her nose adorably scrunched as she awaited his verdict.

Bloody, bloody hell.

"Thank you. I have never received a more perfect gift." He hauled her back into his arms, kissing her crown. "Ara. My sweet, foolish Ara. Why did you come back when I told you I am not the man for you?"

"Why did you?" she returned.

"Because I was hoping you would be here and I could not stay away, wondering if you were." The confession was all but ripped from him. He did not want to reveal the depth of emotion he felt for her, but it was impossible to deny her when she was in his arms.

He would do anything—anything—to keep her there.

The realization sobered him. Terrified him.

"I am glad you could not," she whispered. "I know our fathers have a bitter old grudge, but their enmity does not concern me. Will you come to Kingswood Hall and court me?"

Her question robbed him of the ability to speak for a moment. How could she possibly imagine her father would allow the bastard son of the Duke of Carlisle—a man he loathed—to court his youngest daughter? She was either incredibly bold or incredibly naïve.

With another kiss upon her crown because he could not help himself, he at last set her at arm's length from him, gazing down into her upturned face. "Ara, I am a bastard. Your father would never permit me to call upon you, never mind court you. No father worth his salt would countenance such a match. It would be an insult to both him and you."

He begged her to understand with his gaze. To make this easier for them rather than more difficult and painful. If their last goodbye had not stuck, then this one would have to. For both their sakes.

"My father is in London," she said. "Mama said he had some important matters to attend to, but my lady's maid told me he is seeing his kept woman in St. John's Wood and that is why he has gone. A very lovely French actress, I am told, not much older than I am."

He stared down at her, shocked by her words and her knowledge both. She spoke so calmly of her father's infidelity, as if she spoke of the weather. An innocent girl should never know such ugly underbellies of life.

Of course, it was the natural order of things, and he knew it. His own mother was one such kept lady. But she loved his father with all her heart, and he returned that love. It was why Clay had been raised alongside his half brother Leo in a rather uncommon fashion. But neither that love nor the advantages his father had provided him could expunge the taint of his birth.

"You ought not to know of such things," he said at last. "Your woman never should have gossiped to you in such malicious fashion."

Ara shook her head, the stubborn expression he had come to know all too well in their fortnight of secret meetings coming over her face. "I am glad she did. I do not want to be kept ignorant of the truth. I wish to know all there is to know. About everything."

She took a step toward him, her countenance changing once more. Her eyes darkened to unadulterated violet, and there was something glittering within their gorgeous depths, though he could not be sure precisely what. Unlike his brother the heir apparent, he did not have a great deal of experience with the opposite sex. Under his brother Leo's tutelage, he had visited brothels in town. He had bedded women. But that had been simple, each party understanding what was expected.

He had never courted. Had never *loved.*

Good God.

He loved her.

It hit him, like a clap of thunder overhead—unexpected, a shock to his senses. Loud and angry and threatening and promising change. He loved Lady Araminta Winters.

Her hand was upon his chest now, splayed and open, directly above his hammering heart. "Everything, Clay. Will you teach me?"

Bloody fucking hell.

He swallowed, took her wrist in a gentle grip, but could not seem to make himself pry that hand away. For he liked her touch upon him far too much. "Ara, my love, I cannot teach you anything."

"Please, Clay?" She looked up at him shyly, her pale face trusting and so damn lovely. "My heart belongs to you." With her other hand, she caught his and guided it to her own breast.

He absorbed the steady, rapid thumps. So visceral. So powerful. Here was their common bond, and he had never felt closer to another person in his life than he did then, standing with his hand pressed over Ara's heart and hers to his. How had he ever lived before her, this fierce little woman with the flaming hair and the freckle-dotted nose and the lush mouth that begged for his kiss? This woman who wanted him in spite of who and what he was?

"I cannot do what you ask," he growled anyway, because he may be a bastard, but he was a gentleman. He had scruples, *damn it,* even if it was getting increasingly difficult to recall them. "I cannot court you, and I certainly cannot...teach you anything. You are an innocent, Ara, and that is precisely as it should be. One day, you shall go to your husband with your heart unburdened and your head held high, and you will be glad I did not take what you offered."

Her stare did not waver from his. She inhaled deeply, and he felt the rise and fall as though it were a part of him. "The only husband I want to go to one day is you, Clay. I am in love with you."

He forgot to breathe.

Her words were so beautiful, so glorious, so frightening, so wrong…and yet so very right. It was everything he wanted to hear. Everything he was afraid of. Just as she was everything he could not have.

He should tell her to go. Should tear away from her and flee, never turning back, never returning. He should leave her to the life she deserved, to the loveless match her father would arrange for her with some pale, pampered lord with soft hands and a born-in-the-purple lifestyle.

Instead, he kissed her. He did not mean to. No, his conscience insisted he leave her here, her innocence intact. But his body had decided on mutiny. Or perhaps it was his heart. Either way, he was not leaving her. He *could not* leave her.

The hand over her heart slid to cup her nape. The fingers gripping her wrist released her and found the sweet curve of her cheek instead. There was nothing gentle about his kiss, though he had intended it to be a slow and steady wooing. But the trouble with Lady Araminta Winters was she was like fire, and whenever he was in proximity to her, he too caught flame.

Her mouth opened beneath his, and when his tongue met hers, she moaned. A rush of desire surged to his cock. With one tiny sound and the beginning of a kiss, his ballocks were drawn tight and he was sporting an erection to rival any of the trees in the forest. When her tongue rubbed tentatively against his, slipping into his mouth, he almost lost control.

With a hiss, he yanked his mouth from hers, his breath leaving him in harsh pants as he stared down at her. Her eyes were huge, pools of violet-blue he could easily drown in, her mouth slack, swollen from his kisses. Everything in him screamed to lay her down upon the soft blanket of the moss on the forest floor and take her.

But he could not. She was too precious to him. She was too perfect and good and innocent, and if there was one thing he would not do, *by God*, was ruin her.

"I will court you," he bit out, curling his hands into fists to keep himself from hauling her back into his chest and kissing her into oblivion once more. "Tomorrow. If you are certain I will be welcome?"

She gave him the most glorious smile he had ever seen. "I have never been more certain of anything in all my life. Thank you, Clay. You will not regret it, I promise!"

He hoped to hell she was right, and he would not come to regret this day. More importantly, that he would not come to regret losing his heart to a woman he knew would almost certainly never be his. He tucked her book into his coat, settling it over his heart.

Chapter Seven

For the second time in as many days, Clay encountered the young duke cuddling his cat. This time, it was late evening, and Clay had been returning to his apartments after a long day of making certain there were no weaknesses at Burghly House that could be exploited by the villains determined to do harm to Ara. Just as before, he had not even been aware that the young lad was missing from the place where he was meant to be—sleeping soundly in his chamber at this time of night.

Clay stopped and stared at the sight of the lad sleeping on his bed alongside Sherman. Both dozed peacefully, and despite the intrusion in his personal space and his irritation with the governess who was charged with his welfare, warmth seeped into Clay's heart once more.

Damn it all, he did not want to feel this weakness for Ara's son, the tender feeling, as if the young duke could grow upon him much the same way his cat had: at first always underfoot and then beloved. He did not want to like the boy at all. The lad was a symbol—more than Burghly House, more than referring to Ara as *Your Grace*—of the world she had built without him. A world of liveried servants and a St. James's Square address, of Worth gowns and balls and routs and fêtes. A world he, simple Clayton Ludlow, who had been raised as a duke's son but who would forever be a mere duke's bastard, could never have given her.

She would have been plain Mrs. Clayton Ludlow. Would she have borne him a son as well? For a moment, the odd notion struck him that if Ara *had* given him a son, he would have looked rather a great deal like the lad. Dark-haired and lanky as Clay had been until he had grown into his body. Awkward and quiet as Clay too had been. With a good heart. A tender heart.

Hell no, he thought again, he did not want to like the boy.

Indeed, he wanted to dislike him on account of who his sire was—the man who had taken Clay's place. To say nothing of who the lad's mother was—the woman who had heartlessly betrayed him.

But he could not stop the feeling as he gazed upon the innocently sleeping form, the boy's gawky body curled into a ball as if to protect himself and the white and black cat he cuddled against an unseen menace. Sadly, the menace was real. More real than the lad could possibly know.

And neither a stripling nor a feline could diminish it. But that was a concern for another time. For the moment, the lad was safe, thank the Lord, and he had not been swept away by some unknown Fenian menace whilst Clay had been otherwise occupied. He remained as he was for another beat, watching Ara's soundly sleeping son.

He found himself moving across his chamber, reaching for a spare coverlet and draping it over the boy, taking care to leave Sherman uncovered as the cat did not care for it. Neither the lad nor the feline stirred.

Satisfied of the lad's comfort and safety, he went in search of his mother or governess, whichever he could find first.

He had not far to roam, for a whirlwind of raven skirts collided with him just outside his apartments. Instinctively, his hands settled upon her waist, steadying her as her palms flew to his chest.

The lad's mother it was, then.

Bloody hell, the connection of their bodies, albeit innocent, was enough to rouse the old demons within him. He had not stopped wanting her, it seemed. His cockstand gave painful testimony to that fact, straining against his trousers after no more provocation than her waist beneath his grip and her hands upon his chest. But her waist was perfectly curved. And her lips were so lush and full, begging for a kiss. And she was so beautiful it hurt.

Wide, vibrant eyes settled upon his, sending a jolt through his veins. "Mr. Ludlow," she said, her tone rife with starch. "You are far too familiar with my person, sir."

She sounded like his mother offering him a scold.

His mother had not dared to berate him in at least fifteen years. This woman—this beautiful, feminine creature staring up at him—was an asp fashioned in a goddess's mold.

The heat in his veins turned to ice. He set her away from him as if she were an inferno and he feared getting burned. Because that was precisely what she was to him. Ruination. Destruction. His only regret.

Collecting himself and willing his erection to abate, he allowed his hands to drop to his sides and fashioned his face an impassive mask. "Your Grace, by any chance, are you searching for your son?"

The last two words tasted bitter on his tongue, the reminder of what could have been. He forced it all from his mind. He was here to perform a duty. To keep the duchess and the young duke safe until the dangers of the Fenian menace had blown past like a thundercloud on a summer day. And he could only hope it would, sending him speedily on to his next assignment.

So he could forget the bewitching blue-violet of her eyes and the fire of her hair and pink softness of her lips.

"Edward," she breathed as if it were a sacred word. "Of course I am looking for him! He was not in his bed when I went to bid him goodnight, and his governess has no inkling of where he can be. Have you found him? Is he…safe?"

Despite their history and the way he felt toward her, he hated that she had to think, even for a moment, something ill may have befallen her innocent son. That the actions of some faceless villain who thought he could solve his homeland's problems by slaughtering innocents could impact this mother in her very home enraged him.

He stared down into her arresting face, calming his rage as he crafted a careful response. "Yes. He is sleeping within my chamber."

She inhaled deeply, her nostrils flaring, her wide lips tightening with disapproval. "Your chamber, Mr. Ludlow?"

He hated, bloody well hated, the way she spoke to him. As if he were no better than a servant. As if he were beneath her.

He swallowed. "Yes, *Your Grace*. As I just informed you, your son is safe and fast asleep within. I shall have him removed as it pleases you."

"How did he come to be within your chamber, Mr. Ludlow?" Her voice was cold and scathing but it also held the note of command he had heard so many times before. The tone that said she spoke to an inferior who had no choice save to answer her query in the manner that pleased her.

"I cannot say, madam," he gritted, detesting he must speak to her as if they were strangers. Detesting—worse still—the other troubling conclusion he had reached in his mind: that they had always been strangers. That he had never truly known her.

That everything between them had been feigned and false. Had she been rebelling against her strict papa? Had the notion of allowing a duke's bastard to touch her appealed to some part of her?

He could not ask, and he would never know.

"Why would he be in your chamber, Mr. Ludlow?" she asked, poison lacing her voice. "And for how long has he been there?"

He suspected he knew what she was about, and he would be more than happy to return her volley with some of his own fire. "I have no inkling of why or how long your son has been within my chamber as he is fast asleep. Since my task here is ensuring your safety, I regret to say your son does not fall within my authority."

"Your authority," she repeated, her lip curling as if to suggest he had none.

"Indeed. *My authority*," he echoed coldly. "Fenians murdered your husband in a park, madam, and that same faction of criminals has threatened you. My duty here is to keep you safe, not to maintain a reckoning of your ill-behaved offspring. That task falls to you and to the child's nursemaids."

She flinched as if he had struck her. "I am aware of your role here, Mr. Ludlow. But what I cannot comprehend is how my son was not in his bed tonight as he has been every night for the entirety of his life and somehow materialized within your chamber, of all the chambers in this house."

His lips flattened. "I would never harm the lad, if that is what you suggest. My only sin is discovering him sleeping and curled up with my cat."

An elegant burnished brow raised. "Your cat?"

He met her stare, unflinching. No amount of questions or raised brows would force him to love the creature any less. "I inherited it, you might say," he offered vaguely, recalling his conversation with the lad in the garden.

The duchess frowned. "Its previous owner is dead and you have been forced to carry on with the thing?"

With the thing.

He smirked. "Indeed not. The cat's previous owner gifted him to me. It was quite prescient of her now that I think upon it, for I had not realized just how endearing a feline can be until Her Grace gave me Sherman."

Her eyes pinned his, holding him captive without a touch. "Her Grace?"

"The Duchess of Leeds," he offered smoothly. "A treasured friend of mine."

"I do not care how many *treasured friends* you possess, Mr. Ludlow. What I do care about is how my son came to be within your apartments." Her expression could not convey her disgust for him any more than if she had announced it, baldly. Which she may as well have done. "Furthermore, I require him to be removed at once."

He stared at her, old furies clashing with the new. And for the first time in years, he overstepped his bounds. "If you require his removal, perhaps you can attend to it yourself, Your Grace. I am not your servant but your guard."

Her chin tipped upward in defiance, her eyes flashing. "A guard who lost my son."

"*You* lost your son, madam," he corrected, even as everything within him longed to rail. To touch her again. To—*God forbid*—kiss her. "I found him for you. You are most welcome for my unnecessary service."

Those blue-violet orbs darkened. "How did he come to be here? I still do not understand."

"I would venture to guess you do not understand a great deal where your son is concerned. I suspect, however, he came to see my cat." He took pity on her then, softening in spite of himself and his decree she would have to move the boy herself. She had always been a small woman, but she seemed even frailer now, and he had no doubt she could not haul her lanky lad from here to his chamber on her own. "Would you have me carry him to the nursery, Your Grace?"

But the furrow between her brows only deepened. "How did he know you have a cat in your chambers?"

"I volunteered the information when the lad asked."

Her eyes narrowed to slits of ice. "He adores animals. You must have known as much when you *volunteered* the information."

His patience withered. His presence in Burghly House had been forced by duty. He was not, however, duty-bound to allow her to insult him. "Precisely what are you implying, Your Grace?"

"I am not implying anything," she snapped. "I am asking you. Why, of all the many chambers in this home, would he choose to hide himself in yours?"

Her icy question was not without merit. He had wondered as much himself. But he did not like the accusation in her tone. "Perhaps you would be better served to wake your son and put the question to him directly, Duchess."

The mouth he had once claimed with his own thinned into a harsh, unforgiving line. "I am asking you, however. What occasion did you have to speak to my son, Mr. Ludlow?"

He clenched his jaw, taking her in, wishing he did not still find her so bloody alluring. That after all these years—after the scar on his cheek, after her betrayal, after the way she had savaged his heart—he would no longer be susceptible to her. "You certainly seem to have a habit of misplacing the young duke, Your Grace. He had also gone missing from the nursery when last I saw him yesterday. Mayhap you ought to ask yourself why."

She paled. "He has been distraught. His father was murdered."

"Does that make you any less his mother?" he returned.

"You are overstepping your bounds, Mr. Ludlow."

He did not give a damn. Her frigid bearing skirted the walls of imperturbability he had long ago erected around himself. He hated that she could be so cold when everything inside him was a raging inferno whenever he was in her presence. "I have no bounds here, madam."

"You have those which I set for you, sir." She raked him with a dismissive stare. "You are an unwanted presence within my home, and while I may not have a choice of who the Home Office has decided to install here, I will not allow you to ride over me roughshod."

He closed the distance between them, partially because he could not resist and partially because he wanted to discomfit her. To prove she was not as unassailable as she pretended. That he was not alone in the old attraction that would not leave him, painful as a splinter.

His gaze attempted to bore straight through hers. "There is only one manner in which I would like to ride you, madam, and I assure you it does not involve trading barbs with you over the whereabouts of your son."

Her mouth opened, those pretty pink lips forming an *o* of surprise before she gathered her wits. Her nostrils flared. "How dare you?"

Because he was a fool, he did not look away. Nor did he relent. Perhaps it was pride that spurred him on. Perhaps the awful, throbbing need for her that had never faded. "Have you forgotten, Your Grace?"

Red tinged her high cheekbones. He wanted to touch her. His hands ached with the restraint he exercised, fists curled tight. He would not touch her. Would not lay one finger upon her creamy throat, or the delicious hollow at its base where he fancied he could see her pulse thrum.

"Why would I wish to remember my greatest regret?" she asked, her tone carrying the lash of a whip.

Her greatest regret? *Lord God, woman, you have no idea what a regret is.*

Her words should not hurt. Should not cause a great river of agony to unleash inside him. But they did. What the bloody hell had he been thinking? That she would throw her arms about him and beg his forgiveness for the sins she had committed against him? That she would have changed?

He stepped back, keeping his countenance devoid of expression. "He was in the gardens."

"I beg your pardon?"

"The lad," he elaborated, using a tone as cool as hers. "He was in the gardens when I first came upon him yesterday. The child's governess had been wholly unaware of his absence, from what I gather. When I came upon him, he held my cat in his arms. I can only surmise a maid unwittingly allowed Sherman to escape. Either way, the young duke found him. I told him I have a friend who rescues stray creatures, and she gifted me with a cat who has become my companion."

Her jaw tightened as her gaze flicked over his face. "It is hardly appropriate for you to bring a feline into Burghly House that was given to you by a paramour."

"Her Grace, the Duchess of Leeds, is not my paramour," he corrected, for nothing could be further from the truth. "She is my friend."

Ara's expression remained sour. "As you were once my friend?"

Perhaps she was not as unaffected as she would have him believe.

He stifled the surge of triumph that wanted to rise within him, for he dared not hope she was as haunted by their past as he. Even if she were, it would still mean nothing. The water had passed beneath that particular, ugly bridge long ago. "I thought you did not wish to remember your greatest regret, Ara."

Her eyes flashed. "I have not given you leave to use my name."

"I am not a man who asks permission." He gave her a feral smile. And she would be wise to remember that. He was not the youth who had been easily swayed by her beauty and charm, mad for the twitch of her hips and the curve of her breasts. He was a man now, with a man's desires. A man's body.

And he could have any woman he wanted.

Why, then, do I still want her?

Damn it, but as he stood near enough to touch her, his entire being caught up in her—her scent, the gleaming copper of her hair, the silken rustle of her skirts, how smooth and soft her skin looked—he recognized the heaviness in his loins. The familiar tug in his belly. He remembered how she tasted. How she had felt, warm and wet and so tight he had lost himself inside her far too quickly.

His cock rose against the placket of his trousers once more.

Of all the inconvenient times.

They stared, locked in a battle of wills.

"You *will* ask permission here, Mr. Ludlow," she said suddenly, her eyes deepening to a stormy blue as she took him to task as if he were a recalcitrant youth. "Burghly House is my domain."

"I will never humble myself before you," he gritted, for if she expected him to bow and scrape to her, she would have an eternity to wait.

He was not her servant. Nor was she his better, though she may think it. He had spent the eight years since he had last seen her building himself into the man he was. She had not robbed him of his dignity or his desire to become something more than the bastard son of a duke, though she had tried.

"Then your time here shall be fraught with difficulty, I am afraid." The curt edge to her voice could have sliced open the flesh of a weaker man, making him bleed.

She did not know who he was, what he had become. To her, he was still the young man she had known, the hopeful dreamer who had been about to have his naïveté so ruthlessly crushed. He would tell her now, because he wanted her to fear him. He wanted her to maintain her distance so he would not be forced to look upon her or speak to her. So he would not be reminded of how much he had loved her and how perfectly her body had fitted to his.

He laughed, allowing the blackest part of himself to bubble forth. "Do you imagine, my dear Duchess, that I have been charged with your protection from Fenian cutthroats because I am the sort of man who would be cowed by a tiny, harmless female such as yourself? I could break you in half with my bare hands without exerting an effort. You are like a butterfly flitting about the head of a lion, madam. Spare yourself the embarrassment of attempting to best me, for it will only end in your obliteration beneath my paw."

"It is true then, what Carlisle said." Her expression lost its frosty lines of disapproval, softening with shock. "You are a hired killer for the Crown."

He did not deny her statement, for it was futile. He was not what she accused him of being. Not precisely. The truth was far murkier. He was sometimes spy, sometimes assassin, other times guard. "I am not a man with whom you should tangle." And he had tarried far too long, speaking to her, clashing verbal swords, lingering in her charmed presence, breathing in her rarified air. "Now, shall I carry His Grace to the nursery?"

Ara stared at him without responding. Perhaps it was the newness of hearing her son referred to by his title. Perhaps she was repulsed by the notion of the acts Clay had committed. By what he had become.

The thought should not rankle, but it did.

He frowned, needing to be free of her troublesome presence as expeditiously as possible. "Madam?" he prodded. "What shall I do with the lad?"

She blinked. "I shall carry him to the nursery myself if you will remove him from your…from within."

She could not even bring herself to speak the word *chamber* aloud before him. Did he disgust her that much? Was it the memory of the acts of passion they had committed together that so repelled her?

Or was it that she did not trust herself in the same way he did not? Did she feel the old hunger that had ruled them both so long ago? If he touched her cheek, would the memories haunting him claim her as well?

He would never know.

He did not need to know.

For he had a task at Burghly House, and rekindling the madness he had once shared with the now-widowed duchess was not it.

He offered her a mocking bow and then returned to his apartments, finding the lad still sleeping soundly. For a moment, he stood, taking in the boy's innocent face, relaxed in slumber. The poor lad had been through a great deal of trauma, not only losing his father, but the grisly manner in which it had occurred. The hard angles inside Clay rounded and softened in a way he did not want and could not like as he looked upon the boy.

Shaking himself free of maudlin sentiment, he gently lifted Ara's son into his arms, ignoring the disturbed mewl Sherman gave him at having his slumber interrupted. The lad did not wake, instead curling his warm little body against Clay in blind trust. What would it be like, he wondered, to hold a child in his arms that was his own? To be the protector and defender of his own flesh and blood?

He had not thought about having a child of his own for years now—not since Ara—and perhaps her return to his life was responsible for the odd sense of loss infecting his chest just now. The tightness in his throat. The strange prickling on the back of his neck. This boy, sleepy and warm, his body too long for his years, was Ara's son. A part of her.

And as much as he told himself he hated her for what had happened between them, he somehow still felt a connection to this child. A surge of protectiveness broke free inside him, and his palm flattened over the lad's back, gently patting as if to offer comfort.

Swallowing, Clay tamped down the inexplicable surge of emotion and strode from the chamber, the lad still asleep by the time he reached his censorious mother waiting in the hall. Her mouth pinched into a line of deeper condemnation as she opened her arms and attempted to rescue her son from Clay.

"I will carry him, Your Grace," he informed her, easily stalking past her.

The lad was lean and lanky, but he was heavier than he looked, and the chances of Ara managing to haul him to the nursery without collapsing en route were unlikely. He would not have her falling over or dropping the boy to spare her pride. The stubborn woman would simply have to accept his help.

"Mr. Ludlow, I demand you give me my son," she called breathlessly, chasing after him like a hen pecking at his heels.

"Your demand is noted, madam," he drawled softly, "and denied."

"He is *my* son," she charged, hurrying her pace so she walked alongside him. "You have no right to flout my authority."

"Recall my earlier words to you Duchess," he hissed. "Now do hush unless you wish to wake the boy."

"You beast," she charged.

He ignored her, walking on with a calm he did not feel. Did she suppose he was not good enough to carry her precious heir? That his bastard hands would somehow tarnish the lad? Or did she loathe him so much she would fight him at every turn regardless of the cause?

It little mattered, for she was not a conundrum upon which he should waste his focus or time. His presence at Burghly House had nothing to do with their painful past, nor anything to do with her current opinion of him. Indeed, if she despised him, all the better for his cause and peace of mind. He could not be distracted by her.

The Fenian menace was poised to once more strike. And Clay would be damned if he allowed anything to happen to the lad sleeping trustingly in his arms. That was where his thoughts needed to lie—with the protection of the duchess and the young duke. Nowhere—absolutely *nowhere*—else.

"I will be speaking to the Duke of Carlisle about this," came her threat as he held the boy with one hand and opened the nursery door with the other before stepping inside.

"You do that, madam," he said grimly, for he knew it would not do one whit of good.

His brother and the Home Office had decided he was to

be the guard placed at Burghly house, and so he would be. Leo treated him as an equal. They had grown up in the same home, shared tutors, bonded as true brothers. But duty always took precedence for Leo.

The child's hapless governess appeared then, wide-eyed, hands flurrying in agitation. "You have found His Grace! Oh, thank you, Mr. Ludlow. Where was the naughty boy hiding?"

He lowered the lad to his bed with care before straightening to his full height and pinning the domestic with a glare. "He was hiding in my chamber. This is not the first time His Grace has gone missing, Miss Argent. One has to wonder whether the lad has an affinity for disappearing or if you are deficient in your duties."

Miss Argent gawped at him. Perhaps his plain speaking surprised her. He did not care. The woman had smelled of spirits on at least one occasion, and her propensity for losing her charge was hardly promising. If she were directly in his employ, he would have given her the sack well before now.

"Thank you, Mr. Ludlow," Ara said pointedly. Coldly.

He turned from the sleeping lad back to her. Her fiery hair had never been more at odds with her icy demeanor. How pale she was. How small. How elegant. How regally beautiful. The Ara he had once known had always been beautifully imperfect, her hair cascading halfway down her back, her hem torn or muddied, a spot of mud on her cheek.

The duchess she had become was almost frightening in her effortless perfection. Her hair was ever elaborately coiffed, nary a lock out of place. Her silk gowns, though fashioned for mourning, were the first stare of fashion, never even a loose thread to be seen. Nor would she ever deign to allow herself to become dirty.

She was dismissing him, he realized.

"I will speak with you in the morning, Your Grace," he

returned. "Over breakfast, just as you suggested."

She frowned. "I suggested nothing of the—"

"Until tomorrow, Your Grace," he interrupted with a deep, mocking bow. "Miss Argent."

Stifling the torrent of emotion unleashing itself inside him, he quit the chamber, leaving Ara to handle her ineffectual servant. On the morrow, he would address his concerns regarding the governess. Until then, he needed to find his bed and some sleep of his own, if it would claim him.

More often than not, it never did.

Chapter Eight

ARA HAD NOT been prepared for the sight of Clay holding her son—his son, *their son*—in his arms. The large, hulking figure carting about a smaller version of himself had taken her breath. For the first time since Edward's birth, his father had held him. And he had not carried him with a stiffness of bearing as she had supposed he might, as though Edward was a weight he did not wish to bear.

Of course he had not.

Instead, Clay had carried Edward as if he was precious.

As she went about her morning toilette the next day, watching her lady's maid brush her hair into a semblance of order in the looking glass, she could still recall the sight of his immense hand stroking Edward's back.

Lovingly.

No.

Not lovingly, for Clay did not know. He could never, ever know.

You are like a butterfly flitting about the head of a lion, madam.

His vicious words returned to her. Yes, perhaps she was. Yesterday, she had realized once more just how truly dangerous it was to have Clayton Ludlow beneath the same roof as she and their son. He was an intelligent, perceptive man. How long would it be before he began to make connections between Edward's age and his dark hair and tall, lanky body? How long would it be before he saw himself in the son he did not know he had?

Your fault, whispered a voice inside her. *It is your fault he does not know he has a son. You denied him the right.*

Nay. He did not deserve the right. He had abandoned her. Had left her with no word, no warning, and no explanation. Had disappeared from her life as if she were of no import to him at all.

She could still recall the frowning servant at Brixton Manor, Carlisle's country seat. *Mr. Ludlow has gone abroad. I regret to say that he is not at home.*

Even after he had humiliated her, she had chased after him. But he had been long gone. And then he had returned eight years later, a stranger who was more compelling than ever. More forbidding, more *forbidden.* Still, she wanted him. In the basest, most shameful part of her, she yearned for Clayton Ludlow in a way she had never longed for another man.

Perhaps it was because he was the only man who had ever touched her.

She had never lain with a man other than him. She could have, naturally. Should have, likely, for then she would not be currently cursed with this hungry pulse between her thighs. With this heat pooled in her belly. With this languorous ache in her breasts.

Freddie had given her his blessing. With Edward as his heir, he had decided that a spare would not be immediately required. Perhaps never. And he had been only too eager to continue his life as he had lived it prior to their marriage, spending all his time with Percy. "Take a lover," he had urged her, squeezing her hands and giving her the beatific Freddie smile she loved best. "God knows I would, were I you."

She had toyed with the notion, knowing Freddie, while beloved to her, would never be her match in a physical sense. Knowing he was right to urge her elsewhere. She had attended balls and soirees. Had kissed lords all too eager to take an experienced married woman to their bed. And she had denied each one. They had never been right. None of it had ever been right. Instead, she had devoted herself to being Edward's mother and Freddie's friend, two of the most fulfilling roles she had ever inhabited.

But somehow, so many years later, that wicked hunger was still alive, burning brightly inside her. It had not died or dimmed. If anything, it had grown higher and hotter, and the moment she had first seen him, those flames had threatened to burn her anew. With each time her path crossed his, the fire scorched more than the last.

"Your Grace?"

She blinked at her reflection in the mirror, realizing belatedly that her lady's maid had been endeavoring to garner her attention for some time now, judging from the slight tinge of exasperation in her voice. "Yes, Marks?"

"How shall I dress your hair, if you please?"

"A Grecian braid shall suffice," she answered absentmindedly.

She did not care how her hair was dressed. She did not care how she looked. She had no one to impress—especially not one grim, forbidding mountain of a man she had once known. Her husband was dead. She stared at herself, feeling as though she was trapped in a nightmare. Freddie, the one man in her life who had never disappointed or betrayed her, who had been steadfast and loyal and kind, was gone forever.

And Clay had returned.

Her hands clenched into fists, the crescents of her nails biting into her tender flesh. She must not think of him in such intimate terms. He was Mr. Ludlow to her now. A stranger tasked with her protection and nothing more.

Surely it was Freddie's loss and the aching hole he left in her heart that made her strangely susceptible to her old feelings. Three months had passed since the day of his murder, and the horror of it all was as fresh today as it had been upon the day word reached her.

She had been taking tea.

Edward had been having lessons.

She would never forget the moment her life had forever altered. Her tea had slipped from her hand, spilling on her skirts, the delicate cup hitting a carved table leg and smashing. All she had been able to think about was how terrified Freddie must have been in the final breaths he had taken. The assassin had attacked him from behind. She had been thankful for that one small mercy. That Freddie had not seen the end coming to him.

"Take this handkerchief, Your Grace," Marks interrupted her musings once more, offering her a monogrammed linen square.

She had not realized she was crying, but the return to the present made her aware her cheeks were wet. "Thank you," she said, accepting the handkerchief and dabbing at her cheeks. It was one of Freddie's, for she liked having these small pieces of him about, along with the mourning brooch she wore fastened above her heart that contained a lock of his hair.

"It is horrid, Your Grace, what happened to the duke. I do not know how you bear it. To think these vile murderers would wish ill of you." Marks, not ordinarily an expressive woman, clicked her tongue with disgust, her countenance in the glass softening with sympathy. "They will find their justice at the hands of the Lord."

"Let us hope their justice comes sooner than that," she said quietly.

Thus far, the true culprits responsible for plotting and committing the act remained free. How she hated the faceless, nameless menace. Men who had used Freddie as a political sacrifice, spilling his blood without a thought for the man who had been a gentle and beloved husband and father. Without a thought for how very much he would be mourned and missed.

Marks put the finishing touches on her hair. "There, now. You are ready to take your breakfast."

Breakfast. How had she forgotten Clay's intention to ruin the solitude of her morning routine? It returned to her suddenly, along with the reminder of his silken voice, rife with effortless command.

I will speak with you in the morning, Your Grace. Over breakfast, just as you suggested.

She had not suggested. Nor did she wish to face him again, with her emotions too raw and near to the surface. Seeing him with Edward had affected her in a way she wished most heartily it had not.

"I think I shall take breakfast in my chamber this morning," she said with a forced lightness even she could hear in her tone. "I have some correspondence I wish to read and make, and my head is aching. Would you be so kind as to have a tray sent up, Marks?"

"Of course, Your Grace." The lady's maid offered a quick dip and then left the chamber, hastening to do as Ara had asked.

When she was alone, she exhaled slowly, relief removing a weight from her shoulders. She knew she could not avoid Clay forever. *Not Clay*, she corrected inwardly, yet again. But *Mr. Ludlow.* She could not avoid *Mr. Ludlow* each day, but she could certainly refuse to do his bidding this morning.

Indeed, perhaps the answer was to keep to her apartments as much as possible until the horrible criminals responsible for Freddie's murder were imprisoned and the threat looming over her like a thundercloud would dissipate at last. She stood and wandered to the window, where the curtains had been tied back to reveal the gloom of a foggy London day over St. James's Square. From her chamber, she could spy the familiar bronze statue of William III astride a horse even on days such as today, when the bleak gloom rendered seeing to the other side of the street a nearly impossible feat.

How was it possible her world was the same—the statue, the street below, the sounds of horses' hooves and jangling tack, the yellow fog, the carpet beneath her feet, all of it the same—and yet Freddie was no longer in it? And how was it that the one man she had done her damnedest to forget had returned to her because of Freddie's death?

She wanted to rail against the wrongness of it. The unfairness. Ara pressed her palm against the glass pane, absorbing its coolness. She took another deep breath, wishing she could somehow banish him from Burghly House. That she could rewrite history and undo time so she could save Freddie and never have to see Clay Ludlow again.

A sturdy tap sounded at her door. Likely Marks or another of the domestics, returning with her breakfast tray. "Enter," she called without turning away from her perusal of the street.

She preferred country life to the city, but Freddie had made his home in town, and she had accompanied him. Why did she remain here now? How she longed to return to Kingswood Hall with its sprawling forests and undulating hills. But she could not go back there, not ever again. She was not welcome in her family home, and even if she was, nothing remained for her there. When she had married Freddie, she had severed all ties with her family.

Thank heavens for Freddie. He had been her savior.

The door opened behind her and still she did not look as footsteps sounded.

"You may place the tray on my table and go," she said.

But the footsteps came nearer to her instead of retreating. And they were heavy, not at all the light tread of Marks but the heavy, sure thump of a man. A flash of terror bolted through her. *Good God*, what if someone had somehow slipped inside Burghly House with the intention of doing her harm?

Heart hammering, Ara spun around, a scream in her throat as she launched herself at the unknown interloper. She collided with a wall of chest. Large hands spanned her waist in a tight grip. She clawed at the dark jacket and charcoal waistcoat, tears clouding her eyes as all the fears swirling inside her came to a head.

"Ara, calm yourself."

The deep voice scarcely penetrated the haze of panic infiltrating her mind. She pummeled the chest with her fists, but it was hopeless, for the chest was muscled and broad. This man was immense and immovable. Solid as a mountain.

He was…

"Ara, it is me." He caught her wrists in firm grips, yanking her against him so she toppled into him. And there was his scent, leather and musk. And there was his voice once more, which she should have recognized, rumbling against her breasts. "It is Clay, Ara. You are safe."

She stared up at his familiar visage. The wide, angular jaw covered with dark whiskers, the slash of his nose, his dark, glittering eyes, and the mouth that was wide and full. That she had once loved to kiss.

Tears came. Her entire body shuddered. Great, wracking

sobs emerged, and she could not control them. She had no power over her body's response to the terror that had overtaken her.

"Ara, hush." He cupped the back of her head, pressing her face to his chest. "I would never hurt you. You have nothing to fear from me."

How wrong he was. He could hurt her. Had already done so more than anyone before or after him ever had. But the hurt he spoke of and the hurt he had dealt her were two different forms.

She attempted to stifle her humiliating sobs to little effect at first. The steady thrum of his heartbeat against her ear, reminding her of another time when she had listened to those beloved thuds. Slowly, the madness left her. She became aware of herself in stages. His hands, large and warm through the fabric of her morning gown, stroking her spine with steady, soothing calm. Her arms, somehow wrapped loosely around his lean waist. His mouth on her crown, his hot breath scalding.

"That's it, love. Calm yourself."

Love.

That lone word, emerging from him, pierced a tender part of her she had no longer believed existed. There had been a time when she had been his love. When she had loved him so fiercely it had swallowed her whole, and when she had believed in his love for her too. To hear him say it now, so effortlessly, as though the word carried with it no significance at all…

She jerked away from his hold, trying not to notice how right being back in his arms had felt. As natural as breathing. Shame licked through her as she thought of how much she had revealed. Until now, she had been so careful to hold tight the reins on her emotions with every interaction between them. To never allow him to see how very affected she was by everything around her. Losing Freddie. Clay's reappearance in her life. Just *everything*.

"How dare you enter my chamber?" she demanded, dashing at the fresh tears on her cheeks with the back of her hand. "You have no right to come here unannounced and uninvited, Mr. Ludlow."

"Ara." He moved toward her, a hand outstretched.

She stepped back, for she knew if he touched her one more time, she would be lost. "You will refer to me by my title whilst you are beneath this roof."

He stilled, his expression hardening into the rigid lines she recognized all too well. "Forgive me for the lapse, *Your Grace.* It was not my intention to give you a fright. It was, however, my intention to speak with you this morning as I previously made abundantly clear."

How was it he could suck all the air from her lungs with one biting look, one remonstrating sentence? She gritted her teeth. "I believe I made *my* intention clear to *you*, Mr. Ludlow. I do not wish to speak with you over breakfast. Nor do I wish to speak to you this afternoon, this evening, tomorrow, or any day thereafter. We have said all that needs to be spoken already. You are here to protect me. That does not require an audience with me."

His lips thinned, and she noticed how well-defined his philtrum was, even with the shade of whiskers masking it. Once, she had kissed him there, unable to resist.

"You are correct that I am here to protect you, madam," he agreed, his tone formal and cold and bloodless, much as he would speak to any stranger. "To enable me to perform the task assigned me, I do need to speak with you, however. Regardless of how displeasing you find such a condescension. More specifically, I wished to speak to you regarding the safety of your son, given he has exhibited an alarming tendency to wander and elude his governess."

She stiffened. "The threat was made against me and not Edward."

He shook his head slowly, his dark gaze unreadable. "That is immaterial. I am not as certain there is no danger for the young duke. While I am beneath this roof, it is my duty to see to the safety of him as well as you."

The ominous note of warning in his tone settled into her belly like a leaden weight. It had been difficult enough these last few days, dealing with the fear of an unknown foe wishing to do her harm and take her from her son. But she had foolishly allowed the Duke of Carlisle's words to reassure her Edward was safe. To think now he too could be in danger left her ill.

She swallowed the bile, hating to allow him to see her weakness for the second time since his invasion of her chamber, but unable to control her emotions. Edward was her son. He was all she had, that innocent, brave, beautiful little boy.

"Have you..." she wet her dry lips, struggling to find the words before continuing, "have you found evidence to suggest Edward is in peril as well?"

Her voice broke on the question. More vulnerability she did not wish to show him. But she had no pride when it came to her son. She would crawl on her hands and knees for him. Would beg. Plead. Walk through fires or broken glass. She would lay down her life to save his, and without a thought.

"I have not." His gruff tone held a surprisingly tender undercurrent. "It is not my intention to make you fear, Your Grace, but I am greatly concerned the child's governess is ineffective at her duty. For me to perform my task here properly, I need to know you and the lad are safe at all times.

There cannot be a question of that. There can be no weakness, for if the enemy senses even the slightest opportunity, he will strike."

She could not be certain if she believed he did not want to make her fear. Indeed, where Clayton Ludlow was concerned, she was not certain of anything. The mountain of a man who had stormed her chamber was nothing like the young man who had stolen her heart. He was scarred, savage and intense, arrogant and icy.

His jibe from the night before returned to her.

There is only one manner in which I would like to ride you, madam.

He had intended to shock her, she was sure. To use his vulgarity as a weapon against her. But then he had held her son so gently in his arms. Her son. His son. Their son.

Their son who could be in danger. Her baby boy. Her only light in the darkness of her days. If those murderous bastards harmed him…if they killed him…

Dear, sweet God. She tried to speak, but words would not emerge. Her mouth was dry, her hands clamped on her silk skirts so tightly her knuckles ached from the force. And yet she could not move. Could not speak as her past and her present and her greatest fears collided in one ugly, vicious burst of emotion and pain.

"Ara?"

His worried voice seemed to reach her as if from the other end of a tunnel. Her vision swirled, sweat beading on her brow, a wave of nausea so intense she feared she would cast up her accounts roiling through her. She could not seem to catch her breath. Could not seem to remain standing. Her knees gave out, and she would have crumpled to the floor in a heap of skirts had not those large, strong arms caught her.

Caught her and held her. She gasped for breath, and it

was *him* she breathed in. Only him, always him. The man she had once loved. The man who had abandoned her. The man who had broken her heart. The father of her son.

"Ara," he said again, his lips over her ear. Grazing her. Branding her. "Ara, inhale slowly. Take your time. It is shock. It will pass."

She wanted to obey his soothing voice. Wanted to listen, but her corset seemed to grow tighter with each breath she struggled to make, and darkness clouded her vision. She felt as if there were an invisible pair of hands on her throat, choking the life from her.

"Ara, speak to me. Say something." He gave her a slight shake as if to snap her out of whatever had come over her.

But it did not work. She still could not catch her breath. Could not form a word. Her head seemed too heavy for her neck, and she lowered her forehead to his chest. This madness had seized her once before, on the day of Freddie's murder. It would not leave until she succumbed to the darkness.

"Damn it to hell," he growled against her ear, and then she was being scooped—effortlessly—into his arms, held to his broad chest as if she were a babe. He carried her across the chamber.

As she struggled for breath, she was dimly aware he had not taken her to her sitting room but to her bed. He folded his massive body onto it, still cradling her, whispering in her ear.

"Hush, love, it will pass." His fingers moved with nimble skill over the line of buttons down the back of her gown, opening them.

Her bodice gaped as he made more progress, but she did not protest. Could not protest if she wished. Her every focus was upon inhaling and exhaling, getting her galloping heart to calm, and making her mind and body cease conducting war against each other. She clung to him, wrapping her arms around his neck and burying her face in his throat. Her nose pressed into his flesh. He was so very warm and alive. His skin calmed her, the scent so familiar, the thrum of his pulse reassuring.

Once, she had loved to lay her head over his heart when there had been nothing separating them. She had drawn the shape on his chest with her index finger, a doodled heart that meant he was hers. But he was not hers. He had never been hers at all, had he?

Tremors shook her as he found the laces of her corset and plucked the knot. She ought to be appalled at the liberty he had taken with her. She ought to push away from him, shake this spell of weakness that had attacked her. She should never have allowed him to take her in his arms in the first place, or to remain in her chamber when it was disastrous for him to be here.

It did not matter that she was a widow or that he was charged with her protection. No good could come of his presence in her chamber. In her bed. *Dear God*, they were on her bed. Her heart had slowed now. She was better able to think. To breathe. In, out, slow and deep.

"That's the way of it, love. Steady now. Breathe in and out," he rasped, his hand traveling up and down her spine in a steady, soothing caress. The other hand had found its way into her hair, cupping the base of her skull and gently massaging her scalp with his long, expert fingers.

How did he know just how to hold her? Just how to calm her? She did not want to move. She never wanted to move. His arms were so warm and strong, his touch so much gentler than she would have imagined.

"Protect my son, Clay," she whispered into his throat. It was not a request but a demand. And she did not know why, but her instinct told her if there was anyone who could keep

Edward safe, it was Clayton Ludlow. He may have broken her heart, but everything about him—from his immense size and strength to his undeniable intelligence—promised he was the best protector she could ask for.

"Your son will remain safe, Ara," he said softly, still stroking her. "You have my word I will do everything in my power to see that nothing happens to either of you."

She believed him. Perhaps she was the biggest fool in all London, but she believed this man when he made that promise. If only he had kept another promise. The one from long ago. If only he had never stopped loving her.

If, indeed, he had ever loved her.

"Do you hear me?" His fingers tensed on her skull, urging her head back so she had no choice but to look up into his face and meet his gaze. "While I am here, you need not fear anything."

Oh, but how wrong he was. Her eyes devoured his face, her traitorous body rejoicing at his nearness, and she knew she had everything to fear in his presence. She had to fear her reaction to him. Had to fear her ability to resist him. Had to fear he would ruin her all over again, just as he had eight years before, and she would let him.

I should tell him Edward is his son, she thought suddenly. He deserves to know. Edward deserves to know his father.

She opened her mouth, the confession ready on her tongue. But she could not force herself to do it. Not now. Not yet. Perhaps not ever. "Promise me something," she said instead.

He raised a brow, his knowing fingers still working her scalp and skimming her spine with only the barrier of loosened laces and her chemise beneath separating them. "What do you want from me, Ara?"

Ara. There it was again, her name in his mellifluous voice.

She ought to correct him, but something had changed between them, their walls briefly lowering, and she was loath to erect hers just yet. This closeness felt too good. Too right.

And she needed this promise from him. Needed it more than anything she had ever needed in her life. For even if there was not a threat that had been directly made against Edward, it did not mean he was not in danger. "Promise me if something should happen, and if you are faced with the choice of either protecting my son or protecting me, you will choose my son."

He frowned. "I will protect you both equally, however I must."

She shook her head. "No. It must be him first. Always him."

His lips tightened. "You are a good mother, Ara. Just as I always knew you would be."

The praise took her by surprise. "It is a selfish wish, for my son to be protected. I have already lived my life. He has yet to live his. Whatever danger faces us, he is an innocent. I could not bear it if anything happened to him."

Tears threatened to return.

But he would not allow them to fall. He shocked her by cupping her cheeks, his thumbs tracing her cheekbones in broad strokes that sent a surge of warmth between her thighs. "I promise I will protect your son above all else, Ara," he said solemnly.

Your son, she wanted to say.

But she did not. Instead, she closed her eyes and lifted her face, her mouth finding his cheek. She kissed him there, against logic and reason and most assuredly against self-preservation. Against common sense and past knowledge and her conscience and her pride and…

She kissed him again. Just a gentle press of her lips to his skin. "Thank you," she murmured.

Another kiss. Then another until somehow, she had found her way to his jaw. He was so familiar, and suddenly it was as if the time between them had never been. She was one-and-twenty again, in the arms of the man she loved. Her body took control, and she was helpless. Mindless. It was a bittersweet homecoming.

The rasp of his whiskers thrilled her. His scent invaded her senses. She became aware of everything in that moment. Aware of his hands caressing her face, of his big body burning into hers, of the fact they sat upon her bed, and she was in his lap.

Aware of the thick, hard jut of his arousal surging beneath her.

An answering pang of desire blossomed in her core, a shameful gush of wetness bathing her flesh. She wanted him inside her so much she ached with the need. She pulsed and hungered and longed. More kisses. She moved down his throat. She could not stop kissing him, it seemed.

And then, she was flying. Just for a moment. Just until she landed in a discarded, half-disrobed heap in the center of her bed.

Clay stood over her, his expression dark, fury making his angular jaw go rigid. "I will protect your son, Duchess." His tone was biting. "Save your wiles for a man more inclined to fall victim to them."

He offered her a mocking bow, and without waiting for her response, he stalked from the chamber, slamming the door at his back. Ara flinched at the sound, such finality resonating within it. She had never been more ashamed of herself in all her life.

What had she been thinking?

Why had she kissed him?

She stared unseeing at the intricate plasterwork on the ceiling above her. It did not matter how much time had passed, damn it all. She was still just as much a fool for Clayton Ludlow as she had been eight years past.

If only she could shake him.

Chapter Nine

STRIPPED TO THE waist and covered in sweat, his body aching from the blows he had received, Clay stood in the center of the Burghly House ballroom, facing his next sparring partner. Beauchamps was the fourth man he had faced and defeated this afternoon. Here now was Farleigh, who at least matched Clay in height and brawn, if not in agility. He doubted the fellow would produce much of a challenge, but if it meant more of the distraction he craved, he was willing to give it a bloody try.

He and Farleigh squared off, facing each other, fists raised.

"Are you not growing weary, sir?" Farleigh asked, grinning.

"I never tire," he lied, feinting to his left, fists at the ready. Brilliant attempt at diversion, but his senses were honed upon one thing. "I need to make certain my men are always at the ready."

He often sparred for the rush it gave him and for the manner in which it kept his instincts honed. Today's spate of bouts had less to do with training his men than his own need for a productive manner to occupy his day. Something to keep him from hunting down the Duchess of Burghly and taking what she had been offering that morning.

Damn it, he could still feel the soft warmth of her lips on his skin as if she had branded him.

Farleigh landed a blow to his shoulder. Clay grunted, doubled back, and attacked, knocking him in the jaw. Just a glancing blow. Not enough to do harm. Sparring with his men was of no use to him if any of them were actually injured. It was more for the sport, for the excuse to unleash their bloodlust, to keep them sharp and hungry.

Farleigh gritted his teeth. "Is that all you have to give me, sir?"

No, it damn well was not. He had rage in him that was clawing and fighting to be unleashed. Years' worth of anger for the same woman who had just all but seduced him in her chamber. In the bed she had shared with her husband.

The thought of the Duke of Burghly bedding Ara, claiming her, losing himself inside her body, made Clay want to smash his fists into something. Anything. Anyone. He watched his opponent, looking for a sign of weakness. With a lunge, he took Farleigh by surprise and jabbed him in the midsection.

The breath left Farleigh in a rush, but he did not give in to defeat, instead catching his breath and regaining his stance before striking back. His fist would have smashed into Clay's eye socket had he not been faster. With a lightning-swift blow, he deflected Farleigh's wrist.

"Is that all *you* have?" he returned mockingly.

"What in heaven's name is going on in here?" demanded a husky voice dipped in ice.

A voice he knew too well. The one that haunted his thoughts, waking and sleeping. He glanced over his shoulder to find Ara standing at the threshold of the ballroom like an angry goddess. Her hair was a fiery riot in contrast to her prim black mourning weeds, her face pale, brow furrowed. How was she so damn alluring, even in her disapproval, even dressed as if she were an advertisement for the love she had shared with her dead husband?

The thought made his lip curl. In the next breath, Farleigh took advantage of his distraction, his fist crashing into Clay's jaw with a surprising amount of force.

Pain exploded, radiating from his jaw to his molars. Black specks dotted his vision. Had he been a smaller man, Farleigh would have easily laid him low with such a punch. But it was good. He needed the reminder. Perhaps now his mind and his bloody foolish body would forever equate the sight of her with a blow so hard it rattled his teeth. Maybe he could train himself to be impervious to her.

"Sorry, sir, was that a bit too hard?" Farleigh's voice reached him through the haze clouding his mind in the wake of the initial shock of the blow. "I have never been able to land a blow to your face before. You are far too skilled, and I did not realize you were distracted by the lady."

Rubbing his jaw, he muttered the vilest, filthiest curse he knew, but it did no good, and his jaw still throbbed with an unmerciful intensity. "Her Grace," he corrected Farleigh. After all, she had all but destroyed Clay so she could bear her title. May as well allow her to wallow in it now. She had wasted no time in throwing it before him like a gauntlet. "And no harm done, Farleigh. I think."

Wryly, he tested his teeth to make certain none had been knocked loose as she approached in a swirl of indignant midnight silk. She stood before him, eyes flashing. An errant tendril of hair had escaped her elegant coils and braids, brushing over her cheek.

Blue-violet eyes scorched him. "What is the meaning of this outrage, Mr. Ludlow?"

Odd choice of word in his opinion. An outrage was the woman he loved betraying him. An outrage was what had happened to his face. An outrage was the fact that he was now saddled with the unwanted burden of her.

But they had an audience, and so he flicked a glance at Farleigh. "You may return to your post. We will continue this match again another day."

"Of course, sir." Farleigh bowed and took his leave in a haste likely borne of the combination of the blow he had landed to his superior and the dudgeon the Duchess of Burghly was in.

Clay could not blame the chap. Still rubbing his smarting jaw, he returned his attention to her after the door had fallen quietly closed. "What do you want, Duchess?"

He was curt, but he did not give a damn. He had been in the devil of a mood ever since that morning. Ever since she had pressed her lips to his skin as if he was a sin she could not resist and had kissed him. If it had been one kiss, he could have been able to ascribe it to gratitude or confusion from the fit she had suffered. But it had been more than one. Eight to be precise. He had counted.

She stared at him for a moment, chest heaving, and he swore he could see in her eyes—the large, dark pupils growing round—the memory of their last encounter. But then she stiffened her shoulders like a woman going into battle and sailed forth. "What I want is an explanation for my ballroom being turned into a pugilist club. You may be staying at Burghly House as a guest, but that does not give you leave to commandeer an entire chamber for your savagery."

His savagery, was it?

The laugh that tore from his lips was bitter and dark. "Is that what I am to you, Your Grace? A savage? An animal?"

"You were exchanging blows with another man, and you are positively indecent!" she hollered back at him so loudly her words echoed in the cavernous room.

He glanced down at his bare chest. Somehow, he had forgotten he no longer wore his shirtsleeves and waistcoat. No help for it now. She could claim maidenly modesty all she liked, but she had seen far more than his chest before, and she had been a married woman.

The urge to spar with her instead rose up, fierce and undeniable.

He looked back to her. "You did not seem to think me indecent a few hours ago, madam. In your chamber. Remember? You sat upon my lap in your bed, and I unfastened your gown and corset. Then you put your mouth on me. Here." He slowly trailed a bruised finger over the patch of skin she had kissed first.

Color rose to her cheeks. "How dare you speak of such a thing?"

Oh, he bloody well dared. And he was not yet finished. "Are you ashamed of your actions, Your Grace? Ashamed you touched a savage like me?"

Her lips tightened, but she said nothing.

He stepped closer to her, so near his boots slipped beneath the heavy fall of her skirts. Her scent enveloped him, floral and musk and everything he longed for but could never truly have. He wanted to hate her. Wished he had never loved her. "Or perhaps you are ashamed because before you were the Duchess of Burghly, you were mine."

"I was never yours," she denied then, sudden and sharp. "I was a foolish girl, easily led astray by a man I wrongly believed loved me."

"Is that the fiction you have crafted for yourself, darling?" he asked, touching her at last with the tip of his finger only. Just one callused pad beneath her chin, tilting her head gently back. Taunting her. Taunting him. "Is that what has made sleeping at night easier for you? Poor Ara. Such a victim."

Her nostrils flared. "You disgust me. Clothe yourself and never again dare to use the ballroom of Burghly House as your sparring chamber."

How he longed to melt her ice. To take her in his arms and prove to the both of them that she would melt for him. That her body would still respond to his in the same way his did to hers. But he too had his pride, and so he remained rigid, scowling down at her, his finger still upon her chin. "I will not make such a ludicrous promise regarding the use of this or any other chamber within Burghly House, madam. My men need to remain agile and strong. Daily training is an important part of their ability to protect you."

Albeit not in the extreme he had allowed it to progress today. That had been his own doing, a way to attempt to rid his body of the poison she infected him with.

"You call engaging in bouts of fisticuffs training? I fail to see how pummeling your men and allowing them to pummel you will be beneficial."

"You may be the Duchess of Burghly, but I am the man who has been entrusted with your protection," he bit out, her disdain nettling him though he had tried his damnedest not to allow her beneath his skin once more. "Therefore, I will commandeer the use of any chamber as I see fit."

But she did not relent or wilt beneath his blistering scorn. "This is my home, Mr. Ludlow. You will ask permission before conducting your *training* in future. And you will do it decently, wearing the proper attire of a gentleman, which you most assuredly are not."

No, he was not a gentleman. He never would be one. If he had been born the duke instead of the bastard, would she have loved him? Would she have become his wife instead of betraying him and leaving him with a scarred heart and face to remember her by?

He cast the unwanted questions aside. They were a moot point.

"Do I offend you, madam?" He withdrew his finger from her chin at last, severing the connection that seemed to singe him and throwing his arms wide.

"Everything about you offends me." And yet, her gaze trailed down his bare chest and arms, and lower still, belying her words.

She had kissed him earlier. For that brief moment, it had been as if no time had ever intervened between them. As if she had never been gone from his arms or his heart at all. For the sake of his sanity, he needed to retreat. To step away and ignore the raging tide of lust for her rising inside him. For that was surely all he felt for her now—the quickening of his breaths, the tightening in his ballocks, the twitching of his cock, the all-consuming ache to be one with her, to drive himself inside her body again—pure, animalistic desire.

"Liar," he charged softly.

Her gaze shot back to his. "Pardon me?"

She could kill him with her icy duchess hauteur all she liked. He would not bend, not with this driving force guiding him onward. Whatever it was. Foolishness? Stupidity? Pride? Need?

He took one more step forward, crushing her skirts. His perspiration-glazed chest met her silk bodice. When she would have slipped away in retreat, his hands flattened to the gentle curve of her back, splaying to keep her where he wanted her. The cold gold and glass of her mourning brooch was a shock to his chest.

He ignored it.

Ignored her scandalized inhalation. Her raised brows. Ignored her black mourning gown. Their ugly past. Everything and everyone but them and now. This moment. Her in his arms. Nothing between them.

"Look me in the eye, Duchess," he urged, "and tell me I offend you. Tell me my touch disgusts you. That I am unworthy of you. That you hate me."

Her eyes widened, her expression stricken. She shook her head. "Please, Mr. Ludlow. This is highly improper."

"Tell me," he repeated, the vehemence in his tone shocking even him. He did not know what he sought to gain or why it mattered. Hell, he did not even know what he was trying to prove. All he did know was that this morning, she had kissed him, and his whole bloody world had imploded when he had left her behind on that bed.

As he had walked away, he had been beset by the thought of what could have been. He could have been her husband. He could have made her happy. He would have always been the man who loved her above all else. And her tentative, tender kisses had struck him like a blade to the gut. So very dangerous.

They had not been the kisses of a woman who had been repulsed by him. This he knew.

"Tell me, Ara," he said again, using her name this time, her true name. Stripping the barriers of rank and class. Bringing them back to when they were a simple man and woman, beneath the enchanted branches of a centuries-old forest.

"You must not call me that," she said weakly.

"Why?" He searched her expression, searched her gaze, for an answer. "Why, damn you? Does it make you remember?"

Her eyes glistened now, so blue and vibrant they looked as if they had come from the brush of a master artist. "What would you have me remember?"

Everything. Every. Damned. Thing.

He would have her remember laughter and kisses, holding

each other beneath a blanket of stars. The firelight bathing their bodies in a glow. The way he had felt inside her. He could not parse it in mere words, and if she needed to ask, any traces of the Ara he had once known were forever gone.

"Nothing. I would have you recall nothing, for that is what we were to each other then, and that is what we must be to each other now." He released her, setting her away from him and turning on his heel. Disappointment opened like a broken dam to release its torrent and flood him. He could not get far enough away from her fast enough.

His body returned to him then. His jaw ached. His scar burned. His skin itched. *Fucking hell*, why had he been forced to accept this godforsaken assignment? He should have known he could never remain impervious to her. That the bitterness haunting him would taint all he saw, thought, and touched. That remaining at Burghly House with her would be his ruin.

ARA WATCHED HIS broad back as he stalked away from her. There was precious little resemblance to the young man she'd known in the rippling muscles and barely leashed power she could not seem to stop admiring. Beneath the fine trappings of a gentleman, he hid the body of a warrior. He was somehow even larger without his clothes to detract from his magnificent presence. There was nothing to hinder her view of him now.

When she had first come upon him sparring, bare-chested and graceful, she had momentarily forgotten her ire with him for using her ballroom as if it were a pugilist's paradise. But then she had forced herself to recall how insignificant he had made her feel that morning. How small and foolish and unwanted.

How he was still the same man who had made her burn for him only to abandon her all those years ago. Not a blessed thing had changed. Anger, pure and raw and sudden, struck her.

"Do not turn your back on me," she seethed. How dare he? How dare he return and disrupt her life, hold her in his arms when she was vulnerable, and make her long for him once more? And then to strip half-nude and engage in a pummeling match with one of his men in her ballroom?

He ignored her, stalking to his discarded shirt and waistcoat, no doubt to belatedly make himself decent. If only the notion did not cause a swift spear of regret to course through her. Her heart beat a rapid staccato, a molten bolt of heat sliding through her body and settling between her thighs. Old aches returned. Needs she had not revisited in all the time that had fallen between them.

Calm down, you fool. This man is not for you, and he never was.

"Mr. Ludlow," she called after him, holding fast to her anger lest she allow other, far more dangerous feelings to rule her. "I am speaking to you."

"You are berating me, madam." His motions jerky with his own wrath, he stabbed his arms into his shirt. "I have told you once, and I shall tell you again. I am not your bloody servant to be ordered about. If you wish to play the tyrant, do so with your butler or your housekeeper or a goddamn footman."

Something inside her broke.

Perhaps it was her sanity.

Perhaps her patience.

Perhaps it was simply her, fragile as a porcelain teacup that had been thrown against a stone floor. She was in thousands of shards. Her husband had been murdered. Her life was in chaos. She was in danger. The man she had once loved had returned a cold and angry stranger.

And she was running. Her skirts were clenched in her fists, lifted high. Her feet were moving. Connecting with the polished parquet, hurling her through the air. With an animalistic cry torn from the very deepest, darkest recesses of her being, she launched herself onto his back.

Her abdomen collided with his rigid spine, knocking the air from her lungs in a rush. She looped her arms around his neck, holding on. He grunted, barely flinching beneath the weight of her assault. Of course he didn't. The man was a mountain. But she did not care.

"I hate you!" she shouted at him, wrapping her legs about his waist when her arms threatened to give way in spite of the impediment of her heavy skirts. "I hate you, Clayton Ludlow. Do you hear me?"

He said nothing, remaining still and stiff as the trunk of a tree. His only reaction was the bob of his Adam's apple against her arm as he swallowed and the thump of his pulse. This was not what she wanted. She wanted him angry. She wanted him to say something. To hurt the way she did.

She wanted *him* to break.

"I hate you," she whispered again, pressing her face between his shoulder blades and inhaling his scent, laundered fabric and the tang of male sweat and the musky deliciousness of his soap. His shirt was wet. Her cheeks were wet. Her own shoulders were shaking. Tears, she realized.

She was crying again. Shaking. Sobbing into his back, holding on to his neck as though releasing him would send her careening over a cliff. And maybe it would. Never had a more hopeless jumble of confused emotions crashed through her.

His large hands landed on her stocking-clad knees, gently

forcing her to release him from her hold. Next, he grasped her arms and pried them from his neck, bending until her feet touched the floor once more.

With the same cagey finesse he had displayed during his sparring match, he spun around to face her, his expression thunderous. His handsome face was all sharp angles and harsh edges. His dark eyes blazed. The angry scar bisecting his cheek was pulled taut. "Strike me."

The two stark words were not what she had expected.

She dashed at the tears blurring her vision, swiped the wet trails from her cheeks, and stared at him. "I beg your pardon?"

"You hate me," he said calmly, as if he didn't stand before her with his shirt unbuttoned to reveal a distracting swath of his huge chest. As if she had not just leapt upon his back like a feral cat. "Perhaps it would do you good to relieve some of your anger, Your Grace. Your husband was murdered. You are at the mercy of a vicious band of killers who would make you their next victim. And now here I am, the bastard who once dared to defile you with my touch. Slap me. Punch me. Kick me. I care not. I will not feel it anyway."

She shook her head slowly. "No. I cannot do that."

"Assuage your guilt, madam." He took her hand in his, closing his fingers over hers and exerting enough pressure to force her to make a fist. "I will show you how to hit. You would do well to know how to defend yourself."

His hand over hers, warm and large and familiar in a way that made her ache, was almost her undoing. "I do not want to hit you, Mr. Ludlow."

"Yes, you do." His lips quirked into a derisive half grin. "Else you would not have leapt on my back. You hate me, do you not?"

No. She did not hate him at all.

She wanted to hate him. Needed to hate him.

But all she truly wanted to do was kiss him. *Dear God. This could not be happening.* Her lips parted. Her gaze dropped to his mouth. The air seemed to catch fire around her. Or mayhap it was just Clay. Resisting him was so much easier when he did not touch her. When he was not half disrobed before her.

She tried to respond. Nothing emerged from her. Not a whisper of sound.

"Say something, Duchess."

How she wished he would call her Ara again. Her name in his sinful voice was enough to melt her. "I…"

"Mama?"

That small voice, so familiar and beloved, turned the forbidden passion swirling through her into ice. Tugging her hand from Clay's grasp, she whirled about to find her son had entered the ballroom without her even hearing the door click open. He stood, hesitant and small at the threshold, sending a questioning glance between her and Clay.

He looked so much like his father, wearing a serious expression, lanky and dark-haired and far too tall for his age. Why, he was only seven years old, and it would not be long before he was taller than she.

"Edward," she said, rushing toward her son. Rushing away from Clay and the unwanted way he made her feel. "Why are you not with Miss Argent?"

"You told me you would read with me this afternoon," he said, frowning at her.

So she had. What was the time? Somehow, in the whirlwind of the day, she had lost her wits. She was not ordinarily so distracted. This she blamed upon Clayton Ludlow as well. "Of course I did, and we shall do that. What would you like to read, darling? More of *Alice's Adventures in Wonderland*?"

But her son, an intelligent boy, was not so easily distracted. "Mama, why does Mr. Ludlow want you to hit him?"

She blinked, grateful he had apparently not entered the room in time to see her full ignominy as she pounced upon Clay's back as if she were no better than a wild animal. Her cheeks went hot. What was wrong with her? She had a reputation to maintain. She was a widow. She had a child. She could not allow herself to become ensnared in the same madness she had once fallen headlong into with Clay.

"I wish to teach the duchess to defend herself, Your Grace," came the low rumble of his voice behind her before she could answer.

"Because of the bad men who killed my father?" Edward asked.

The bad men? Her heart froze. She had not spoken to her son of the circumstances surrounding Freddie's death. What use had a child for such information? It would only haunt him, give him nightmares, and fill him with more fright than he already possessed.

"No," Ara denied hastily.

"Aye," Clay said, hunkering down before her son and meeting him at eye level. "Because of the bad men. It is best to be prepared, Duke. It is my duty here to keep you and your mama safe, and part of keeping her safe means showing her how to fight off anyone who would wish to do her harm."

That was not what he had been about with his little demonstration. Or was it? Had she read too much into his actions and his words? Did her proximity to him rob her of the ability to conduct coherent thought?

Either way, it mattered not, for she did not wish Edward to know anything more about what had befallen Freddie than necessary. There need be no talk of dangerous men or killers or her defending herself. How dare Clay reveal such damning information to her son? It was not his place.

Her lips tightened. "Mr. Ludlow, that is more than enough of troubling thoughts. Edward, we ought to adjourn to the library so we can continue our reading."

"No," her son said. "I want Mr. Ludlow to train me as well so I can defend you. I must act in Papa's stead now that he is gone."

Her heart gave a pang at the sincerity in his boyish voice. Guilt hit her anew at the deceptions she had perpetrated. Edward had lost the only father he had ever known, and Freddie had undeniably been a wonderful, doting papa. But here before her son stood the father who had sired him, neither knowing their true relationship to the other. No one had ever known the truth except for Ara and Freddie. Even Percy, for all that he knew Freddie was not Edward's father, had no inkling of the true identity of the man responsible.

She could confess everything now. Here. Perhaps she should.

But the words would not form on her tongue. No, she could not be yet another earthquake in her son's already fragile world. He needed stability and reassurance now. He needed solidity and love, and the last thing he needed was to be informed that the man he had loved as his father for his entire life had not, in fact, shared his bloodline.

"You are a brave lad." Clay was telling Edward, clapping two enormous hands on his thin shoulders. "I will teach you everything I know. How does that sound?"

"You will?" Edward beamed.

Clayton Ludlow spending a prolonged amount of time with Edward could not be productive in any fashion. Ever. Clay was far too wily and intelligent, and Edward was not far behind, though he was a boy. He had a knack for observing those around him and listening. Sometimes she forgot just how much he saw and heard.

"No, he most certainly will not," Ara interrupted, her tone a trifle more stinging than she had intended. But there was no help for it. Her territory was being invaded more by the day, and she did not like it. She needed to take a stand, as much for her own sanity as for Edward's wellbeing. She pinned Clay with a glare. "My son will not be engaging in fisticuffs at your direction, sir. He has no need of such worries. I am safe here at Burghly House under your protection. *He* is safe here. Is that not right?"

Clay threw a look at her over his shoulder, his dark eyes assessing. "Would you not rather he be prepared, Your Grace? Your safety and the lad's safety are hardly trifling matters, after all."

"Yes, Mama," Edward added. "I need to be certain I can protect you. Papa would want that. Mr. Ludlow will show me all I need to know."

Ara's gaze flicked from Clay to their son. *Dear heavens.* The similarities between them were more apparent than ever. Devastatingly so. Her heart clenched painfully. "How do you even know of such matters, Edward?" she demanded.

"The servants speak when they think I am not listening," he told her without preamble and without a hint of remorse. "I understand more than you think me capable of, Mama. I am nearly a man fully grown."

"In good time, Your Grace." Clay gave Edward's hair a playful ruffle, and Ara's heart broke then and there. "You have a deal of growing yet before you become a man, I should say. Though you are well on the way, and I am sure your mother could not ask for a better son."

Clay was so tender. So gentle. So very good with Edward, who had always been awkward and quiet. "No, I could not ask for a better son," she agreed past the lump in her throat. Past the guilt and the fear threatening to crush her. Fear Clay would look into the face of his son and see himself. Fear all her carefully crafted lies would one day fall down around her like so much dust. "But that does not mean I wish for him to engage in violence in my name, Mr. Ludlow."

"I want Mr. Ludlow to teach me," Edward insisted, his stubborn streak making an appearance. "I do not want to lose you, Mama, for you are all I have left in this world."

Oh, my darling boy. If you only knew.

"Come here, my love." She sank to her knees alongside Clay, doing her utmost to ignore his big, burly presence, and opened her arms to their son. Edward launched himself into her in that unselfconscious manner that only children possess. She hugged him tightly, burying her face in his mop of unruly dark hair. "You will never lose me, Edward. Do you understand? No matter where we are in the world or how much time has passed, I shall always be in your heart."

Aware of Clay's gaze on her, she glanced up to find him watching her, intent.

"I want to learn, Mama," Edward said into her bodice, hugging her tight with his skinny arms.

Clay raised a brow, as if daring her to defy him, and how she wished she could read the emotions glittering in the dark depths of his eyes. "I will teach you, lad."

Chapter Ten

Eight years earlier

HE HAD NOT come to court her.

She had waited. And waited. Then, she had waited some more.

A week had passed since she had last seen Clay. Since he had given her his promise. And he had not come to call at Kingswood Hall. Not on Monday or on Tuesday. Not Wednesday when the sky had been lit with a brilliant sun. Nor Thursday when a thunderstorm ripped through the countryside. Friday and Saturday had passed, leaving her with Sunday and no choice but to find him.

Each day with the exception of the day of the deluge, she had found an opportunity to slip away to their meeting place in the forest. Each day, she had been as disappointed as the last.

Mama had gone to pay a visit to her sister, leaving Ara unattended for the afternoon and evening. Perhaps even through the night if she grew fortunate and Mama decided to say on with Auntie Charity as she often did. Ara had seized her chance, knowing it may well be her last.

And now, here she stood, before the massive hewn doors of Brixton Manor, the country seat of the Duke of Carlisle. She had slipped away from her chamber without notice, saddling up her favorite mare and making the journey on her own. Her mare was tethered to a tree in the sprawling woodland that abutted the park, and she had walked for some distance on damp ground, much to the peril of her boots and hem.

Her hand shook as she knocked, tentatively at first. She was not even certain this was where Clay resided. It was entirely possible he was kept far from the main house because of his status. It was definite that her presence here, unchaperoned, unannounced, and uninvited, would raise brows and cause a stir. She was in danger of doing her reputation irreparable harm.

But he was worth it.

And she deserved an answer.

She knocked with greater conviction.

The door swung open, and a silver-haired butler frowned down at her. "How may I help you?"

"I am here to see Mr. Ludlow," she announced, as if she were not likely bedraggled from her travels and her traipse across the park. As if it were perfectly proper for an unaccompanied young lady to appear at the front door of the Duke of Carlisle's home and demand an audience with his bastard son.

She swallowed.

The butler's frown of disapproval intensified. "Mr. Ludlow is not at home."

Ara remained undeterred. "Where has he gone?"

The butler blinked, obviously not being accustomed to such dogged persistence. "I am afraid I cannot say."

The man was bluffing, and she had not risked everything to come here to find Clay only to be turned away at the door as if she were a beggar woman asking for coin. "If you please, sir, let him know he has a friend calling. I am certain he will see me."

His eyes narrowed. "Does this friend have a name, madam?"

She stared right back at him, unrepentant. "No. Tell him it is a friend who was expecting to see him, and he will know precisely who I am."

"You may wait within," he announced haughtily, as if he were the duke himself, allowing her entrance at last.

Giving the butler her sunniest smile—one she did not feel in the least—she swept over the threshold and fussed with her dress as she waited. *Oh heavens*, she must be a sight. Grass blades were stuck to the ribbon-trimmed hem of her riding habit, and her smart little boots felt sodden. Inhaling deeply in an effort to wrangle her misgiving, she shook the wrinkles from her two-tiered skirts and tried to squelch any worry longing to rise to the surface and consume her.

The butler's reluctant decision to attempt to locate Clay seemed promising. If he would see her, that was. She cast her eyes about the entrance hall, which was a great deal grander than the entry Kingswood Hall boasted. It rose two stories so it could be overlooked from a variety of alcoves and arches above. Marble statues stared blankly down at her, as if judging her for her rashness. Perhaps former Dukes of Carlisle? She could not be certain. Or Greek gods and goddesses, those remaining fragments of belief in the fantastical.

The black and white floor glistened with polish. Footsteps could be heard somewhere, far off, echoing in the cavernous interior. Was it the butler? Clay? Other servants? Ara looked all around, feeling like an interloper. Feeling like a fool.

She ought to leave. Could she simply go? Quietly exit through the door she had so recently traveled past? Race across the park with what remained of her pride still intact, find her mare and ride home as fast as she could manage before anyone was ever the wiser of her imprudence?

Ara inched toward the door, even as more footsteps echoed. It was not too late. She could flee, and no one needed to know…

The footsteps were coming faster now, matching her breath and her frantically beating heart. *Go, you fool! Run!* She picked up handfuls of her habit, ready to flee.

"My lady."

His voice stayed her, low and warm and so very welcome.

She spun about, and there he was. Her Clay. Today, he was dressed to perfection as a proper gentleman. No shirtsleeves rolled back or a lack of a waistcoat. No indeed. As she drank him in, she had to admit he looked every bit the duke's son. And here in the grandeur of the Brixton Manor entry hall, she felt, for the first time, the disparity of their situations. Not because he was illegitimate, but because he was the son of a wealthy and powerful man. Though her father was wealthy, the opulence of Brixton Manor was beyond anything he could dream of owning. Kingswood Hall was a mere shack in comparison.

Her gaze clashed with Clay's. His the darkness, hers the light. She wished she could read the emotions hidden in their glittering depths. "Mr. Ludlow," she said stupidly, staring at him as if he were the first gentleman she had ever seen.

He was not, of course, but he was the most beloved.

"Why have you come?" he asked next, dashing her maudlin sentiments.

The blood leached from her cheeks. Yes, this had been a mistake. Perhaps he had merely been entertaining himself with their interactions. Perhaps he had been bored, and she had been too forward, and she had forever made a fool of herself. Perhaps he had not wished to hurt her feelings, and so he had allowed her to believe there was something more.

How wretched.

How humiliating.

But he had kissed her with such passion, as if he wished to steal her soul and hold it for ransom. Could she have been wrong?

"I..." She struggled to form words. Now that she was here, standing before him in her sodden skirts and ruined boots, her mind seemed to have taken its leave of her. She felt as inadequate as a discarded pair of stockings. "You said you would come to Kingswood Hall."

"Aye." He nodded, his jaw going rigid. "And so, I did."

She shook her head, frowning at him now. "No, you most assuredly did not."

"I did and was denied."

The insistence in his tone. The starkness of his expression. The firmness of his words. It all added up to one conclusion: he was telling the truth. But how could that possibly be? She had never received word of his visit. She had spent many an hour gazing out various windows, hoping she might catch sight of him, his horse, his carriage. Anything to do with him.

No indeed, he had not come. She would have known.

Wouldn't she?

"Three days in a row, Lady Araminta," he confirmed coolly. "I may be a bastard, but even I know when I have been made a fool. I chose not to return on the fourth day, on account of my pride."

Three days? Her heart thumped and fluttered with a wild, silly hope. He had come calling upon her three days in a row?

And then, just as abruptly, her hope died, for she realized if he had been turned away day after day, it could only mean one thing.

Her mother had acted in her father's stead and refused to grant him entrance to Kingswood Hall, keeping it from her. Had it been the grudge he had with the Duke of Carlisle or the fact that Clay was not the duke's rightful heir? She did not know. Indeed, it rather startled her to imagine her mother had even engaged in this level of interference, and without uttering a word to her…

Unless Clay was prevaricating.

Yes. That had to be it. She seized upon the explanation. "I had no word of a visitor, and believe me, I asked. I asked, and I watched, and I waited. Still, you did not come for me as you swore you would."

A strange expression transformed his features. He closed the distance between them, grabbing one of her hands in his. His hands, unlike hers, were ungloved, and the heat of his touch upon her absorbed into her skin, settling with the delicious ferocity of a brand. Their fingers tangled. Intertwined. Just like that, she was where she longed to be. With him again, beneath his spell, following him to wherever he would take her.

"Come," was all he said.

And she followed, allowing him to tug her from the entry hall. Allowing him to lead her past more judgmental statues and busts, white and perfect and marble, all of them warning her not to allow herself to be led too far stray. But it was too late for that. Too late for caution. For regrets.

She hoped.

Her hand in his, him tugging her, guiding her, their fingers laced…shocking. Improper. Altogether wrong. She should not be here, at the Duke of Carlisle's home. Should not be with Clay. Ought not to allow him to lead her away from the place where eyes and ears could see and hear.

But she went with him. Trusting him. Through halls and past shocked domestics who did their best to rearrange their expressions into neutrality. Until all at once, they were in a chamber, the door shut behind them. The room was cavernous and masculine, and it smelled of him, musky and wonderful and so very male.

So very Clay.

Their fingers were still tangled together.

They stood, side by side, neither of them talking. She understood she had breached a boundary from which there was no return. She was standing in Clay's bedchamber. Holding his hand in hers. She knew not where his father the duke was, but she was certain neither Carlisle nor her father would approve of what she and Clay had just done.

It was ruinous.

Reckless.

No one knew who she was, and yet this was the country. Domestics had ears and eyes. They spread rumors. This—Clayton Ludlow and her weakness for him—would be the end of her.

"Why did you bring me here?" she asked softly, her gaze immovable, fixated upon the large, dark bed at the opposite wall. *His* bed. It was where he slept. Where he laid his head. Did he take off his clothing to lay in it? Did he remove his shirt?

His chest was so lovely.

She was not meant to have seen it, but she had, and now she could not help but long to see it once more. To touch it. Taste it. Her cheeks blazed with the fires of her shame. She could not control herself. Could not tame herself, it would seem. He had made a wanton of her. There was no going back.

"Bloody hell, I don't know." He scrubbed his free hand over his face as if it could erase some of the tension that threatened to choke them both. "Your mother told me I was not meant for you, and she was right. You deserve someone of your station, Ara. I will forever be a bastard, forever walking in shame, and you do not need to suffer in silence alongside me.

My father treats me as an equal in his household, and it makes it easy to forget the way of the world. It was wrong of me to consider, even for a moment, courting you."

Her mother. There was all the confirmation she needed. Anger rose within her, stark and swift and strong. "How dare my mother say such things to you? She had no right."

His thumb traveled over the back of her hand in a slow, steady caress as he turned to face her, looking down solemnly. His expression was grave. "She had every right, Ara. She is your mother, and she is looking after your best interests. She is not being selfish as I was. As I am."

"I did not know you came to see me, Clay." Her fingers tightened over his as she willed him to believe her. "If I had an inkling—any notion, whatsoever—I would have been there within an instant. I would never have turned you away. You are the man I love."

"I cannot be." He released her hand and turned to walk away from her, his large frame tensing with anger. "Do you not see? No one will allow me to even court you, let alone wed you because of who I am. And they are right. They are right, damn them."

"No," she denied just as vehemently, going to him and throwing her arms around his waist from behind. She pressed her face in the dip between his shoulder blades, inhaling deeply of his scent. He was so vital. Everything she needed. All she ever wanted. "They are all wrong, because nothing has ever been more right in my life than you, Clayton Ludlow. Do you hear me? I do not care if you were born illegitimate to the Duke of Carlisle or to the queen herself. I will not give you up. Not now. Not ever."

A knock sounded at the door then, interrupting the solemnity of the moment.

"Brother, what is the rumor I hear about you hauling a

mysterious village girl into your chamber? Father will have an apoplectic fit." The sardonic voice was muffled.

Ara stiffened as the seriousness of the improprieties she had committed returned to her anew. She had waltzed through the Duke of Carlisle's home with shocked servants looking on, holding Clay's hand, allowing him to lead her to his *bedchamber*. There were eyewitnesses to her shocking lack of shame.

If anyone discovered who she was, she would be ruined.

"Damn," Clay cursed with quiet vehemence then, echoing the vein of her thoughts aloud. "I do not know what I can have been thinking, bringing you here. You make me lose my head, Ara."

"Tell me you are not bedding the girl in there," his brother said from the other side of the door. "You ought to know better than to bring quim here. Father has eyes and ears everywhere."

She did not know what *quim* meant, but she was certain it was not a complimentary word. Before she could contemplate the matter further, Clay tugged free of her grasp and spun to face her once more, his face set in severe lines.

His dark gaze plumbed hers. "Your mother was right to send me away. There can be no future for us. No hope."

She shook her head as tears stung her eyes, refusing to believe his words. "There is always hope. Court me in secret if you must. We will find a way to be together."

Another insistent knock intervened. "Brother, I must insist on rescuing you from your folly. I know of just the place to take your lightskirts. Bodesly Inn. The serving wenches are most accommodating. I once had two in my bed—"

"Stubble it, Leo," Clay hollered in the direction of the door.

She searched his face, desperate for him to see how deep

her feelings for him ran. He had become a part of her. The notion of never seeing him again filled her with a hollow ache. "Meet me in the forest tomorrow," she said. "Please."

He touched her cheek with the backs of his fingers. Just once. The ghost of a caress. "Ara."

But she would not give up on them. "Please, Clay. I will be there. Waiting for you."

I will always wait for you.

I love you.

She tucked the remainder of what she wanted to say inside herself.

He stared at her, his face harsh. Inscrutable. "You must go, Ara, before anyone realizes who you are."

"Tomorrow," she repeated. "Let me make my own choices, Clay. Let me choose you, if you dare."

Chapter Eleven

"HERE YOU ARE, lad. This knife is for you."

Clay handed the young duke his favorite blade. Small yet capable of inflicting damage on any assailant, the knife featured three blades that folded inside a golden case accented by repoussé. Each blade was of varying length, and it had served him well on many occasions over the years.

Yet surprisingly, as he placed it in the lad's palm, he felt not even a hint of sentiment. Gifting it to the boy had been a sudden decision, but it was the right one. Here was a young lad whose father had been slaughtered in a most brutal fashion, and there were now strangers infiltrating his home because of threats made against his mother. Perhaps the blade would enable him to feel some measure of reassurance, however small.

"Thank you, Mr. Ludlow, but he cannot accept such a gift," came the wintry voice of the lad's mother from over his shoulder.

He ground his molars. Of course she would object.

He had just spent the better part of an hour training the lad in the art of fisticuffs and defending one's self. Naturally, the duchess had insisted upon observing his lessons with the young duke, and to that effect had taken up residence in a chair on the far side of the ballroom, a book in her lap.

He knew the reason for her presence.

She did not trust him. How dare he, a bastard, presume to train a peer of the realm? Likely, she feared he would somehow corrupt the lad. That he would taint him. How thoroughly she had fooled him once, with her proclamations of love and her promise she would choose him. That she loved him in spite of the circumstances of his birth that would mark him for the rest of his life.

"But Mama," protested the lad now, his blue-violet eyes pleading with his mother. "Mr. Ludlow has given it to me, and you said one must always appreciate a gift and be thankful for it. I cannot return the blade to him now."

"The blade belongs to you now, Your Grace," he said solemnly. "I could not take it back even if I wished it."

"No?" The lad's eyes went wide, his eyebrows climbing up his small forehead toward his shock of dark hair. "Why not, sir?"

"Once a warrior gives a gift to another warrior, it is bad luck to take it back," he lied, casting a glance toward the lad's mother.

She scowled and rose from her chair, shaking out her skirts with an elegant gesture before gliding toward them. The way she moved was always effortless, filled with grace. "That is pure nonsense, Mr. Ludlow."

"I am a warrior now, Mama," the lad said triumphantly, and it was the most animated Clay had seen him since his arrival at Burghly House. The dark husk that once had been his heart warmed at the sight.

"You are not a warrior," she snapped at her son. "You are a duke. Dukes do not go about carrying weapons upon their person."

"Perhaps if Papa had, the bad men would not have killed him," the lad countered stubbornly, his fist closed tight around the closed blade as if he feared his mother would wrench it from his grasp.

She paled, stopping midstride, her black skirts swaying about her. "How do you know of such things, Edward?"

"You must not think in that fashion, lad," Clay intervened, lowering to his haunches so he could look the boy in the eye. "Your papa was a brave man, and the men who attacked him were cowards. They came upon him from behind. Even if he'd had a blade, he would not have been prepared for their attack."

"Edward, I need to speak to Mr. Ludlow alone." The duchess's voice cut through the air, as sharp as any of Clay's blades. "Why don't you run along to Miss Argent and return to your studies? Leave the knife with me, if you please."

"Please, sir, tell her I must keep it," the lad whispered to Clay.

His eyes—Ara's eyes—were huge, pleading. A shift happened inside Clay. A sensation blossomed. There was a name for it: fondness. Yes, he liked the lad. More than liked him, actually.

"He must keep the blade," Clay reasserted, giving the lad a bolstering wink before glancing up at the duchess.

She watched him with ice in her eyes, her face a pained, ashen mask. "He is a boy. He cannot have a blade."

Clay rose to his full height, never taking his gaze from her. "I shall teach him how to use it properly."

"It is not your place to teach him anything," she snapped, her tone biting. She held out her hand to the lad. "The knife, Edward. Give it to me."

No, it was not his place. He had no claim upon her son. No claim upon her. He was the bastard she had once scorned and betrayed. He wondered if she felt any guilt, even the slightest hint, when she looked upon the handiwork of her father's mercenary. Likely not, and the thought provoked the banked fires of his rage toward her into a freshly burning flame.

"But Mama," the lad protested, dragging Clay from the depths of his thoughts.

Taking pity on the lad, Clay intervened once more. "It is not bad luck if the blade is held in trust for the warrior by the warrior's mother, however," he invented.

He had not much experience with children, but it had become apparent to him that they were eternally hopeful, their hearts filled with innocence and beliefs that had yet to be dashed. The day would come when that would happen. But it would not be today for the lad, damn it. He needed to believe in something. He needed to cling to his bloody hope, for it was all the boy had left.

Ara gave Clay a sour look. "The blade, Edward."

"Very well, but only if you are certain, Mr. Ludlow, that a warrior's mother can hold the blade for him without it causing misfortune?" the lad asked.

"Aye," he said past a sudden thickness in his throat. "I am sure, lad."

As if his blessing was enough, the lad acceded to his mother's wishes and deposited the folded blade in her waiting palm. "Very well, Mama, but I shall want it back. Mr. Ludlow will show me how to use it, and I will be requiring it then."

Her fingers closed over the blade with so much force her knuckles went white. "Thank you, Edward. You may return to Miss Argent now."

"Yes, Mama, I shall." He slanted another glance toward Clay. "Until our next lesson, Mr. Ludlow."

Clay bowed. "Of course, Your Grace."

The lad offered a hasty bow in return and then took his leave of the chamber, closing the door quietly behind him. Silence descended for several heavy moments. Clay swung his attention back to the duchess. She stood within reach, not even an arm's length away. Near enough to tempt him, even after everything she had done.

His eyes dipped to the ever-present mourning brooch on her bodice, and for the first time, he noted the color of the hair trapped behind the glass. Golden. The Duke of Burghly must have been as flaxen-haired as a wheat field. How odd the lad was so dark in contrast, possessing neither Ara's flaming locks nor his father's blond.

"You have no right to give my son anything," Ara said then, dragging his gaze back to her face with her venom.

"I did not think the gift would be so poorly received," he said drily, crossing his arms behind his back and taking a wrist in one hand.

It was not a gentlemanly pose, but it was necessary if he wished to refrain from doing something foolhardy like touching her. Or something ludicrous like taking her in his arms. Or something as bloody stupid as kissing her lush, pink lips and backing her up against a wall so he could ravish her mouth as the savage inside him longed to do.

"Blades are dangerous," she argued. "He is only seven years old, Mr. Ludlow."

Seven years old. Why had he never given a thought to the lad's age before? Of course he was young, but not so young he could not be entrusted with a blade. Why, Clay himself had been similar in age when his father had first taken him on a hunt. Seven years was almost a lifetime. It was almost eight years, in fact, which was the last time Clay had seen the lad's mother. Since he had kissed her. Held her. Lain with her.

Clay froze.

Holy God. His mind sprinted through facts, attempting to make sense of the ugly, jumbled mess that had only just begun to take shape.

Seven years old. Dark hair. Gangly limbs. Tall.

Clay had seen the pictures of the Duke of Burghly, and while he had not been able to discern how light the man's hair had been, his facial structure was clear. The lad did not resemble Burghly in the slightest. Indeed, the lad resembled...*sweet Jesus*...he resembled...himself.

Seven years old.

Seven.

Years.

Old.

Why had it never occurred to him before this moment? Why had he never realized? *Good God*, all the signs were there. He had seen himself in the lad. How many times had he looked upon him and been reminded of himself as a youth? And not just that. They had bonded. They had connected.

The boy was his son. The duke. The lad. *Bloody hell*, the name Clay called him mattered not. Only one thing did. One truth he was beginning to think irrefutable: Ara's son was *his* son.

The only time they had made love, he had lost control and spent inside her. It had been but the once, and he had not thought a babe would be likely. And then, after she had betrayed him, he had never thought of a babe at all. He had tried to think as little of Ara as possible.

But now... Now, his heart thumped madly in his chest as if he had run a great distance. Now, it seemed such a circumstance had not been as unlikely as he had believed. It seemed he had left behind a part of himself on that night, one he had never dreamed existed.

He struggled to calm himself, for he did not yet possess enough facts—enough ammunition—to serve him. "The lad is seven years old," he repeated slowly, lingering on the number, his eyes burning into hers, looking for the slightest hint of a reaction.

Her nostrils flared. "Yes, Mr. Ludlow. My son is seven years of age, far too young to be entrusted with a dangerous blade he does not know how to wield."

"When is his birthday?" he asked with deceptive calm.

"Why?" she asked, her full lips pursed into a thin line.

Damn it, he did not have the patience for her games.

"When?" he repeated through gritted teeth.

"I do not need to linger here and subject myself to your interrogation, Mr. Ludlow." She pinned him with a glare, grasping her skirts in the hand that did not contain his knife and giving them an agitated twitch as she spun to present him with her back. "If you will excuse me, I have many important matters awaiting my attention, sir."

No.

He was not allowing her to leave this chamber until he had answers. Until he knew, irrevocably, that what he already suspected was true.

No. Bloody. Way.

He followed her, seized her waist in his hands, and forced her to face him once more. She gasped, her head tipping back as he spun her more harshly than he would have needed to, her fingers finding purchase on his shoulders. Violent anger careened through him. If she had kept his son from him…if she had lied…for years…*eight fucking years*…and allowed the lad to believe another man was his father…

"Is there something you would like to tell me, Your Grace?" he asked, unable to keep the barely leashed violence from his tone.

She was so small in his hands, like a bird, so fine-boned and slim. He could crush her with such ease. He was a large man, he knew, and he was ever cognizant of his size, but she had driven him to the edge of reason. He would never hurt her, but if she feared him, so much the better.

Her eyes were wide, her pupils dilated. And yet, she said nothing.

Hungry for her words—nay, for her admission—he tightened his grip. "I repeat, madam, is there something you would like to tell me?"

Her eyes, flat and cold, met his. "There is nothing I want to tell you, sir."

He shook his head. "No, my dear. I am afraid that simply will not suffice. Try again."

She threw back her shoulders and tipped up her chin, the picture of elegant, wild defiance. It took him back to the mad days of their youth, just for a beat, until he banished the thought. He did not want to recall the girl he had thought he'd known, for she had been a chimera, and he had already paid his penance for his stupidity long ago.

"Go to hell, Mr. Ludlow," she said coldly.

His patience died. His reason disappeared. In that instant, he could do nothing but feel, and the anger and resentment and unadulterated fury rising in his chest would not be denied. He drove her backward. Mindless, spurred by need and anger and Lord knew what else, he gripped her waist and stalked forward, moving them as one. Moving until her back was against the wall.

He did not even bother with pretense. Instead, he sank his body into hers so that every part of him—all the sinews, all the angles and planes, all the hardness and steel, fitted itself against her malleable curves. Their lips were scandalously close, their breaths mingling. Hers emerged in harsh pants to match his.

"I have been in hell these last eight years." The admission was torn from him. "You sent me there without a moment of remorse. But I will forgive you for all your sins against me save one. What I cannot forgive, Ara, is you keeping *my son* from me."

"He is not your son," she denied, an edge of desperation entering her voice. "I insist you release me at once and cease your manhandling of my person."

She was lying. He could see it in the way her eyes refused to focus upon him. In the way she held herself. In her every protest. The rage beating inside him was palpable. So too the devastation. He had thought she had betrayed him before, but this—keeping his son from him for seven bloody years and raising him as another man's child—this revelation flayed his skin from the bone. It was as if she had taken his blade and sunk it deep into his chest.

"You, madam, are a liar," he bit out, rage coursing through his veins. It was so strong, so violent it left a bitter taste in his mouth. Or perhaps that was her breath, scented with tea and fear.

"And you are a bastard, Mr. Ludlow." She maintained her poise, even as he crowded her against the wall, even as he sensed the anxiety roiling through her. "Now that we have traded insults, would you mind removing your person from mine so I may exit the chamber and distance myself from your insufferable presence?"

He slid his right hand from her waist up her bodice. Over black silk he coasted, absorbing her heat, the softness of the fabric, the boning of her corset, the fullness of her breast. He did not stop until he reached her heart, his hand splaying over it, her mourning brooch a cool reproach, providing slick contrast to the warmth radiating from her. Her heart pounded, steady and hard. No indeed, she was not as unaffected as she pretended.

"Aye, I am a bastard," he said. "That was the trouble for you, wasn't it, Duchess? You wanted me, but when you realized how hard life would be as the wife of a bastard, you found yourself a duke instead. Did the poor devil ever know the lad was not his, or did he believe you went to his bed an innocent?"

It would not have been the first time a lady of quality went to her husband's bed carrying another man's seed. The notion of Ara marrying Burghly and deceiving him into believing Clay's son was his made him ill. As did the thought of her lying with him. She had gone to her marriage bed carrying his babe, and she had chosen to bear and raise that babe with another man.

Her brilliant eyes settled upon his at last, bright in her pale face. "Edward is Freddie's son."

"*Freddie* is dead," he spat.

She flinched. "I am aware my husband is gone, Mr. Ludlow. If he were here, you would not be."

No, he would not. He would be assigned to a different mission, somewhere else. He would be going about his days without knowing he had a son. A son who thought his father had died three months ago in a Dublin Park at the hands of assassins.

Damn it, he hated Burghly as much as he envied him, for the man had been a father to the lad for seven years. He had usurped Clay's place in his son's life. In Ara's life. Because she had chosen the duke instead of Clay. The knowledge made her betrayal so much worse than he had supposed.

She had lied to him. Lied to their son. To hell with the scar on his face. It was a trifling matter compared to the loss of seven years with Edward. Seven years he could not regain and she should not have stolen from him. But to think, had he not come here to Burghly House on this assignment, he never would have discovered the truth. He never would have met his awkward, sensitive, big-hearted lad with the blue-violet eyes and frame that was too large for his body. Such a vital part of himself—as necessary as his damn heart—and he would not have known.

Because of her.

All because of one woman.

"You would have allowed the lad to think Burghly was his father for the rest of his days," he observed with a coolness he did not feel. Inside, he was raging. He was every emotion he had ever felt multiplied by a thousand and then set on bloody fire.

"Because Burghly *is* his father," she insisted, clinging to her lies. "I married Freddie shortly after you left for the Continent. It was a whirlwind courtship as we fell madly in love. You are mistaken in your assumptions, Mr. Ludlow."

After her betrayal, he had needed to flee. With stitches yet in his cheek, he had gone as far and as fast as he could go. He had landed in France, then on to Italy and Prussia before settling back in Paris for an extended stay. He'd spent nearly six months as a wanderer, living life by the moment, some days drowning in his grief and others determined to purge Ara from his mind and heart however he could.

It had been a sinful time, most of it a blur as he looked back upon it. And all those lost months, as he had been trying to remove every remnant of her from his memory, his son had been growing in her womb while she had become another man's wife. When he had returned to England and found his purpose in the Special League, his son had been a babe. Clay had been robbed of the opportunity to watch him grow. To hold him in his arms.

Her words struck him then. "How did you know I had gone to the Continent?"

"I went to Brixton Manor," she said quietly. "I was informed of your departure."

No one had ever spoken a word of her visit to him. He supposed they would not have. His father had been furious with him for dallying with the daughter of a man he loathed.

"Why did you go there?" he asked, though he knew he ought not. Her reasons no longer mattered. She had allowed another man to raise his son for seven years and had every intention of perpetuating that lie now.

"Because I was a fool." Her tone was bitter. "I have long since grown weary of answering your questions, Mr. Ludlow. I have a great deal of correspondence awaiting my attention, so if you will excuse me?"

Did she truly believe, even for an instant, he had believed a word of her nonsensical denials? That he would allow her to scurry away so she could *write letters* when the most important question of his life went unanswered? Did she not think he had wits about him or eyes in his head? The truth did not need her voice, for it was in everything, and he could not believe he had not seen it sooner. Perhaps he had been too blinded by the task assigned him. Perhaps he had been too distracted by her. Whatever the case, he knew now, without her acknowledgment, the lad was his bloody son.

But he wanted to hear the truth from her. She owed it to him.

She moved to squeeze herself between him and the wall, attempting a side step so she could slink away. There was no way in hell she was going anywhere until she confirmed what he already knew. He blocked her, kicking out a booted foot, his long leg trapping her. Unfortunately, the movement also brought their bodies even closer together, until she was flush against him.

"I will not excuse you, madam," he warned, his hand moving from her heart to her throat. His fingers curled lazily about her neck, his thumb dipping into the hollow where her pulse thrummed a frantic staccato. "Do not think for a moment you will be leaving this chamber until I have my answers."

"I have already given you your answers," she insisted, swallowing in a ripple against his thumb.

"No, my dear Duchess." He shook his head slowly. "You have given me falsehoods."

Her lips parted. "Let me go or I shall scream."

He almost laughed, but levity was not in him. Not when he felt so torn up inside he could scarcely gather his thoughts. "Scream away, madam. You will only send my men raining down upon us, and then we shall both have to explain why we are here against this wall."

"Because you are holding me prisoner," she gritted, lashing out at him for the first time by striking his chest with the heels of both hands.

For such a small thing, she had a surprising strength. But she was no match for his larger frame, just as he had never been any match for her cunning betrayal. "Nay, Duchess. We are here in this battle because you insist upon deceit. I will give you one last chance to be honest with me. Who is the father of your son?"

She stared over his shoulder. "My husband, Mr. Ludlow."

Stubborn to the end. Did she think she could fool him? Or did she fancy he would relent and believe her lies? Was she that arrogant, or simply that desperate? He searched her face, seeking an answer and finding none. Here was the woman he had once loved, a woman, as it turned out, he had never truly known at all. Time had worn by, but she was as calculating and selfish as she had been all those years ago.

He stroked her throat slowly, moving from her pulse to her jaw, and then back down, once, twice, thrice. Again and again, for now that he was touching her—part caress, part threat, he could not seem to stop himself. She was pale and soft, her skin luxurious as velvet.

"Such vulnerability here," he said lowly, the pent-up anger inside him wanting to alarm her. "You are completely at my mercy, Ara."

He could not bring himself to refer to her by her title. Not now. Not with so much unspoken between them, the memories of everything they had shared and what they had been to each other pulsing in the air.

Her eyes flew back to his, wide and vibrant. Solemn. "I have always been at your mercy."

There she was wrong, for in truth, it was the opposite. He was at her mercy, as ever. From the moment he had first seen her pale face and vibrant hair in the forest, he had been helpless to resist her. She had been like a sylph, wild and lovely and so very intriguing. He'd lost his heart to her. Believed in her, in their love.

But love was a myth.

And Ara had chosen a life of comfort and ease instead of him.

The rage inside him had abated, as had the shock. In their places was a desperate need of knowledge. He wanted her admission. Her acknowledgment. Enough of her lies. He wanted—deserved—to know the truth.

And so did the lad.

"Tell me the truth," he commanded her. Begged her. He lowered his head until his forehead almost touched hers. "Tell me I am Edward's father."

Chapter Twelve

"TELL ME I am Edward's father."

Clay's demand resonated in the chamber, so forceful and stern it echoed through the ballroom. It repeated itself all around them, haunting, insistent.

Dogged.

Though she tried not to be affected by the emotions she thought she heard in his voice, she was.

Longing. Hurt. Betrayal. Desperation.

Ara's heart nearly stopped beating. Or perhaps it was beating so fast it threatened to stop. His hand was on her neck, huge and hot, caressing and threatening all at once. The Clay she had once known—or rather the Clay she had thought she'd known—would never have hurt her.

Not physically, anyway.

This Clay was a world away from the young man who had gently wooed her with his wit and humor and lively smiles. Of course, she now knew he had merely shown her the face he wished her to see so he could gain what he wanted.

He had taken everything from her: her heart, her innocence, her trust. And had left her with a bitter, empty shell. How dare he reappear eight years later, demanding to know he was the father of her son? Where had he been when she had been frightened and banished from her father's home, unknowing of where to turn, when she had disgraced herself and had to find a way to live through the consequences of her actions?

He had left her when she needed him most.

She did not owe him anything, least of all the truth. If he had wanted to be a part of Edward's life, he should not have gone away. He should not have fled to the Continent. He should never have left her waiting on the day he had promised they would run away together to be married.

Tears stung her eyes as she shook her head, not looking away from his dark intensity. "No."

"No?" he repeated as though he could not believe her refusal. "Then tell me I am not his father, Ara."

She swallowed, her gaze straying from his. She stared at the protrusion of his Adam's apple. "You are not Edward's father."

"Look me in the eye when you lie to me, damn you," he growled, releasing her neck and taking her chin in a firm grip instead. He forced her head back, until she could not look anywhere but at him. "Try again."

"Freddie was his father," she said instead, for that much was true.

Freddie had promised to raise Edward as his own, and he had held firm to his vow. He could not have loved Edward any better had he been the product of their own marital bed, and Ara knew it. He had been a good man. Compassionate and munificent. Unlike the man before her.

Clay sneered down at her now. "I will give you one more opportunity, Duchess. Tell me the truth, or I shall take the matter to Chancery Court. I will petition that Edward is my rightful son, and you have wrongfully kept him from me. I will attest to our affair, and the date of the lad's birth will lend credence to my claims. I will also have him removed from your custody and placed into mine."

She had not considered the possibility he would wish to take her son from her. The thought of such a private matter going before the court made her ill. If the court sided with him, Edward would be disinherited and she could lose her son. And the court always favored the rights of the father above those of the mother. Her mouth went dry, a sharp stab of fear cutting through her.

Surely, he had only issued such threats to force her to give in and admit Edward was his son.

"You would not do something so reckless," she countered. "My reputation would be ruined. Edward's inheritance would be called into question."

"I don't give a damn about your reputation, madam. I care about the truth you've been hiding for eight bloody years." His expression was as rigid as the big, powerful body keeping her pinned to the wall. "I will not let you leave this chamber until you admit it."

Anguish mingled with her fear. "You cannot take my son from me. I will not allow it."

"You have already taken him from me for seven years," he countered. "It will be your turn to see how it feels to have your child robbed from you, and you will be helpless to stop me. Is that what you want, Ara? Is that what you will force me to do?"

His questions hung in the air, sharp and angry and damning.

She could hold fast to her assertion Freddie was Edward's father and pray Clay would not do what he warned and take the matter before the court. Or she could reveal the truth and hope he would be merciful. Why had she allowed him to give Edward lessons? Why, oh why, had her foolish tongue slipped, revealing his age? She should have known better. This entire, sordid mess was her fault.

And it seemed there was no good resolution.

No option save one.

"Ara? Answer me."

"You are his father," she whispered.

There. It was done.

Eight years of holding in her secret, and in a scant handful of seconds, the truth had been revealed. It felt simultaneously freeing and terrifying. Freeing because the weighty guilt that had been her constant companion, lurking in her heart whenever she thought of the father Edward would never know, could at last be banished. Terrifying because she had confirmed what Clay had only suspected. He could still attempt to take Edward from her. He could still ruin her.

He released her so abruptly she almost fell to her knees on the parquet before he turned to stride away from her. Blinking, she raised two fingers to her chin where his touch had been. She still tingled from the contact. Her body was a quivering mess of agony and dread and a tiny, unwanted surge of longing.

What would he do?

As she looked on, he stalked from the ballroom, slamming the door behind him with so much force it rattled in its hinges. She flinched. And then she gave in to the overwhelming emotions roiling through her. She slid down the wall, her skirts billowing in a puddle of jet silk, and wept the same bitter, wracking sobs she had cried on the day she had discovered Freddie was murdered.

CLAY REQUIRED MOTION, and he required distance.

Specifically, he needed distance between himself and the Duchess of Burghly, the mother of his child, and the woman who had been withholding his son from him. Because if he did not leave her presence—leave her goddamn house, in fact—he would not be responsible for his actions. Because he had been installed at Burghly House to protect her from Fenian murderers and not to throttle her with his own bare hands.

So, he moved. He made certain his men were stationed and aware of his departure, because even as irate as he was with the woman, he would not have her death on his bloody conscience or his pristine record of service for Her Majesty. And then he walked. His legs ate up the streets of St. James's Square. He paced. He wandered. He found his way back to Burghly House in a daze. He saddled a horse.

And then he rode.

He rode and rode.

Even when a driving rain unleashed its torrent, he did not halt until finally he found himself ensconced in Leo's study. His brother, ordinarily unemotional and detached, had taken in his drenched body and thunderous expression and frowned with concern, ordering him to sit while he fetched him a whisky.

Clay did not accept orders from his little brother outside the Special League, so he ignored the directive. Instead, he paced the confines of Leo's study like a lion stuck inside a cage, which was precisely how he felt. He wanted to rip something apart with his teeth. He wanted to destroy.

"What in the hell has you so agitated, Clay?" Leo demanded, appearing before him with two glasses in hand. He offered him one. "Here you are. Take a head-clearing draught first and then answer me."

He accepted the whisky and sent the lot of it down his throat. It singed a path to his gut, but he still felt numb. "I have a son," he announced baldly.

The word felt strange and foreign on his tongue.

Son.

He thought of the lad, and finally, warmth trickled into his heart.

Leo nodded, taking a sip of his own whisky before answering. "The Duchess of Burghly's boy."

What in the bloody hell?

He froze. "You knew?"

His brother raised a brow. "You did not?"

"Of course not, damn your hide." In typical Leo fashion, he gave no answer. Clay's hand balled into a fist at his side. "Explain yourself, brother. I am not in the mood to play your games today."

"I saw the boy when I first went to Burghly House after learning of the threats against the duchess," Leo explained, apparently taking pity on him for the first time in their lives. "He is your image, poor lad."

He ignored his brother's slight, focusing instead upon the first half of what he'd said. Clay stalked forward. "You mean to tell me you knew before you assigned me to protect her?"

Leo took another sip of his whisky, eyeing him. "You are awfully thirsty, brother. Shall I fetch you another?"

"Answer the bloody question," he gritted.

"Yes."

Clay's patience snapped, and the last vestige of his control went along with it. He hurled his empty tumbler against the wall. "Damn you, Leo. Why did you not speak up? Why did you not say something?"

Leo frowned. "It was not my place to intervene. I am not responsible for managing your by-blows."

"Edward is not a bastard," he roared.

And thank the Lord, too, for illegitimacy was not a curse he would willingly place upon any of his progeny. Though their father the duke had loved Clay's mother, and he had been raised alongside Leo like an equal, that had not changed who he was to polite society, nor the way he was received or looked upon.

"Forgive me," Leo drawled with patent insincerity. "How shall I refer to a seed you planted in the womb of a lady without first being wed to her?"

He supposed he deserved his brother's scorn. He should never have taken Ara before they had married. He most certainly never should have gotten her with child. Nor should he have left without making certain there were no such repercussions. But he had been young and stupid, thinking first with his prick and then with his pride. He had not been able to stomach remaining after Ara's betrayal.

"Fair enough," he rasped. "I was wrong to do what I did. I have no defense of my actions. I was young and bloody reckless, and I did not know there would be a child. But for Christ's sake, Leo, why would you send me there without warning?"

His brother calmly sauntered to the sideboard, filled a fresh glass, and returned to him, holding it out in offering. "How should I have known you were unaware?"

He checked the urge to throw the tumbler against the wall to join the first, accepting it with great reluctance. "Did you not think I would have mentioned it to you at least once in these last eight years?"

Leo returned his stare, unflinching. "Do you think you are the only man in London who has fathered a child with another chap's wife? Half the sons and daughters of the *ton* do not resemble their supposed sires in the slightest."

It was true, and Clay knew it. The way of the world, or at least of the privileged world. "She was not another man's wife then."

"No, but she became one."

His brother was only stating fact. It should not feel as if he had plunged a dagger into Clay's heart. But yet it did. Ara's betrayal ran so much deeper than he had ever fathomed. He had thought nothing could be worse than the twin scars he bore from her—the one on his face and the one on his heart—but he had been wrong. Keeping his son from him, willfully allowing another man to claim the lad as his own without ever breathing a word of it to Clay…

Little wonder he had needed to flee Burghly House. He itched to shake her. And then raise her skirts and drive himself so deep inside her she would never forget he had been the first one to claim her. To make her his.

But he could not do either of those things.

"Yes," he agreed, heaving out a sigh borne of the magnitude of his whirling thoughts and emotions. "She married Burghly, and she passed my son off as his."

"It has been done before," Leo said quietly. "Many, many times. Why should this one be any different?"

"Because he is *my* son, damn it." His grip tightened painfully on the glass, and still he did not take another drink. "I did not know, Leo. I *should have* known. If I had, I never would have left for the Continent. And if I had not gone, I would have realized she carried my child. I would have married her myself."

"Why did you not?" Leo asked, taking another sip of whisky, eyeing him with that penetrating stare he had. "Marry her, I mean. You were mad for her then, and you had obviously ruined her. Why did you go?"

He had never confided the truth of his scar to anyone but his mother years later. When he had returned to Brixton Manor bloodied and shaken, he had been too ashamed to admit what had happened.

Clay took a long draught of whisky once more. Perhaps this was a day of catharsis. It certainly seemed so. He swallowed, relishing the burn of the spirits down his gullet. Mayhap this would help him heal.

Or forget.

He touched a finger to his scar. "This is why I left, and she was responsible."

Leo did not seem particularly surprised by this revelation either. "Do tell, brother."

"I was going to marry her." Memories he had suppressed for so many years returned, visceral and vicious. "Until the day she betrayed me, and everything changed."

Chapter Thirteen

Eight years earlier

LET ME CHOOSE you, if you dare.

Try as he might, Clay had not been able to expel Ara's fierce words from his mind.

He had gone to her the next day as she had asked, against his sense of honor. Against his better judgment. And against everything he had been taught, he had lost control. One kiss from her was all it required for him to vacate his sanity.

One kiss had led to another. Then another. Then another.

Until they had fallen as one to the blanket she had spread on the forest floor. Until he had lifted her gown to her waist and kissed his way up her beautiful legs. Until he had pleasured her with his mouth so thoroughly, she had spent twice, writhing and crying out beneath him like a beautiful sylvan goddess.

Afterward, she had asked to touch him, and he had allowed her to free his aching cock from his trousers. He had shown her how to pleasure him, how to stroke him, and he had come in her hand like a callow youth. It had been the most blisteringly satisfying experience of his life, and he had not even been inside her.

For he had not taken her innocence. Not entirely. But he had gone beyond the pale. He had behaved in a dishonorable fashion toward her. He had been weak and sinful, and he had not been able to resist wanting her when he knew he ought to leave her the hell alone.

Ruining Lady Araminta Winters that day would have been bad enough. But he had continued his folly. For weeks, they had met in secret. In the forest. In a hunting cabin on his father's estate. Thrice, he had even smuggled her back into his bedchamber by using the servant's stair with no one being the wiser. With each assignation, they grew bolder and his ability to keep from sinking home inside her diminished in increasing increments until he knew he had to act or the day would come that he committed the worst sin of all.

So today, *he* was choosing *her*.

He stood in the ante-room of Kingswood Hall, pinned beneath the contemptuous glares of half a dozen lords and ladies from previous centuries. There was also a picture of the Nativity and one of the Holy Family, having no less censorious an effect.

It was not that he hadn't wished to choose her from the start. His heart had always known Ara was for him. But gaining the courage to approach her father had been another matter. He had the modest means his father had settled upon him, no title to speak of, and he had been born a bastard. Add to that the old, persisting feud between Ara's father and his, and his prospects were as sterling as counterfeit candlesticks.

The pompous butler returned then, his expression revealing nothing. "I am afraid His Lordship is not at home."

The refusal to grant him an audience was expected. There was no reason for it to sting, and yet it did. He'd be damned if he would allow anyone to see it, however.

He straightened to his full, formidable height. "I shall wait for him to return. As I said, the matter is of grave import."

The domestic looked as if he had stepped in something

undesirable. "I regret to say the earl will not be returning today."

The devil he wasn't.

"Tomorrow, then," he suggested through gritted teeth.

The butler did not blink. "That will not be possible. His Lordship has a great deal of estate matters which will occupy his time."

Ara's father would not speak with him, and he hadn't even an inkling of Clay's reason for requesting to see him. There was no help for it. He was in love with the man's daughter, and though part of him knew any attempts on his part to be granted her hand in marriage would prove futile, he was willing to do anything to make her his.

She was the first thing he thought of when he woke each morning and the last thing on his mind before he faded into slumber. She was smart and witty, lovely and charming, everything he could hope for in a wife. More than he could hope for, actually. So much more.

He made up his mind.

Striding past the gawping butler, he made his way down the main corridor, throwing doors open as he went. The servant was at his heels, protesting profusely along the way.

"Sir, this is truly extraordinary."

Clay found an empty main saloon. The library.

"I must ask you to leave at once," the servant demanded.

He turned, towering over the fellow easily with his formidable size. "You can tell me where he is, or I can continue my search, chamber by chamber."

The man huffed.

He didn't have time for theatrics. He spun on his heel and resumed working his way through the chambers. Finally, he threw open a door to reveal the study. A thin-haired man was seated behind a large, ornate desk within. He had found his quarry at last.

"Lord Wickham." He bowed formally. "I am Mr. Clayton Ludlow, and I request an audience with you."

"I am sorry, my lord," the butler intervened, sounding much aggrieved. "He would not listen to reason."

"Of course he would not," drawled the earl in a nasty tone, standing. "He comes from tainted stock and was born on the wrong side of the blanket. Why should he possess any breeding at all? You may go, Burton. I shall speak to Mr. Ludlow so he may be on his way once more."

Clay waited for the butler to leave, closing the door softly behind him, before speaking. "My lord, I realize you did not wish to see me, but I must beg an audience of you."

"You are damned right I did not wish to consort with the Duke of Carlisle's bastard," sneered the earl.

Bastard.

The word had followed him like an epithet all his life.

It was unchangeable, a part of him just the same as his bloody hands, and yet it rankled to hear it thrown at him now by Ara's father, as if the word left a disgusting taste in his mouth.

He remained unflinching, however, determined to persevere. Determined he would do his utmost to win the woman he loved. "I am aware you have a quarrel with my father."

"I do not quarrel." The earl flashed a smile that resembled a snarl. Even his straight teeth appeared sharp, and though he was a small man—here was how Ara had inherited her tiny frame—he was nonetheless intimidating. "I loathe Carlisle, because he is a snake in the grass. He stole something from me once, and I shall never forgive him."

"I am not my father, though I cannot fathom what he could have stolen from you," he defended. "Nevertheless, I am my own man, and I come to you independent of him."

"You truly do not know, do you?" Wickham asked, disbelief marking his tone.

What the devil? Was Ara's father mad?

He shook his head slowly. "I am afraid I do not, my lord."

"Your mother," the earl elaborated, bitterness resonating in his words. "He stole your mother from me. I loved her, and he took her away. If you think I would ever give the misbegotten product of their unholy union the slightest courtesy, you are wrong, you insolent whelp."

Shock permeated Clay. His mother had been a celebrated songstress in her youth, but he'd had no notion she was the reason for the feud between his father and the earl. Dread settled into his gut like a leaden weight, for whilst the likelihood of Wickham giving his blessing upon a union between Clay and Ara had been tenuous at best before, it now seemed impossible.

But he had not come to Kingswood Hall to walk away without trying. "My reason for seeking an audience with you today has nothing to do with grudges you hold against my mother and my father. Rather, it pertains to your daughter, Lady Araminta."

Wickham stiffened. "I cannot conceive of a reason you would need to discuss Lady Araminta with me, Mr. Ludlow."

"I wish to marry her, my lord," he revealed, deciding to make the leap. The opportunity and his reception could not be worse. He had nothing to lose.

Except Ara.

And he would not—could not—lose her.

The earl's expression hardened. "You cannot imagine, for even one moment, I would allow my lady daughter to wed a bastard."

He was prepared to make his argument. He had spent the last sennight practicing. "Kingswood Hall borders an estate adjoining Brixton Manor that my father wishes to settle upon me. I also have a generous income per annum that I feel confident would enable Lady Araminta to a life of reasonable comfort."

"You have not even been introduced to my daughter." The earl's gaze narrowed upon him. "Why would you wish to marry her? Undoubtedly, you are aware of her dowry. However, she is already all but promised to the Marquess of Dorset. Surely even one such as you can comprehend that a marquess and a bastard do not equate. Therefore, I could not countenance the mésalliance as you propose, even had I been so inclined, which I most assuredly am not."

All but promised to the Marquess of Dorset?

This information gave him pause.

But it was something he would address with Ara later. In private. It was possible that her father bluffed. Or perhaps it was a match he wished for her to make. She had certainly not spoken of an imminent betrothal aside from their own.

"I beg you to reconsider, my lord," he tried again. "While I may not be a peer of the realm, I would treat Lady Araminta with fairness, respect, and above all kindness."

"As will Dorset," Wickham snapped. "You have said your piece, which is more than I was initially willing to allow. Consider yourself fortunate and take your leave."

There was an air of finality in his tone. In the moment.

Clay felt as if the air had been stolen from his lungs. The embittered man before him would never allow him to wed Ara. Part of him could not blame Wickham, for Lord knew if he had a daughter of his own, he would want her to marry a wealthy lord who could provide for her rather than a duke's by-blow who had been scorned all his life.

Nothing he could do or say would change Wickham's mind. There had to be another way.

He bowed, sickness swirling in his gut. "Thank you for your time, my lord."

And then he stalked from the study and from Kingswood Hall altogether.

But he had not given up on Ara. Not yet. Somehow, by some means, she would be his wife.

ARA RACED THROUGH the darkness and collided with a wall of chest.

Strong, familiar arms banded around her.

"Steady, Ara love," Clay whispered.

She embraced him tightly, burying her face in his coat. It had been two days since she had seen him, and the intervening hours had been interminable. Finally, at last, here he was.

"I missed you so," she murmured back, rising on her tiptoes to press a kiss to his corded neck. Here, the bristle of his whiskers pricked her lips, and she could open her mouth to taste the salty musk of him. His pulse pounded. She flicked her tongue over its steady throb.

He issued a low sound of need. "Minx. You must not or we shan't make it to our destination."

That simply would not do.

With great reluctance, she stopped her exploration of his skin and allowed him to take her hand and tug her into the copse of trees where his mount invariably waited. The moon was full and high, unnaturally bright overhead as they made their way to his horse. He slung his large body into the saddle first and then held down a hand, hoisting her with ease and settling her before him, between his powerful thighs.

The late August air was cool, but Clay's body was a furnace of warmth, and she nestled against him, relishing the closeness they could share, however fleeting. He rode to the hunting cabin, an easy silence falling that was interrupted only by the steady plod of his horse's hooves. Now and again, she caught a glimpse of the night sky through the boughs overhead, their twinkling lights like charmed beacons overhead.

She could ride with him like this forever, she thought wistfully. Like every other stolen moment with him, she wished it would never end. But the ride came to a halt, Clay slowing the mare to a trot before stopping her and dismounting.

He reached up for her next, helping her down and hauling her against him. For an indeterminate span of time, they simply held each other, breathing in and out, relishing the secret chance to be close. How she ached to be so free with him every day. To live her life with him, never leaving his side.

She shivered.

He rubbed her arms through her pelisse. "Are you cold, love? Come, let us go within. I'll build a fire."

She was not cold, not in the way he meant, but Ara did not wish to spoil the loveliness of their tryst with heavy thoughts. Instead, she allowed him to lead her inside the small, neatly kept cabin. An oil lamp flickered to life when he lit it, bathing the chamber in a golden glow. He drew her against him and kissed her sweetly before striding to the grate and crouching down to begin building a fire.

He was such a capable man, and it was one of the many traits she admired in him. He did not shy from performing tasks himself, unlike the lords who had courted her. He wore his industriousness with honor.

"I wish we did not have to meet in secret," she said suddenly, hugging her arms about herself as she watched him.

For some time, he did not respond, the only sound between them the rustling of logs, followed by the gentle crackle of the kindling as the flame came to life.

"I went to see your father two days ago," he said at last. His back was to her, his hands busy with working the flames higher.

"You did?" An instant burst of hope flared in her breast. "Why?"

"To ask for your hand in marriage," he clipped.

There was something different in his tone, a lack of joy, that warned her to temper that hope with caution "And what did he say?"

"He said you are to wed the Marquess of Dorset." He had yet to turn back toward her, and she could not see his expression, but she could well imagine what it contained.

Her heart gave a pang as she went to him, falling on her knees alongside him at the hearth. She did not care if her silk became crushed or otherwise befouled. All she cared about was him.

"Clay." She touched his bicep, firm and powerful beneath his coat. "Will you not look at me?"

He took his time with the fire, waiting until it crackled merrily into the silence, radiating a warmth she scarcely felt, before he turned back to her. "Have you anything to say about it, Ara? Were you intending to go from my arms to another man's bed?"

"Of course not," she said softly. "I do not want to wed Dorset. The marquess has been pressing his suit, but I do not care for him at all. There is only one man I would have as my husband, and Dorset is not he."

"The earl was adamant in his disapproval." Clay cupped her face with a large, callused hand, his dark gaze searching hers. "I am beneath you, Ara. I have no right to be here with you now. No right to want you as I do."

"How adamant was my father?" she asked, desperation making her mind whirl. There had to be some way she could make her father listen to reason. He was a harsh, stern man. But surely if she could convince him she was in love, he would relent. Surely she could force him to realize she and Clay were meant to be together.

That they were each other's fate.

He ran the pad of his thumb over her lower lip, his countenance pained. "Extraordinarily so. Not only does his quarrel with my father still rankle him, but he has vowed he will not ever grant me your hand."

"No," she denied, launching herself at him without a thought. Though she was small, her momentum took him by surprise, and they toppled as one to the demi-lune rug laid before the hearth. His thighs splayed wide, and she settled between them, only the impediment of her skirts and his trousers in her way.

"His words, love. Would that I could change them." He was somber.

She stared intently down into his ruggedly beautiful face, and her heart knew there was no other man for her. "I will change his mind, Clay. I will speak with him."

"And tell him what, love?" A bitter laugh escaped his lips, but he caressed her hair reverently just the same. "That while we have never had a proper introduction, we have been meeting in secret and engaging in all manner of wickedness and we now wish to be properly wed?"

"It is not like that between us." She frowned down at him. Yes, they had been wicked, though she would not regret a moment of the time she had spent in his arms. "I will tell him I love you, and I will not be happy unless I am your wife."

"If only it were that easy, Ara mine." His strokes slowed.

"Apparently, your father and mine vied for my mother's hand years ago. My father won, and yours will not forgive him for it. You see, I am not just a bastard but the bastard born to the woman he once loved. He loathes me, and he has assured me he will not give his consent."

"Fortunately, I am of age." Her tone was firm, her decision made. If her father would not approve of a match between she and Clay, they would simply do what they must. "I can marry whomever I wish."

"Aye." Clay's fingers had found their way into her carefully wrought coif now, plucking pins and sending heavy curls falling around them like a curtain. "He could disown you. Refuse to speak to you. What would you do then, Ara? I hardly think you would be prepared to lead a simple life, possibly stripped from all friends and family. I will taint you. Ruin you far worse than I already have."

"You could never ruin me," she whispered before kissing him as she had been longing from the moment she had walked into his chest earlier. Their mouths clung as if this kiss was their last, but for her it was everything. It was the beginning. She opened for him, surrendering to his tongue, his gentle owning of her lips.

With a growl, he suddenly rolled, until her back was upon the carpet and he straddled her with his thick, muscular thighs. He broke their kiss, staring down at her with so much naked need she lost her breath.

"Then marry me, Ara. Come away with me," he said. "Will you?"

She did not hesitate. "I love you, Clay, and I would go anywhere as long as I was with you."

"Bloody hell," he cursed, merging their lips for another long, heady kiss. It was fiery and raw, tender and sweet. "I do not want to wait any longer, Ara. I will need a day to obtain a license. Two days from now is not soon enough, but it will have to do. Meet me near the north road leading from Kingswood Hall the day after tomorrow. Pack what you can in a small valise. We shall figure out the rest."

The hope she had ruthlessly tamped down sprang forth once more, filling her with buoyant, radiant light. "I will be there at dawn," she vowed.

"Yes?" A boyish grin lit his features.

Her arms twined around his neck, guiding him back down to her. "Yes. I will be anywhere you are, whenever you wish me there. Now kiss me, Clay."

Still smiling, his mouth found hers. Their lips fused. On a liquid sigh of want, she opened for him. His tongue plundered, and he tasted sweet, like sugar. If love had a flavor, it would be this, she thought, it would be him.

She had been sleeping before he came into her world. He woke her heart, her body. He had unleashed *the despicable thing*, and now it could not be contained. Through him, she learned *the despicable thing* had a name.

Desire.

They kissed and kissed. Kissed until she was breathless. Until the pulsing between her legs grew heavy and warm, until need for him transformed her. She knew what the sensations burning through her meant now. She needed him to touch her. They kissed until he rocked against her, and she felt the lengthy protrusion of him through her skirts, so close to where she wanted him most.

Though she had touched him, bare skin to bare skin, he had never made love to her fully. She knew it was what her body longed for, what made her restless and achy. It was what she had imagined so many nights, lying awake alone in her bed in the dark stillness. Wondering where he was. Wondering what it would be like to touch him whenever she chose.

To take him inside her. To become his in every way.

"Ara." Her name was a groan as he tore his mouth away at last, his breathing as ragged as hers. He cupped her face in his big hands, staring down into her eyes with his dark gaze, and there was a rawness she had never before seen in his expression.

An intensity. A tenderness.

He looked at her as if he loved her too. He had yet to say the words. Her heart was strong enough for both of them. Perhaps he was not yet sure how to define what he felt for her. She would wait. She had never been more certain of a decision in all her life.

"I never wanted to feel this way." He shook his head. "Not for you, and not for anyone. But when you look at me as you do, when you touch me, when I breathe in your scent—bloody hell, even when you are nowhere near me—my chest aches."

"Clay," she whispered, her fingers working through his luxurious hair, writing tender patterns of love over his scalp. She could not stop touching him. She never wanted to stop. He was *hers*, this man. And she was his. "You do not need to explain. I feel the same."

He dipped his head, ran his nose along hers in an unexpected caress, then kissed her tenderly once more before rising to look down at her again. His eyes glittered like the stars that watched over them in their midnight races to be together. "My mother told me love would be like a stream after days of pouring rain, that it would rise and overflow its banks, that something violent and magnificent would replace what had been there before. That one small stream can become a rushing river, transforming everything in its path."

She stroked the back of his neck. "Your mother sounds like a wise woman."

His thumb traced her cheek with such slow gentleness she could not look away. Did not even dare breathe for fear she would break the spell that had fallen upon them. "I never understood. Why would she choose to live with a man who could not marry her? Why did she accept less than she deserved? But now I know, Ara. Because she was in love, and I know she was right because I feel it too. I would give anything to be yours. I vow to you I will always love you, Ara. You will have my heart forever and the century next."

"Oh Clay, my love." She hauled his mouth back down to hers, and they kissed again. His lips found her neck, open and hungry, feasting on her. His breath was hot and moist, and it sent a fresh pang of need straight to her core.

"Damn it, Ara. I wanted to be a gentleman tonight," he murmured against her skin.

"I do not want a gentleman." Her fingers traveled, finding his wide shoulders. Such confined strength. She could feel the ripple and flex of his muscles, but there was too much fabric between them, and if she had to wait two whole days to become his wife, she wanted so much more than passionate kisses. "I need you, Clay. Please."

"Ara." He groaned. "We cannot."

"We can." Her fingers found buttons, slipping them from their moorings. "We will be married in two days' time. No one will ever be the wiser."

"*I* will be, my darling." He made a suffering sound. "As will you."

Ever waging war against his interminable sense of honor, her Clay. She moved against him, instinct guiding her. One slow arch of her body into his. Her breasts brushed his chest. The part of him she wanted most pressed against her. It was not enough. Like the fire he had lit in the grate, she was aflame. Burning for him.

"I want to feel you inside me," she whispered, holding his gaze.

Another sound emerged from low in his throat, like a strangled growl. "You do not know what you are asking."

She moved again, undulating her body. Already, she had his coat and waistcoat undone. She pulled both from his shoulders until he was clad in only a shirt, and then she grew bold. Ara knew how to touch him, what he liked, what made him lose himself until his big body shook and bliss rocked through him and he spilled his seed into her waiting palm. Once when he had managed to sneak her into his chamber at Brixton Manor, she had raised her hand to her mouth and licked the creamy spend he had left behind, curious, wanting every part of him she could have.

And he had grown rigid again, rolling her to the bed beneath him, and lifting her skirts. He had buried his face between her legs, licking and sucking her hungry flesh until she had writhed and cried out beneath him. He had not stopped until three simultaneous quakes had roared through her. The traces of him remaining on her hand had been crushed into her skirts as she held them to her waist for him, and she'd hidden the gown from her lady's maid as a precaution, lest the woman make a query about the stains on the pink silk.

She worked open the placket of his trousers now, and he was not wearing smalls beneath them. He sprang free, hard and thick and so very beautiful. Her hand found him. She stroked.

The breath hissed from him. His head dipped. His mouth returned to her throat before rising again. His jaw clenched. "Damn it, Ara."

"I want you to take me, Clay." She ran the pad of her thumb over the smooth firmness of his shaft, feeling moisture gathering at the tip. Feeling bolder still, she brought her thumb to her lips. Licked the wetness from her skin.

She tasted him, tart and bold and delicious. Sucked her thumb. Looked deep into his eyes, telling him without words what she wanted. She loved him. He loved her. They would be wed in two days. There was no sin tonight.

She would not leave this cabin until she was his in every way.

"I am yours," she murmured. "Make me yours forever, Clay. I want you to be my first, my only."

"Fuck."

The vicious epithet rent the air, but it did not shock her. Rather, it inspired her. It empowered her. That one word, so rough, so crude, meant he waged a losing battle to keep from giving them both what they wanted. She reached between them, grasping his velvet hardness, pleasuring him as he had shown her.

His hips jerked. And then he tugged her wrist gently away from him. His fingers went to her simple bodice. Buttons popped free. Like a wild man, he dragged her gown down her body. Like a wild woman, she tore away his shirt, ripping a long strip right down the center when she could not open the buttons as quickly as she wished.

His bare chest was bathed in golden firelight, all the contours delineated—the slabs of sinew and muscle, the breadth of him. Her hands couldn't get enough of his skin. She ran them over him, absorbing his heat and strength, the fine dusting of hairs, the beautiful grooves on his abdomen. She wanted to run her tongue all over his body, to taste him everywhere. Just gazing upon him filled her with a heady, delirious want.

"Yes, love." He caught her hands in his with those handsome long fingers. Fingers that knew just how to touch her, how soft, how fast, how rough. "I am yours."

He was hot and sleek. Perfection. Like a marble warrior come to life. Even better, for she had seen him in action. He was *her* warrior. And he would soon be her husband.

"I never want to stop touching you," she confessed, her cheeks warming after the words left her.

But he was not ashamed. "I never want you to stop either, love. Touch me all you like, for the rest of our lives."

Oh, yes.

She would accept his directive without question.

"Where?" she asked, her hand traveling back to his length, which had only grown in size. How would it fit inside her body as he had told her? She could not imagine, and yet she wanted him inside her with an aching persistence. Anticipation, anxiety, curiosity, and need collided. "Here?" Her fingers tightened around him, stroking.

"Hell, Ara," he growled, and then the last shred of his restraint finally gave way.

He found ties and buttons and hooks, and he began undoing. With speed and deftness. With an almost desperation that told her he was as frantic for her as she was for him. She hadn't worn a corset, and she was glad for it as he made short work of her chemise, drawers, and stockings, leaving her utterly bare before him. He shucked his trousers.

And then he was on his knees between her spread thighs. His beautiful face lowered. He kissed her mound, directly above the bundle of flesh capable of such intense sensation. Lower still he kissed, over inner thighs, and onward, pressing chaste, tempting kisses all the way to her…

To her *pearl*, the word he had taught her—one of many initiations between them.

His mouth closed over her, and he sucked.

She moaned, caressing his hair, his shoulders. Any part of

him she could reach as he laved, his tongue slicking the plump bud. His teeth nipped. Just a soft exertion of pressure before his tongue swirled again, working her into even more of a frenzy. He licked down her seam, his knowing tongue parting her, teasing where she ached.

"You taste so bloody good, Ara," he murmured into her desperate flesh. "And you're so hungry for me, so responsive, so wet. I could keep you like this forever."

If she had possessed the ability to speak, she would have quipped that she wouldn't object to such a fate. But he was inflicting his divine torture on her again, and all she could manage was rolling her head on the carpet, arching her back, and moaning. The pressure built inside her, coiling like a spring as he licked and gently bit.

A great, frenzied rush swept her away. The pleasure burst. She cried out, tremoring with the power of her release, her fingers tightening in his hair. He rode out the storm of her climax with her, caressing her thighs, making a deep rumble of satisfaction she felt in her core.

And then he was kissing back up her body, settling between her thighs, the thick head of him rubbing over her in a delicious temptation. His tongue swirled around her nipples as he slid his fingers over her sex, sending sparks shooting through her. He stroked her pearl in exquisite torture, suckling the stiff peaks of her breasts.

"Ara mine," he murmured against her skin, his breath and lips a brand. "You must be certain. I cannot maintain my control for much longer. I want to be a gentleman. To treat you with the honor and respect you deserve."

He was such a good man, so honorable. She had no question, no doubt in her soul. Her hands were on him, touching him everywhere she could. "I want you now, Clay. Inside me. You are the husband of my heart, and I don't want to wait two days."

He buried his face in her neck, kissing all the way to her jaw as he rocked his body against hers, slowly and tentatively. "Certain, Ara?"

His skin was hot and smooth, his shoulders hard slabs, his biceps flexed as he held himself above her, keeping his full weight from her body. It seemed impossible a man so large and powerful could be capable of such gentleness, and yet he was. He touched her with a reverence that shook her.

"Certain," she said.

His mouth claimed hers at the same time as he thrust inside her. One quick pump of his hips. Pain sliced through her at the intrusion. She flinched beneath him. The hand between their bodies stilled.

"I'm so sorry, love," he said against her mouth. "Shall I stop?"

"No." She kissed him again, moving beneath him. An aching burn tore through her, chased by spirals of pleasure as his fingers plied their sensual torture. How odd this claiming was, half pleasure, half pain. And yet, incomplete somehow. She wanted more. She moved again. He settled deeper inside her.

He groaned. "You feel so damn good. Too good for me, Ara. Too good. I do not deserve you."

Yes, she wanted to say, *you do*. But she could not seem to speak.

He thrust deeper, stretching her, taking small, slow strokes until he was all the way inside her, and she was so full. Her body adapted to him. As he worked her with his clever fingers, the pain receded. In its place was *the despicable thing*, accompanied by the need for friction. For more.

They kissed and kissed. Slowly, he began to move, giving her what she wanted. In and out he thrust, unhurriedly at first but then faster. Kissing her with such aching tenderness that tears leaked from her eyes and trailed down her cheeks. He found them, caught them with his lips.

"Am I hurting you, my love?" He stilled, gazing down at her, concern furrowing his brow.

"You could never hurt me," she said, managing to find her voice. She urged him to continue by undulating her hips, bringing him deeper once more. "I am happy. So very happy."

He found her lips, fed her his tongue, his kiss firm and demanding, yet giving and sensual all at once. She never wanted him to stop kissing her, just as she never wanted his body to part from hers. She wished she could keep him here forever, their skin melded together, bodies as one with him inside her, his tongue and his taste in her mouth.

He was her entire world. He was the sun and the moon and the stars, the days and the nights, and every breath.

And she was coming undone. Flying. Her body exploded like firecrackers in a dark sky. With him inside her, the pleasure was even more intense. She tightened, losing herself, shaking, crying out. He slid in and out, faster and faster, and then he thrust deep inside her one last time as bliss rippled through her, curling her toes.

He tore his mouth from hers and threw back his head, crying out her name as he spent inside her. Another tremor hit her, and she was helpless. Mindless. Filled with love and filled with Clay.

"I love you," she whispered, holding him tightly to her as their hearts pounded in unison.

They held each other in silence for a long time, nothing but the crackling of the fire and the steady reassurance of their breaths interrupting. When they did not dare tarry any longer, Clay tenderly cleaned her with a handkerchief and they helped each other to dress.

The ride back to Kingswood Hall was over too soon.

They parted with a long, slow kiss in the darkness. When Ara slipped back inside her chamber, she could not sleep, the happiness within her so strong she vibrated with it. She stood at the window for a long time, fancying she could see Clay standing below, watching her in return, as reluctant to leave her behind as she was him. The moon bathed the park in a silver glow. The stars seemed brighter than she had ever seen them.

At last, she forced herself away from the window, sat at her writing desk, and confessed her elation in the only fashion she dared trust: to the pages of her journal. She signed her name at the bottom with a flourish.

Mrs. Clayton Ludlow.

Chapter Fourteen

One moment, Ara had been alone in the garden, staring into the sculpted hedges and trying to calm her racing heart and mind. The next, a crunch of tread on gravel alerted her to another presence.

She turned, expecting the interloper to be Clay, returned from wherever he had disappeared to in the wake of her revelation. Hours had passed. Rains had come and gone. And still he had not reappeared. She was desperate to know what his next move would be. Terrified of how her admission would impact Edward. Frightened of the power Clay could wield over her.

But when her eyes settled upon the unfamiliar face and form of a stranger, all her terror and fear turned into abject horror. The man stood at a distance, a bowler hat pulled low over his brow. His countenance was grim. Menacing. Dark-red splatters stained his coat and trousers. *Blood.* The hilt of a vicious-looking blade glinted in his hand, also dripping with gore.

And she knew.

She knew he was here to kill her.

Ara screamed, snagging fistfuls of her skirts and running in the opposite direction. Clay had men stationed everywhere. She could only guess that the blood on the stranger's clothing was from one of them.

He had murdered one of her guards. And now, he would murder her.

No.

She would fight. She would run.

As fast as her feet and her legs would take her, she raced. Into the maze of carefully manicured hedges she went, knowing the path by heart. Heavy footfalls followed, echoing in her ears. All she could hear was the pant of her own breaths, the thudding of her heart, and the sound of the stranger following her. Gaining on her. Closer and closer he came. Her heart hammered. Her breaths became increasingly shallow until she was gasping. She was losing speed and he was gaining.

The garden was not large. She reached the center of the maze. He grew closer. Closer. Closer. But she was determined. Desperate. The footfalls sounded heavier now. She had a son to live for. She had everything to fight for. She pushed herself, ran faster, her heavy skirts and corset twin impediments to her progress.

Until her foot caught in her hem. She lost her balance. Tripped. Fell headlong into the gravel path. A fresh wave of fear hit her as she collided with the earth. Her hands caught most of her fall, keeping her head from slamming into the ground. But the footsteps were upon her now, and she was lying prone, helpless.

A lamb for the slaughter.

This was it for her. She had reached the end. Edward's face flashed through her mind. *No*, she had to be brave for her son. She had to escape. She would live for him. She *had* to live for him. She scrambled to her hands and knees, desperation coursing through her.

"Ara."

Huge, boot-shod feet appeared before her.

This was not the voice she had expected to hear. This voice was familiar. Dark and low. Reassuring in a way it ought not to be after all these years and everything that had come between them.

Hands gripped her, hauling her upward.

And there he was. Clay. She had never been more relieved to see another person in all her life. She threw herself into his arms. "Th-there is a man. He's f-following me."

The words would not emerge without the trembles wracking her body. Terror still clawed at her. Where was the man? He had been so close on her heels. Clay's touch swept over her back, up and down in soothing motions.

"He will not follow you again," he promised, a lethal note underlying his voice.

Good heavens, had Clay killed the man? She was afraid to ask. "P-please. Edward…is he safe?"

"Yes, the lad is safe." He continued to stroke her back, holding her tightly. Almost as if she were precious to him, though she knew the truth was he loathed her. "Did that bastard touch you?"

She shook her head, inhaling deeply of his reassuring scent. Musk and man and leather. And Clay. "I ran from him. H-he was getting closer. He was c-covered in blood, Clay. H-he had a blade."

"Aye. He almost killed one of my men. I'll be requesting more guards forthwith." His voice rumbled in his broad chest.

Her body went cold, and she could not seem to stop trembling, her teeth chattering. The threats against her, while concerning, had been faceless and intangible. Now, she had seen a man who intended to murder her, just moments after he had attempted to kill another.

"Ara, you are safe now. You have my word." His tone was grim. He stroked her hair with such tenderness her heart ached.

She did not trust his word. He had given it to her before, and his promise had been a lie. But the truth was, she had no one else. He was all she could rely upon, the only hope she could cling to.

And so, she clung. She clung as if he were the side of a boat and she was in danger of being swept away into the sea. She clung to his strong neck and his massive chest. Clung as he bent and scooped her effortlessly into his arms. Not a hint of a protest left her lips as he stalked back along the path she had just run down.

Though she pressed her face against him, she saw the fallen figure of a man in the path. More blood.

"Avert your gaze," Clay ordered curtly.

But it was too late. She recognized the still form, the bowler hat lying next to his lifeless body. Clay had killed for her. Silently, savagely, and without hesitation. He had saved her life, but to do so, he had needed to take another.

A shocked gasp tore from her, and she forced her eyes away from the dead man.

"It was necessary, Ara." Clay's deep voice vibrated against her cheek. "If he had reached you, I would not have been able to save you."

She swallowed, knowing it was the truth. "Thank you, Clay."

"It is my duty to protect you," he said tightly. "You need not offer me your gratitude."

His sudden coolness felt like a rebuke. "You may put me down now," she said, her pride reasserting itself now that the danger seemed to have been extinguished for the moment.

"No," he bit out.

She glanced up at him, finding his wide jaw rigid. "I wish to walk on my own. I do not require you to carry me about as if I am an invalid."

"The matter is not open for discussion. I am carrying you, and that is final."

What a stubborn, vexing man. So changeable. One moment, he held her as if she were dear to him, and the next he withdrew even as he insisted upon carrying her back into Burghly House.

She wriggled in his arms, trying to get free. "You do not have the right to order me about. Put me down now, Mr. Ludlow."

He did not even pause his stride. "Cease squirming or I shall drop you."

Naturally, she did not heed his warning. Instead, she moved about, pushed at his chest, doing everything in her power to make him release her. But he held firm. She felt as ineffectual as a butterfly flitting about the head of a lion, just as he had once said.

As they re-entered the house, one of his men approached, wearing a forbidding expression. The servants were nowhere in sight, the house eerily silent.

"We have searched the entire home, sir," said the man. "We cannot find the assailant responsible for stabbing Beauchamps."

"The young duke," he barked, never breaking his steady pace. "There are two men guarding him?"

"Aye, sir. Two men at the nursery, another on the ground below watching the perimeter."

"And Beauchamps?" Clay asked.

"He's in a bad way. There's a doctor seeing to him now, sir," answered the man. "We have also sent word to the Duke of Carlisle. I expect he will be arriving within the half hour."

"I've found the assailant, Farleigh," Clay said then, apparently satisfied by the reports he'd just received. "He's in the gardens."

"In the gardens? Shall I interrogate him, sir?"

"This bird won't sing, Farleigh," Clay said harshly. "I am afraid I had no alternative. Perhaps you might see to the body. I would not have the child or an unsuspecting domestic seeing it. Search him for any hint of information."

"Aye, sir," chirped the man called Farleigh, heading off in the direction from which they had just come.

Clay was like a general commanding a field of battle, and her glimpse into the man he had become left her shaken. So shaken she forgot temporarily her struggle to be released. Until her wits returned to her, and with them, her outrage. "Release me at once."

He ignored her, stalking to a small saloon she scarcely ever used, and elbowing the door open. Once they were over the threshold, he kicked the portal closed at his back and released her so suddenly that when her feet met the plush carpet, she almost tumbled backward in a heap of skirts.

Smoothing her dress into place, she glared at his back, for he had turned away from her to pace the length of the chamber. "I am grateful to you for saving my life whether you like it or not. But you, sir, have no right to cart me about. Who do you think you are?"

He spun on his heel, bearing down on her, eyes blazing. The ferocity in his expression stole her breath. "I am the man who just killed for you. The man who is charged with your wellbeing and safety. I have every right to protect you as I see fit."

"And yet you left me hours ago, with no word of when you would return," she charged, her shock giving way to anger. Anger was far easier. She could cling to it. Hide herself in it. Wear it like a shield.

"I alone am to blame for this breach, and I know it." He

raked a hand through his hair, looking every inch the dark, dangerous warrior. "I should not have abandoned my post. I would never have done so under ordinary circumstances."

The reason for his abrupt departure hung between them, unspoken and heavy.

He had discovered he was her son's father.

But she could not think about the magnitude of her revelation to him now. Not when a man who'd wished to murder her lay dead in the gardens. Not when she had almost been in that man's place. When she had almost been the one whose blood had spilled. The one who breathed her last breath.

Clay had saved her. And despite his highhandedness, she could not deny he had spared her life today. Without him, she would not be here before him in this small chamber, wanting to kiss him and rail against him.

"I am thankful you returned when you did," she managed to say softly. "How did you know where to find me?"

He swallowed, his expression becoming pained. "I heard you scream. I had returned to find Beauchamps badly wounded, and I knew I had to find you and the lad as soon as I could. I made certain the lad was safe. You screamed. I ran. I was…Jesus, Ara, I was afraid the bastard would reach you before I could."

She stared at him, reading the emotion in his countenance, hearing it in his voice. Her foolish heart longed to believe that a part of him could still care for her, at least in some small measure. Because she realized in that moment, shock still making her weak, part of her had never stopped caring for him.

That her heart still beat for him.

When he was in a chamber, he was all she saw.

When he was gone, he was all she thought of.

He had been back in her life for scarcely any time at all,

and she was as weak for him as she had ever been. Young, foolish Ara had believed this man her destiny. She had thought they could never be torn apart. Older, harsher Ara could still fall prey to the same fanciful notions, it would seem.

"Clay," she began, but there was no opportunity for her to complete her thought, for he was upon her.

He caught her waist, guiding her with sudden force, not stopping until her back met the door. There was no gentleness. No lover's finesse in his touch. It was pure and wild. Raw need. Hunger and desperation, fear and life and death and the frantic desire to celebrate taking a breath.

And she felt the same. Felt the furiousness of her emotions. Felt it all return to her in a flash, if indeed it had ever truly been gone. There was nothing and no one but Ara and Clay. No past. No present. No future.

There was the moment, and then there was his mouth.

Hard and firm, insistent and demanding, his lips crashed into hers. She wanted it. Welcomed it. Needed the mercilessness of his claiming. Her hands sank into his hair, her body arching into his. Her breasts crushed against his chest. She opened for him, sucked his tongue into her mouth. He tasted of whisky and bitterness and sin.

He tasted of life and raw emotion and the sweetest passion.

He tasted of the past she had never truly left behind.

She grabbed fistfuls of his hair, tugging, angling his mouth to hers, struggling to control him. They savaged each other. Ara bit his lower lip. He nipped her back with a growl. His long fingers sank into the braid pinned to her crown, pulling with just enough force to move her mouth back to where he wanted it. His subtle domination—on the verge of painful pleasure—made her knees go weak.

She moaned, kissing him back with ruthless abandon. His other hand slid from her waist to her breast, cupping her through her bodice and corset, making her ache. This was not the touch of the young man she had once loved but the bold, commanding caress of a man. He had changed. So had she. And yet this—the conflagration between them—remained the same.

Or perhaps, it was more.

She had never burned for him the way she did now. Her cunny was slippery with need, aching and pulsing and yearning. She wanted him to lift her skirts, find the slit in her drawers, and slide home.

It was wrong, and she knew it.

There were so many reasons why they could not. Why she could not. Should not.

As if he sensed the tumultuous nature of her thoughts, he tore his mouth from hers, breathing heavily. His dark gaze burned into hers. She could not look away from him. He was glorious, his mouth swollen from their kisses, ruby-red where she had bitten into his sensual lower lip. His face was all harsh lines and angles, his expression inscrutable.

She fought to regain her breath, the madness receding proportionally to the distance between their hungry mouths. Her first thought was of Edward. Though Clay had reassured her he was safe and Farleigh had reiterated the same, she would not be satisfied until she could be certain herself. "I need to see my son now, Clay. Please."

He stiffened, his eyes darkening, his mouth taking on a harsh flatness. "*Our* son, Ara. He is mine as well, and you must accustom yourself to it. I'll not press the matter with him now, but in time I will want him to know who I am."

Of course he would want Edward to know he was his father. She had expected and feared as much. "He is a boy,

Clay, and he has just lost the only father he has ever known. I do not know when, if ever, he will be ready for such a revelation."

A muscle ticked in his jaw. "He will know who I am."

"When the time is right," she agreed quietly.

"When I decide the time is right," he snarled. "You have kept him from me long enough."

"Out of necessity alone," she defended. "I gave him a father and a home when he would have had neither."

"You gave him what you wanted, and the one thing I could never have given you—a bloody title." His lips twisted, and he released her, moving away as if he could not bear to be in such proximity to her now that he had regained his senses.

"No," she said, shaking her head. "How very wrong you are."

He could have given Edward far more than any title. And if he thought that marrying Freddie had given her everything she'd ever wanted, he was sorely mistaken. She had loved her husband, but as a friend. No man before or after Clayton Ludlow had ever made her feel the way he did, as though he was the other half of her she had never known was missing. Until he had left her behind with nary a goodbye.

Until he had left her to find a way of raising their son on her own.

There was so much more she could say to him, but she did not. Her foolish weakness for him knew no bounds, it would seem. Otherwise, she never would have allowed him to kiss her. She never would have kissed him back.

"It would seem we have both been very wrong," he said then with a funereal air. "Come, madam, I will take you to our son."

She ignored the arm he proffered, running her tongue over lips that still felt the brand of his kiss upon them. "I do not require your escort."

How she wished she had not kissed him.

His lip curled. "You shall have it whether you require it or not."

How she wished she did not long to kiss him again, even now.

Oh, heart. Do be quiet. We cannot afford to indulge in your particular sort of trouble. Not now, and not ever again.

But as he trailed her all the way to the nursery, she knew instinctively that her heart and her common sense had not waged the last of their war against each other. Instead, she had a weighty feeling that the real war had just begun.

Chapter Fifteen

Clay helped Ara down from the carriage, trying to ignore the old sensations a mere touch from her gloved hand elicited in him. The moment her boot-shod feet touched the gravel drive, she released him and swept away, as if his touch had scorched her. Mayhap it did if she felt even an inkling of the need coursing through his veins after their kiss.

It took every shred of his control to keep from following her with his gaze. Even in a black travel gown, her copper locks covered by a demure midnight hat, she was so bloody lovely it made his chest ache. But the sight of the small, solemn face exiting the carriage next made his chest ache in an entirely different fashion.

"Welcome to Harlton Hall, Your Grace," he said, striving to keep his voice good-humored for the lad's sake. He had already been through hell, and the sudden departure from London following an attempt on his mother's life could not have been easy on him. "Though it be humble, I hope you shall find it to your liking."

"Thank you, Mr. Ludlow," the lad said seriously as he stared up at the looming, partially resurrected home at Clay's back.

He had bought the sixteenth century manor house and its two hundred acres with a notion to restore it to its original glory. He had been drawn to its forest, which had reminded him of the lush woods at Brixton Manor. But his familial home and the adjoining estate his father had settled upon him had never appealed to him in the wake of losing Ara. Harlton Hall had been his chance for a new beginning, far from the memories haunting him. The west wing was still in a sorry state of disrepair, but the main hall and east wing restoration had been completed, meaning that there would at least be a comfortable space for Ara and the lad to spend the next fortnight.

In the wake of the attempt on her life, Clay and Leo had decided the best thing to do was remove her and the lad from London. Oxfordshire was not nearly far enough, but the Fenians would not be searching for the Duchess of Burghly at a dilapidated old hall on the Isis.

The situation remained grave. Beauchamps had miraculously survived the attack, but he was still weak and unable to provide any meaningful information regarding the man who had stabbed him from behind. He thought he had heard two pairs of footfalls in the moments before the blade cut into his flesh, but he had not been certain.

As for the knife-wielding villain Clay had dispatched, there had been not a stitch of identification on his body. Nor had there been even an address or an epistle or a newspaper clipping tucked into a pocket.

With so much uncertainty, risking another attempt on Ara's life had been unthinkable. And so it was that he welcomed his son and the woman he had once loved—the last two people he had ever fancied would pass between Harlton Hall's Doric columns and step inside its centuries' old halls. It had been meant to be his haven from the world. A place for his mother to spend her dotage comfortably since she did not wish to be present at Carlisle House for all the licentious gatherings Leo held as a ruse to deflect from his work in the

Special League.

Ara too stood, gazing up at Harlton Hall, her expression shielded by the brim of her hat as he approached her once more. Formally, he offered her his arm to escort her. Without sparing a glance in his direction, she placed a light touch—so light it may have almost not been there at all—upon his arm. With her free hand, she reached for Edward, touching his thin shoulders in a motherly fashion, as if to reassure him.

Clay watched the simple interaction, a painful wrenching in his gut. He was reminded he was an outsider in their lives. That he was a father who had never been able to reassure or comfort his son. That his son, even now, believed he was another man's child. All the pain and resentment festering inside him toward Ara returned tenfold, and he welcomed it, for perhaps it would chase away the pathetic longing for her he could not seem to shake, regardless of what she had done.

"Where have you brought us, Mr. Ludlow?" she asked coolly as the three of them started forward, crossing the drive to the steps that led to the double doors of the main hall.

"To a home where you will be safe," he hedged, for though he owned it, Harlton Hall had never felt like his. He was a pretender within its walls, and though he had worked hard to amass the funds necessary to purchase it by making sound investments in property and businesses, he would always be the bastard who bought a home where a king had once stayed.

"It is not fair for us to burden a strange household. We could have traveled to Kingswood Hall instead," she pointed out.

Over his dead, blood-soaked corpse. The day he saw her father again would be the day he left the coldhearted earl with a scar to match his own.

"Your familiar routes of travel, your familial connections,

will all be common knowledge to the Fenians," he said smoothly instead, fighting against the rage that still threatened to consume him. His scar itched, but he refrained from touching it. "One cannot hide in the precise location where one's enemy will first look, Duchess."

"Will the bad men find us here?" the lad asked.

Clay felt Ara's hand tremble on his arm where she hesitantly rested her hand. And his own gut clenched at the lad's query. "Not if I can help it, Your Grace."

How bloody odd that title felt in his mouth, on his tongue, speaking it to his own son. How wrong. But before he could dwell upon the injustice, the doors to Harlton Hall opened.

He had not sent word ahead of their travels, needing to keep Ara and Edward's locations as secret as possible. Thankfully, his mother—a more than capable lady of the house—had outfitted the hall with a full staff of domestics, all of whom, it went without saying, she held to the strictest standards.

Lily Ludlow may have been a duke's mistress and never his wife—Carlisle's death before his duchess's had rendered that dearly longed-for goal of hers unattainable—but she was a lady to her core. She knew how to dress, how to conduct herself, and she had the biggest, most giving heart he had ever known. She also sang like an angel, but that was another talent entirely.

As if his thoughts had materialized her, there his mother stood, alongside his butler, Keynes. She wore a golden-yellow day gown, her dark hair streaked with gray, her warm brown eyes sparkling with unabashed delight as they met his.

"Clayton, my darling," she greeted, rushing forward with her signature exuberance and enveloping him in a perfumed embrace. She kissed his cheek. "I cannot believe my eyes. And you have brought company for me. Oh, how lovely."

She extricated herself and cast a curious glance toward Ara.

He stiffened, hoping she would not prove as discerning in this instance as she so oft was. "Mother, I present Her Grace, the dowager Duchess of Burghly, and her son, the young duke. Your Graces, I present my mother, Mrs. Ludlow."

Though she had never married, she had adopted the Mrs. before her surname many years before, in an effort to distance herself from the scandal she had once been embroiled within.

His mother beamed at Ara. "Such a pleasure to make your acquaintance, Duchess." Her attention turned toward the lad, and her welcoming smile faded. She flicked a questioning glance to Clay before pasting the smile back on her face. "And you as well, Your Grace."

Bloody hell, she had seen the resemblance. Of course she did. The lad was his image, from his dark hair and tall, skinny body to his long blade of a nose, slashing cheekbones, and too-wide jaw.

"The duke and his mother will be our guests for the next fortnight," he forced past lips that had gone dry. Damn it, how had he forgotten how very shrewd his mother was? How had he ever imagined bringing Ara and her son—rather, *their* son—here to Harlton Hall would work?

But she said not a word of her suspicions. And once again, of course she did not, for his mother was a consummate hostess. She had spent her entire life being reviled for who and what she was—first as a songstress, then as the mistress to a duke. Such a woman, it seemed, could either harden with bitterness or turn her sunshine outward, sending her rays over everyone in her presence. Mother had always chosen the latter.

She sent the lad a mischievous wink. "Oh my, how fortuitous. You see, the cook just made lemon and chocolate tarts, and there is nothing I love more than nibbling on some lemon tarts and telling stories. You do not happen to enjoy lemon tarts or stories about knights and dragons, do you, Duke?"

For the first time since his arrival, the lad grinned. "I love lemon tarts and stories, Mrs. Ludlow."

"How wonderful. My son always preferred lemon tarts to the chocolate ones when he was growing up. I don't suppose you are the same?" She placed a hand on Edward's shoulder. "I am so dreadfully happy you like stories, as I have not had a young man eager for my stories in years. Would it be acceptable to you, Your Grace, if I took the duke into the kitchens so he may sample the lemon tarts whilst you settle yourself? Cook does make the most divine tarts, and I promise I shall have him returned to you in no time."

Ara nodded stiffly, her expression uncertain. "As long as that is what Edward wishes. Traveling does have a way of wearing one out, and I suppose the reward of a tart would not be remiss."

"Shall we, young Duke?" his mother asked the lad.

"I should like that," the lad said quietly, sounding younger than he looked. Sounding like a boy who had suffered far more pain, fear, and loss than he should have at his tender age.

Clay watched his mother and his son disappearing from the main hall, bemused.

Ara turned to him, her violet-blue eyes cool and assessing. "I shall oversee the unpacking of the carriages."

"No," he denied softly before turning to the ever-efficient butler, who hovered nearby. "Keynes will oversee the unpacking while I escort you to your chamber. Will you be so kind, Keynes?"

The butler bowed. "It will be my pleasure. Welcome to Harlton Hall, Your Grace."

The matter settled, Clay hastily conferred with his men

about their posts before proffering his arm to Ara once more. "Come, Your Grace. I shall show you to your chamber."

He was aware that taking Ara to a chamber—any chamber, anywhere, on any day, at any time—was a dangerous prospect for him indeed. How he wished the anger and resentment still burning in his gut for her had a dousing effect on his raging lust. Alas, it did not, and though they walked in silence, a respectable distance between them, everything in him screamed with the need to haul her into the first empty chamber he could find and kiss her senseless. To finish what they had begun with their frenzied passion at Burghly House.

He hated what she had done to him, to them, and most of all to their son. And yet there was an undeniable part of him that would always feel she was his. She was the first woman he had ever loved—indeed, the only woman he had ever loved—and nothing she did would change that. His heart had once beat for her, and it remembered still.

"This is *your* home," she observed, a bite of accusation in her tone as they walked beneath the carved stone galleries of the main hall and ascended the grand stair.

"Aye," he agreed, slanting a glance in her direction. Her cheek was pale, her lush mouth drawn thin with what he could only presume was disapproval. Did she fancy herself too good to stay in his bloody home? "Harlton Hall is mine."

As are you, something inside him said. But he had never felt such a primitive possession for this home and its sprawling acres as he did for her. He ignored the voice. He damn well never should have kissed her. His weakness was spreading like a weed that began as one seed and soon took over an entire garden with its promulgation.

"You should have made me aware before our departure," she said lowly. Angrily. "I would never have agreed to come here."

Irritation blended with resentment and unwanted lust. On the inside, he was a sick stew of uncontrollable emotions, all caused by one woman. They reached the top of the stairs and he ground his jaw down, quickening his pace so he could sooner deposit her in the chamber and rid himself of her disturbing presence.

"You were almost murdered in London," he reminded her tightly. "Harlton Hall—where no one will expect you to be—is the safest place for you until the Home Office has some answers about who is behind the attack."

"Why did you not tell me you were bringing me to your home?" she snapped, stopping in the upstairs hall and turning on him.

Because he still did not think of it in those terms, not truly. He was a bloody usurper, claiming a life he could never truly own. Wanting what would forever be beyond his reach. Stupid. Foolish.

Weak.

So damned weak when he needed to be strong.

"You already indicated you would not have agreed to come here had you known Harlton Hall is mine," he said instead, unwilling to confess his vulnerabilities to her.

She crossed her arms over her chest in a defensive posture, her eyes flashing. "I wish to leave."

"No," he bit out.

Color rose to her cheeks at last. "You cannot command me."

She was stubborn, the bloody woman. But she was no match for him. "Try to leave and see what happens."

Her nostrils flared. "Perhaps I will."

When she made as if to storm away, back down the hall to the staircase, he caught her arm. His grip was tight, though not punishing. "Ara, stop."

"Do not call me that, and do not presume to touch me." She attempted to sidle free of his grasp but he held firm.

"Do you know what I think, Ara?" He stepped forward, into her body, her skirts crushed between them, the brim of the hat she had yet to remove nearly grazing his jaw. "I think you have forgotten you truly are at my mercy."

Her eyes spit fire at him. "Release me."

He would not let go of her. He never had, and he never would. Not in this moment. Not in the matter of her safety. *Good God*, not ever. They were inextricably linked now, for the remainder of their lives. Their son was the common bond between them.

But not the sole one.

The sound of footfalls and commotion reached him before he could respond, and he recognized it as domestics making short work of the trunks, beginning to unpack the carriages they had brought from the train station. He was not finished with her or this dialogue yet, and so he marched into the nearest chamber, pulling her behind him and closing the door at their backs.

Locking it.

Perhaps the time for their battle had come at last.

"What do you think you are doing, Mr. Ludlow?" Her voice was unnaturally high, breathless.

He pivoted back to her, wondering if she was nervous to be alone with him. Surely she did not think he could possibly do her harm? He was duty-bound to protect her. He studied her face, searching her gaze, trying to make sense of the dynamic between them.

"I am taking the opportunity to have the dialogue we should have had days ago, when you admitted I am the father of your son." Though he strove to keep his voice cool, he could not quite excise the slight edge from it.

Her countenance turned wary. "As far as I am concerned, we have nothing left to say to each other on the matter."

"I beg to differ." He stalked closer to her, unable to keep his distance.

He wanted to undo the ribbon ties of her hat. To tear it from her head and reveal her lustrous copper locks. To kiss the frown from her lips, to lift her skirts and bury his aching cock deep inside her.

Realization hit him as he reached her, the scent of roses and a crisp summer day seeping back into his senses. The sweet, luscious scent of Ara and love and the forbidden. Of the young woman she had once been, of the nights when they had learned each other's bodies.

Her transgressions against him did not matter as he stood there before her. His want for her was elemental. She was all he had ever desired, from the instant he had first spotted her watching him in the woods that fateful day. He had returned again and again, knowing she had been waiting, watching. Needing to know her. Longing for her.

Her eyes burned into his, and he had to touch her. He lost all control of himself, his hands framing her lovely face. The same face he had loved so long ago, only now she had lines etched ever so faintly alongside her mouth and her eyes. Were they the marks of laughter or sadness? Why did he envy whoever had made those marks? Why did he hate all the years that had kept him from her?

"Clay," she whispered.

There, before him, her façade crumbled and fell. He saw not the Duchess of Burghly but a woman who was frightened and alone. He saw the girl who'd claimed his heart. He saw, simply, Ara. His anger remained, swirling in his gut, but it was supplanted by the overwhelming need to take her in his arms.

He had to know one thing. His heart, body, and mind clamored with the need.

"What we had, Ara, did it ever mean anything to you?" he asked hoarsely.

Part of him hoped her answer would be no. But the other part of him, the part that had not entirely forgotten the young man he'd once been, hoped otherwise.

Say yes.

Say yes.

Please.

Clay did not know where the words emerged from. Or if he spoke them aloud. All he did know was that he was falling into her. Mayhap, in a sense, this had been inevitable. Mayhap she would always be his, and he would always be hers.

Her expression turned stricken. "It meant everything to me."

Bloody hell, I am lost.

For the truth of it was, it had meant everything to him too. It still did. He had spent eight years trying his damnedest to forget her, only to find her again. With a simple sentence, he was back in the hunting cabin with her, secluded in the ancient woods. The last time he had ever truly been happy had been there, the night she had said she would marry him.

He wanted to stop there, on that memory, and not move forward. Not in this moment. This moment wanted no heaviness, no grief or despair. It wanted only a physical relief. And here was the greatest comprehension of all: perhaps he could finally purge her from his life if he bedded her. If he took her until there was nothing left for either of them to give.

He kissed her, deep and hard and ruthless. His lips melded with hers, his tongue sinking into her mouth, her breath mingling with his. She kissed him back, a soft sound of want emerging from deep in her throat. Her fingers sank into his hair, anchoring him to her, and her tongue boldly slid against his. She wanted him every bit as much as he wanted her. It was the way of things between them. How it had always been—raw and real and powerful.

He went mindless.

The ability to think fled him. His body ached and hungered. Eight years of longing reawakened, just for her. All for her. A hot, pulsing need began in his ballocks and made his prick rise stiff and hard against the placket of his trousers. Just kissing her was enough to make him lose the last of the reins he had upon his control.

Every word he had intended to say was dashed, like a ship upon the rocks of a treacherous harbor in the midst of a storm. He had to be inside her. He was a locomotive, barreling down a track. The years, the pain, the scars, the ache, the worry, the fear, the wonder, the lies and betrayal, all fell away.

They were man and woman.

Need and want.

Hunger and touch.

Clay and Ara, just as they once had been. Before broken hearts and betrayal had torn them apart.

Damn it all, he had never been so hungry in all his life, filled with an ache only she could assuage. He sucked her tongue, bit into her full lower lip. She moaned into his mouth, and he drank it in, savored it as if it were his own. Drew it deep down, all the way to his soul.

As one, they moved.

Providentially, Clay had chosen a bedchamber to enter. And though it had been entirely unintentional, he had forced them both inside what would be his bedchamber when he actually lived at Harlton Hall. There was a bed, large and inviting, occupying the far wall. He had never slept in it. He supposed he would have to now. But she would take the chamber adjoining though she did not know it yet, and that would help him ease to sleep at night.

Their kisses never stopped. His hands tore away her layers—her hat, pelisse, gloves. All the way across the chamber they traveled, kissing and nipping and licking as one. When they finally reached the bed, he planted his hands on her waist, spinning her around. He did not wish to look into the face of the woman he had once loved. He needed her back to him, and he needed to take her from behind.

There would be no question what this was—an exercise in unadulterated lust. Need simmered between them still. A hunger he could not deny. But that was all this was. All it could be.

Just this once, he promised himself. *And then never again.*

He wanted her. Had never stopped. But this was not eight years ago. He was not a fool. Or at least, he was not as great a fool as he had been then. His fingers tightened on her. He found her ear, licking the shell, biting the whorl. "Tell me what you want."

She did not speak, but her fists caught in her skirts, raising them. There was no mistaking the gesture. They moved against his trousers, traveled past her knees, and then on to her thighs. "You."

His cock twitched and his mouth went dry, but he required more from her than that simple admission. He fought the urge to grind himself into her skirts. "More specific, Ara."

"You inside me," she murmured. "I want you inside me, Clay."

Finally, he was no longer Mr. Ludlow, the man she disdained in her frigid duchess tones. But some instinct inside him, depraved and sinful, wanted to prolong her submission. To heighten his own arousal by making her beg.

He needed to hear her full confession. He wanted more. More desperate longing. More signs that what he felt for her was reciprocated. "What part of me inside you?"

His left hand remained on her waist while the right found the hemline of her gown, just about over the delectable swells of her rump. He worked his hand higher, taking her ribbon-trimmed hem, finding her curves through the softness of her drawers, absorbing her heat while he held his breath. She was so bloody beautiful, a marvel of femininity and wit and everything a man could ever want.

Except loyalty.

But *fucking hell* if that did not matter now, not when his cock was ready to sink inside her. "Ara?"

"I want you, Clay," was all he could wrangle from her.

For now.

He was determined. He wanted her complete surrender. Today, he was storming her battlements. Destroying every impediment between him and what he wanted so badly he could taste it.

Her. Her capitulation. Her surrender. Her sweet release. Her desperation. *Bloody hell*, he wanted to make her sorry for making him love her, for turning her back on him, and raising his son with another man. For leaving him with a scarred face and an even more mangled heart. For never trying to find him. For lying to him even when he had come back into her life. For every. Damned. Thing.

He tongued the sweet dip of skin behind her ear, his hands never straying from her waist. "How?"

A soft sound emerged from low in her throat, half purr, half moan. "You know how."

"No." He kissed her throat, sucked her flesh. Tomorrow, she would bear a bruise here, and she would have to cover it with pearl powder or a high-necked gown. She would see it and think of his mouth on her skin, of how she had been desperate for him to take her. "I do not know how. Tell me, Ara. Do you want my tongue inside you?"

She inhaled sharply, as if he had shocked her. But she was not a stranger to such loving, and he knew it. Here and now, he could still recall how she had bucked and writhed beneath him, how her fingers had twisted in his hair. How slick and plump her clitoris had been, how she had shuddered against him when she spent on his tongue.

When she did not speak, he grinned, nipping her neck. "Or perhaps my fingers?"

"Please," she whispered, her head falling back against his shoulder to grant him greater access to her throat as he feasted on her.

He slid his hands from her waist until they settled atop hers, still gripping her skirts. "Higher," he commanded.

She raised her hem, not hesitating. Her travel gown was not as full and cumbersome as most fashion, and he was grateful for that now as she lifted her skirts to her waist. He stepped back, tearing his lips from her skin, and took her in. Her lustrous copper locks remained perfectly coiffed in a Grecian braid and coil. From the waist up, she looked as composed as ever, her shoulders straight, her gown of black silk with box pleats and lace trimming the bodice and sleeves.

But from the waist down, she was a dream. He drank in the sight of her with her skirts raised for him. Black boots, narrow ankles, red stocking-covered calves, lacy white drawers. Her bottom was round and full, despite her small frame.

A fresh bolt of need spurred him on. He caressed her hips, running his palms down her curves, relearning her. Her warmth permeated the fine fabric of her undergarments, burning into him. Breath hissing from his lungs, desire burning like a fire straight through him, he stepped closer. He kissed her bare nape.

"Clay," she said his name again, a plea, a prayer.

"You never answered me, Ara." He grazed her soft skin with his teeth. Then, he cupped her arse, his fingers trailing where they wanted in lieu of her answer. He found the slit in her drawers and dipped inside, skimmed over her hot, slick seam.

Damn. She was drenched.

Ara moaned.

Lord God. His erection swelled. His ballocks pulsed. It had been a long time since he'd had a woman, but it had been eight godforsaken years since he'd had *Ara*, and he could not restrain the ferocity of his hunger for her now.

He sank a finger inside her. So warm and delicious. She gripped him.

"Are you always this wet, or is it just for me?" he growled, making his way, kiss by kiss, to her ear.

What he wanted to know—and what he *didn't* want to know—was if she had ever been such a conflagration in another man's arms. For him, it had never been the same. The passion had never been so desperate, so all-consuming. For Ara, he would fight an entire army just to claim her as his. Nothing else—no one before or after her—had ever come close.

"Only for you," she admitted then, her voice throaty with want.

He bit the shell of her ear. A second finger joined the first, sinking deep. In and out, he moved them, her cunny so soaked the erotic sounds of him thrusting into her mingled in the chamber with the sounds of their mutually labored breaths.

"You are mine, Ara." He did not mean to say the words, but once they fell from his lips, there was no rescinding them.

He'd lost control over himself. Lust and desire, resentment and rage: everything in him that had built for years coalesced then and there, with his fingers buried inside her, the dew of her desire running down his hand. He wished she had only ever been his. That she had never betrayed him to her father, that she had run away with him as she had promised.

"Yes," she said weakly, bending forward and planting her hands on the bed as if she had lost control of her body as well. Her skirts remained pinned between their bodies, anchored even without her grip.

But her acquiescence was not enough. He hated the mourning weeds she wore. Hated the brooch pinned over her heart. Hated she had married another man. Hated she was the Duchess of Bloody Burghly. Hated she had ever been another man's wife, even if that man had been moldering in the grave for the last four months.

He was jealous of every day Burghly had spent in her presence—every smile she had given him, every sigh, every morning he had risen to spend with her at his side. He should not feel so possessive of her, and he knew it. He had not the right. Indeed, he had never had the right. She was as good for him as poison.

"Say it," he demanded, curling his fingers and working them in steady, rhythmic pulses. Here he was at the heart of her, where she was so soft and warm, and he had not forgotten how to touch her in all this time. What made her weak. What made her spend.

"I am yours." She gasped when he found the most sensitive part of her, teasing her in exquisite torture for the both of them.

"Again." He thrust into her harder, faster.

"I am…oh…"

She was on the verge of coming, but he could not resist

making her wait. Prolonging the pleasure. He removed his fingers. "Say it," he commanded into her ear.

"I am yours." Her every breath was labored, her pulse pounding against his lips as he kissed back down her throat.

"*Yes.*" The lone word escaped him, a hiss of triumph. She was his, *damn it*. Had been his first. Would forever be *his*, and he knew it somehow with an unassailable certainty. "You are mine, Ara. You will always be mine. Never forget it."

Damn her for tearing them apart. For turning her back on him. For making him bleed. For taking his son and marrying another man. For everything. She had brought him to his knees, had devastated him. Her betrayal had left him broken. Now he would break her the only way he knew how, with his body. By giving them both what they wanted and needed.

It was long overdue.

Years overdue.

Necessary.

"I need you, Clay," she whispered.

"Are you sure?" he gritted, needing to be certain she wanted him as much as he wanted her.

That this wild passion between them, even eight years on, remained mutual.

"Yes, Clay." His name was a whimper on her lips. One filled with hunger and need and rampant desire. "I need you inside me, please."

Fuck, he liked the way she begged. But he still wanted more. He wanted everything. He wanted her on her knees.

He skimmed the curve of her waist and hip before moving toward what he truly wanted. His hand trailed over her thigh, gliding inward in search of her mound. Her legs parted. He located the slit in her drawers from the front, and then there she was, his for the taking.

He cupped her, found her pearl. She was swollen with

need. So wet and plump. He wanted to lick her, to suck her bud into his mouth until she came, to lap her creamy spending like the finest dessert. To make her scream with nothing but his lips and tongue.

But his need for her was a fire in his blood. If he waited much longer, he would spend in his trousers like a callow youth. Without even sinking his cock into her body, and he needed to be inside her so badly he ached with it.

Only she could slake his hunger.

His anger was another matter.

It could not be appeased. Nothing and no one would tame it, but he could subdue it for now. For this moment. For the chance to have Ara once more.

To lose himself inside her.

Wet. She was so wet.

He worked her clitoris, stimulating her with rhythmic surges of his forefinger, applying greater pressure when she seemed within reach of her release. And then she was coming, shaking, tremoring against him. He rubbed her, his fingers bathed in her wetness. Her hips rolled against his hand, asking for more. Begging for more as she reached her peak. She cried out, collapsing upon the bed, her entire body stiffening as sweet release washed over her.

Her desire gushed over him. *Damn it. Damn her.* He ground his jaw down, trying to temper his need. He wanted inside her. So badly he could scarcely think.

"Last chance to change your mind," he forced himself to say.

"Mmm." She rocked against his hand, still enjoying the aftershocks of her spend.

He stroked her, letting her ride the waves of her climax. His fingers dipped into her cunny. She was so damn tight, tremoring around his fingers, sucking him deeper still. His other hand released the fastening of his trousers, allowing his rampant cock to spring forth.

She angled her hips to meet his questing fingers, which could not seem to let her cunny alone now they'd touched her once more. "I want you so much I ache with it. From the moment I saw you in my drawing room until now, I have not stopped wanting you. I have not stopped wondering what it would be like if we were to be free with each other again. If we were to be as we once were."

Neither had he. And that was the crux of the matter, wasn't it? For now, it didn't matter. Nothing mattered but the need pulsing between them. The hunger that would not be denied. She had been lost to him for eight years, and his body remembered what they'd had. His heart remembered too.

"It would be like this," he murmured as he withdrew from her and coated his erection with her juices. In one swift thrust, he was sheathed inside her. She was hot and slippery, squeezing his cock so hard she almost pushed him from her body. The breath fled from his lungs. She felt so bloody good, so bloody perfect.

It was like coming home.

For a beat, he held still, buried deep, half afraid if he moved, it would be over. Or this was a dream and he would wake in his empty bed, alone and desperate for her. But then, a sigh escaped her, along with a one-word demand.

"More."

Yes. Bloody hell, yes.

He stroked her pearl as he slid his cock almost completely from her sweet cunny only to slide inside again. A grunt tore from him. A moan emerged from her. His control broke. A flood tore through him—memories, desire, need—and he was awash in it. He was lost. The delicate nuances of lovemaking were beyond him. He pounded into her, not giving a damn about anything other than their mutual hunger.

He was savage in that moment. He became an animal. His hips pumped. The rhythmic, wet sounds of their fucking filled the chamber, mingling with her breathy pants and his harsh breaths. He bit her ear, wishing he had her entirely naked and beneath him. Wishing she was his.

But she was not, and she never had been.

And this was all they had, this mad desire, this frantic rutting between two strangers. But she wasn't a stranger, was she? She was a warm body against his beneath the midnight stars. She was laughter and frantic kisses. She was sunshine and roses. She was his first love, his only love.

The mother of his son.

He increased his pace, taking her with such frenzy the bed creaked. She arched her back, meeting him thrust for thrust, the soft sounds hatching from her throat making him even more mindless. In and out, hard and fast. Long and deep.

She clenched on him suddenly, crying out as a new release claimed her. She trembled, a fresh wetness spilling down his cock. Her body slumped forward, her face pressed to the counterpane, which muffled her cries as she spent all over him.

He wanted to hear her moans. He wanted to remember them, to plant them in his memory for when he slid from her body and he was once more the man tasked with her protection.

He sank his fingers at last into the glorious temptation of her hair. It was silken, so damn soft, and he tugged gently, bringing her head back as he fucked her harder still. Her cries were loud, echoing in the chamber.

It was all he could take, hearing her throaty moans, feeling her climax tremor through her as she milked his cock. His ballocks drew tight, and he could no longer avoid his own release. With one last, unrestrained thrust, he withdrew, gripped his cock, and spent all over her lacy white drawers.

Chapter Sixteen

"HOW ARE YOU settling in here at Harlton Hall, Your Grace?"

Ara glanced up from the untouched food on her dinner plate to find Clay's mother giving her a warm smile. Her thoughts took a moment to gather themselves, to form a semblance of coherence. For a beat, all she could think was this woman's son had made love to her. Had been inside her hours before. Had spent all over her drawers before tearing from the chamber and disappearing.

She had not seen him since. How awkward this dinner was, two women who were utter strangers, one mother and the other lover, though she felt certain his mother was blissfully unware of what had transpired earlier. Edward had gone to bed early, tired from their travels, and her host had not reemerged since their frantic coupling of hours before.

And then another strange thought walloped her with the force of a storm gale. This woman was her son's grandmother. Had Clay told her? Would he tell her?

She swallowed, wondering how much his mother knew. "Very well, thank you, Mrs. Ludlow."

"I am so very sorry to hear of the circumstances which have necessitated your stay here," Clay's mother continued, seemingly unaware of Ara's extreme discomfit.

Clay's mother preferred bold colors and made no effort at

subduing them, her evening gown a rich, bright shade of red. She was lovely and elegant, a radiant woman with a melodious voice. She resembled Clay, her almost ebony hair shot with silver, her eyes dark, her nose the same slashing blade, her mouth held in almost the identical, stubborn fashion.

The same as Edward's.

Ara reached for her wineglass, bringing it to her lips for a long and indelicate draught. "It has been a difficult time indeed."

"I can only imagine," his mother said, her expression one of commiseration. "I am so very sorry for your loss, Your Grace. The Duke of Burghly was an excellent politician."

Yes, Freddie had been.

He had fought valiantly for the causes in which he believed. She inclined her head. "Thank you, Mrs. Ludlow."

"You may call me Lily," Clay's mother invited, her eyes assessing.

Ara replaced her wine goblet on the table. "Thank you, Lily."

"You are the Earl of Wickham's daughter, are you not?" Clay's mother continued in a conversational tone as she returned her attention to her dinner, cutting a slice of veal.

Ara lifted her wine back to her lips for another healthy swallow. She was beginning to feel lightheaded, the dining hall swirling at the edges of her vision. Perhaps she ought to eat a bite, but she was at sixes and sevens. First, she had been stalked by a killer, then she had relocated to the country, Clay had made scorching, frantic love to her, and now she was faced with his mother whilst he hid himself only the Lord knew where.

The wine was strong. She needed more. Needed distraction. Fortification. Anything.

She took another sip.

Then another.

"Yes," she forced herself to say at last. "I am the Earl of Wickham's youngest daughter."

It would be the height of impoliteness to point out she knew Lily had once been her father's paramour. Or at least the paramour he had wanted for himself. She knew not the details, nor had she ever presumed to ask. She would not dare.

"I knew your father once," Clay's mother said softly. Almost sadly.

Ara glanced back up, shocked to hear the open acknowledgment. "Oh?" she asked politely. Noncommittally. For what could this woman possibly say that she needed to hear on the matter?

Nothing, she was sure.

"Yes," Clay's mother continued, surprising her. "We did not part on good terms, unfortunately."

It was difficult indeed for Ara to picture her stoic father falling beneath the spell of a woman like Lily Ludlow, who was almost exotic looking, bold and beautiful, frank and unapologetic. Ara's mother was nothing like her—an icy, pale blonde with a determination to be proper at all costs.

"I am sorry to hear that," she said at last, worrying a slab of veal with the tines of her fork.

"It was your father's choice," Clay's mother said, watching her with a shrewd gaze. "I do not think he ever forgave me."

Ara did not know what to say, so she maintained her silence, cutting a bite of veal and raising it to her mouth at last. Nothing had ever been more tasteless.

"I am sure he must have," she said at last with an attempt at a smile.

"No." Clay's mother shook her head slowly, her gaze stern and steady on Ara's. "He did not. I know because of the way he treated my son."

Clay.

Ara stiffened, wondering where this particular line of conversation would proceed. "In what way is that?"

Clay's mother gave her a forlorn smile. "As if he did not matter."

How bitterly familiar, for it was the same manner in which her father had treated Ara after he had learned she carried Clay's child. She could still recall the twisted rage on his countenance. Could still feel the sting of his slap across her cheek. The vicious lash of his words.

No daughter of mine makes herself a bastard's whore. You will go abroad and be rid of your sins, or you will marry. But whatever choice you make, know you will not be welcome within Kingswood Hall with your bastard's bastard.

Ara's fingers rediscovered the stem of her wine goblet, clenching on it. She had not forgiven her father. Was not sure forgiveness of a betrayal so deep was even possible. Edward had never met her family, and she was happy to keep it thus. Her mother cared only for her own entertainment, her father for his pride. Her brother had sided with their father, and her sister had died birthing her lover's babe some six years ago.

She returned to the present with a jolt. Clay's mother's gaze remained intent upon her. Seeing far too much, she was sure. "Mrs. Ludlow, I do not wish to revisit the past."

Revisiting it was far too painful, like a wound that had been sliced open all over again. She had not known, on the day she had discovered Clay had gone abroad, that she carried his child. But in the weeks that followed, her illness and lack of courses had spurred her lady's maid into action. Mama had been summoned. Her father had been notified. She had been sent to live with Rosamunde, and it was through her sister that she had met Freddie.

"Please, call me Lily, my dear," Clays mother urged again

into the silence that had fallen between them. "Forgive me for broaching a painful subject. I did not intend to cause you distress."

She raised her wine back to her lips, took another bracing sip. "My father and I have not spoken in years," she admitted for reasons she could not fathom. She had not confided the rift with her family to anyone except Freddie in all these years. Why would she unburden herself now to Clay's mother?

"Such a division in a family makes me sad, Your Grace." The look Clay's mother bestowed upon her was warm, sympathetic.

Ara inhaled slowly to stave off a wave of unwanted emotion. It had been seven years since Edward was born. The knowledge her father and mother did not wish to meet their grandson would forever be a knife in her gut. "I have learned that time forces us to accept the pains we are dealt, but it cannot make us forget them."

The moment the words left her, she wished she could recall them. Wished she could tuck them back into her heart, back into her mind. For Clay's mother was eyeing her shrewdly, as if she understood all the things Ara left unsaid. As if she saw and knew far too much.

For Ara was not just speaking about her family. She also spoke of Clay. She had accepted that he left her. She'd had no other choice. She had been alone, a babe in her belly, nowhere left to turn. But even now that he was back in her life, even after she had allowed him back inside her body, she did not know if she could forgive him for leaving her. For turning his back on her. For letting her wait for him that long-ago day and then leaving before she could speak to him once more.

"I understand such sentiment more than you can know," Clay's mother said softly. "Do you know, Your Grace, how my son's face was scarred?"

The abrupt change of conversational direction—returning to *him*—unsettled her. She shook her head. "I would not presume to ask him such a question, as it would not be my place. Nor has he ever offered the information of his own volition."

The older woman's expression changed. A new light entered her eyes, but Ara could not be certain what the emotion was, or what it meant. Clay's mother could be as difficult to read as he was. "He was cut with a blade, Your Grace. He was attacked from behind, cudgeled over the head, and woke to the knife on his cheek."

Ara shivered at the thought of some unseen foe laying Clay low. It seemed so impossible to imagine, that her mountain of a man could be overpowered by anyone. Not *her* mountain of a man, she reminded herself. Merely a man. She could not let their foolish, frenzied coupling affect her. Could not allow it to throw her. She had too much at stake. Everything, it seemed.

Her stupid heart. Her stupid, mad heart.

Oh, but why had Clay chosen such a dangerous path? She could not shake the question, for it bothered her every bit as much as her capitulation to the desire between them did. "His work for the Home Office is perilous indeed. I do hope the villain responsible has long since been sent to prison."

Clay's mother gave her an odd look then. "No, the man responsible has not been imprisoned. Indeed, he continues to live with impunity."

"How horrid." Despite herself, and despite everything that had come to pass between her and Clay, she knew a surge of rage on his behalf. How dare someone cut him, attack him and slice his beautiful flesh with a blade, and go about life without consequence? "Is there nothing that can be done?"

The elder woman returned her attention to her dinner

abruptly. "There is something, perhaps."

Something was better than nothing, Ara supposed, but this newfound knowledge still disturbed her. "He knows then, who the assailant was?"

Another strange, probing look. "Yes, Your Grace. He does."

"When did it happen?" she asked, curious though she knew she ought not to be.

She was curious about everything that had happened to Clay in the years since she had known him last. In the years since he had been hers. It was ridiculous. Ludicrous, even. But she was desperate to know, hungry to learn the missing pieces of him. Where had he gone? What had he done? Why had he left her?

A slight frown curved Lily's lips. Melancholy swirled in the depths of her dark eyes. "Perhaps you should ask Clayton. The story is not mine to tell."

Ara nodded, forced herself to consume a few more bites of her dinner, and wondered. What had happened to Clay? And why did she care so damn much?

SHE HAD BEEN given the apartments of the lady of the house.

Ara paced the floor. The hour was late. The night was dark beyond her window. She should be sleeping, regaining her rest after the travel that had brought her to Oxfordshire and Clay's home. She should not be thinking of him. Should not be wondering what he was doing. Wondering if he would come to her. If she should go to him.

Should not be imagining his body on hers, atop hers, inside hers.

Should not be wanting him.

The chamber she had been assigned disturbed her. It ate at her, pricked at her, prodded and goaded and taunted.

From the moment she had entered the sumptuous chamber, she had known it was one of the best in Harlton Hall. She had not initially, however, realized it was *the lady's apartments.* That a door adjoined her chamber with the one next, and that one likely belonged to the man who owned the entire home.

To Clay.

She had lain awake. Tossed and turned. Had attempted to read a book and surrendered. Had reverted to the years of her youth and tried to abolish the *despicable thing* by appeasing it as she had oft done in the past. But her body knew Clay's was near, and it wanted him now more than ever.

Her feet seemed to move of their own accord, eating up the distance between them. Her senses were overly aware of everything: the plush coarseness of the carpet beneath her bare feet, the cool evening air bussing her cheeks and kissing her throat, the scent of the fire in the hearth, the pounding of her heart. Her hand found the latch.

The door had not been locked.

It opened. Swung wide with a slight creak.

Her breath caught. There he stood, bare chested in the golden glow of the fire in his hearth, wearing only trousers. Even his feet, long and masculine, were bare. It was the first she had seen him in dishabille since the day she'd caught him brawling in her ballroom. And this time was different. More intimate. They were the only two occupants of the chamber, and they were not in the daylight of an empty ballroom. They were in the quiet promise of a bedchamber with nothing and no one to come between them.

She feasted on the sight of him, because while he had made love to her earlier, he had been behind her, and she had been denied this opportunity. She allowed her hungry gaze to rake over every bare swath of skin, every sculpted muscle. *My God*, he was beautiful. Glorious in a way she could not deny. Every inch of him was warrior—wide shoulders, defined chest, the muscles of his abdomen like cut ropes etched in stone, the strong arms.

"Ara." Her name uttered in his low, dark drawl was her undoing.

Time fell away. Years ceased to exist. The aching void in her life that had been left by him was whole once more. She flew to him as she had so many times before. As she had when they had been young and innocent. When they had been forbidden but it hadn't mattered because their hearts had been wild and their hands and mouths had been greedy and they had not wanted anything at all but each other.

When they had been a man and a woman who had found love, against all odds, in the delicious shade of a forest, and they had fallen hopelessly under each other's spells.

She threw herself into him, leaping through the air. As she made impact, she hooked her legs around his waist. He caught her, his arms going around her like bands. Her arms twined about his neck.

"Fuck, Ara."

She slammed her lips into his. It was the only answer. The only thing she could do. All she wanted. Precisely what she needed. His tongue was inside her mouth, his hands kneading the flesh of her bottom. Even though it had been mere hours since their furtive coupling, they were ravenous. He bit her lip. She sucked his tongue. Teeth crashed together.

She moaned. He groaned. Her fingers sank into his hair. Still holding her in his arms, he walked them across the chamber effortlessly, as though she weighed nothing. And then she was on his bed, on her back. He had tossed her there. With a rush of desire, she watched as he shucked his trousers and smalls until he stood by the bed, naked.

His cock was huge and hard and thick, jutting against his lean abdomen. He took her breath. Every bit of him was strong. So strong. So vital and powerful and gorgeous. She grasped handfuls of her nightrail and pulled it up over her head, throwing it to the floor where it landed in a wispy heap.

And then she was naked.

On Clay's bed.

It was wrong, and she knew it. Wanting him this much, letting him back in, was a grave error. But she couldn't stop. He was here, and he needed their lovemaking as badly as she did—before her stood stark, glorious evidence of just how much.

He lowered himself to the bed at her feet, his large, warm hands on her ankles. His gaze burned across her body like twin, live coals, feasting up over her legs, lingering at the apex of her thighs, trailing over her breasts to her lips and at last meeting hers. "This is madness."

It was, and yet it wasn't. She had fought for so long—against him, against the feelings he inspired in her, against her desperate need for him. But they had always been fire, and she was ready and willing to catch flame once more for him. With him.

It would always be him, she realized. Clayton Ludlow was her fate. He was stolen kisses and furtive assignations. He was the first man who had ever made her body come to life. Her only lover. Her every sin. He was the man she had never forgotten. The one she had despaired she would ever find again.

"No one has ever felt right but you." She made the confession almost involuntarily. Her lips moved, her tongue formed the consonants and vowels. Her voice produced the sound. But she had not meant to blurt them aloud.

"Damn it, Ara." His touch glided up her calves, and he lowered his mouth to her skin. He rained kisses on her anklebone, her shin, the sensitive swells of her calves, the dips behind her knees. "You should never have come here tonight."

No, she should not have. Opening the door between their chambers had been a mistake. Allowing him to take her earlier had been a mistake. Hungering for him the way she did—also a mistake.

The biggest mistake of all? Her words. She should never offer up such revelations. Not to him, not to Clay, the man who had left her once before. The man who had fled, taking her heart with him. Why had he gone? And where? Ara wanted to ask, but the sight and sensation of him slowly pleasuring his way up her body stole her breath.

He kissed a trail over one hip, then the other, nipping her with his teeth. The hum of satisfaction deep in his throat rumbled through his body, and she felt it in his lips as they opened on her skin. Felt it in his tongue as it licked a path of fire over the protrusion of her hipbone. His breath was hot and moist, so near to her throbbing center and where she wanted him most.

Not close enough.

"You left the door unlocked," she reminded him breathlessly. He could not pin this on her. The naked want on his face when she had stood on the threshold had been her undoing.

"For if you required me."

Oh, she had *required* him, but perhaps not in the manner he had originally intended. Ara bit her lip, saying nothing as he kissed higher, over the faint white lines that had scored her skin from carrying Edward. She stiffened when he lingered there, stopping to skim his palm over her belly. The marks had been purple and angry once, but they'd had seven years to calm and fade.

No one had ever seen them before, and she knew a flutter of embarrassment, chasing away the need.

"What happened here?" he asked softly, tracing the lines with his long fingers, looking up at her. "These are new."

"Not new." A rush of heat flooded her cheeks. "They are from bearing Edward. He was a large babe, as one might expect."

His eyes darkened, and he lowered his head, kissing each mark as if in worship. He said nothing, his hands bracketing her hips, his mouth finding its way to the dip in her belly. His tongue slid inside, making a wild current of pleasure rocket through her.

A rush of air burst forth from her, half sigh, half moan. "Clay, please."

His mouth moved lower. "Please what, Ara?" he murmured against her. "Tell me what you want, what you need. Tell me why you came to my chamber and leapt into my arms. Tell me why you cannot stay away."

Because she loved him.

Because she had never stopped.

She swallowed violently, pushing away the errant thought. It was wrong. It had to be wrong. She could not still be in love with Clay. Not after all he had done. Not after all these years. No, it was that she wanted him. Her body remembered all the sinful, exquisite tortures he could visit upon it.

That was it.

That was all.

"I want you," she said instead, and even that was an admission she hated to give.

He coaxed her legs to widen. They glided across his coverlet, opening her to him completely, and she almost trembled with need. She imagined he could see her folds, plump and slick, the aching bundle of flesh between them, eager for his tongue. He tormented her by kissing everywhere—her inner thighs, the juncture where her thighs met her mound, the swell just above her cleft.

"What do you want?" he asked. His fingers raked up and down her outer thighs, lightly dragging his nails over her sensitized flesh.

"Your mouth," she whispered, cheeks growing hot. "Your tongue."

The words fled from her. They could not be contained. Long ago, he had used his lips and tongue upon her, making her spend with nothing else. It had been so many years…it had been forever, it seemed, since she had last been pleasured. Eight years, to be specific. She did not know what it was about this man that turned her into a wanton, that made her so weak, that made her flesh come alive and her lust boil out of control, but she could not help herself.

There were some facts she had come to realize were indisputable.

The sun rose in the east.

London would forever be rife with fog.

And as long as she lived, Clayton Ludlow would make her body sing.

"Do you want me to lick you, Ara?" he asked, his voice so gruff and low and decadent that it emerged as a growl. His kissed a circle lovingly around her pearl, avoiding it. "Do you want me to take your sweet, swollen bud into my mouth and suck you until you spend?"

Oh. Good. Sweet. Merciful. Heavens.

A tiny spasm ricocheted through her with such sweet pleasure she could not keep still. Her hips jerked. A burst of wetness rushed from her core. His words were so erotic. His teasing so unbearable. She swore she would die if she did not have his tongue on her, stroking her. Inside her. If he did not do as he had asked and suck her until she came again.

"Yes," she cried out. "Please, Clay."

"I like the way you beg, Duchess."

His words were hard. Harsh. A vivid reminder that this was not eight years ago, and they were not the same people as they had been then. That those young fools were forever lost to the ether, replaced by hardened, sharper versions of themselves. That time could change everything, and some things were not meant to be revisited. That practicality and reason could outweigh fate. She would have withdrawn from him had he not lowered his dark head at last and run his tongue along her slit. One hot, wet pass was all it took.

She was mindless again, moaning, arching her back. Her hands sought him. One landed in his luxurious hair, the other found his splayed over her belly. Their fingers tangled and held. He licked her again, another long, slow swipe.

A moan rent the air. She did not know if it was hers or his. She rocked against him, pelvis thrusting against his face. The *despicable thing* was at work within her, and it wanted satisfaction. It wanted Clay Ludlow taking her apart, climax by climax.

At long last, he gave her what she wanted, taking her throbbing pearl into his mouth. He sucked long and hard, and this time there was no doubt who the cry echoing through the chamber belonged to. It was hers. And he was…*oh*, he was…

He was far too much. And not enough. And everything all at once. The world fell away. Everything disappeared, even her surroundings. All that remained was him and his glorious mouth, bringing her to her peak.

He worked the underside of her bud with his teeth. Gently nipped before flicking his tongue over her in steady, fast pulses. The hand that was not entwined with hers moved from her hip to between her thighs. He traced her seam, parted her flesh, and sank a finger deep inside her.

She clenched. Bucked, took him deeper. A second finger joined the first, sliding in and out as he alternated between sucking and licking her swollen pearl. His knowing probe found a place inside her she had not known existed. In and out he pumped, curling his digits, her channel growing wetter and wetter until the sounds of him pleasuring her filled the chamber.

Her breathy moans of helpless need. The sodden harmony of flesh colliding, of licking and sucking and claiming. Of receiving pleasure and giving pleasure. Of surrendering to the passions that had always been simmering between them, just beneath the surface of their every interaction since he had reappeared in her life.

Something deep inside her tightened like a knot. She was on the precipice, the place between her legs throbbing and heavy. Her nipples hard, her breasts achy and full. Even her skin seemed as if it were on fire.

"You taste so good," he whispered, his tongue flicking back over her again.

Her release jolted through her, sudden and ferocious. One moment she was undulating her hips against his delicious ministrations, and the next everything had exploded. She had exploded. Pleasure roared through her, white hot and overwhelming, so strong her shoulders curled forward, rising off the bed. Her body gripped his fingers, bringing him deeper. More wetness rushed from her, bathing his fingers, soaking his mouth.

And then, he tore away from her with a warrior's fierce roar. He rose on his knees, gripped his cock—so magnificent, so engorged—and positioned it at her entrance. The aftershocks of her release were still tremoring through her but she wanted more. She wanted everything. All of him.

Everything he had to give.

She moved beneath him, bringing the tip of him inside her.

They sighed as one.

Clay lowered his large body over hers, his face hovering above. Dark eyes seared hers with unabashed heat. "Is this what you want, Ara?"

She did not think she could manage a coherent word, so she made a sound of approval low in her throat and undulated her hips, bringing him deeper inside her.

"Say it," he commanded, his expression as intense as his gaze. "I need to hear you."

"Yes," she forced out, and it was natural, so natural for her to wrap her legs around him. It was as if time had never passed. As if they were back to the Clay and Ara they had been. Back in the hunting cabin. Back when they had been free. When they had been young and desperate for each other. When everything had seemed possible. "I want you. Only you."

It had only ever been him.

Would only ever be him.

Damn him, what was it about Clayton Ludlow?

He thrust inside her, his cock sliding deep and slow. His movements were controlled. "Only me?"

"Always," she promised before she could think better of what she'd said. Her arms locked around him, holding his huge, powerful body tight to hers. He was so large and she was so small. She loved their dichotomy. "You are my fate, Clay, and I am yours."

Right or wrong, it was the truth. They were inevitable. Years and betrayal could not keep them apart. They still wanted each other as much, if not more, than they ever had.

"Yes," he hissed, taking her deep, withdrawing, and then sliding home inside her again.

His mouth found hers. Their kiss was as frantic as it had been earlier, just as hungry, every bit as ferocious. She tasted herself on his tongue. Ran her fingers down the strong planes of his back. Marked him. Taunted him. Met him thrust for thrust.

And then they were flying together. It was elemental. Give and take, bodies pumping, tongues mating, hands roaming every inch of skin they could find. They slammed together, moved as one. Harder, faster, his strokes growing more deliberate, more prolonged.

She fractured again, splintering into a thousand different shards of herself, coming over him, around him, milking his cock as stars and light flashed through her. She cried out into his mouth, and he swallowed them, took them, made them his just as he made her body his. Wetness gushed from her.

She was lost. Helpless. This was not just pleasure. It was not just release. It was all-encompassing. It was as if she had found herself, here and now, with his body planted over hers, his rigid cock inside her.

As the shudders of pleasure wracked through her, he stiffened and withdrew, gripping his cock as he spent all over her skin. He painted her belly, her abdomen, and even her breasts with streaks of his seed. Groaning and rolling away from her, he fell onto his back, his breath emerging in heavy pants.

Heart hammering, she lay alongside him, reluctant to move. Reluctant to wash the traces of him away from her skin.

"You should never have come here tonight," he said again into the silence.

She stared at the ceiling, her fingers trailing through the evidence of their latest sin, rubbing it into her skin. "No," she agreed. "I should not have."

But she had, and they *had.*

And nothing would ever be the same.

Chapter Seventeen

Eight years earlier

TWO DAYS AFTER he had watched her slip away from him beneath the full moon, Clay was waiting for Ara again. Those bloody days had stretched into an eternity. Because he did not want to risk their discovery, he had been forced to temper his need for her, which only seemed to grow with each hour he was not at her side.

He had punished his body by running until his lungs ached. He had sparred with Leo and bloodied his knuckles and bruised his jaw. He had performed every exercise he knew until his muscles shook, until he was covered in sweat. Until his heart threatened to pound straight through his chest. But using his body as a weapon to fight his tension had failed.

In between attempts to work the nerves from his body, he had applied for and acquired a marriage license. He had also spent a good portion of his time with pen and paper at hand, planning. He had funds at his disposal: meager, but enough for several months at least.

After they were wed, he would seek employment at the Home Office. His father had wished to settle Marchmont on him, a property that wasn't part of the entail. Though his pride had forced him to decline Marchmont previously, he would accept it for Ara. It would not be as fine as Brixton Hall or Kingswood Manor, but it would suffice, and he would do anything for her.

He was going to become a husband. Today. He was going to be *Ara's husband.* He grinned into the night as he waited, knowing he was an hour ahead of their appointed meeting time. He had been unable to remain at Brixton Hall a moment longer, knowing the rest of his life awaited him. She had his heart. Now and forever.

She was his fate.

The sudden, soft crunch of a footfall behind him alerted him he wasn't alone.

Before he could react, violent pain slammed through his skull, accompanied by the sickening sound of something heavy and hard connecting with his flesh. A thousand tiny stars swirled before him.

Bloody hell, was he being robbed? *What in the hell? Who in the hell?*

He reached out, his mind swimming with agony and confusion. He was blinded, off-kilter. He tried to grope for his attacker. Met with empty air. Another swing of the weapon hissed through the air, landing on his already battered head. He raised his arms, trying to deflect the blows that kept coming. But he was slow, his body sluggish and weak from the grueling pace he had set for himself. From shock and surprise and the effect of the blows he'd suffered.

Another.

He fell to his knees.

Another.

The world went black. He pitched forward into nothing, and his last thought was of Ara. He had to protect her. He had to keep her safe. But the blackness called, and the anguish was a tide, pulling him under.

TODAY WAS THE day. The first day in the rest of her life. The best day. *No, scratch that.* It was the beginning of the best of her days.

She was going to be a wife.

Clay's wife.

Mrs. Clayton Ludlow.

Ara's hands shook as she retrieved her small valise from its hiding place beneath her bed. Small enough to carry. Large enough to contain a few of her most precious possessions: her journal, a simple gown, undergarments, two pairs of stockings, and Volume II of Elizabeth Barrett Browning's *Poems*, the match to the volume she'd given Clay.

She was early, she knew. Clay had instructed her to meet him at dawn, which would not yet arrive for another hour. But in the dark stillness of Kingswood Hall, so much change about to unfurl, she could not sleep.

Energy quaked inside her like a spring blossom prepared to burst forth and bloom. In the time since they had parted, she had done her best not to show a hint of the tumult rioting inside her—the sheer, unadulterated joy. As she breakfasted alongside her mother and father, she wondered if they noticed a difference in her.

She wondered if her smiles were too bright, too wide, if she seemed too eager, too carefree. Too alive. She feared they could sense the love burning inside her, filling her, overwhelming her. Transforming her. Changing her from Araminta, proper and well-behaved, dutiful daughter, into Ara.

Ara was the woman who found love like a wild rose thriving amidst weeds and plucked it to make her own. Ara was brave and bold. She was the one who left Kingswood Hall in the night and wrapped herself in the arms of her lover. She was the one who dared.

And Ara was loved. She was going to make a happier life for herself than her mother and her sister had found. One of her own choosing. One of her own making. She did not need a title or wealth. All she needed was Clay and his large, reassuring body, his knowing hands, his gentle strength, his tenderness. His teasing.

His kisses.

His love.

How she adored his mouth. His fingers. His dark hair, the scruff of his beard, the scuff on his boots. He was going to be *hers*. Hers to touch and love, though it still seemed an impossible fantasy as she made one more cursory check of the items she had stowed inside her valise.

But it was true.

She was going to be a wife.

Clay's wife.

Mrs. Clayton Ludlow.

No matter how many times the thoughts rained through her mind, she could not seem to imagine the reality of it. The bliss of being free to be with the man she loved. Of no longer having to hide in forests and hunting cabins, living for the night and the darkest hour when no one would discover what she was doing or where she was going.

She sat down on the edge of her bed, valise at her side, and waited.

HE WOKE TO his hands bound. To the sting of a cold metal blade on his cheek. To the lash of something tight around his chest and waist. To the scent of stale sweat and gin and old boots.

To a warning.

"You will leave Lady Araminta alone."

The voice was gruff. Nasally. Unfamiliar.

Pain swam through Clay, nausea roiling in his gut as he slowly became aware of his body once more. His eyes blinked open. The world was blurry and dark. A shadowed face loomed over his. Something cold and wet hit him in the cheek.

Spittle?

Bloody hell, where was he? What had happened?

"Ara," her name was the first word on his lips, a cry into the night. "Where is she?"

"She is not here," the stranger clipped, digging the blade deeper into Clay's skin.

Fuck, it hurt. The pain of his head met and swam together with the pain in his cheek. A fresh roil of nausea rolled through him. He choked back the bile. Swallowed it down. He had to be strong. For Ara.

Everything for Ara. Always.

But the blade pressed deeper. He was being cut apart. Flayed. Laid open. A warmth slid down his face, dripping, dripping. Wetness coated his neck. The knife sliced deeper.

"There now, not so pretty anymore are you?" the voice asked.

He blinked, tried to see the face of his assailant. Nothing made sense. His mind was jumbled. All he could think of was Ara. She was to meet him here. They were to be married. What had happened to her? Where was she? Had she come?

"By God if you have harmed her, I will tear you limb from limb," he managed, though the words were weak. The blows he had taken to the head had made the world seem like it was distorted. Everything hurt. He hurt.

His face. His head. His back. Why the hell couldn't he move? He struggled, trying to free his arms, to defend himself.

Realization sank through the murk. He was bound. He was helpless. All the strength he had honed, all the ways in which he had built his body so it would never fail him, were useless to him now. With a few blows to the head, he had been felled.

The blade sank deeper. Slowly, slowly, deeper, stroking downward. And the pain was fierce and his blood ran, hot and sticky and wet, down his throat, soaking into his coat.

"Won't be so easy to charm the ladies after this, Duke's Bastard. You'll be marked forever now."

He tried to speak again. "Wh-where is she?"

"She is where she belongs, you son of a whore," his attacker said. "She's safe in her bed at Kingswood Hall, regretting the day she ever spoke your name. You will leave her alone from this moment forward."

"No," he denied even as the man's knife cut deeper into his flesh. He would not believe—could not believe—Ara would do this to him. To them. She loved him. He loved her. They were meant for each other.

"A letter from the lady." The man tucked it rudely into his coat. "Read it at your leisure, *Your Grace*."

He did not miss the scorn in his assailant's voice, even as the blade continued its slow and steady path of destruction.

"Cannot be," he muttered, though half his face felt as if it were on fire. The pain was blinding and numbing and hot all at once.

"Your blood for the blood you spilled," the man said as he finished drawing the knife down Clay's face. "The earl considers the debt paid now. You will never speak to Lady Araminta or look upon her again."

"I…no." It was all that would emerge. He was losing blood. Growing dizzy. The pain sank its fangs so deep into his belly it gave a violent heave. He was going to vomit. To cast up his accounts.

"Believe it. The lady confessed all to her father. She has realized the error of her ways, and she wants nothing more to do with you. Read her letter. She will not be coming to meet you, Duke's Bastard. Not today. Not ever."

No.

Not Ara.

He could not believe her capable of such treachery.

She was going to become his wife. Today. The license was in his pocket.

The blade reached his jaw, slicing deep. So deep. So much pain. He would never be the same, and he knew it all the way to his bones. He would be disfigured. Forever changed.

But who else would have known? How else would he have been found here? How would the earl know? Nothing made sense. And the sense it did make was more horrible than the knife cutting his flesh, making him scream.

Making him bleed.

The world turned black again, and no matter how hard he tried to fight it, he couldn't keep himself from succumbing to the abyss.

ARA ARRIVED AT the designated meeting place with one quarter hour to spare. The early morning air was biting, but she scarcely felt the cold. Her body vibrated with expectation. She clenched her valise and exhaled a breath, grateful she had not been discovered. They had not been thwarted, and nothing and no one could stop them.

Now that she had reached her destination, a sweet sense of peace settled over her. The rightness of it all sank into her bones, becoming a part of her. It was as if she had waited her entire life for this moment. For this man.

Within hours, they would have their freedom. Within hours, they would be wed, and they would have the rest of their lives to learn and love each other. To grow together. To find their own happiness.

Her heart gave a pang as she waited, eyes searching for a beloved, tall figure emerging from the mists.

"Mrs. Clayton Ludlow," she whispered to herself with a small, satisfied smile.

WHEN HE CAME to next, he was on his back. His body felt as if it had been decimated by a locomotive. Head, face, arms, legs—everything throbbed and ached. *Holy hell*, his teeth hurt. His mouth tasted of blood. His mouth struggled to form words, but searing pain shot through his cheek to his jaw, burrowing itself inside him with such ferocity he almost cast up his accounts.

"Christ on the cross, is that you, brother?"

Clay blinked. His vision swirled. The sky was bright. Too bright. Everything hurt. Where was he? And how? And why? Three Leos hovered over him. All of them appeared concerned, which was unusual for Leo, who made an art of disillusionment and detachment.

"L..." he attempted to say his brother's name and failed. His mouth failed him. Or his face. Or his mind.

He couldn't be sure.

"Jesus, don't try to talk," Leo said, dropping to his knees. "Clay, don't close your eyes. Can you hear me?"

Tired. So tired. Clay's eyes didn't want to stay open. They were heavy. Filled with the weight of a thousand stones. He hurt. Everything hurt. He had lost Ara. There was a letter in his coat. From her. A goodbye.

He couldn't bear it.

"How did you come to be here?"

"Where?" he managed to croak.

"Brixton Hall," his brother clipped.

Clay opened his eyes long enough to see Leo's face swimming before him. Worried.

Leo never worried. Leo was *Leo*. Cold and arrogant and cynical, detached as a grave robber. How could this be right? How could any of this be right?

"Fuck, Clay, your face is…" Leo's words trailed off, and then he touched Clay's cheek gently. "Someone cut you badly, brother."

The pain was so intense he couldn't control himself. His body twisted on the ground where he had been left—somewhere on the outskirts of Brixton Manor, but Lord knew how—and he retched.

"Jesus, what happened to you?" his brother demanded.

When the heaves subsided, he spat into the dirt. Dark-red blood stained the ground. "Robbed. I was robbed."

And he had been.

In the truest sense of the word. His vision narrowed as if he had entered a dark tunnel. Or a chamber of hell.

Then, he passed out once more.

HOURS.

That was how much time had passed since she had arrived in the early morning's ethereal glow and now. Ara hadn't a timepiece, but she guessed by the position of the sun, the pain in her feet and back, and the crushing, bitter weight lying heavy on her heart, that it was at least noon.

Fears, dark and painful, threatened to consume her. They

swirled through her mind, resounding, mocking, and bitter.

He isn't coming for me.

He has changed his mind.

He does not love me.

As the sun had begun to rise and he initially failed to arrive, she had contented herself with a waterfall of reasons why he had been delayed. Perhaps he overslept, she reasoned. Perhaps he had forgotten. Mayhap his horse had gone lame. But time had lolled slowly on, the sun ticking its way across an overcast sky.

Her naïveté continued to provide her with a fountain of hope for some time. Had she gotten the day wrong? Maybe he had told her three days instead of two. Was it possible she was a day early? What if he had been robbed? Thrown from his mount? What if he had fallen and struck his head on a rock, and he was bleeding and in need of her assistance?

As time stumbled on, her confusion melded into worry. Valise still in hand, she had trekked about as much of the dense undergrowth as she could manage, bogged down by her case and her travel skirts, searching for his fallen form. Her search had turned up not a sign of him, and, fearing he would arrive at their appointed place and she would not be waiting, she returned, solemn.

And waited.

Waited some more.

Her feet began to throb. She paced until her left boot wore a blister in her heel. She stood until twinges in her back and the pain in her feet led her to settle her bottom upon her valise. More time passed. Her chin fell into her hand, and in this miserable fashion she passed at least another hour.

All the while, her mind turned into a tempest. Excuses and worry and fear faded. In their place, came realization. Sobering, numbing realization.

Clay had jilted her.

He did not want to marry her.

Indeed, perhaps he had never intended to wed her at all. Or perhaps in the last two days, while she had been dreaming of becoming his wife, he had changed his mind. Or mayhap her wickedness at their last meeting had disgusted him. Maybe he regretted making love to her.

She could only guess at his reasons, for he was not here to ask.

And he was not coming.

Ara finally admitted it to herself after a few more hours had passed, and she was thirsty and hungry and so very tired. At first, all she knew was a great, billowing swell of numbness. But all too quickly, the pain followed.

The horrible, agonizing pain as realization turned into undeniable fact.

He isn't coming for me.

He has changed his mind.

He does not love me.

She was not going to marry Clayton Ludlow today. She had a packed valise, a heart filled with dreams, and nowhere to take them. She had begun the morning in secret smiles and tentative happiness, but the Ara who had awoke in the night, so eager to become Clay's wife that she could not sleep, did not resemble the Ara who stood alone with her valise in the waning hours of the afternoon.

Though she tried to contain them, the sobs inevitably came. She did not know how long she sat on her valise alongside the road, crying into her skirts. When a familiar carriage ambled into view with her father's crest emblazoned on the side, she did not bother to run. Nor did she stop her tears from flowing.

The carriage halted alongside her. She did not even protest when her mother escorted her inside. As the carriage rattled back to Kingswood Hall, she closed her eyes tightly, refusing to speak.

He was never going to come for you taunted the rolling wheels.

He didn't want to marry you whispered the creaking conveyance.

He never loved you, said her broken heart.

She was a fool, and all the love sonnets were wrong.

Chapter Eighteen

I LOVE THEE with the passion put to use / In my old griefs, and with my childhood's faith.

For some reason, the words of an Elizabeth Barrett Browning poem returned to Clay in the aftermath of his wild, foolish, impassioned lovemaking with Ara. He had read the book she had given him all those years ago. Of course he had. Had kept it with him, the last part of Ara he had left. Perhaps the only true part of her she'd had to give.

The book had traveled alongside him through the Continent. It had spent many nights beneath his pillow. The spine had cracked, lines underlined by his pen, corners carefully folded down to mark his favorites. He had railed over some, revisited others. He had run his finger over the careful dedication she had inscribed more times than he cared to admit or count.

To Clay from Your Ara. When you are ready for Volume II, you know where to find it.

But she had never been his, had she? And though he had known where the second volume was, he had never searched for it. Absurd, but he wondered as she rose from his bed now if she still had it tucked away somewhere. If she had ever looked upon her matching volume and thought of him.

If she had ever thought of him at all.

But why the bloody hell should he give a damn either

way? Why should it matter? She had betrayed him. Hurt him. Broken him. Had withheld his son from him. He did not owe her a bloody thing. The lust between them had always existed, and it had not changed.

If anything, their circumstances served to heighten the tension disproportionally, and it was surely that which fogged his brain now, which made him remember the sonnets and the poems and the way he and Ara had once been together. They had been a fiction. She had manipulated and used him, betraying his trust and changing him forever in the process.

He had already shown her more kindness and leniency than she deserved.

And yet, the sharp knife of guilt stabbed him in his gut.

Why did he feel like such a cad?

Why did the way she held her shoulders, curled inward as if to protect herself, the sheen he thought he'd seen in her blue-violet eyes before she rolled away from him, the almost violent way she had fled the bed, affect him? Why did he find himself weakening for her, wanting her, needing her the same way he once had when he had been too innocent to know better?

There was something about the sight of her pale back and thin arms and legs, the indentation of her spine, the curtain of her copper curls, the way she scrambled to her nightdress—*my God*, she was as small as a bird, every bit as dainty—something that hit him simultaneously in the gut and the heart. She seemed so alone. So helpless.

He couldn't shake the notion he had somehow hurt her with his words. And he hated hurting her. Could not bear the thought. Every instinct in him cried out to protect her. To keep her at his side. In his bed. To hold her to him and never let her go.

He had learned nothing in eight goddamn years.

Still as bloody stupid as ever. But he could not seem to save himself. She would always be his ruin. His temptation. His Achilles heel.

"Ara," he found himself saying. "Do not go."

She ignored him, threw her nightrail over her head, stabbing her arms into the sleeves.

"Ara," he said again, rising from the bed, stalking to her without a stitch.

Wordlessly, she spun on her heel, retreating from him, her small feet softly padding across the carpet, back to her chamber. His legs were longer, his strides easily eating up the advantage she had on him.

But then she stopped suddenly, her back still to him, her entire body going still, her gaze settling upon the battered volume he had placed, unthinkingly, upon a side table. He realized the moment she recognized the book. Shame replaced the myriad other emotions whirling through him.

"That is the book I gave you." Her statement emerged as half question, as though she could not believe he would have kept the thing all these years.

He did not blame her, for he could scarcely believe it himself. But he had carried the book—Volume One—about with him, unwilling to part from it. It had been a reminder of the man he had once been, the man who had believed in love and second chances and good hearts. The man who had believed in the heart of a slip of a thing, a small flame-haired goddess who had appeared in the forest one day and had made him believe he could be worthy of her love.

Until she had stripped him of his beliefs and his hopes.

Until she had taken his love and crushed it beneath her dainty heel.

"Aye," he bit out reluctantly.

She spun about, facing him, then averting her gaze when

she realized he was indecent and unrepentant, his entire body on wanton display. Her cheeks turned a shade of scarlet to match her hair. "You kept it?"

His cock was beginning to stir, and he could not face her or this dire conversation whilst sporting a prick that was hard enough to hang a bucket of coal from it. "I…found it recently, and I thought perhaps you would like it returned to you. It is yours, after all. The volumes go together."

Why did he feel as if he was talking about the two of them rather than the bloody poetry volumes? And why had he offered to return the book? *His* book? He had read it so many times that he could recite any number of the poems verbatim. She had gifted it to him.

"It would seem the years were not kind to this little volume." She offered him a slight, tentative smile. "Why did you keep it?"

Because he was a fool.

Because he was bloody stupid.

Because it had been *hers*.

Initially, he had hated the thing. He'd thrown it against walls, had tossed it into a puddle—the corners of pages eighty-three through ninety-one remained slightly rippled despite his efforts to dry and flatten them afterward. He had left it in a hotel, only to retrieve it some two hours later, unable to part with it. He had carried it across seas, across borders, had read it frontispiece to back cover again and again. Once, during a mad bout of drinking champagne in Paris, he had decided to burn the thing at last.

And so, he had tossed it into the fire, only to have second thoughts and retrieve it—drunkenly—from the flame. It had survived far more unscathed than his hand, which still bore several faint scars from the burns. The book had suffered some slight scorching on the red leather cover. It was fitting, he thought—the book wound up as bruised and battered as his heart.

"Clay," she prodded, and she had the journal in her hands now, stroking it, this relic from their past. This unwanted part of them that would not seem to go away. "Why did you keep it?"

"I…" He could not think of a damned thing he wished to say in his defense. "You may have it back. Take it, Duchess. I have no need of the volume any longer."

Nor did he have a need of her.

She could take back the bloody poetry. She could disappear through the doors connecting their chambers. He had no need of her beyond slaking his hungers inside her willing body.

I loved her once.

God, how I loved her.

Until she had betrayed him, he reminded himself, adding an inward *sod off* to the weakness inside him for good measure.

"I do not want it back," she said. "You may keep it, Clay. By now, it is far more yours than it was ever mine."

If only my heart could be the same bloody way, more mine than yours.

If only I had stopped loving you.

No, damn it. He did not love her. Not any longer. He tamped down the maudlin sentiments. They were not only unwanted, but they made a man weak.

"I don't want it," he bit out. Not the book, not the way he felt for her, nor all the old, long-buried, long bitter emotions she unleashed in him. Not the memories. Not her.

She smiled sadly. "Someone told me that when a warrior gives a gift to another warrior, it is bad luck to take it back. You must keep it forever now."

His chest hurt. "This is not a blade but a book."

He could say she was not a warrior, but that would be wrong, for she was. She had been through so much upheaval in the last few months—Burghly's murder, the threats and danger surrounding her, nearly being attacked by a would-be assassin—and her resilience had shown through it all. He admired her strength, even if he could not forgive what she had done.

"Words are every bit as powerful, every bit as dangerous, as weapons," she said then, her voice quiet. Steeped in regret.

He thought of the words she had written him. He had long ago shredded the letter, tossed its pieces into the grate. But he had not forgotten them.

"Perhaps you are right, Duchess."

They stared at each other, tension heavy and thick in the silent stillness of the chamber, the rumpled bed at their backs a reminder of their folly. A reminder of his inability to resist her.

"I must return to my chamber," she said then, her gaze flitting from him, to the book, and then back again. They were wide and bright. Curious and questioning. But also dark with something indefinable.

Melancholy? Longing? The invisible fist holding his heart squeezed tighter.

"Don't," he said, the word torn from him, a plea. It was not what he had intended to say. Not what he should say. Not what he should want.

"I must." She caught the fullness of her lower lip in her teeth, hesitating. *Damn it*, tears glistened in her eyes. A knot rose in his throat and he could not speak past it. Could not do anything but gently take her in his arms and hold her.

"No," was all he said.

He buried his face in her wild curls, drinking in her scent. Roses in bloom. Ara. Young love. Recklessness. Stolen kisses beneath a thousand leaf-covered branches. How the hell had they ended up so far from where they had begun?

"Release me, Clay," she whispered against his chest, her breath warm. "You said yourself I should not have come here, and you were right. It was wrong. You and I are all wrong."

Of course they were. Chasing after her, holding her, wanting her still, it was as wrong as a snow squall in the summer. He was not meant for her, nor was she meant for him. He should release her. Let her go—not just for tonight but forever.

And yet, his arms only held her tighter. His foolish mouth opened. "We were not always wrong."

Her arms slid slowly around his waist, as if she was at war with herself over whether or not she ought to, as if she could not resist. "No," she surprised him by softly agreeing. "We were not."

Bloody hell.

A sudden rush of longing splintered inside him. He felt bloody and raw, like his innards were comprised of nothing but jagged shards. How was it possible for this tiny slip of a woman to tear him apart?

"Stay with me," he breathed into her hair. It was his turn to beg, and he didn't know where the inclination had emerged from or why. But something in him said he could not allow her to walk back through the door. Some part of him, long buried, had been resurrected, and it could not bear to watch her go, to close the door, to give this madness between them the finality it deserved.

"Why?" she asked quietly, her hands moving on his back, caressing him in an echo of the way his traveled up and down hers. "You detest me, Clay. Why would you want me here when you just told me to go?"

"I never told you to go." He pressed another kiss to her

hair before rubbing his bristly cheek against its silkiness. "I told you that you should not have come here, and I was right."

She stiffened in his embrace.

"Because I cannot be near you, Ara, without wanting more," he continued. "Because you make me weak."

"Nothing could make you weak." Her fine-boned hands continued their exploration of his bare skin, trailing over his muscles. "You are so strong."

Not when it came to her, he wasn't.

"There are different kinds of strengths, different kinds of weaknesses." He swept his hand up her spine, sinking beneath the heavy, soft waves of her tresses to find her bare nape. Here, his fingers gently worked her flesh. The cords beneath her skin were taut and strained. "My body is no match for you. You could bring me to my knees with the ease of an avenging army."

A quiet sound came from her then. Not an exhalation, nor a sigh, but…he listened closer. His ears were not mistaken. She was laughing.

It occurred to him that he had not heard Ara laugh since the carefree days of their youth. Hell, she scarcely even smiled unless it was for the lad's benefit. Was her sadness all the result of Burghly's murder? He did not want to think of her dead husband now, not in this moment of uneasy truce. Not when she was a warm and soft blessing in his arms. Not when he could hold her and touch her, kiss her and soothe her as he pleased.

Not when he could hear the sweet, tinkling strains of her levity cutting into the heaviness that seemed to forever follow them. He did not know what to do with a laughing Ara. Was she delirious? Was she laughing at him? Had she imbibed too much wine at dinner?

Hell. Even if she *was* laughing at him, he didn't give a proper goddamn. Her laughter was beautiful. Always had been, and his cock twitched to life in answer. He was still naked, after all, and Ara wore a thin scrap of a gown.

He looked down at her, tilting her chin up with a gentle touch so he could see her face. So he could bask in the undeniable brilliance of her smile. The ever-elusive dimple in her left cheek was a charming divot in her smooth, creamy skin. He wanted to kiss it.

Instead, he raised his brows. "What is so bloody amusing, Duchess?"

"The notion of me bringing you to your knees," she said, her laughter subsiding as quickly as it had burst forth. The shadows in her eyes returned, dimming their sparkle. "You are so big and strong, and I am weak and slight. You do not even like me."

He liked her, *damn it all to hell.* He liked her far, far too much. Always had. Always would. Time, distance, betrayals—nothing had squelched the burning need inside him to claim her. To make her his. To keep her.

Clay stared down into her upturned face. "You are stronger than you think, Ara, and I…I do not dislike you."

Her delicate brows furrowed into a frown. "Such a heartwarming confession, Mr. Ludlow."

"It was not meant to be one, Duchess." It was all he dared reveal to her. All he dared admit to himself, for if he were to hold a candle to the darkness inside, bathe it in light, he was afraid of what he would see. Terrified he would discover his love for her had never fled him at all, but that it had simply been buried beneath the twin weights of grief and hurt.

"Thank you for bringing me to your home," she said suddenly. "I did not feel safe at Burghly House. Not after…" A tremor shook her. She swallowed.

Rage burned inside him still for the man who had chased her through the garden with a knife after savaging Beauchamps. If he could slay him again, he would. Her scream had filled him with an inhuman surge of strength, and he had torn down the path, determined to find her and keep her safe. The day still haunted him, for he hated knowing he had been the one to fail her.

"I am sorry, Ara," he said, caressing her smooth cheek once, twice. "If I had not left that day, none of it would have happened."

Her lips quirked into another ghost of a smile, but this time it was sad. "It would have happened regardless of where you were. You are not at fault. The men who murdered my husband are. It is as you said, they will do anything, commit any sin, to further their cause."

My husband.

He hated those words in her voice, on her tongue. Hated that another man had known her as intimately as he had. Hated that she had loved him. He was bloody jealous of a dead man, and how foolish. How ridiculous. But there it was, a knife in his chest.

"Did you love him?" he asked, and he did not know why. The question had no bearing upon him. Her answer would not change anything. He had no right—no reason—to know. Except for the envy eating him alive.

Her expression shifted, shuttering. "Of course I loved Freddie."

Fuck. Why had he asked? Why had he wished to know?

Those five words dug the blade so deep he could feel it in his skull. Yes, of course she loved goddamn Freddie, whose locks of hair she carried about on her person morning, day, and evening. Why, it was a mercy she did not have the bloody brooch pinned to her nightrail. Freddie the duke. Freddie the heir born on the right side of the blanket. Freddie who had likely never had a modicum of hardship in his life until the day he'd been stabbed to death by a Fenian assassin.

And yet, while she wore her mourning weeds and sported her brooch and proclaimed she loved her husband, she had allowed Clay to make love to her. Twice. Why?

Bile rose in his throat. "Was it him you thought of when I was inside you, Ara?"

He did not want to know, but at the same time, he *had* to know. Perhaps this was the answer, the way he could finally free himself of the hold she had upon him. Perhaps this was how he could let her go, regardless of how much he wanted to hold on forever.

Her lush, pink lips parted, as if she struggled to form an answer. He could kiss her now, punish her with the bruising of his mouth and the claiming of his tongue. Or he could wait, listen to what she would say. His heart thundered in his chest.

"No." She closed her eyes for a moment, as if suffering an inner anguish she wished to keep hidden from him. When her long lashes swept upward, her frank, unwavering gaze took his breath. "It was you. It has always been you, Clay. Only ever you."

What the bloody hell?

"Ara," he rasped, not certain if he should kiss her or shake her. Or both. "You *married him*, for Christ's sake. You loved him."

"Yes," she said, pushing at his chest suddenly, and he released her, watching as she slipped from his arms. "I married Freddie. I loved him too, and he loved me. Most importantly, he loved Edward. He saved us when you were long gone. If it had not been for Freddie, I would have been forced to go abroad and give Edward away."

Her voice trembled on the last few words.

He noticed.

But he was also absorbing the rest of what she had just said. Anger returned to him. "I would have saved you. I never would have bloody well left had you not gone to your father. Tell me something, Duchess, did you ever spare a morsel of sympathy for me? Did you know even a moment of guilt whilst you slept in your warm bed and your father's henchman sliced open my face and left me for dead?"

Her lips parted. For a beat, she said nothing, simply stared at him, eyes wide and unblinking, traveling to the scar on his cheek before returning to his. "What did you say?"

"This," he said, tapping his scar, "is the last gift you left me with. This and the book. As you can see, I still bear both."

She shook her head slowly. "I do not understand, Clay."

Was it possible she hadn't known? That when she had experienced her change of heart and ran to her father to confess their plan of running away together, she had imagined her father would not retaliate against Clay? Could it be true she hadn't realized the depth of her father's hatred for his, and vicariously for Clay?

He ran a palm over his cheek, the scar feeling suddenly as if it scorched his flesh. "When you told your father about what we planned, did you not think he would take action? Did you truly imagine he would not make me pay for daring to try to take you from him?"

Chapter Nineteen

IT WAS AS if she had stepped into a dream.

A nightmare.

She must be sleeping, trapped helplessly inside the nonsensical meanderings of her mind. That was the only explanation for what was happening now. For what Clay was saying.

Your father's henchman sliced open my face and left me for dead.

This is the last gift you left me with.

His words, bitter and dark with accusation, echoed in her mind as his gaze trapped hers. But how could it be possible that her father had…what? That her father had paid someone to attack Clay?

"No," she whispered, her hand flying to her mouth in an attempt to hold back a sudden, violent sob.

His mother's words at dinner returned to her as well.

Do you know, Your Grace, how my son's face was scarred?

He was attacked from behind, cudgeled over the head, and woke to the knife on his cheek.

The man responsible has not been imprisoned.

That meant…*my God*, it meant…

"No," she said again, louder this time. "No, I will not believe it."

"You will not believe what?" He was before her, his expression fierce, jaw rigid, eyes burning with intensity. But when he took her face in his hands, it was with the gentlest of touches. "Tell me you didn't know. Tell me you didn't know he would send someone after me."

"I…" she began, only to falter. She reached up, stroking slowly over the vicious scar. A scar he wore because of her. But his explanation did not make sense. "I never told my father, Clay. I never told anyone what we had planned. Even when you didn't come for me and my mother's carriage found me, it was because she was traveling to visit my Aunt Charity and not because they knew I was eloping with you."

He stilled. "Of course they knew, Ara. They knew because you confessed everything to them. It was all there in your letter. Perhaps you have forgotten what you wrote in the years that passed since, but I can assure you I have not."

Icy tendrils of dread shot through her. Nothing made sense. And yet it did. "Clay, I never wrote you a letter. How did you receive it?"

His lip curled. "The man who attacked me from behind while I waited for you was kind enough to slip it inside my coat."

Dear God.

Her mind struggled to comprehend the gravity of what all these unfettered revelations meant. "But you were not there when I arrived, Clay. I waited for hours."

She wanted to believe he had been there, that he had gone to meet her with every intention of making her his wife, just as they had planned. But if that was the truth, it also meant he had been savagely attacked and taken away before she had arrived. And worse, that it had all happened because of her, that her own father was responsible. The dread blossomed and grew, spreading in her chest, lacing around her heart.

"You went to meet me?" he rasped, his voice low, redolent

with a host of emotions she could not identify.

There was no way to answer other than honestly. "I waited and waited for you."

"Ara." He closed his eyes for a moment, wincing as if he were in physical agony. "Bloody hell, Ara. All this time…all these years, I thought…the damned letter said you felt guilty and ashamed, that you did not wish to shame your parents or your family. It said you never wanted to see me again, that you were going to marry someone from your station, that you had seen the error in your judgment. That I was beneath you."

Each sentence he uttered was worse than the last, sinking into her with the painful proficiency of an assassin's blade. *Dear God*, little wonder he had loathed her on sight. He had spent all these years thinking she had jilted him because she was ashamed of him, that she had been complicit in her father's plan to have him attacked.

She caressed his scarred cheek slowly, tenderly. "I would never say those things. I never did. The letter was not from me. Tell me what happened, Clay. Please, I need to know."

His eyes slid closed once more. A long exhalation escaped him, as if in preparation. When his eyes opened again, they glinted with so much naked pain she almost had to look away. "I was waiting for you. I was early, and it was dark. I heard a footfall behind me, and then pain exploded in my head. When I came to, my hands were bound, and then he was carving my face."

"No, Clay." The pitiful denial was all she could manage to say, and it was not a denial of his story but of what had happened to him. What had happened to the both of them.

Tears blurred her vision as she thought of the young man he had been, handsome and honorable and sweet. Of the Clay who had given her his heart and his body. Of the man she had loved waiting for her as he'd promised, only to be so brutally beaten, his beautiful face cut and marred for life. How betrayed he must have felt, how alone.

He gathered her to him, tucking her head beneath his chin and holding her tightly against his warm, bare chest. His heart thumped into hers in steady reassurance. She wrapped her arms around his waist, holding him every bit as much. And then she wept. She wept for the Clay and Ara they had once been, she wept for the lies they had believed, she wept for the time they had lost.

He held her in his strong, beloved embrace, his hands stroking over her back in comfort. He held her as if she were the one who had endured what had befallen him rather than the opposite.

"Do not cry for me, Ara mine," he said softly, kissing her crown and breaking her heart with the old diminutive he had once given her. "I have had eight years to heal."

Eight years.

That was how long they had been apart.

Eight years too long.

She could never regret knowing Freddie—he had been a light in a time of bleak darkness for her. But she did regret all the minutes, hours, days, weeks, months, and years she had spent living her life without Clay in it.

"Please believe that had I known—had I an inkling—I would have done anything and everything within my power to keep you safe." She understood why he had believed her complicit all this time. They had been so careful with their assignations. How else would her father have known when and where to find Clay? Of course he would have believed her guilty. He had been given a letter he thought was from her. "I wrote everything in my journal. My mother or father must have been reading it without my knowledge. I never told them about that day. I never would have. You were all I wanted, all

I needed."

He was still all she wanted, all she needed.

But she kept that to herself, for whatever it was that had sparked to life between them, she had no inkling of where it would go. If it could be anything more than these precious, stolen moments. She did not dare believe he still cared for her all these years later. They had both changed.

So much had come between them. And for all that the connection they shared had never faded, they were both very much strangers to each other in so many ways.

"I believe you, Ara." His hands continued up and down her back, soothing her. Calming her. Making her feel cared for in a way only he could. "I believe you."

She held him tighter still, her face buried in his hard chest, and even with the shock of everything she had just learned, even with the specter of the men who wanted her dead haunting her, she had never felt more comforted and protected. She had never felt more at home.

CLAY WOKE TO a dream.

It was a dream he'd had countless times over the years. He was lying on his back in his bed, and his bed was dressed with the most sumptuous of linens, and his mattress was a soft cocoon around him. He had slept more deeply than he had in as long as he could remember.

Most miraculous of all was the lovely feminine form draped over him. One of her legs was tangled with his. Her breasts were crushed to his side, her head lay on his chest. Copper-colored curls spilled over him like fire.

He plucked a curl between his thumb and forefinger, rubbed it slowly, pulling it straight and then letting it fall to his chest. Summer roses in bloom perfumed the air, and it was coming from her. Roses with a dash of something else. Sunshine? The gloriousness of the sun? The sweetness of Ara?

All of it.

He stroked her hair. Watched her sleep. Tried to ignore his cock, which was painful, erect proof he was not dreaming. Rather, he was awake. He was awake, and he was grateful. So bloody grateful.

And angry too. So bloody angry.

Angry at himself for believing Ara would be capable of such treachery. For leaving when he should have remained and demanded answers. It did not matter that he'd been beaten and carved like a damned Bayonne ham. He ought to have known better. He ought to have been the man who married her.

He had missed so much.

Watching her belly grow full with his child. Loving her. Thousands of kisses and nights spent with her in his bed. Holding his son in his arms. Seeing the lad toddle on his legs for the first time. Hearing the lad call him *Father*.

Damn it. He wanted the lad to know he was his father.

He wanted to be a part of Ara and Edward's lives forever, and not just as their protector but as husband and father. He wanted to give her another babe, a daughter with her ethereal eyes and fiery hair. Another sylph for him to love. And then at least a half dozen more babes after that.

He wanted them to be what they were always meant to have been. A family.

He swallowed down the lump in his throat, still playing with Ara's hair and listening to the rhythmic sounds of her breathing. The vehemence of his emotions as he held her in the early morning light surprised him. Their late-night revelations had rocked him.

But not just him. They had rocked Ara as well. She had been shocked to realize the full extent of her mother and father's betrayal. She had spent eight years believing he had taken what he wanted from her—her innocence—and then fled to the Continent, leaving her to contend with a babe in her belly, parents who threatened to turn her out, and scarcely anyone to trust.

Mutually drained, they had fallen into bed, holding each other. Inevitably, comforting had turned into something more. Their mouths had fused, and their hands had begun to wander, and he had rolled her gently to her back, sliding home inside her as she writhed beneath him.

She stirred on his chest now, making sleepy kitten noises in her throat that were so bloody adorable he could not contain his smile. His fingers sifted through her hair, discovering her bare back. It was too soon, he knew, to feel this much for her again. But he could not seem to help himself where she was concerned.

She had ever been his weakness, and nothing had changed.

She moved restlessly, and then woke with a jolt. "Clay!"

He could not seem to stop grinning as she blinked sleep from her eyes, her cheeks flushed, her lips full and pink and deuced inviting. "Ara."

Her brows shot up her forehead. "I am in your bed."

His grin deepened. He could not help it. "Aye."

"I should return to…the other chamber," she stammered, blushing furiously. "That is, to the chamber you assigned me. Over. There."

"Or you can remain in this chamber," he said, feeling wicked. One hand found the sweet nip of her waist and the other found her thigh. He guided her until she was atop him. "Right. Here."

As he said the last, he rocked against her, suppressing a groan when he felt her slick heat on his cock. She gasped, her own hands flitting to his shoulders to steady herself. "Clay, what are you doing?"

For a widow, she was certainly an innocent.

He did not mind being the one to debauch her. In fact, it would be his greatest pleasure. In this moment, there was no pain, no danger, no impediment to them both getting what they so badly wanted and needed—each other. What they had been denied all these years.

"I am attempting to keep you here with me for as long as possible," he admitted, moving a hand between them.

His fingers parted her, found the bundle of flesh that was so deliciously responsive, and stroked. She bucked over him, a gasp tearing from her throat. Aye, this was a dream to be sure. A dream to be waking up with her in his bed, with the chance she could be his again.

But he could not rush either of them, he knew. So, he focused on this simple truth between them: pleasure. His need for her. Her need for him. It was the one thing that had never dimmed, despite the betrayals each thought the other had committed. It had always been there, humming beneath the surface of their every interaction. And now it was theirs to unlock.

"Oh," she said as she rocked over him, dragging his hard cock over her seam.

Oh indeed.

He was going to spend all over her if she continued this torture. "I need to be inside you, Ara."

No sight had ever been more beautiful or more arresting than Ara nude and astride him. Her hair was a vibrant cascade of curls down her back, her full, pink-tipped breasts thrust forward like ripe offerings. He could not resist sucking a rosy nipple into his mouth. *Perfection.*

"Clay," she gasped, undulating her hips again as she shuddered against him, finding her release as he rubbed her pearl and gave her breast a gentle bite.

He waited until the waves of pleasure had subsided for her, and then he gripped his cockstand, positioning himself at her entrance. "Do you want this?"

Her blue-violet eyes were steady on his, her pupils dark, large, and glazed with desire. "Yes."

No hesitation, and thank God for that. He thrust upward and brought her down on him at the same time. In one breath, he was deep inside her, and she was hotter and wetter than she had ever been. She clenched on him. It was just so bloody good.

So bloody…

Damn it, he could not even think. His entire world became the connection between their bodies. The pleasure burst open inside him like a firework display on the inky canvas of a night sky, one moment blank and the next color, spark, *boom.* They found their rhythm, his hands on her hips helping to set the pace. Showing her how to move, how to ride him.

Bursts of memory shot through him as he rocked beneath her sensual onslaught. He remembered the first time he had seen her watching him in the trees. He remembered their first kiss. Remembered the night he had made love to her before the crackling fire when he had been certain he would be her husband in two days' time and the future was theirs. Recalled their goodbye kiss in the moonlight, the way it had felt to love Ara, as if the sun shone only for him. As if he were as lofty as a cloud.

He shook himself from the past. Her cunny was so slippery, tightening on him so deliciously it took his breath. *To hell with the past.* He wanted her future. He wanted her mornings, her days, her nights. He never wanted to leave her bed, her side.

Because he had not stopped loving her.

The realization hit him. He did not just want to make a life with Ara and Edward. He loved her. Had always loved her. Would always love her. Araminta Burghly was his, and he wasn't going to let her go. Not ever. Soon, she would be Araminta Ludlow, just as she was always meant to have been.

The thought made his ballocks draw tight, and he almost spent inside her then and there. He surged deep, and she clenched around him once more, a shudder of release sending her collapsing to his chest. Their mouths fused, and he rolled them both to their sides, withdrawing from her body at the last moment to fist his cock and spill his seed into the bedclothes.

In the aftermath of their swift passion, they lay together, their sweat-slicked bodies intertwined. Their gazes locked and held. A small, shy smile curved her full lips.

"Good morning, Clay."

He kissed her nose, adoring the smattering of freckles on the delicate bridge. "Morning, Ara mine."

Her lips parted. Sadness clouded her gaze. "I never thought to hear you call me that again."

He ground his jaw against the reminder of what had been robbed from them. "You have always been mine, Ara. From the moment we first met beneath the shade of the trees until this very moment. Nothing has changed."

And yet, everything had.

Truth could be so strange, as freeing as it was confounding.

Tears shone in her vibrant eyes, clinging to her long, dark lashes. "I am so sorry, Clay."

The tears spilled down her cheeks in slow, fat droplets.

He kissed each one, licking his lips, tasting the salt of her pain. "Do not cry, darling. And do not be sorry. I am not sorry at all. Rather, I am glad."

"Glad?" Her brows arched.

"Glad you are here. Now. We cannot change what has happened, but we can grow stronger from it." He smoothed a stray tendril of hair away from her face and admired her, the sylvan goddess from so long ago back in his arms. "We can go on, as we must."

He drew back slightly so he could absorb every detail of her in the early morning light. Her face had not changed, still as interesting and lovely as ever, accented now by a few faint lines that had not existed eight years before. Her breasts were fuller, rounded and womanly.

Her waist was narrow, and he could see her rib bones as she breathed in and out. She needed to eat more. Needed to look after herself. Undoubtedly, it was the strain she had been under in the last few months.

Reality returned, intruding upon their false idyll.

It settled into his stomach like a cold, dark weight. The threat against her remained, just as real and terrifying as ever. There were men who wanted to spill her blood. Faceless, nameless enemies who would slay her in the same coldhearted fashion they had assassinated the duke.

This was no dream after all.

"Why do you frown?" she asked softly, her fingers brushing over his furrowed brow.

He did not want to speak of the ugliness surrounding them, did not want to bring the darkness into their light. At least not for this moment. Not while he could keep it at bay. And so, he caught her fingers in his, brought them to his lips for a kiss. "I do not want to make you the cause of speculation or gossip. The servants will soon be about."

She was silent for a beat. "Yes, of course. You are right. I must go. I daresay I have already tarried far too long as it is."

She rolled away from him in one swift motion, rising from his bed. His eyes devoured her—the copper curls that hung past her arse, the petite legs, the trim ankles. All that mouthwatering expanse of creamy skin. Tarts, he decided. Cakes and tarts were what she needed. Some indulgence.

Did he detect a stiffening in her posture? She paced the chamber, looking for something. For her nightrail, he would guess. It was currently crumpled and wadded beneath his pillow. He retrieved it and rose from the bed as well, going to her, staying her with a gentle hand.

"Ara."

She stopped. Looked over her shoulder, worrying the delectable fullness of her lower lip. "It is as you said. I need to go. Why do you delay me?"

Ever stubborn. "Ara, look at me," he demanded softly.

She did at last, her expression guarded.

"You are all I care about," he explained. "Your reputation. Your safety. Your happiness. *You*, Ara. I never stopped caring about you, not in all these years."

She bit her lip again before answering, so quietly he could scarcely hear the words. "I never stopped caring about you either, Clay."

She threw her nightrail over her head, and without bothering to free her bold locks from the constraint of the fabric, she turned and fled to the door joining their chambers. All he could do was watch her go, knowing she took his heart with her.

Chapter Twenty

WHAT HAD SHE expected?

A proposal?

A declaration of love?

He had not offered tender words of undying devotion. Instead, he had offered nothing. No hope. Oh, he said he cared about her, that he had not stopped. But one cared about whether or not it may rain on a Tuesday when one was invited to a garden party that day. One cared about whether or not a pair of boots caused blisters. One cared about too much pepper in a dish and not enough salt.

Foolish, foolish Ara. You are older, wiser. You are not the naïve young girl who fell in love with him. What did you think you would accomplish by falling into his bed? And even if he does care for you, you are in mourning. You cannot marry now even if you would wish it.

Ara poked at her breakfast as if it were her enemy. She did not want to eat. Did not think she could possibly stomach a bite.

Her world was in disintegration.

She had risen from Clay's bed that morning, alive with the realization that her entire life—and the ruin it now was—had been orchestrated by her father and mother. Embittered by the knowledge she had allowed herself to be so easily manipulated.

Dear God, she could not stop thinking about her father hiring some cutthroat to beat Clay and carve open his face. Could not stop thinking about the deliberate betrayal that had prompted either her mother or her father to read her journal without her permission and then use what they had read to keep her and Clay apart. To hurt them. A choked sound tore from her before she could contain it as she recalled Clay's recollection of that day, the violence done him.

"Your Grace?"

Ara glanced up from the eggs she had been so liberally stabbing to find Clay's mother watching her with a smile affixed to her lips. Looking as if she had asked Ara a question.

"Are you well, Your Grace?" his mother queried, polite concern underlying her mellifluous voice.

"Forgive me," she said hastily. "I was… I am… Since the incident in London, I have not been myself. I fear I swallowed my eggs wrong."

Lily raised a dark brow, looking very much like her son with her impenetrable countenance. "Oh? How odd. I do not believe you have taken a bite to eat, Duchess."

Ara's face heated as she realized Clay's mother had been observing her far too closely during the course of their quiet breakfast. She wondered if her guilt showed in her expression. If Lily had any inkling what had occurred the evening before.

And that morning.

Her cheeks burned hotter still.

"My appetite has not been as rigorous as it ought to be given the tumult of the last few weeks," she forced herself to say, donning a polite smile.

Lily studied her solemnly. "My dear, you must look after yourself, for the sake of that darling boy if no one else."

Her heart warmed to think of her son, who had been soundly sleeping when she had checked on him before descending to breakfast. Clay's cat had been curled up alongside Edward, and the picture the two of them presented had brought a rush of maudlin maternal tears to her eyes. She rather had a feeling the feline was no longer Clay's at all.

"For these last few months, I have been all Edward has left," she acknowledged before keeping herself from revealing more. Already, she had said too much, and she was not prepared to confess all to Lily. She did not yet know how the other woman would take the news, and Ara did not think herself capable of handling any more conflict and unrest.

Not now.

Not after everything she had been through.

She was still partially in shock from it all: the grief, danger, revelations, and change. She scarcely recognized her reflection in the glass. Somehow, she had not realized she had lost weight, but she could feel it now, in the way her dresses hung on her slight frame. In the way her corset could lace without any slack.

"But now you are here," Lily intervened in that lovely, lilting voice of hers, her tone infinitely kind. "The two of you are not alone any longer, Your Grace."

For now, Ara wanted to say, because Clay had not made her a single promise. She considered his mother, resplendent this morning in a bright emerald gown that set off her dark hair and eyes. She was lovely, and Ara could readily see how the Duke of Carlisle would have fallen in love with her. She had been nothing but welcoming, giving, and warm. Like the flamboyant dresses she wore, she possessed a signature brightness and warmth that drew others to her.

She wondered if Lily suspected Edward was Clay's son. She had no notion of how close he was to his mother. But she could not quite suppress the suspicion that the woman offering her a compassionate smile across the breakfast table knew more than she alluded to. Perhaps it was a mother's instinct.

Ara swallowed past the sudden lump in her throat at the elder woman's empathy. "We are grateful indeed for your hospitality, Lily. I no longer felt safe at Burghly House after…the incident. Being here at Harlton Hall is a refreshing change of pace from the city."

As she said the words, she realized just how deeply she meant them. Despite her inner turmoil over Clay and what the revelations of their past meant for them moving forward, she was calmer here. Her shoulders did not feel quite so tensed. She breathed easier. Harlton Hall felt like a home. It was filled with Lily's warmth and innate sense of style—each chamber decorated sumptuously without being overbearing—and the park was verdant and vibrant, and so very alive.

She felt as if she could belong here.

As if it could be *her* home.

But that was rather silly of her, wasn't it? To develop a fondness for a collection of stones and wooden beams after a mere day? Especially when she did not know where she stood with Clay.

"This is not my home, Duchess," his mother said, her smile turning wistful. "It is my son's. Of course, he has not yet *made* it his home, but there is ample time yet for that. I do keep hoping that one day he will marry and provide me with a gentle and tenderhearted wife so that I may at last have a daughter as well. A grandson in Clay's image would be a gift in equal measure."

Dear God.

Clay's mother *knew.* There was no question of it. She knew she ought not to be surprised, for she herself had seen the undeniable similarities between Clay and Edward. Her son was his father's mirror, in miniature. But somehow, the knowledge that the generous, wonderful woman before her knew the truth of her sins took Ara's breath.

She did not know what to say. Panic scrambled up her throat, for she was not ready for this. The assault she had almost faced had left her badly shaken, and her mind and body did not wish to absorb one more trauma.

Fortunately, Lily spared her the decision.

She directed another sincere smile Ara's way. "Of course, a grandchild in Leo's image would be equally as welcome. But Carlisle is decidedly different from Clay. He assures me he is in no position to settle down with a wife, regardless of how happy it would make me."

Though Ara knew she should not be surprised, she was nevertheless taken aback by Lily referring to the Duke of Carlisle as her son. It was a unique situation, the topic a delicate one.

"Of course," she said mildly, attempting to hide her discomfit by shoveling a forkful of eggs into her mouth and chewing. The dish had long since gone cold. *Oeufs cocotte* had never appealed to her. Less now that they had been too long untouched upon her plate. She stifled her moue of disgust and reluctantly lifted another bite of cold eggs to her lips.

"Our family is unconventional, I know," Clay's mother said then, seeming to read Ara's thoughts yet again. She gave Ara a sad smile. "Pray forgive me if I make you uncomfortable but I do so wish Reggie could have met you, Duchess, and your son as well."

Ara supposed that Reggie was Clay's father, the former Duke of Carlisle. Edward's grandfather. "We would have been pleased to know him, I am sure," she said softly. For a brief moment, she considered confessing all to Lily.

But she thought better of it and forced another bite of cold eggs into her mouth instead.

IN THE BRIGHT morning light outside Harlton Hall, Clay feinted left, then struck Farleigh with a clean blow to the jaw.

Farleigh's head snapped back, but he surprised Clay by recovering with speed and precision, delivering a blow of his own to Clay's chin that rather stung. *Damn it all to hell*, either the man was getting better at sparring, or Clay was getting worse.

"You seem distracted today," Farleigh taunted then, as if sensing the vein of Clay's thoughts.

Distracted.

Hell yes, he was distracted.

"Distracted men are dead men," he said neatly, sidestepping Farleigh's next blow and landing another of his own.

Farleigh grunted. "Truer words were never spoken, sir."

Clay swung again, but his opponent performed a neat block. Trying to oust Ara from his mind was futile. She was a part of him, like his scar, like his heart and lungs and blood. There would be no excising her now, if indeed he had ever been capable of such a thing.

No, he realized as he pivoted on his right foot and avoided another swing from Farleigh.

He had never been capable of cutting Ara from his thoughts or his heart. Even in her eight-year absence from his life, she had still been there. She had been the reason he had never found another who could own his heart. She had been the reason he had roamed. The reason he had accepted mission after mission, putting himself at risk, not having a care for whether he lived or died. She had been the reason he had never loved anyone else. The reason he had never wanted a wife or children of his own.

Because any wife he would have chosen would not have

been *her*.

And any child he sired would not have been *hers*.

Because she had been the other half of him, always. And she still was now. Would be, forever.

She had been gone, and yet she had been the driving force. The reason behind his every decision.

A blinding pain tore through him as Farleigh's fist connected with his eye socket.

"Sodding hell." The epithet was torn from him. It was the second time he had allowed thoughts of Ara to distract him so thoroughly that Farleigh was able to sneak past his defenses and land a solid fist to his face.

"I beg your pardon, sir." Farleigh sounded genuinely contrite. "I expected you to move."

Damn it. He could not continue to go about being defeated by the men he led. It was a hell of a blow for morale for one thing and an even bigger blow to his already wounded pride for another. Here he stood, mooning over Ara so pathetically that Farleigh had planted him a facer.

His eye smarted, and he was certain it would change color on the morrow. Precisely what he needed when he was attempting to woo Ara. At least, that was what he intended to do. She had been far too eager to leave his chamber this morning, and he had been haunted by questions from the moment he had watched her hips swaying back over the threshold between their chambers just before she'd slammed the door.

"Sir?" Farleigh persisted, dragging Clay's attention back to him and away from Ara, where it wanted to stray.

And linger.

"Aye?" He rubbed his eye, shooting his man a wry grin.

"I did not expect you to sustain the blow."

That made two of them.

He had thought he was impervious to the forceful yet relatively unskilled fisticuffs of Farleigh. Then again, he had also fancied himself impervious to the Duchess of Burghly. The mother of his son. The only woman he had ever loved.

Ara.

It did not matter what he called her or how he thought of her, she was his every distraction. She was the reason… She was everything he wanted, everything he needed.

"Sir?"

He was mooning again, rubbing his throbbing eye socket and thinking of her. This simply would not do.

"Clayton?"

His mother's voice hit him then, soft and familiar and deceptively sweet.

Sodding, bloody hell.

"Do not concern yourself, Farleigh," he managed hastily. "Perhaps you have at long last managed to retain something I have taught you."

Farleigh grinned. "Or perhaps you are distracted just as I thought."

"Perhaps you would like me to feed you your teeth?" Clay gritted in a deceptively pleasant tone. The man was trusted and formidable, but by God, he was wearing on Clay's patience something fierce.

"Clayton Ludlow," his mother admonished, reaching his side in a blaze of swirling green skirts.

His mother certainly did have an affinity for bright colors. And intruding when she was least wanted. Not to mention being far too perceptive. She had been attempting to get him alone ever since his arrival at Harlton Hall, and he had been doing his damnedest to avoid it. She knew too much. Saw too much. And he had no wish to be dissected by her today.

Or any other day for that matter.

"You may return to your post, Farleigh," he ordered his man before his mother made a complete fool out of him before his subordinate.

Farleigh wisely bowed out of the tête-à-tête, stalking away across the expanse of early spring lawn and leaving Clay alone to face his mother. He loved his mother. But he could not help but feel this interview would require some answers he was not entirely prepared to give. Some answers he was not prepared to face himself. For how was he to know where he stood with Ara?

His mother waited just until Farleigh was beyond earshot.

"When were you going to tell me I have a grandson?" she asked.

He clenched his jaw, wondering if Leo had been in her ear or if Edward's paternity was so bloody apparent to everyone who looked upon the lad except for Clay. "Has my brother been writing to you?"

His mother shook her head with a slow, tender smile. "Leo has not written in at least a week, and I shall take him to task for it at the first possible opportunity."

Her words caught him off guard. "He writes you regularly, then?"

"Oh yes." Her smile changed, her voice tinged with undisguised fondness. "And visits whenever he can, unlike another son of mine."

His ears went hot. *Damn it,* since when did the heartless Duke of Carlisle send letters and visit Mother? As they had grown to manhood together, he had been keenly aware that his mother—who possessed the heart and tolerance of an angel—treated Leo as if he were her own son. She considered him her son. Leo's mother the duchess was a cold and uncaring sort of female, the kind who considered her child an inconvenience rather than an extension of herself to be cherished and loved. She had borne him for the sake of her marital duty.

But still, he had not realized Leo and Mother remained in such close contact.

"I would visit if he did not forever have me assigned to his missions," he griped without heat, rubbing a hand over his scarred cheek.

"He could not have assigned you to a better mission than this one," his mother said softly, touching his shirtsleeve, for he had stripped off his coat and his waistcoat.

He stiffened, not ready to examine his feelings for Ara any more than he was eager to recall that the danger facing her had not been vanquished. Word had come from London just that morning of a failed Fenian bomb attack on the Mansion House, the home of the Lord Mayor of the city. This hell was far from over, if indeed it would ever completely be eradicated.

"This is the last mission I would have ever hoped to serve." The hoarse admission was torn from him. He scrubbed a hand over his face, wishing for clarity. Wishing for answers and reassurance where none could be had.

"You still love her, don't you?"

It had begun the moment he had first seen her again in the drawing room of Burghly House, and last night, it had culminated in a crashing crescendo.

His Ara.

The feisty flame-haired sylph with the blue-violet eyes and the full pink lips he could never kiss enough. The first woman who had ever looked upon him and seen him as a man, nothing less. The only woman who had ever owned his heart. It had always been hers. Would forever be in her keeping.

Lies and betrayals had taken them from each other.

But the time had come to grasp what was theirs.

He swallowed and met his mother's knowing gaze. "Aye."

"My darling son." His mother's expression turned anguished. She had ever worn her heart on her sleeve. Neither the years nor the loss of his father had changed her. "Perhaps you ought to move past those old hurts. She loves you too. It's plain as day on her countenance. More to the point, I do not believe she had anything to do with her father's actions. When I spoke to her yesterday at dinner, she revealed she has not spoken with her father in years. She appeared to have no inkling what had happened to you."

He sighed heavily, feeling every one of his one-and-thirty years. "She did not. We…had a discussion yesterday, and we both made some realizations that were rather damning. Her parents acted on their own to prevent her from marrying me. She came to meet me that day as we had planned, but I was already gone. She waited for hours."

Bloody hell, the notion of Ara waiting for him, spending hours alone, thinking he had jilted her—that he cared so little for her he had not even bothered to appear—still made him long to tear her father limb from limb. The man had cost them eight years.

"Oh, Clayton." His mother pressed a hand over her mouth. "From the moment I met her, I knew she could not have been capable of such a thing. She is a tenderhearted woman, and she is a good mother to your son."

Your son.

The words still rattled him.

But they felt right. They felt good.

He nodded, and the warmth of the sun—unprecedented after so much spring chill and fog and damp—left him feeling flushed. Or mayhap that was merely thoughts of Ara.

"She is that," he agreed, pausing, striving to find his words. Ordinarily, he was not a man given to sentiment, but this was different. This was Ara and their son, and everything he had ever wanted within his grasp. It rocked him to the core. "Damn it, Mother, I do not know what the hell to do about her."

His mother's lips pursed and she treated him to a raised brow and the stern expression he recalled from his wayward youth. "First, you need to curtail that language of yours. You ought to be ashamed, Clayton. Second, marry her."

The proclamation did not alarm him. Rather, it imbued him with a vast, swelling tide of hope. But he didn't wish to unburden his every intention to his mother. Not yet. "She is newly widowed, mother."

"Months have passed, have they not?"

For all that his mother detested profanity, she remained a rebel in other ways.

Four months had gone by since Burghly's murder. He had counted more than once, and it had never increased on any occasion.

"Not enough. Moreover, we scarcely know each other. The lad does not even know I am his father yet."

"Have you told the Duchess how you feel?" his mother asked next, knowing him all too well.

"No," he bit out. For he scarcely knew how he felt himself. Indeed, he had spent the better part of the morning engaged in bouts of fisticuffs so that he could distract himself from all such thoughts.

"Do you not think you ought to, Clayton?" His mother bestowed an arch look upon him, the sort that could only come from a mother who always thought she knew better than her offspring. He knew it well.

"No," he denied, feeling stubborn as he crossed his arms over his chest. "I do not. I do, however, think you ought to muddle in Leo's life a bit. He requires a mother's guidance far more than I do."

"Fear not." His mother winked. "When the time comes for your brother, I shall guide him in every way possible. Until then, I have a grandson I dearly wish to know and a future daughter who must be wooed. Kisses would be quite estimable, I think. But nothing more, Clayton. Do be on your best behavior. I shall be watching—do not think I won't. Take her for a drive. Bring her flowers. Sing to her. Your voice is so deep and lovely, and I just know she will love to hear it. Too much time has been taken from you already, and you must do this right."

He sighed. Mother had always possessed a flair for the dramatic, God love her. "This is not a love sonnet, Mother. I do not have the liberty to court her. She is only here at Harlton Hall because she is in danger, and though I may harbor feelings for her, she does not necessarily feel the same."

There was no question that she wanted him. Their bodies had found their old rhythm with ease, sparking up a blazing inferno from a small flame. But beyond the base need between them and a handful of allusions to tender sentiments, she had given him nothing to suggest his courtship of her would be welcome.

And he was…

Well, bloody hell.

He had spent so many years fearing no one and nothing—thanks to his immense size and his intensive training with the League—but he found himself terrified. Afraid to offer her his bruised and battered heart, his scarred face, his simple last name, the tumbledown estate he was rebuilding much as he had rebuilt his life. Afraid she did not love him in return. That she had merely been overcome by a rush of old feelings that had never quite dissipated.

That she would tell him *no.*

His mother gave him a searching look. “She cannot deny you if you do not ask her. But neither can she say yes.”

Why did his mother seem to possess the capacity to read his mind? He grunted, aware he was being a beast, but too overwhelmed to continue the conversation any further. “If you have finished admonishing me and ordering me to court the Duchess of Burghly, I will take my leave. I must see to my men.”

Without bothering to wait for her reply, he turned to flee. *Bloody hell*, he was a man fully grown, and he was retreating from his own mother. It was a hell of a day.

“Clayton,” she called after him in her most authoritative tone.

Blast. No one called him that but his mother. He spun on his heel, facing her once more. “Yes, madam?”

She smiled. “Be happy. You deserve it. The three of you are a family, and you belong together. Don’t tarry. Life is too short, too precarious. Far too precious.”

Damn it, those words hit him, poking beneath his armor to find the most vulnerable parts of him. Because she was right. Every bit of it. But he didn’t know what to do next or how to find his happiness after so many years living without it. All he knew was that he wanted Ara as his wife. He wanted the life together they had been denied.

He nodded jerkily and offered her a half bow, all he could manage. “That it is, Mother. Life is entirely too abbreviated. I can only assure you that I will do as I must, when I must. I will be a part of the lad’s life going forward. I will have him know I am his father when the time is right. As for the lad’s mother, that remains to be seen. Good day, Mother, I really must attend to my men now.”

“Of course, my son. One more thing: be brave.”

Chapter Twenty-One

ARA STALKED THROUGH Harlton Hall, determined to find Clay. Already, she had checked the fledgling library—not yet brimming with books but an excellent beginning. She had examined his study, which looked as if it had never even been entered by him. She had searched in antechambers and the main saloon and everywhere she could fathom he might be hiding.

She could only reach one conclusion.

It was possible—likely, in fact—that he was avoiding her. She had spent the afternoon with Edward and Clay's cat Sherman since Edward's new governess, Miss Palliser, had yet to arrive from London. In the uproar before their abrupt departure from Burghly House, Ara had discovered Miss Argent kept a bottle of gin in her apartments, and that the woman had been sleeping during each of Edward's romps from the schoolroom, suffering the ill-effects of imbibing too much the night before. She had dismissed Miss Argent immediately, but there had not been time for the woman's replacement to accompany them on the journey to Oxfordshire.

The afternoon alone with her son had been a much-needed reminder that life could be normal for them. That it would once again return to normal for them one day, God willing. It had also proven to her that the time for telling

Edward the truth was long overdue.

He needed to know Clay was his father.

When she had exhausted every last corner of Harlton Hall in search of Clay, she found herself outside. Alone. The sun was bright and high in the sky. The air was so quiet, sweetly perfumed with freshly budding fauna, and altogether distinct from London's familiar busy sounds and lack of fresh air. Being outside was invigorating. She stretched her arms wide, threw her head back, and tilted her face to receive the sun.

And then she realized she was not alone at all.

Two of Clay's men stood sentinel nearby.

Her brief moment of freedom was effectively dashed. But perhaps she could locate her quarry at last. She straightened into a semblance of what a proper duchess ought to look like, dropping her arms to her sides and otherwise composing herself.

"Excuse me, sirs," she addressed them. "Where might I find Mr. Ludlow? I have an urgent matter I must discuss with him."

Two pairs of eyes shot to her. A dark-haired man with a build similar to Clay's—though not as large—spoke first. "He is in the copse of trees on the eastern side of the manor house, Your Grace."

Ah, Clay was in the trees.

How fitting.

How utterly perfect.

It was where they had first met, after all, beneath the leafy boughs a lifetime ago.

She cleared her throat. "I shall go and search for him there. Thank you, kind sirs."

"I'm afraid we can't allow that, Your Grace," one of the men said hesitantly.

She raised a brow, giving him her most frigid expression,

daring him to deny her free will. "Oh?"

The man swallowed. "Well, perhaps we can as long as you remain within eyesight."

"Just so," she agreed, flicking her skirts and descending the front steps. "I will be safe with Mr. Ludlow. You need not fear on my account."

At least, that was what she hoped.

But her legs were already moving, carrying her to Clay, her heart thumping with the knowledge she was about to lay her heart bare at his feet. And pray he didn't crush it beneath his heel. The walk from the steps of Harlton Hall, across the gravel drive and a well-manicured swath of lawn, felt as if it were endless. Until she reached the forest and found him standing there, a tall, hulking, beloved figure, and it felt as if the journey to his side had taken no time at all.

He saw her at once, just as he had so long ago, his keen senses alert. He wore no hat and neither coat nor waistcoat, the ends of his longer-than-fashionable hair brushing his shoulders. In the cool shade of the forest, his white shirt was like a beacon stretched over his broad chest. He looked fierce and uncontainable.

As wild and necessary as the vegetation serving as his backdrop.

"Ara."

He opened his arms to her, and she caught her skirts in both her hands, running until she reached him and threw herself into his chest. His embrace was sudden and strong, keeping her pressed tight to him. He kissed the top of her head, for she was not wearing a hat either. The warmth of his mouth infused her with a fresh throb of longing. She was glad she had wandered to him. And she did not care if his men could see her embracing him. All she cared about was being in his arms.

He felt like home. His scent filled her—leather, musk, soap, and man. She wrapped her arms around his lean waist, holding him for a moment, savoring the freedom to touch him as she wanted. Savoring him. Savoring life and the possibility for the future.

Mayhap, just mayhap if she dared.

She *needed* to dare.

"What are you doing out here, Clay?" she asked. "I've been looking for you everywhere."

"Taking the air. Walking. Thinking. What are *you* doing out here, my dear?" he asked, the sweet, low rumble of his voice sending a shiver through her. "You ought not to be wandering about, unescorted." His arms tightened even more over her. "I will have Farleigh's hide for allowing you to flit away from Harlton Hall without accompaniment."

"You will have no one's hide." She took another surreptitious inhalation of his shirt and sighed. "I browbeat your men into allowing it, and they knew I was coming to find you."

"You browbeat them?" He chuckled, the velvety timbre sending a spark of pure desire shooting through her. "Darling, you are smaller than a dunnock. They are trained and armed. They are not meant to be browbeaten by you. They are meant to hold firm."

"Nevertheless, here I am," she said, feeling quite pleased with herself. Clay had called her *darling*, and she liked it far too well. Wrapped in his hold, his warmth burning into her, his scent filling her senses, and the quiet cover of the trees around them, it seemed almost as if they had stepped back in time. Here, she could forget—if even for only a short while—all the ugliness in her life. "I had them quivering in fear."

"Of course you did." He pressed another kiss to the top of her head, his hot breath fanning over her part like a benediction. "You have me quivering in fear as well."

She swallowed, her smile deepening as hope sparked deep within her. "What if I told you I felt the same?"

He inhaled, his chest expanding beneath her cheek. "I would say it is only fair that you must be tortured as well."

Ara closed her eyes, reveling in this quiet moment, in the unfettered tenderness. Perhaps he had been avoiding her all day. Perhaps he was as shaken by their newfound circumstances and the revelations between them as she was. But everything about this felt as right as drawing her next breath.

"I do not know where we are," she confessed softly.

"We are here, standing beneath the trees together." A smile permeated his voice.

His gentle teasing put her at ease. "Yes. You have a beautiful estate, Clay."

"I bought it because of the forest." His voice was a low rasp. She almost had to strain to hear him. "And then I could not come here for the same reason. The forest was you, Ara. It still is, but now you are here, and you are in my arms where you belong. You are here at Harlton Hall."

Yes. Precisely where she belonged. She wanted to say it. Wanted to ask him. But even as close as she felt to him in that moment—physically as well as emotionally—she was uncertain of herself. This was all so new to her. He was new to her. Old and beloved yet new and different. Clayton Ludlow had changed in the eight years since she had known him. He had lived life, fought battles, traveled. Perhaps he had fallen in love. So much of the time denied her was a mystery, just as she must be a mystery to him.

"Thank you for welcoming me into your home," she forced herself to say then before shifting to a different subject—the reason she had sought him out in the first place. "I had dinner last night with your mother and breakfast with her again this morning."

"I am aware."

When he said nothing else, she continued, the question that had been nettling her ever since breakfast returning. Needing to be answered. "Does she know, Clay?"

He was silent for some time, the only sound between them his steady inhale and exhale, almost as if he were asleep. "Elaborate, if you please," he said at last.

Ara sighed, her arms tightening around him, wishing she could stay thus forever, connected to him. That they could never again be torn apart. "About us…our past?"

He took his time answering once again, leaving her waiting, staring into the sunlight-dappled forest with nothing but the thrum of his heart for comfort. "She knows I wished to court you all those years ago. That I was denied. She knows what happened that day and why."

"Does she know about Edward, Clay?" she asked. His mother had seemed to know far too much, but she could not be certain whether it was her guilty mind at work or Lily Ludlow truly did know all.

"She has surmised." His voice was decadent and low, a delicious rumble. "I could not deny it. The lad is my image, and my mother and brother both took note. You need not fear, however. She is aware that Edward does not know I am his father, and that we are waiting until the timing is right."

The timing would never be right for her to reveal to her son that she had lied to him for his entire life. That Freddie had not been his father by blood, but that he had been his father by choice and deed.

The thought of revealing everything to her son continued to fill her chest with a gripping, tight anxiety. But her earlier realization stayed true and firm, unwavering as ever. As did her determination to begin the process of undoing all the wrongs her family had perpetrated upon herself, Clay, and

Edward.

To make everything right.

She took another deep, steadying breath. "The timing is…it will never be… We should tell Edward now, Clay. I want him to know you are his father. You and your mother…you are Edward's family. He needs that now more than ever. He needs you both."

"Are you certain, Ara?" His voice was conflicted. "I would like nothing better, but I do not want to frighten the lad, or upset him in any way."

Of course she was not certain. She had kept her son's true father from him for his entire life. Edward would be angry. Confused. Upset. But the time had come for the truth. She may have been a young lady with no options when she had married Freddie, pregnant with another man's child, but much had changed since then.

She nodded slowly. Tears pricked her eyes and she blinked them away. Something about this felt so very right. Frightening, but *right*. "Yes. Edward deserves the truth."

"Aye." Clay's voice was thick. He swallowed. His heart drummed. *Thump, thump, thump* against her ear.

"Before we tell him, however, I will have your promise," she said, knowing she had to protect her son as best she could. Clay had left her once. Had disappeared from her life for eight years. She understood the reasons. He had been beaten, disfigured, and left to believe she had betrayed and abandoned him. But he was also not the same man now as he was then. She had only known him for weeks after eight years of separation. There remained so much of him that was a mystery, so much of him that was a stranger.

She was still a mother, above all. She had to put her son first. He depended upon her. He needed her. And he had already been denied so much.

Accordingly, she had to be certain he was willing to remain in her and Edward's lives now, despite the dangerous missions he undertook. In spite of everything. "Promise me you will not disappear from his life, and that you will stay a permanent part, just as he needs you to be. I do not think he can bear to lose you."

And neither could she, but she kept that bit to herself. Silence was better. Sometimes, silence was necessary. It kept her from saying too much. From revealing all the humiliating, dark recesses of her heart.

"You need not ask it of me. I give my promise freely. I could not ask for more than to be a part of Edward's life. He is my son." Pride rang in his voice. "You have raised a good lad, Ara. You can be proud of him. *I* am proud of him."

She smiled again. "Yes, he is a very good lad. Let's go tell him now, Clay. Together."

He tensed beneath her touch. "You're certain, Ara?"

"Certain," she echoed.

He set her from him, and then his mouth came down on hers, firm and hard. The kiss was swift, ruthless, and beautiful in a way that took her breath. It claimed. It promised.

It healed.

Their lips parted. She met his gaze, nose to nose, she on her tiptoes, her hands roaming the rigid planes of his back. She had never been more certain of anything in her life. And though she had no notion of how Edward would react to the news, the time had come. The truth needed to be told at long last.

"Thank you," he whispered against her mouth. "Ara mine."

She kissed the corner of his lips. "It is long overdue."

Hand in hand, their fingers intertwined, they made their way from the protective shade of the forest and into the dazzling sun.

CLAY STOOD IN the library alongside Ara, facing her son.

His son.

Their son.

How surreal to think the lad was his own, and that at long last he would know the truth. Within seconds. Mayhap minutes. Clay was sweating. His scar itched. He had never been so nervous in all his life.

And then, Ara slipped her hand back into his. Her fingers delivered a tentative squeeze. He swallowed, squeezing back, grateful for her. Grateful she had been strong enough to keep their son when he had been absent from her life. Whether or not it was of his own volition no longer mattered. He could not change it, but he could appreciate the fight Ara must have waged, unmarried and with child, doing her utmost for Edward.

The lad eyed their laced fingers, his brow furrowing. He was an observant little chap. Damn, but he reminded Clay of himself.

"Mama, why are you holding Mr. Ludlow's hand?"

"Because I…" Ara turned to Clay, her expression seeking.

Bloody hell, he did not know what to say either. What to do.

He improvised.

"Because we care about each other." Lord knew he was more in love with the maddening woman than he had ever been before. "And because we have something we wish to tell you."

"You are going to marry each other," the lad guessed, his expression solemn.

Ara jerked her gaze back to their son, wetting her lips. "Not precisely, Edward."

"Yes," Clay gainsaid her without a dash of compunction. "We are."

A gasp flew from her throat as her eyes snapped to Clay once more. "We are?"

The decision had come to him without thought, without hesitation. The words simply fled him. He didn't regret them. Ara had always been meant to be his wife. She was the other half of him, and he knew it with a certainty that was elemental, as natural as his knowledge that the sun would rise each morning. No one would ever complete him as she did.

"If you will have me," he said softly.

Emotion shimmered in her eyes. "Oh, Clay. Of course I will."

He pulled her into his arms for another embrace, burying his face in her silken hair. Gratitude washed over him. He was so damn thankful for her, to have found her again, to have found their son. He'd never known such joy, and he was terrified and elated all at once. He kissed her cheek. "Thank God, Ara mine."

Suddenly aware of their audience and the real reason they stood in the library—not his impromptu proposal at all, but rather to tell their son the truth—he stepped back, putting a respectable distance between himself and Ara. Half of him was bloody tempted to haul her back into his arms and kiss her silly, even with the lad looking on.

She wanted to be his wife.

Just as she should have been eight years and a hell of a lot of scars ago.

Clay sank to his haunches before Edward, looking his son in the eye. "I know this will be more change for you, lad. You have endured a great deal in the last few months, and your mama and I do not wish to upset you, but there is something else we must tell you as well."

Edward regarded him seriously. "Do you want your cat back now?"

A reluctant laugh tore from him. "No, lad. You and Sherman have bonded, and it is plain the feline prefers you to me."

His son gave him a shy smile. "Thank you, sir. When you marry Mama, will you be my father?"

Emotion swelled inside him, constricting his throat. He glanced back at Ara for assistance. Every carefully planned word he'd prepared had vanished from his mind.

She placed a soothing hand on his shoulder, granting him her support. "Yes, Mr. Ludlow will be your father, Edward. But not just because I am marrying him. Mr. Ludlow *is* your father."

Edward's brows furrowed as his mind absorbed Ara's words. "I do not understand, Mama. Papa was my father, and he is gone."

Clay found his voice at last. "Before your mama married the duke, she and I were in love. We were going to wed, but then...circumstances would not allow it. The duke graciously stepped in when I could not. He will always be a father to you. Nothing will change the love he had for you or the love you have in your heart for him. But I am your father, lad."

"Mama?" Edward looked to Ara, shock on his small, pale countenance. "Why did you never tell me?"

Ara sank to her knees on the thick carpet of the library, her jet silk skirts pooling around her. "I was not able to tell you. I am so sorry, Edward. I acted in my best capacity as your mother to provide for you and keep you safe. I did what I had to do, but now the time has come for you to know the truth."

"Then I am not the Duke of Burghly," Edward said slowly. "I am Edward Ludlow."

"You are both of those titles," Ara said, gripping the lad's thin shoulders. "There is no surviving male heir but you. Freddie wanted you to be the next Duke of Burghly, to keep the line going. He made every provision for you accordingly. You must honor his wishes, though you now know the truth."

Clay gritted his teeth against the notion of the lad never taking his surname, but he knew that perpetuating the lie was necessary to avoid ruin and scandal for both Ara and Edward. Since Burghly did not have a rightful heir, no one was being harmed by it. Only his pride suffered. But there was also a certain, delicious irony to the notion that the son of a duke's bastard would be a duke himself. One day, Edward would lead the life Clay had always wished could have been his.

And he was grateful for that. Grateful his son would never know the scorn that had dogged him his entire life. Humbled that the Duke of Burghly had been a kind and loving father to his son when he had not been able. All the anger and jealousy seething inside him dissipated, vanquished by happiness and love and a great, abiding sense of peace.

The past was over.

The time to move forward had come, and he was walking into it, headlong and openhearted.

"I am sorry, lad," he said, his throat still thick with more pent-up emotions than he knew he possessed. "I know this must be a shock to you."

"Did you not want me as your son?" Edward asked, hurt and confusion lacing his voice.

"I have never wanted anything more," he assured him. "I am honored to have you as my son. I did not know about you. If I had, nothing would have stopped me from coming back to you and your mama both."

"It is a long and difficult story, what happened in the

past," Ara added, a frown creasing her brow as she met Clay's gaze once more. They had decided there was no need to reveal the full extent of the ugly truth to Edward. One day, when he was old enough to understand, they might. For now, they would offer him only as much information as he needed. "What's important is that you know the truth, and you keep this truth to yourself. Tuck it into your heart, my love."

Edward nodded slowly. His eyes flitted to Clay once more. "Does this mean I can have my knife back now?"

A laugh tore from him. "No, lad. You must still heed your mama."

He was silent for another moment. "Is Mrs. Lily my grandmother? She tells stories about knights and dragons and gives me sweets. I like her."

"Aye." Clay grinned. Thank God for his mother. The woman was an angel, and he had no doubt she would help to ease the transition for the lad.

Edward cocked his head then, giving Clay a bashful half smile. "I like you too, sir. Having a warrior for a father is just as honorable as having a duke for a father."

Warmth exploded in Clay's chest. His eyes stung. His vision blurred.

He blinked.

Tears.

Tears of happiness. He ruffled the lad's dark hair, so like his own. "Thank you, son."

Chapter Twenty-Two

ARA HAD BEEN waiting for the knock on the door adjoining her chamber to Clay's for what seemed like an eternity. She had prepared herself, she thought, for the dialogue they would have. They had not been alone since she had found him in the copse of trees earlier that afternoon. The rest of the day had passed by in a frenzied blur. The new governess, Miss Palliser, had arrived, sending the house into a flurry as the small staff of domestics saw her settled. She was set to begin her new position tomorrow, and Ara had met with her accordingly, doing her best to make certain she had not hired another Miss Argent.

Miss Palliser was dark-haired and lovely, soft-spoken and pleasant, and she seemed genuinely excited to take on Edward as her charge. Only time would tell, but it was a promising start, at least. After sending Miss Palliser off to get her belongings sorted and brush off her travel dust, Ara had joined Clay, his mother, and Edward for an informal dinner. Lily was a lovely woman with a heart as big as England. Her adoration for Edward was plain, and likewise his for her. It was as if the lost time between them had never existed.

Ara had sat at the dinner table, basking in the warmth, feeling for the first time in a long time as if she were a part of a family again. *Her* family. It was not that Freddie had not loved her or that she had not loved him, but rather that their love had been platonic, and he had made his home with Sir Percy, the one he loved with all his heart. Being with Clay, watching him interact with their son, watching his mother's eyes well with tears of maternal happiness, had been humbling indeed. And gratifying as well.

But not another word had been spoken between them regarding his sudden marriage proposal. *Heavens*, if one could even refer to it as such. Rather, it had been more of an announcement than a question. She had not minded. Her heart—always his, still his, forever his—had leapt, eager to agree. Sitting alone in the silence of her chamber, however, brushing out her curls before the long, beveled glass, gave her time to fret.

She fervently hoped he had not changed his mind.

What if he does not wish to marry you after all, an unwanted voice inside her asked. Then her mind started churning, doubts and more questions brewing. What if he spoke out of the abundance of emotion coursing through him in that moment? What if he had simply gotten carried away?

What would she do if he—

Knock, knock, knock.

There he was, one piece of wood and a dozen steps separating them, and though she had been expecting him, anticipation skittered through her all the same. For a beat, she felt as if she were the same girl she'd been eight years before, stealing away from Kingswood Hall beneath the cover of darkness and running to him. Tonight was different, however. She was older. Wiser, she hoped. More in love with him than ever. She had not stopped loving him. He had always been a part of her, and she had carried him in her heart all this time.

She stood, shaking out her dressing gown, flipping back her long hair, surveying herself in the mirror for a moment longer than necessary. She had never been a vain woman.

Indeed, she did not think she had even noticed her appearance in some time. But tonight, she wanted to look as well as she could.

For Clay.

Knock. Knock.

The raps on the door were a bit louder this time, suggesting he was growing impatient. She tightened the sash belting her waist for good measure. One last look in the glass—pale face, wide eyes, bright-red hair she had always loathed, a smattering of freckles on her nose she could never successfully cover with pearl powder, lips that were too large—and she sighed, willing her heart to calm itself.

"Enter," she called, attempting to strike a nonchalant pose.

Dear Lord, what if he realized she had been assessing her reflection? How embarrassing. How silly of her. Nine-and-twenty years old, vicious assassins threatening her life, her entire world in shambles, and here she was, worrying about if her robe accentuated her waist enough, counting the spots she had always reviled. *You are a ninny, Ara. A complete and utter fool.*

But then the door opened, and Clay strode through it, and she forgot to think. Forgot to breathe. Forgot everything and simply drank him in. He wore a dressing gown as well, fashioned of navy silk, and it hugged his powerful body in a way that made her mouth go dry.

His chest was exquisite. *He* was exquisite. Flawless. He was not the same young man she'd fallen in love with, but this man was so much more. The scar on his cheek only accented his beauty, for it told the story of who he was. It showed his resilience and determination. His strength and fortitude. She hated how he had received it, and she would never forgive her father for the grievous sins he had committed, but all the same, she would not trade the Clay before her now for the Clay she had first fallen in love with.

They were the same, and yet they were different. So different. Both beloved. Both hers.

He did not hesitate or waste time. His long legs ate up the distance between them until he stood before her, close enough to touch, the decadent scent of his soap wafting to her.

"Ara mine." He opened his arms.

Every part of her sighed *yes*.

Her heart.

Her body.

Her mind.

She stepped into them, into him, wrapping him in her embrace as his strong arms banded around her, anchoring her to him as well. He felt so right, so wonderful, so strong and warm and sure. Her ear was pressed to his heart again.

Thrum, thrum, thrum.

How thankful she was for that heart. For the lifeblood it sent through him. For the fact that he was here, alive, holding her. And he was hers. Words bubbled up inside her. A confession. She could not stay them or keep them within any longer.

"I love you, Clay," she said.

His arms tightened on her. "I love you, Ara mine."

Ara closed her eyes, savoring the words she had not dared to imagine she would hear again. "I never stopped loving you. Even when I thought you had betrayed me, I ached for you. I longed for you. I was so hurt, so angry you had left me behind. I had to put you out of my mind, to keep you locked away, and I focused instead on Edward. Being his mother was all that I had."

He tensed ever so slightly. "What of Burghly? You loved him, did you not? You wear your mourning brooch for him like a shield."

"Yes, I loved Freddie." She paused, hesitant to betray Freddie's secret but knowing she needed to be honest with Clay.

"It is wrong of me to be jealous of a dead man," he said lowly, his hand traveling slowly up and down her spine in a caress that was as comforting as it was maddening. "Part of me is grateful to him for being the husband and father you and Edward needed. Part of me hates him for the time I lost. For the love you gave him. It is weak and wrong of me, I know, but I wish to God I had been the man holding you and loving you these last eight years instead of him."

"The love Freddie and I shared was different, Clay," she said softly. "It was not like what you and I have."

"How so?" he asked quietly.

She would trust Clay with her life. Indeed, she had already entrusted her life to him, and he had saved her. There was not a finer, more honorable man she knew.

She stepped back in his embrace, looking up to meet his dark gaze. "Freddie was not attracted to me. He was already in love with another when I met him. I was… After you left for the Continent and my parents discovered I was with child, my father told me I must either marry in haste or leave, bear my babe in secret, and give him away. I chose to find a husband." She hesitated as old, painful emotions resurged inside her. "I went to my sister because I could not bear to marry Dorset. I would have, if I had needed to, but I was hoping to find someone more amenable. I found Freddie. He was in my sister's set, and he was looking for a wife to assist with his political ambitions. He was kind and sweet, and when he proposed, I confessed everything to him."

Clay made a low sound in his throat. "Damn it, Ara, it kills me that you had to endure that rot. I never should have left. I should have bloody well known better. I should have known you better than to think you capable of such duplicity."

"You had been attacked, and you were hurting and confused." She raised a hand to his cheek, loving the bristle of his whiskers against her open palm. "I cannot fault you for reacting as you did. I am sharing this with you to explain, Clay, not to bring judgment. Freddie and I enjoyed a friendship rather than a true marriage. He confided in me that he was in love with Sir Percy Dorwood. Freddie was a politician, and he was just rising to prominence. He could not afford for anyone to discover the true nature of his friendship with Sir Percy, or he faced not only social and political ruin but the potential for so much more ill to befall him. So, you see, he needed me as much as I needed him."

"Your marriage—it is between you and Burghly," Clay rasped, his jaw tensing. "You do not need to explain a bloody thing to me, Ara. I failed you. You needed me, and I believed the worst of you."

"You did not fail me, Clay." Her thumb traced the proud, high slash of his cheekbone. Her gaze locked on his. "We were both the victims of circumstance, misled by others and left broken and wounded. I am telling you this because I want there to be no secrets between us. I loved Freddie as a friend, as a man who was always respectful and caring and considerate, who gave me and my son everything he could. But he was not you. There is only one man for me. There has only ever been one man for me, and that man is Clayton Ludlow. And he's standing before me now, though I still feel as if I am dreaming him and he may not be real."

He pressed a worshipful kiss to her palm. "He is real, and he is all too fallible, and he is so damn sorry for the last eight years."

She kept her gaze intent upon his. "Those years made us who we are now. I regret nothing if it means having you here with me. If it means I can love you for the rest of my life. I would bear every moment we spent apart all over just to have you here in my arms now."

"My God, Ara. I do not want to spend another breath without you as my wife." He paused. "I will for your sake, of course, but if I had my way, I would marry you today. Here and now. As it is, I would never wish to be the cause of scandal. In two months, you will have been in mourning for long enough. It is still a shortened period, but do you think you might—"

"Yes!" She launched herself back into his arms, locking her arms around his neck.

"You do not even know what you are agreeing to, Duchess."

For the first time, her title felt wrong. "Do not call me that, for it is not who I am. I am Ara, your Ara, just as I have always been, and I cannot imagine an honor any greater than becoming your wife. If that is what you were asking, of course. I will marry you tomorrow. Two days from now. Whenever you can acquire a license. I am yours, Clay. I do not want to wait any longer than absolutely necessary. Freddie would understand, and I do not owe anything to anyone other than you and our son."

"Ah, Ara mine." Closing his eyes for a moment, he dipped his head and pressed his forehead to hers. "All I have wanted, for as long as I can recall, is to have you by my side, in my bed, to touch you and kiss you, to hold you and keep you safe, to be yours in every way. Of course that is what I was asking, in my brash and unsophisticated way. I fear I will never be a duke. I will never be noble. That is not who I am, but I am the man who loves you. I am the man who would die for you."

She caressed his scarred cheek, love for him blossoming so big and beautiful and true it left her transformed. "You have just described the noblest man I know. And I would be honored to be your wife. To be Mrs. Clayton Ludlow. There is nothing I want more."

His lips found hers. He kissed her with such slow, gentle tenderness she ached. A sound of need emerged from her throat. Her senses were awash with him, her heart filled with love. He told her without words how much he loved her. How much he needed her.

She opened for him, their tongues invading each other's mouths, and their kisses turned deeper. More demanding. Her hands were in his hair, traveling the broad, sculpted planes of his shoulders, claiming him everywhere she could. Desperation gradually superseded their leisurely explorations. Kissing became insufficient.

Wet heat pooled between her thighs where she throbbed for him. Every part of him was hers, and she wanted it all, and she wanted it now. His scar. His mouth. His beautiful body. His dark hair. The blade of his nose. The abrasion of his whiskers. His tongue.

The hard, long length of his cock jutting against her belly.

She couldn't resist stroking him as they kissed, fingers curling about his thick erection. An answering pang settled deep in her core. He growled into her mouth, and she tightened her grip, the soft silk of his dressing gown aiding her movements as she worked him the way she knew he liked. She had not forgotten.

But like their frantic kisses, caressing him with a barrier of fabric keeping her from his smooth, hot skin left her aching for more. She wanted to worship him as he had her, to give him mindless pleasure. To show him with her body just how completely she loved him.

Feeling bold, she released his shaft, gripping the knot of the belt on his dressing gown instead. She tipped her head back to look up at him. His eyes were dark, pupils obsidian, his expression more relaxed than she had seen it in as long as she could recall. His breathing was ragged.

Good.

"Come," she said simply, taking a step backward, in the direction of her bed. The word was not a question or an invitation so much as it was an order. She tugged him along with her, and he followed.

How she reveled in the power she had, capable of making this hulking, fierce warrior, this mountain of a man, do what she wished. His gaze never left hers as she pulled him to where she wanted him.

"Get on the bed," she said softly. Having him at her mercy gave her a new, intense sense of pleasure, heightening every tiny pulse of desire inside her into a wild flame.

"Ara," he protested, and she could not be certain if it was because he was so accustomed to being the one in command or if it was because he suspected her intentions.

She changed her mind. "Take off your robe first. I want to see you."

And she did. His body was glorious, huge, and masculine. She had seen it many times, but she could never admire him enough. He was beautiful, and she was feeling brazen. She had never felt more powerful, more desired, or more alive.

She wanted more.

She wanted Clay naked on her bed. She wanted to kiss and lick him everywhere, to taste him, to pleasure him with her mouth the same way he had done to her. She wanted everything, to make him lose himself.

"Ara." Once more, he attempted to take control of the

moment.

But she was relishing her power far too much. She was so wet, so hungry for him, that if he stroked her pearl but once, she would spend. She wanted to prolong the intensity and the desire.

"Off," she insisted, pulling on the end of his belt. "Do it, Clay."

His eyes burning into hers, he did as she bid, pulling the belt open and shrugging his dressing gown from his wide shoulders. It fell to the carpet almost soundlessly. Her eyes drank in the sight of him, every part of him. Well-muscled shoulders, broad chest, strong arms. Even his abdomen was hewn perfection. His cock rose thick and long and hard. The *despicable thing* inside her returned tenfold.

Good, sweet heavens.

"Get on the bed," she demanded.

He reached for her but she stepped away, enjoying this far too much. "On the bed, Clay."

"I want to touch you, love."

The smile she gave him was wicked and she knew it. "You will. Just do as I ask, please."

His smoldering gaze never leaving hers, he lowered his large frame onto the center of her bed. With a deep breath, she untied the knot on her dressing gown as well. It fell from her in a silken whisper. And then she joined him on the bed, making a place for herself between his legs.

Her gaze fell upon his cock. Dipping her head, she kissed the broad tip once. Twice. Flicked her tongue over the slit, hungry to taste him. His groan rewarded her along with the taste of him on her tongue.

"Bloody hell, Ara. There is no need…you do not have to…"

His words trailed off as she grew more adventurous and

sucked him the way he had done to her pearl. Just once, testing, to see if the effect was the same for him. His hips jerked, driving his cock deeper into her mouth.

She released him and looked up the expanse of his exquisite body—all hers. "Tell me what pleases you. I want to bring you pleasure."

"Holy God, woman, if you bring me any more pleasure, I will spend like a callow youth down your throat," he rasped.

Oh.

That meant she was doing something right. She took him in her mouth once more, alternating between sucking and licking. Listening to the cues of his body—when his hips pumped against her, when his breathing became harsher, when growls of pleasure emerged from him, she knew she had found her stride.

"Ara." Her name was a moan on his lips.

Her mouth was filled with him, and she could not speak. Wetness kissed her tongue, and it was not just her saliva, she realized, but a part of him as well. He was coming undone. Losing his control. Humming her satisfaction, she touched the heavy sacs beneath his cock, gently testing their weight.

"Ara, I'm going to come in your mouth if you do not stop," he said.

She did not stop. She wanted his seed in her mouth. Wanted to taste him, to swallow him. She wanted every last drop, as much as she could get. The flesh between her thighs swollen and needy, and he had yet to even touch her there. She moaned and instinctively took him deeper, bringing him into her throat. His fingers sank into her hair, tightening.

"Damn it, Ara," he gritted through clenched teeth as he seemed to give in.

He guided her, showing her how to set the rhythm he wanted. She savored him, reveled in her ability to make this big man give in to her. He had stripped away his dressing gown for her. Had lain on the bed for her. He allowed her to have her way with him.

And she loved it. Loved him in her mouth, hard and tart and thick. Loved the sounds he made, the restless pumping of his hips. Loved his fingers tugging at her hair. Loved it when he surrendered completely.

"Ah, fuck." He pumped harder, his cock surging so deep her throat constricted around him. "I'm going to…"

His warning was cut short by a flood. Wet heat spilled inside her, tangy and earthy and heady. She swallowed it, took all of him he could give until the last spasm rocked through him and he caught her upper arms in a gentle yet firm grip, hauling her atop him.

His breaths were harsh and ragged, his heart pounding with a fury she could feel against her breast as she draped herself over him, relishing the way their skin came into contact, so that there was not an inch of her that didn't touch him. This was what she had been made for, loving this man.

"You did not have to do that," he said softly.

She cupped his scarred cheek in her hand. "I wanted to. I love you, Clay Ludlow, so much it hurts."

"I love you too, Ara mine." A gleam entered his eyes. "Where does it hurt?"

His fingers traced her seam, parting her folds to tease her pearl. Her breath left her. He rolled them suddenly as one, until she was on her back on the bed, him settled atop her. He intensified the pressure and pace ever so slightly. "Does it hurt here, love?"

"It aches," she whispered.

"Perhaps I can ease the pain," he murmured, kissing her throat and then making his way down her body to the curve of her breast. First one nipple, then the other, his tongue flicking out to swirl around the sensitive buds before sucking. Lower still, over the curve of her belly to where she yearned the most.

She was so starved for him that when his mouth met her slick flesh, a small tremor coursed through her. She was on the precipice, ready to spiral into the abyss. A finger entered her, gliding with ease. She tipped her hips, bringing him deeper as he suckled her, and then added a second finger, working them in and out her slick passage as he worshipped her.

She came undone in a flash, the pleasure so violent and intense that as it rollicked through her, tiny pinpricks of light burst in her vision. He made a low sound of approval, not stopping his sinful torture until he had wrung the last ripple of pleasure from her body.

He fell to the bed alongside her, drew her into his arms, and they lay together, sated and happy. She wrapped her arms around him, vowing inwardly that she would never let him go. No one and nothing would ever tear them apart again.

"Ara," he said tenderly. "My Ara. Just as you always were. Just as you were always meant to be."

She kissed his chest. "At last."

Chapter Twenty-Three

FINALLY.

One fortnight later—and *eight bloody years later* than he had originally intended—Clay was Ara's husband.

He could scarcely believe it was true. That the goddess seated at his side was now his wife seemed an implausible dream. An impossibility he could have never hoped to attain. And yet, she sent him a beaming smile, radiant in her happiness and in her unfettered love for him both. A river of gratitude washed through him, leaving him momentarily breathless. It was a hell of a thing.

"Felicitations on your nuptials and to the future Lord and Lady Stanwyck," Leo said with as much warmth as Leo was capable of mustering.

A hearty chorus of affirmatives sounded all around the table.

When his brother had arrived at Harlton Hall for the intimate wedding celebration, he had come bearing startling news. The Crown had deigned to bestow a viscountcy upon Clay in recognition of his service. He was to become Lord Stanwyck, and Ara would be his viscountess rather than mere Mrs. Clayton Ludlow after all. It seemed surreal.

Not so much the title, though he would accept it graciously as he must.

But that Ara—the only woman he had ever loved—was

well and truly his.

That he was seated at his wedding breakfast, surrounded by his family and a miniscule gathering of his friends—the Duke and Duchess of Leeds only—filled him with an immense sense of awe. Fear for Ara and Edward's safety remained a knife lodged in his chest. But the presence of Leo and Leeds at the wedding breakfast, along with a cadre of armed men scattered throughout Harlton Hall's demesne, left him feeling as secure as he possibly could.

Tomorrow, they would face the reality of the Fenian menace once more. Today, he was a man in love, his bride at his side, and nothing had ever felt more right. Today, he would not allow those fiendish villains to infringe upon what he shared with Ara.

"You are frowning," Ara observed softly, so that only he could hear. "Are you not happy?"

"On the contrary," he reassured her, reaching discreetly beneath the table to tangle their fingers together and give hers a squeeze. "I have never been happier, my love."

His only cause for worriment was the wellbeing of her and their son.

"You are worrying about them," she guessed.

Bloody hell, of course he was. His wife and his son were in danger. He would not rest until this madness was done and he could go about the business of being Ara's husband and Edward's father rather than their bodyguard.

"Perhaps you need not look so grim-faced, brother," Leo said then, raising his glass in a salute. "I received word not long ago of arrests having been made in Dublin."

The words had scarcely permeated Clay's brain when the sound of a glass upending ruptured the silence. His eyes swung to the source—the new governess, her countenance pale, had dropped her wine goblet. A dark red stain spread over the white table linen.

"I do beg your pardon," she muttered softly, her expression stricken, as she attempted to use her napkin to dab at the offending spill. "I am not ordinarily so clumsy."

It was unusual for a governess to attend a wedding breakfast, so perhaps, unaccustomed to such a circumstance, her nerves had caused her to grow clumsy. Clay could not blame the girl, for he felt ill at ease himself in this august assemblage. She was surrounded by no less than two dukes, two duchesses (one former, one current), and a presumed viscount.

"You must not concern yourself with such trifles, Miss Palliser," Ara was quick to reassure the embarrassed governess. "Today is a day of joy, and not even a thousand spilled glasses could spoil it."

Clay's eyes returned to his brother, seeking an explanation, only to find Leo's hard stare focused upon Miss Palliser. For a moment, he swore he detected something in his brother's harsh countenance—a glimmer of interest, a spark of something—but it was quickly banished when Leo wrenched his gaze away from the governess at last.

"The men responsible for the outrage against the Duke of Burghly have been captured," Leo elaborated succinctly. "Just yesterday. A treasure trove of information has been discovered along with them, and my Dublin sources assure me that more arrests will inevitably follow. This nightmare is at its end. I was saving the good news for after the nuptials."

Holy God.

Clay stared at his brother, unseeing. It was as if his mind and his body had become separated. The one could hear and comprehend and understand. The other had fled him entirely. He could not move. Could not speak.

He felt...numb.

And then he felt a rush of relief so intense it rattled

through him like a locomotive, leaving him trembling in its aftermath. He was still gripping Ara's hand beneath the cover of the table, and he was not certain which of them was crushing the other more.

He turned to her.

She had raised a free hand to her mouth, stifling a sob—half joy, he suspected, half weariness. "Oh, Clay. Does this mean we are free at last?"

"It is my greatest hope." He could not resist tugging her to him, pressing a tender kiss to her forehead, even before their guests. How he wished he could ravage her mouth as he wished, haul her up in his arms and carry her to his chamber. He wanted her all to himself, and he did not want an audience.

"This is wonderful news indeed," Clay's mother said. "I could not be more pleased. I only wish your father could be here now. How proud he would be of his two sons. How happy he would be to welcome Ara and Edward into our family."

"My Mama says that everyone in heaven is still with you in your heart," Edward offered solemnly. "They will always be there, and no one can remove them or their love."

"How right your mama is," Clay told his son, giving Ara's hand another surreptitious squeeze. "No matter how great the distance or how long the time apart, the ones you love will always be there in your heart."

"I love you so," Ara whispered to him.

"That is certainly true," added the Duchess of Leeds, offering her husband a look that shone with unabashed adoration "Would you not say so, my husband?"

The look Leeds gave her in return was every bit as love-sick. "I would most certainly concur."

Clay found himself grinning, well pleased that the two

who had begun their marriage as one of convenience had found happiness in each other after all. Once, he had disliked and distrusted Leeds, but Leeds had proven himself to be a trustworthy and devoted friend, and Clay was happy to count him one. The duchess with her heart of gold had won him over from the start of their unlikely friendship.

"Forgive me," drawled Leo then with the full icy hauteur only he could affect. "Excessive sentiment makes me bilious. Let us carry on with the breakfast before I lose my appetite, shall we?"

"You do not appear to have lost your appetite, Your Grace," Edward observed out of turn, and it was quite true for despite the maudlin vein of their conversation, Leo had cleared his plate of this course.

"You may call me Uncle Leo, scamp," Leo admonished Edward without a trace of heat, his ordinarily hard exterior softening ever so slightly. "And I will thank you kindly to mind your own plate. I do not suppose you can finish yours and watch mine at the same time, can you?"

Edward smiled, undeterred. "No, Uncle Leo."

"Just so." Leo's attention returned to Miss Palliser, and Clay did not think he was mistaken this time about the flare of interest he saw in his brother's expression. "Perhaps your governess ought to teach you about manners if she has not yet done so."

That was unexpectedly churlish of Leo, even by Leo's standards. Clay frowned at his brother.

"Miss Palliser has only just joined us recently," Ara spoke up before he could, flashing the quiet governess a reassuring smile.

"Plenty of time then," Leo said mildly, his stare lingering on the governess, who flushed beneath his scrutiny. "Plenty of time."

Clay motioned discreetly for the next course to be served. "If you were hungry, brother, you would have only had to speak for yourself. No one knows better than I what a bear you become when deprived of nourishment, and we cannot have that on a day of such unmitigated celebration."

Leo turned his attention back to Clay, grinning. "Today is not about me, brother dear. It is about you and your lovely bride. I wish you happy, today and every day that follows."

"Thank you, Your Grace," Ara said.

Their fingers laced even more tightly together.

"Yes," Clay agreed. "Thank you, brother." For he wished the very same.

EIGHT YEARS AGO, she had written it in her journal with a flourish and a foolish heart brimming with yearning and hope.

Today, it had become a reality.

Today, she had become Mrs. Clayton Ludlow. Soon to be the Viscountess of Stanwyck, though the title mattered not to her. She was not the name she wore. She never had been. She was Ara. Ara who loved Clay with all her heart. And though everything else around her had seemingly changed, that fact had not. She was still his, now just as much as she had ever been.

She had learned a new truth in the weeks since Clay had returned to her life, and it was that though years may pass and two hearts in love may be torn apart, nothing could vanquish the fire of a love that was meant to be. Not time. Not distance. Not misunderstandings. Not lies or betrayals.

Not anything.

"Ara."

She spun, hand on her heart, to find him there, his presence larger than his size. *Dear God*, how she loved him. She wanted to say something meaningful, something appropriate to the occasion. Something he would remember years later, when they were silver-haired and coddling their grandchildren. But he took her breath. He robbed her of speech. There he stood, hers at last.

"Ara."

He opened his arms, and she raced to him as if she were a young girl of one-and-twenty all over again. As if they had never lost each other. As if this was all they had ever known. She was in the air, launching herself at him, and he caught her with ease, holding her in his arms.

Her love for him was uncontrollable. It was like a small stream that became a rushing river after a deluge of rain, transforming everything in its path. Just as he had described to her once.

It was a force all its own.

Their mouths met in a kiss of tongues and teeth and lips. Of hunger and savoring and desperation and frantic need. It was a culmination of every second they had been apart. She could not kiss him long enough or hard enough. Her hands sank into his hair. His hands clamped on her waist, holding her in place. Her legs wrapped around him.

She felt so small in his arms, and yet so fierce, so revered. So loved, so needed, so wanted. Every part of her cried out for more. She took her mouth from his to rain kisses on his face—his eyebrow, his cheek, his rigid jaw, down his chin. She found his throat and his racing pulse and licked, then gently bit.

He rewarded her with a groan. "I wish we were off on our honeymoon now. I wish we were not bound to remain here by our circumstances."

"Mmm." She licked a path down his neck, finding his

prominent Adam's apple. "I do not need to be anywhere other than here. Now. With you."

And it was true. She had no desire to travel to the Continent. Having him as her husband at last was gift enough.

"Ah, Ara." His hands slid from her waist to her bottom, cupping and squeezing and settling off a delicious waterfall of sensation skittering through her.

Want.

Need.

Desire.

All she wanted was this man: his taste, his touch, the scent of him, his broad chest, his muscular arms, his long legs, powerful thighs, his lean waist and barely suppressed strength. All she wanted was him. Now. Forever.

"You are mine," she told him, reveling in the words. In the truth of them. "Mine, Clayton Ludlow."

"I have always been yours, my darling," he said, walking with her in his arms to the bed. "Always."

He laid her down as gently as if she were made of the finest Sèvres porcelain. She wasted no time in opening the knot on her dressing gown and spreading it wide. He shucked his and she had a moment to admire the beauty of his body before he joined her on the bed.

His mouth was everywhere, delivering heated kisses to the bare skin of her legs, belly, breasts, and throat before settling upon her lips at last. She sighed into his mouth. He tasted sweet, like the wine he had consumed at their wedding breakfast. Their tongues tangled.

His hands took up where his mouth had left off, stroking and caressing. He found her nipples and rolled them between his thumb and forefinger. His heated touch skimmed over her belly, and knowing fingers parted her folds.

"You are so wet for me, Ara," he whispered against her

mouth. "So perfect."

She was desperate for him, her hips seeking more. Ara kissed him everywhere she could reach—his jaw, his neck, his shoulder, his lips—and still it was not enough. Restlessness built within her. She was starving for his touch, for the fulfillment only he could bring her.

"I need you so much, Clay." She reached between them, taking his thick, hot length in her hand.

"Put me inside you," he ordered lowly.

His directive made the slick flesh between her thighs throb. She didn't hesitate, guiding his cock to her entrance. He thrusted as she arched, and he was seated deep inside her. So deep. So good. She was full, stretched.

His mouth slammed back down on hers as a growl tore from him. He moved, slowly at first, but as the pleasure built, he increased his pace. They made love frantically. Mouths, tongues, hands everywhere. She reached her pinnacle, her inner muscles contracting on him as pure ecstasy shot through her. In the next breath, he was coming undone too, and with a low moan he spent inside her.

He collapsed atop her, his breathing heavy, their skins slicked with sweat. They kissed again, slowly, languorously. His heart beat against her chest. She held him to her, and there was no need for words.

She was home.

Chapter Twenty-Four

CLAY WOKE HAPPY and sated as he had not been for as long as he could remember. He woke to soft red curls tickling his chest. To a warm, feminine body draped over his. He woke to Ara, naked. To Ara, his wife.

Ara, his *naked wife*. It was a blissful combination. He would never grow weary of Ara and her capable mind, her sizzling wit, her loving heart, or her delectable body, it was certain. They had spent the entire day following the wedding breakfast inside her chamber and his, alternating between making love and holding each other and talking. They had not even left for dinner, taking trays in their apartment instead.

But as he lay there in the early morning light, reliving the heaven of the day before, a troubling sense of disquiet entered his mind. He thought of the governess. Of her spilled wine. Of how odd the timing of it had been, just after Leo's revelation regarding the Fenians who had murdered Burghly. Of the pallor she had displayed.

He could not sleep, thinking of it. Could not rest. Could not allow himself to give in to the desires burning in his blood for his wife. He would love nothing better than to wake her with kisses, tease her until she quivered with need, sink home inside her.

But questions and misgivings churned in his mind, unrelenting. His ardor was eclipsed by his concern, that niggling voice inside him telling him something was wrong. Something about the governess was somehow off, and the more he thought about it, the more convinced he became that his instincts were not failing him.

Dropping a kiss on his sweetly sleeping wife's lips, he extricated himself from her embrace and left the bed, tucking the bedclothes over her before he hastily dressed himself. The misgiving built as he left his chamber and headed for the nursery, all the while praying he was wrong.

Taking care to be quiet lest he wake Edward, he opened the door. And was met by a loudly meowing Sherman. The feline raced out the door and into the hall, as if spooked. Inside Edward's chamber, his fears were realized when he discovered the lad's empty bed.

"Edward," he called, his fears mounting.

Panicked, he rushed to the governess's chamber, knocking loudly at the door. "Miss Palliser?"

Sherman followed, brushing against his ankles, meowing again. There was no answer from within. He rapped once more. When he was met with silence, he entered. Though it was the height of impropriety, the swiftly rising tide of fear within him would not allow the time to locate a female domestic to perform the task.

His intrusion would not have mattered anyway, for Miss Palliser was nowhere to be found. Indeed, the chamber looked as if she had never even inhabited it. With a vicious curse, he left and jogged down the hall, telling himself to be calm all the while.

That his fears were likely groundless. That Miss Palliser and Edward were probably breaking their fast at that very moment, and he would race into the breakfast room to find the lad flashing him a grin. The Fenians who had murdered

Burghly had been arrested. Surely the end had come to this madness. Surely, he was overreacting.

But the breakfast room was empty. Keynes appeared, the ever-efficient butler sporting an air of perplexed concern. "May I be of assistance, sir?"

"The young duke," he bit out. "Have you seen him this morning?"

Keynes's eyebrows snapped together. "I cannot say that I have, sir."

The misgiving in his gut deepened into fear.

"Damn it." He raked his fingers through his hair. He was going to have to wake the household. Where in the hell could Miss Palliser and the lad be?

Leo entered the breakfast room just then. "Clay, I need to speak with you. Would you excuse us, Keynes?"

Clay had never been more relieved to see his brother. The butler bowed and disappeared.

"I'm glad you are here," he said hoarsely, about to enlist his brother in helping him to find Edward and the wayward governess. Or to assure him that he was mad and the lad was safe and sound.

"Not the usual reception I receive, but I will take it," Leo said drily before Clay could continue. "I'm afraid the news I have is not good, brother. I've just had word from Leprechaun."

The news made Clay's skin go cold.

Leo referred to their mutual friend Padraig McGuire by the name the League had assigned him. McGuire had successfully infiltrated the most militant faction of Fenians in New York City, his work so sensitive and dangerous that he had nearly been killed on more than one occasion. The information he fed to the League was invaluable.

Dread made Clay's mouth dry. An invisible fist clenched

on his heart. Information from Padraig could only mean one thing. The Fenians were plotting again. And if the Fenians were plotting again, Ara and Edward could be in grave danger.

Which meant it was entirely possible the disappearance of his son and the new bloody governess was not innocent as he had so desperately hoped.

"They have sent a female," Leo continued, oblivious to the fear paralyzing Clay. "She was working with the man you killed at Burghly House. She's the last of the ring of plotters, and she has infiltrated your household already. We need to interview the entire staff. Each domestic will be subject to scrutiny. We need to find out who she bloody is before she can do any irreparable harm. I would like to begin with them, interviewing each servant. Females only, starting with the new governess, and...bloody hell, Clay, why are you so pale?"

Because his brother had just confirmed his greatest fear.

Miss Palliser, or whatever the bloody hell her true name was, was not a governess at all. There was no innocent explanation for her disappearing with Edward. She was the female. The female who had infiltrated his household without a moment of resistance from him. *Jesus*, had he been so relieved to replace the incompetent Miss Argent with her love of getting soused nightly that he had failed to notice he had allowed a fox into the henhouse?

"She is...damn it." He closed his eyes for a moment, sucked in a frantic breath. Fear and terror and panic and worry and every bad emotion he had ever experienced hit him full force, straight in the chest. For a beat, he could not find his voice. Could not even find his mind. He was adrift in a sea of blackness, helpless.

"Clay." Leo's voice was stripped bare, rife with emotion.

He had never seen or heard his brother so affected. "It is the governess, Leo. She has him. She has my son."

The color leached from Leo's face. "Fuck."

"Yes." *Fuck* and every other epithet that had ever been invented had never been more appropriate. "We have to find them, Leo. I have to…I cannot let anything happen to him. This is all my bloody fault, and I will not forgive myself if…if…"

"Do not say it," Leo interrupted, his countenance as grim as his tone. "Do not even think it. We will find him, Clay. We will find him and bring him home where he belongs."

Clay swallowed hard and could not keep himself from dragging his half brother into an embrace. They had never hugged before. Leo despised outward displays of affection. But Clay didn't give a damn.

To his surprise, Leo hugged him in return, clapping him on the back.

"I swear to you, Clay. We will find your son. He needs to get more acquainted with his dastardly Uncle Leo, yes?"

"Yes." Clay closed his eyes. "Yes, he damn well does."

"Then there is no time to waste. Let's gather the men."

"Ara."

She woke from deep, dreamless slumber to Clay's voice. There was something wrong, she realized as her eyes flew open. He was fully dressed, standing over her bed with a grim expression.

Fear gripped her. "What is it, Clay? What's happened?"

"The governess has taken Edward," he said.

Ara felt as if her stomach had been tossed from a cliff. She wanted to retch. She wanted to scream. Terror clawed at her throat, all the horror she had been holding at bay since the attempt on her life at Burghly House—nay, ever since

Freddie's vicious murder—returning to her a thousandfold.

How could this be?

"Why?" she managed past lips and a tongue that had gone dry with shock.

Clay's gaze met hers, and what she saw within those dark depths shook her to her soul. "Leo has received word from one of his sources that there is a female Fenian in our midst. I believe it is Miss Palliser."

Dear God. "She cannot be one of them," she said, shaking her head in denial. "She is a woman. And she is polite. Beautiful, actually. Soft-spoken. She seems so kind…"

Ara pressed a hand to her lips, stifling the flow of words. She was rambling. Making little sense. None of the things she had mentioned had any bearing on Miss Palliser's true nature, and she knew it.

What if the woman was a Fenian sympathizer who had taken Edward to do him harm? Evil could lurk behind a pleasant smile and a calm demeanor. It could hide behind false kindness and humility, behind compliments and good manners. Evil could be female as well as male, could it not? That was the thing about it—evil had no face, no indication, no warning or outward sign, until it was too late to stop it.

Until it was a runaway locomotive barreling down tracks.

Destroying everything in its path.

Clay caught her to him. She clutched his arms, struggling to gain her breath. She had never considered herself a weak woman, before, but the events of the last few months had made her feel small and trifling and insignificant. They had made her realize how powerless she was.

But not her son.

She could not accept that the Fenians would take an innocent boy. Why would they wish to hurt him? How could they? And a woman? Miss Palliser? Why would the new governess wish her beloved boy harm? It made no sense. Or it made horrible, awful sense. The sort of sense she could not comprehend.

"Say something, Clay," she begged in a hoarse whisper, searching his beloved face for some small sign of comfort. Anything.

"I will find him, Ara." His jaw clenched. "I swear to you I will find him, and I will bring him safely home to you. Leo and I are riding out now."

"I will come with you," she said. "Let me dress, and I—"

"No, Ara," he said gently. "There isn't time to waste. I must go now."

Tears blurred her vision. He was right. She did not want to be an impediment. "Go, Clay. Bring our son home."

He kissed her once, swift and hard, and then he strode from the chamber, leaving Ara alone in the bed that had been filled with such love and joy just the day before. Her son was out there, somewhere in the world without her. Shaking, she stood and began to hastily dress herself. Of one thing, she was utterly certain. She could not bear to stay behind and wait.

THEY CANNOT HAVE gotten far, Clay reassured himself as he raced hell for leather down the road alongside Leo. Leeds and the rest of the men had split up, determined to cover every square mile of the land surrounding Harlton Hall. Meanwhile, he and his brother had decided the best course of action for them to take was to head for the rail station. If Miss Palliser was indeed a Fenian sympathizer who had infiltrated his home with the goal of abducting Edward and either ransoming him or far worse, she would not remain in Oxfordshire. She would be fleeing to another city, and with all haste.

The key was to find them first. If Miss Palliser spirited him away in a train car, their ability to disappear would be infinite. But Clay would not think that now, not as he spurred his mount down the road at breakneck pace, desperation and fear a sick soup swirling inside him.

The head groomsman had reported settling them into a gig early that morning, Miss Palliser volunteering to drive. The governess had announced they were off on a learning expedition. The lad had been cheerful and smiling, eager for his lesson. So bloody trusting. Such a good-hearted lad. The notion of Edward being led away to danger by someone he had trusted infuriated him. He deserved better, by God.

The lad had already suffered enough in his young life, and Clay had only just begun to know him. He could not bear to lose him now. He would do everything within his power—*every bloody thing*—to ensure his son's safety.

They raced around a bend in the road, and his heart slammed into his throat when he spied the gig pulled off to the side of the country lane, empty, the horse pulling it browsing in some grass. Apparently anticipating they would be followed, Miss Palliser had chosen to disappear into the dense undergrowth of the woods bookending the road.

As he rode, he scoured the surrounding land for any trace of the governess or the lad. And that was when he spotted a flash of movement in the distance. Keeping his eyes pinned to the spot, he called to Leo, gesturing in the direction he had spied it.

He and his brother reined their horses and dismounted, tying them off to nearby trees. "I saw movement," he told Leo hoarsely. "It could have been them."

Leo nodded, his expression tense and grim. He extracted his pistol from his coat. "You head in from the road, and I will run ahead and attempt to double back. If it is them, I can approach from behind, perhaps get in a shot at her."

His brother's words made a wave of nausea roil through him, but he forced it back, nodding. He had to be strong. To gather his wits. He had to fight for the lad. To put an end to this madness once and for all.

Without another word, he extracted his own weapon and ran into the tangled undergrowth, going full speed toward where he had seen what could have been a dove-gray gown. He ran until his pulse pounded. Until his lungs ached and burned. Briars clawed at him, tearing at his coat and trousers, slicing into his flesh. He was impervious to them all, single-minded in his pursuit.

He found a path and followed it, praying it was not a deer trail. It twisted and curved, and then, suddenly he found himself in a clearing. And there, in the midst of it, stood Miss Palliser facing him, her arm around the lad's thin shoulders, the barrel of a small pistol pressed to his son's temple.

"Do not come any nearer," she warned. "Stay where you are, and the young duke will remain safe."

His breath left him. He had a pistol in his hand, but he dared not raise it for fear the unhinged woman might pull the trigger, killing Edward.

"Papa," Edward called, hiccupping, his eyes—Ara's eyes—wide with fright.

It was the first time his son had referred to him as his father. It should have been an occasion for joy. A celebration. Instead, he was gripped with horror. The sight of his son, terrified and helpless and in the clutches of this madwoman, nearly undid him.

He forced his numb lips to speak. His training had taught him the best method of defense when the enemy had the upper hand was distraction. Distract, make them weak, and then press your advantage at just the right moment.

"You may as well surrender yourself now, Miss Palliser," he said with a calm that was far from the dread and terror rioting inside him. "As you are aware, your compatriots have been arrested in Dublin, and the man sent to harm the duchess in London is dead by my hand. You are the only conspirator remaining. What do you think you can accomplish when everyone else around you has failed?"

"Do you truly think I am so easily fooled?" the young woman asked, her face an emotionless mask. "I will not be surrendering. I promise you the boy will not be harmed as long as you do as I say."

"What would you have me do?" he asked, playing along, his mind whirling with possibilities, the options he had to sufficiently distract her so that he could rescue Edward. He could shoot at or near her, but that would put his son in danger. One instinctive tensing of her finger on the trigger, and the lad would be...*no*, he would not think it.

There were other ways. Leo was resourceful. He should be coming upon them from Miss Palliser's rear at any moment.

"Place your weapon on the ground before you," she ordered, her voice cold.

He could detect it now, the faint tinge of an Irish accent where before he had noticed none. What a proficient actress this woman was. How bloody dangerous.

He did as she asked, lowering the gun to the ground slowly before standing upright, his hands raised, palms facing outward. He had another pistol hidden on him and three blades, but she needn't know that.

"There you are, Miss Palliser," he called. "I have done what you wished. Now you must give me my son."

"No." She shook her head. "He cannot go with you, I am afraid. He must remain with me. But after I am finished with him and he is no longer useful to me, he will return to you unscathed."

"Like hell I will allow you to take him from me," he ground out, taking a menacing step forward. If the woman thought he was about to allow her to abscond with his son now that he had found them, she was mad and witless both.

She took two steps in retreat, hauling Edward with her. "Remain where you are or I shall hurt him," she warned, her voice a lash.

Behind her, on the other side of the clearing, he saw leaves rustle. Leo. He would bet his life on it. *Thank Christ.* He would continue to distract her.

"What do you hope to accomplish?" he asked. "Do you truly believe the harming of an innocent youth will make Home Rule possible?"

"What I hope to accomplish and what I believe are two different beasts, sir," she said, taking another slow step and pulling Edward with her.

"Papa," his son called, pleading. "I do not want to go with her. She said she will take me on an adventure, and then I can go home again. But I don't want to do that. I want to go home to you and Mama."

"Silence, Your Grace," Miss Palliser ordered Edward, her gaze never leaving Clay. "I must take the boy with me, but he will be returned."

Sounds reached him then, the rustling of someone racing through the dense forest toward him. Could it be another of Miss Palliser's confederates? Heart hammering, he spun on his heel to find his wife racing toward him, holding her skirts high in clenched fists.

Bloody hell, Ara had followed him. He might have known.

A shot rang out suddenly, echoing in the silence of the forest.

Clay turned back to Miss Palliser, shock and dread rocketing through him. He saw her stunned face, a dark stain spreading on her upper arm, the pistol falling from her slack hand. She went pale, looking down at the blood coating her hand, and then her eyes rolled back in her head and she crumpled into a heap on the ground.

Everything happened in a flurry.

Edward raced toward him, shouting. "Papa! Mama!"

Leo burst forth from his hiding place, binding Miss Palliser's hands and ankles.

Ara was beside him now, sobbing. He was sobbing. His cheeks were wet. Relief hit him, vast and sudden. He fell to his knees, opened his arms, and his son launched himself into him. He buried his face in the lad's soft hair, holding him as tightly as he dared.

"You are safe now, son."

"Oh, thank God," Ara cried, throwing her arms around Clay and Edward at once. "Thank God!"

Leo approached them, ruffling the lad's hair affectionately. "You are unharmed, Duke?"

"Yes," Edward said, sniffling into Clay's waistcoat. "M-miss P-palliser was not u-unkind to me. But she w-wouldn't t-take me h-home."

"She will never be able to frighten you again, lad," Leo said softly, his jaw clenched. "I promise you. Nor will anyone else. This is the end of the road for these villains."

"Thank you, brother," Clay said, gratitude rushing through him, fierce and strong.

"I told you he needs more time to get to know his dastardly Uncle Leo, did I not?" His brother sent him a cocky half grin.

"Yes," Clay agreed, bone-numbing relief joining the gratitude. "You certainly did."

"Thank you," Ara sniffed up at Leo. "You are not a dastardly uncle at all, but a hero."

Leo was solemn. "Some would call me a villain, my dear sister, and they would not be far from the mark. Forgive me for not seeing the evil in our midst until it was almost too late."

"Nonsense," Clay said gruffly, still hugging his son tight, relishing the sweet sensation of the lad's arms linked about his neck. "None of us saw it."

"The most important thing is that she cannot hurt anyone else, and Edward is safe," Ara said, smiling tremulously. "I cannot thank you enough for saving him."

Leo nodded, looking uncomfortable at the open displays of emotion. "It was my duty, and I am happy to say this is all over now. She was the last of the ring of plotters. My hunch is she thought to use Edward as a shield so she could return to Dublin unimpeded. But I'll be taking her to London now, where she will receive swift and unmerciful justice."

It was indeed over.

Edward was safe. Ara was safe. Miss Palliser would be on her way to rot in prison, and with the men responsible for Burghly's death in custody and the last, rogue Fenian related to the plot aside from Miss Palliser dead, their days of living in fear were finally at an end.

"I love you, Papa," Edward whispered, just loud enough that Clay could hear it above the frantic beats of his heart.

"I love you, son," he said. "And your mother as well."

Ara smiled at him, and it was beautiful, so deep and true that her dimple made another rare appearance. "I love you both with all my heart."

Clay hugged his family to him—Ara in one arm and his son in the other. "Come," he told them. "Let's go home."

The past was done. The danger was ended. And it was time to move forward, together, into the endless possibilities of the life that lay ahead of them.

Epilogue

ARA HAD A surprise for her husband. One she hoped would please him.

The sickness she had been experiencing in the last few days, coupled with her missed courses, were all too familiar. She would wager Harlton Hall that she was with child.

Clay was going to be a father again, and this time, he would not miss a single moment of their child's life. Edward would be receiving a younger sister or brother. Their beautiful little family was going to grow in size by one. It was soon, she knew, the ugliness of the past and the Fenian plots against her not far behind them. But the notion of having another babe to dote upon filled her heart with a flood of contented joy.

She knocked at the door of Clay's study, where she knew she would find him poring over old Harlton Hall ledgers and records. He had made the decision to cease his career as one of Her Majesty's covert agents on his own, wanting to keep Ara and Edward free of any future threats, and his choice relieved her. She had experienced all the upheaval she ever wished to know, and there was nothing she wanted more than to settle into a peaceful, calm life with their growing brood of children and each other.

In lieu of the League and its intrigues, he had thrown himself headlong into learning the history of the estate and researching crop yields with the intent to make Harlton Hall as profitable as possible. She was about to knock again, assuming him so focused upon the records before him that he missed the sound of her rap when the delicious, velvety rumble of his voice reached her.

"You may come in, Ara mine," he called.

The smile that curved her lips would not be suppressed as she opened the door and crossed the threshold. His study was one of her favorite chambers at Harlton Hall, as it smelled of him and everything about it—from the heavy, ornate desk to the oil landscapes hanging on the walls—was so very Clay. They had spent many pleasant hours ensconced within it, wrapped up in each other, sharing a brandy and talking well into the night. On more than one occasion, they had made excellent use of the thick, new Axminster.

He stood at her entrance, dressed in black trousers, his shirtsleeves, and a black waistcoat, so handsome he took her breath. Sometimes, it was still difficult to believe the large, powerful man striding toward her was hers. That they were husband and wife. That this new life she found herself in was not a dream flitting through her mind in the night, but was real.

And wonderful.

And true.

"How did you know it was me?" she could not resist asking as they reached each other halfway, in the middle of the chamber. Her arms wrapped around his waist as he drew her into his embrace.

"I recognize your knock," he said, his hands slid up and down her spine. "And I know you cannot resist venturing here for late-afternoon wickedness every now and again."

Her cheeks burned, and she was grateful her face was pressed to his chest. "I do not recall hearing you complain about my visits."

"Never." He kissed the top of her head. "You may visit me every day. Twice, if you like. I will happily choose making love to my wife over researching historical yields of wheat and corn."

Giving him an affectionate squeeze, she tipped her head back to gaze up at him. "Your life here at Harlton Hall will be staid and boring compared to what you are accustomed to, I have no doubt. Do you miss it?"

He swept the backs of his fingers down her cheek in a slow caress, his dark gaze unwavering upon hers. "Never. I have everything I could want—more than I could want, in fact—right here within these crumbling old walls. I love you and our son, and you both are my life. You are all that matters to me."

She could not resist nuzzling her cheek into his hand. "What if your life were to change?"

His brows snapped together. "In what fashion?"

She swallowed, excitement mingling with trepidation inside her. "What if your life were to encompass more than just myself and Edward? Have you room for...perhaps, one more?"

Ara saw the moment her words sank into his mind. The expression on his face shifted from one of sensual promise to dazed happiness. "Ara, what are you saying?"

"I'm saying you are going to be a father again, Clay."

"My God, Ara." His lips slammed down on hers in the next moment, hard and possessing and hungry.

She kissed him back with all the love bursting inside her. Kissed him and kissed him until she had to pull away and catch her breath. "Are you happy, my love?" she asked.

"Happy does not begin to describe the riot inside me," he murmured, shaking his head. "I am bloody elated, Ara. A babe. Another son or a daughter—I can scarcely believe it. Are you certain?"

He pressed his hand to her stomach, reverently caressing her though the layers of fabric, undergarments, and boning separating them.

Ara nodded. "The signs are the same as they were with Edward."

"You should not be on your feet," he said. "Are you tired? Thirsty? Overheated? Your cheeks are flushed, darling." His other hand went to her forehead. "You are not feverish, are you?"

His frenzied rush of concern made her heart feel warm and impossibly full. Love for him swelled inside her. "I am perfectly well, Clay. You need not fear. If I am overheated, it is merely down to my proximity to a certain tall, handsome, mountain of a man who regularly ravishes me in this very chamber."

"Minx," he said without heat, bringing their mouths together once more for a kiss that was unhurried and impossibly tender.

"Mmm," she hummed her pleasure against his lips. "I am *your* minx."

He lifted his head, gazing down at her with such naked, unfettered love that she feared she would melt. "Forever, Ara mine."

"Yes," she agreed, smiling, tears of pure happiness pooling in her eyes and blurring her vision. "Forever."

"God, Ara," he said. "I am terrified. Thrilled and terrified and in complete awe all at once. We need to tell Edward and my mother. Leo too. He shall wish to know he is to be an uncle again."

"Of course we will tell them all, together." A naughty coil of heat snaked through her then as she gazed up at the masculine perfection of the man she loved. "But first, perhaps we might involve ourselves in a bit of *afternoon wickedness.* What do you say?"

The look of sensual promise he gave her set her ablaze. "I say that is a capital idea, my Lady Stanwyck."

His lips claimed hers then, hot, insistent, and hungry. Laden with the promise of a love that had lasted eight years and had only grown more resilient for the time and distance they had faced.

He broke the kiss to scoop her effortlessly into his arms. "I love you, Ara."

She linked her arms around his neck, heart bursting with happiness. "I love you more."

THE END.

Dear Reader

Thank you for reading *Nobody's Duke*! I hope you enjoyed this first book in the League of Dukes series and that you loved Clay and Ara as much as I loved writing their hard-won happily ever after. After everything they had been through, they deserved to have their second chance at love. When Clay first appeared in *Her Deceptive Duke*, I had no intention of writing his story, but it didn't take long for me to realize that the first book in the League of Dukes series had to be his.

As always, please consider leaving an honest review of *Nobody's Duke.* Reviews are greatly appreciated! If you'd like to keep up to date with my latest releases and series news, sign up for my newsletter (scarlettscottauthor.com/contact) or follow me on Amazon or BookBub. Join my reader's group on Facebook for bonus content, early excerpts, giveaways, and more.

If you'd like a preview of my upcoming standalone *Heartless Duke*, Book Two in the League of Dukes series featuring Leo, Duke of Carlisle, and the plucky Irish lass who melts his ice with her fire, do read on.

And if you're in the mood for another, extended sneak peek of *Heartless Duke* plus a swashbucklingly sexy novella, check out *Lord of Pirates*, coming in February 2019.

Until next time,

Scarlett

Heartless Duke
League of Dukes Book Two

BY
SCARLETT SCOTT

He's a heartless cad. A relentless rake. Dangerous to know. As hardhearted and cruel as can be.

He's the Duke of Carlisle, leader of a secret branch of the Home Office charged with keeping the peace amidst great peril and upheaval. By day, he hunts anarchists and murderers with savage intensity. By night, he rules over London's darkest, most depraved souls.

But he's about to meet his match in his latest prisoner.

She's a strong, independent woman. Fearless and determined. Unlike any lady he's ever known. As unfettered and plucky as can be.

She's Bridget O'Malley, a trusted member of the underground organization to gain Irish independence. By day, she is a respectable young woman of modest means, attempting to make her way in the world through honest employment. By night, she is embroiled in a world so treacherous and dangerous that even she finds her own life at risk. To save herself, she will commit any sin.

When the heartless duke and the fiery rebel clash in a fierce battle of wills, unexpected passions flare to life. Threats lurk at every turn, and no one is as they seem. Will they be each other's ruin? Or is love enough to become their salvation?

Prologue

Oxfordshire, 1882

THE DUKE OF Carlisle landed at his half brother's estate in Oxfordshire with a small cadre of servants and one armed guard, dusty, travel-worn, and weary. It seemed wrong somehow to arrive at Clay's wedding after having spent the previous night surrounded by the most depraved and licentious acts imaginable.

Or at least those imaginable to Leo, and his mind was blessed with a boundless creativity for the wicked.

But here he was, prepared to do his duty.

Duty was everything to him, for it was all he bloody well had.

He was also late, the hour approaching midnight, but he had allowed himself to be distracted at a tavern blessedly in possession of a hearty store of spirits. It was possible that he was drunk as well, having consumed roughly enough ale and wine to float the Spanish Armada.

A poor decision, that. He ought to have arrived earlier like a gentleman.

He flung open his carriage door and leapt down without waiting for it to reach a complete stop. Fortunately, he was blessed with a cat's stealthy reflexes even when bosky, and he landed in the gravel on two booted feet with effortless grace.

Farleigh, one of the men standing guard over Harlton Hall whilst his brother's wife-to-be continued to be in danger, approached him first. The political assassination of her husband had left her a target for a particularly ruthless ring of Fenians.

An unfortunate business, indeed. One Leo was doing his utmost to rectify. The criminals would be brought to justice by his hand, one way or another. Death was just as swift a sentence as prison. He would choose death for the miscreants over imprisonment every time.

"Your Grace," Farleigh said, bowing. "You ought to take better care. You could have been injured."

Leo flicked a cold gaze over the man. "Yet, I was not. Is the entire household abed, sir?"

"There are some who have awaited your arrival. They will see to it that your belongings are taken to the proper chamber and you are settled."

Leo's lips thinned. Apathy, as vast as it had ever been, was a chasm inside his chest, threatening to consume him. Likely, he ought to find his chamber, order a bath, and scrub himself clean of the stink of London and the road.

But all he truly wanted was more liquor and some distraction, not necessarily—but preferably—in that order.

"Have there been any incidents since the relocation from London?" he asked sharply.

Even in his cups, he could not shake himself of the burden of his duties. He was the leader of the secretive branch of the Home Office known as the Special League. The safety and wellbeing of England's citizenry was in his hands. And the plague of the Fenian menace was evidenced everywhere these days: bombs exploding across England, vicious murders carried out, all in the name of Irish nationalism.

Some days, he needed to over imbibe.

He allowed such a weakness once per month, no more.

"There have been none, Your Grace," Farleigh confirmed. "The decision to leave town and come here with Her Grace was a wise one."

"Of course it was," Leo drawled. "I made it."

Aware of his rudeness and not giving a good goddamn, Leo stalked past Farleigh, his long legs taking him up the stairs leading to Harlton Hall. He did not bother himself with the details of his trunks or even which chamber had been assigned him. Instead, he went in search of his quarry.

Whisky. Brandy. Ale. *Holy hell*, even Madeira would do at the moment, and he disliked it intensely. He was in a foul mood, and he did not know why, other than that the Fenians continued to outmaneuver him.

No one outmaneuvered the Duke of Carlisle, by God.

He stalked through the entry and main hall, and was about to acknowledge defeat when he strode into a darkened chamber and collided with something soft. Something feminine and deliciously scented. *Ah, lemon and bergamot oil.* Something—his hands discovered a well-curved waist—or rather *someone*.

"I beg your pardon," the lady said with a huff and the slightest lilt to her accent he could not place.

"You may, but perhaps I shall not grant it," he said, feeling like the devil tonight.

"Grant what, sir?"

"My pardon." He dipped his lead lower, drawn to her warmth. Though he could see only faint outlines of her as his eyes adjusted to the dim light—a cloud of dark hair, a small, retroussé nose, a stubborn chin—he was nevertheless drawn to her. "Have you done something requiring it?"

She made a sound of irritation in her throat. "Release me, if you please. I have neither the time nor the inclination to play games with a stranger who arrives in the midst of the night, smelling of spirits."

"Allow me to introduce myself." He stepped back, offering her an exaggerated bow. "The Duke of Carlisle, m'lady. And you are?"

She moved forward, into the soft light of the hall. With the gas lamps illuminating her fully at last, he felt as if he had received a fist to the gut. She was striking, from her almost midnight hair, to her arresting blue gaze, to the full pout of her pink lips. And she was proportioned just as he preferred: short of stature yet shapely. Her bosom jutted forward in her plain dove-gray bodice.

Damn him if the woman wasn't giving him a cockstand here and now, at midnight in the midst of the hall with the hushed sound of servants seeing to his cases fluttering around them. They were not alone, and yet they might have been the only two souls in the world.

Her eyes sparkled with intelligence, and he could not shake the feeling that she was assessing him somehow. "I serve as governess to the young duke."

Governess.

That explained the godawful gray gown.

It did not, however, explain his inconvenient and thoroughly unwanted attraction to her. He did not dally with servants.

More's the pity.

Leo frowned. "What is the governess doing flitting about in the midst of the night, trading barbs with a stranger who smells of spirits?"

He could not resist goading her, it was true.

Her brows snapped together. "You waylaid me, Your Grace."

He would love to waylay her. All bloody night long.

But such mischief was decidedly not on the menu for this evening. Or ever. He had far too many matters weighing on his mind, and the last thing he needed to do was ruin a governess. He had come to celebrate his brother's nuptials, *damn it*, not to cast the last shred of his honor into the wind.

"Whilst you are being waylaid, perhaps you can direct me to the library," he said then. "I am in need of diversion. My mind does not do well with travel."

The truth was that his mind was not well in general, and it hadn't a thing to do with trains and coaches. But that was his private concern, yet another weakness he would admit to no one.

He expected the woman to inform him which chamber he sought and how he might arrive there. He did not expect her frown to deepen, or for her to turn on her heel and stride away down the hall in the opposite direction.

"Follow me, if you please," she called over her shoulder. "I shall take you there."

Leo followed, admiring the delectable sway of her hips as they went.

The governess intrigued him far too much, and he hoped to hell it wasn't going to become a problem. As it stood, he would only be at Harlton Hall for a few days' time. What could possibly go wrong?

Lord of Pirates

When a dangerous-looking stranger raps on Lizzie Winstead's door in the middle of a stormy night, the peace of her humdrum life is shattered. She's shocked to discover her visitor is Captain Edmond Grey, one of the most feared pirates of the realm. But he's also her lost love.

Edmond is a wanted man throughout the Colonies, but despite his formidable reputation, he desperately needs help to nurse his wounded brother back to health. Only Lizzie can be trusted not to turn Edmond over to authorities for the price on his head.

Lizzie can't quell the feelings Edmond stirs in her heart or the fire he ignites in her blood. Before long, both succumb to the reckless desire renewed between them. She follows him aboard his pirate ship and sets sail into a world rife with passion and peril.

Together they brave fierce battles and frightening storms, determined to discover whether the love they once shared is strong enough to reunite them forever and conquer the demons of Edmond's past.

Chapter One

Philadelphia 1719

AT FIRST LISTEN, Lizzie mistook the commotion for thunder from the angry spring rainstorm that had been assaulting the city since sundown. She stilled at her writing desk, pen poised above the notes she'd been transcribing on one of her father's medical treatises. No indeed, the loud pounding sound was not caused by a storm, she realized with growing concern, but someone at the front door.

She dropped her pen in its inkwell and stood. Only a desperate person would call at the house of a physician at this hour, someone in dire need of aid. With her father gone to Boston to visit with an old associate from London, Lizzie would have to see to the patient as best she could. Although she had not been permitted to attend university, she had served as her father's apprentice for nearly half her twenty-eight years. She only hoped the problem was one with which she was already familiar. After all, she was unaccustomed to practicing on her own.

The knocking grew in intensity. There was no time to tarry. She secured the wrapper she'd donned over her night shift. Although she was hardly dressed to receive a visitor, she had little choice. Taking a candle with her, she left her bedchamber and navigated her way downstairs.

By the time she reached the front hall, the ever-efficient Jeremiah and Judith, her father's faithful retainers, waited.

"Shall I answer, Mrs. Winstead?" Jeremiah asked in grim

tones.

Philadelphia was still relatively young and could, at times, be quite rough. However, Lizzie could never deny care to someone in need on account of a misplaced sense of caution. Indeed, her father had asked her to carry on in his absence should the need arise.

Praying it was not some drunkard or scoundrel at their door, she nodded to Jeremiah. "Please do, Jeremiah. I'm certain it must be one of Papa's patients."

"Yes, madam." Raising his candle high, he swung open the front door to reveal a large silhouette.

"I need to see Dr. Crawley at once," announced their guest in a voice as low as it was commanding.

"He's not at home," Jeremiah responded. "Can I help you in some way, sir?"

"Rouse him from bed if you must. Damn my blood, I don't have time for a servant with a cane up his arse."

Irritated at the man's rudeness, Lizzie swept forward. Jeremiah was of slight build with graying hair and a gouty limp. If their unexpected guest wanted to cause trouble, he easily could. Best to try to tamp down a problem before it began.

"I'm afraid my father is out of town, sir." She tried to peer through the murkiness of the night to see the man's face but could discern only long hair too straight to be a wig. The brim of his hat hid all else from her view.

"Lizzie?" Disbelief underscored the stranger's tone.

Something about that rough, demanding voice sent a trill down her spine. A trigger of remembrance flared in her stomach. His use of her father's pet name for her more than startled her. She could not shake the sense that she knew this man.

But how, and who?

She stiffened. "Sir, do I know you?"

"Indeed." Silence descended for a beat, interrupted only by the slashing rain and violent rumble of the storm beyond him. "I'm an old family…friend. Might I have a private word with you?"

When she hesitated, he spoke again, cajoling. "I beg of you, Lizzie. It is a matter of life and death."

He spoke like a gentleman but hardly looked like one, even in the dim light. That he would not reveal himself before the servants was particularly telling. Her instincts told her to shut the door in his face, bar it, and never think of him again. But there was an urgency in his tone, a pleading almost. Her heart was ever too soft.

"You may come inside," she conceded after a long pause. "Judith, please put on a pot of water for tea."

"Mrs. Winstead," Jeremiah protested, giving voice to her private concerns.

"Our guest is a family friend, Jeremiah. Please stand by should we need you." She would give the man the privacy he requested, but not the opportunity to do mischief. If Jeremiah remained within earshot, she would feel somewhat safe, at least. She inclined her head to the mysterious man before her. "Follow me, sir."

Lizzie led him into her father's study and lit a handful of tapers. The light afforded her the opportunity to make a closer inspection of the man. He wore a greatcoat over the customary jacket of seamen, and a pair of breeches and boots much finer than the rest of his garments. He appeared thoroughly sodden from the rains. His hair was dark, perhaps black, his features mostly obscured by a beard. He looked, in fact, like a man who was dangerous.

She placed her candle on her father's desk and clasped her hands at her waist, trying to staunch the unease sliding through her. "Pray explain who you are, sir, and what brings you to our door at this time of night."

"First, I must have your word that what I tell you remains between us only."

Lizzie scoffed. "I hardly think you're in a position to make demands of me."

In two strides he closed the distance between them. His large hands clamped on her waist, which was nearly naked without her customary stays and stomacher. She felt the heat of him through the thin fabric as the salty scent of sea water assailed her. He yanked her flush against his body.

Excitement mingled with fear as he held her. It had been years since a man had touched her so intimately and she was shocked to discover a stranger could have such an effect upon her.

"Listen closely, Lizzie. You've a gouty old man and woman for protection and nothing else. I haven't the time to play bloody games with you. I'll have your promise or you'll pay the price," he growled.

Beneath the commanding boom of his voice hid a lingering sense of familiarity. Comprehension hit her with the force of a runaway stallion. She knew the man before her. Hand shaking, she reached up and traced the strong edge of his jaw. The bristles of his beard tickled her fingertips. She studied his eyes, his sensual full mouth. He had changed much, but beneath the grizzled façade of a seaman she recognized the first man she'd ever loved.

"Edmond," she whispered. "Can it be? Is it you?"

Don't miss Scarlett's other romances!

(Listed by Series)

HISTORICAL ROMANCE

Heart's Temptation
A Mad Passion (Book One)
Rebel Love (Book Two)
Reckless Need (Book Three)
Sweet Scandal (Book Four)
Restless Rake (Book Five)
Darling Duke (Book Six)

Wicked Husbands
Her Errant Earl (Book One)
Her Lovestruck Lord (Book Two)
Her Reformed Rake (Book Three)
Her Deceptive Duke (Book Four)

League of Dukes
Nobody's Duke (Book One)
Heartless Duke (Book Two)

Sins and Scoundrels
Duke of Depravity (Book One)
Lord of Pirates (standalone novella)

CONTEMPORARY ROMANCE

Love's Second Chance
Reprieve (Book One)
Perfect Persuasion (Book Two)
Win My Love (Book Three)

Coastal Heat
Loved Up (Book One)

About the Author

Amazon bestselling author Scarlett Scott writes steamy Victorian and Regency romance with strong, intelligent heroines and sexy alpha heroes. She lives in Pennsylvania with her Canadian husband, adorable identical twins, and one TV-loving dog.

A self-professed literary junkie and nerd, she loves reading anything, but especially romance novels, poetry, and Middle English verse. When she's not reading, writing, wrangling toddlers, or camping, you can catch up with her on her website www.scarlettscottauthor.com. Hearing from readers never fails to make her day.

Scarlett's complete book list and information about upcoming releases can be found at www.scarlettscottauthor.com.

Connect with Scarlett! You can find her here:
Join Scarlett Scott's reader's group on Facebook for excerpts, giveaways, and a whole lot of fun!
Sign up for her newsletter here.
scarlettscottauthor.com/contact
Follow Scarlett on Amazon
Follow Scarlett on BookBub
www.instagram.com/scarlettscottauthor
www.twitter.com/scarscoromance
www.pinterest.com/scarlettscott
www.facebook.com/AuthorScarlettScott
Join the Historical Harlots on Facebook – It's a super fun group for lovers of steamy historical romance, packed with takeovers, teasers, giveaways, book talk, and more!

Made in the USA
Middletown, DE
20 July 2019